NOW OPEN YOUR EYES

nicole fiorina

NOW OPEN
YOUR EYES

Now Open Your Eyes

bohobooks
est. 2019

Barnes & Noble Edition | Paperback
Publication Date: February 9th, 2019
ISBN: 9798609211521

Published by Nicole Fiorina Books | Poetry by Oliver Masters
Proofreading by Annie Bugeja | Cover by Nicole Fiorina Books

n i c o l e f i o r i n a

NOTE FROM AUTHOR

Now Open Your Eyes is the third and last book in the Stay with Me series. This series must be read in order for it to be understood.

A lot of research went into this entire series, beginning with Stay with Me and continuing throughout the trilogy. Please keep in mind that the discussion regarding medication is based on my personal experience with it over the years, and how it affected *me*. Medication reacts to everyone differently. I am not a doctor or licensed psychiatrist, and I do not recommend altering medication without first speaking with your doctor. Between my personal experiences, as well as speaking with those who have lived with the subjects discussed, and countless hours of research, I've learned that every person's experience is unique in their own way. No two journeys are the same. This story isn't meant to change your mind, but to open your mind. For you to embrace those who are different, and see that there are two sides to every story—both sides being correct depending on how you look at it.

Difficult topics are discussed in this story. *Their opinions may or may not reflect my own.* Mature content, adult language, graphic sexual content, and disturbing matters may trigger an emotional response. Read at your own risk.

I hope you enjoy my creative spin and this world I've built.

Playlist available on Spotify:

https://spoti.fi/2GytbGj

You can also stream from
https://www.nicolefiorina.com

For my son who feels *too much*,

Never be ashamed of showing your emotions or tears.
One day, there will be someone who needs every single one.
In the meantime, yes, baby, you *can* handle it,
and you are nothing less than
b e a u t i f u l.

PROLOGUE

"The greatest measure of man
is what he does next after
everything has been
taken from him."

OLIVER MASTERS

Ethan

Seven Months Ago - September

had three hours.

Initially, I'd come here with one goal in mind. But I'd been putting it off. Mia had become a distraction. Or perhaps a savior, depending on how you look at it.

Either way, I couldn't waste another day.

It was mid-evening, and everyone should have been in their rooms. For fifteen minutes, I'd been standing before a mirror in an empty bathroom on the third floor with my conscience left somewhere on the second—wherever Mia was at the moment. Hopefully, in her room, but she had a habit of wandering, getting herself into trouble.

Haden Charles felt no remorse. Absolutely none. Haden walked these halls as if he owned the rights to every swirl in the marble laid out before him. He went on with his life as if nothing ever happened. But something had happened. Haden Charles was one of the five men who'd taken the life of my sister, Livy. I'd watched and studied the bloke for the last seven months. He didn't cower to himself after murdering my sister. Haden woke up, ate breakfast, went to class, played cards in the garden, living as if Livy never existed, as if he had not taken part in her death.

While staring into my eyes in the mirror, my heart hardened with every passing second. Anger filled the places where my baby sister used to, and the feeling was colder, heavier, and rougher around the edges. Anger consumed me, threatened me, taunted me. This anger fucking changed me, long forgotten was the man I used to be. All I knew was this rage, forgotten what it was like without it.

Then I found Livy in my eyes. *"Let it go,"* her voice chanted inside my head. But I couldn't let it go. The monster inside me was hungry, the whisperings of "tick-tock" growing louder, drowning out Livy's sweet voice.

Tick-tock.

The bag resting beside my boot over the dirty bathroom floor contained everything I needed to get the job done. Over a year, I'd been planning. Haden had a mum, a dad in prison, a little sister, and a Golden Retriever named Poncho. Nothing I did was half-arsed, fully aware of the life I was about to take from this world—from a family.

But he had a little fucking sister. He should have known better. And God? I'd given him over a year to make things right. Either God turned a blind eye … or God was waiting for me to do his bidding.

Pushing off the sink, I straightened my back before swooping up the black duffel in my fist.

Tick-tock.

My clothes blended in the dark halls. Black shirt, black jeans, black boots. Black soul. Each step I took toward the second wing, my heart warned me, but Karma sang its sweet song over and over again, and there was only one way I could sedate the monster.

It had to be tonight.

Jerry had this wing, but once a week, he smashed Rhonda in her office at the Nurse's station behind locked doors. The only reason I knew this was because he was a bit gobby in the break room, which Rhonda didn't deserve. But I didn't come here to make friends.

With Jerry busy, and halls empty, I didn't have much time.

I had swiped a generic guard badge from the Dean's office, one linked to no one's name, and scanned the card to Haden's door, sucked in a deep breath, and pushed open.

Haden Charles didn't expect death to knock, did he?

"What the fuck?" Haden shouted, sitting up from his bed. His dark and confused eyes roamed over my black attire, trying to place me and piece together my intrusion at once. But before Haden had a chance to stand, I bombarded the bloke, digging my knee into his chest and wrapping my fingers around his throat.

"Three questions, and you *will* be honest with me," I commanded into his ear as he fought against me. He was no match for my size, the monster inside, and the adrenaline jetting through my veins. "I'll know if you're lying." Haden's eyes bulged as he tried twisting out of my grasp. Knowing how much air supply to leave, I tightened my grip.

The junkie had been here at Dolor for three years for shooting up and dealing. Most students were in for two, but lucky for me, these fellas couldn't pass a class. Haden was twenty now, hardly a boy any longer. Men had to take responsibility for their actions. "Olivia. Did you rape her?"

Haden violently shook his head and tried to reach for my face, his turning blue, but I was far enough where he couldn't reach me. I was no stranger to death, and this wasn't my first kill. My arms were in a deadlock, but I let up a little for him to speak, and he gasped for air. "Who the fuck is Olivia?"

"Livy," I growled. "Answer me."

"Everyone fucked that slapper," Haden spit with humor in his eyes, proving, once again, how he viewed women. "I'd hardly consider it rape when she laid there and took it. Like a champ, too."

The monster inside me bared his teeth, and I should have snapped his neck right then and there. It wouldn't have taken much effort, considering I already had him by the throat. But I had more questions for him and needed more answers.

Releasing one hand, I shoved it into my pocket and flicked open the pocket knife, hovering the sharp point over the bloke's bulging eye. "Did you kill her?" Surprisingly, my voice stayed calm, my words direct, but I couldn't mask the slight tremor in my knife-holding hand. Haden's movements stilled under my grasp, and fear materialized from his watering eyes beneath the tip of the blade. The plan wasn't to use the knife on him. Only a means to get the answers I needed to justify what I was about to do. "The fucking truth."

"I'm not a rat," he croaked in a husky breath.

"Did you hang my baby sister?" The grief and heartache threatened to show, jeopardizing my patience. My hand trembled around the tight grip of the knife, ready to carve Livy's name into his face so, dead or alive, he would never forget what he'd done—so everyone would know what he'd done.

"Drew!" Haden rushed out with a shocking revelation in his eyes. "Drew was the one."

The monster inside me laughed at his audacity. Tommy, Livy's boyfriend, had killed Drew, and Haden knew it would be easier to throw the one person under the bus who wasn't here to defend his name. "Let's try this again." I already knew the names. When I'd visited Tommy in jail, he ran me off a list of the five boys who gang-raped her. Drew, Haden, Chad, William, and Lionel. But I needed Haden's confession. I wanted to hear him say it. "Did you murder Livy?"

Haden squeezed his eyes closed before he opened them and locked his dark gaze on me. "You want me to tell you how I watched Lionel and Drew suffocate her? How her freckled face turned blue, and arms went

12

limp? How I helped lift her body so Lionel could pull the sheet around her neck? How she was already dead before she was flying? Do you think I'd honestly admit to something like that? You'd have to fucking kill me before my arse is going to that hell of a prison."

His sorry excuse for a confession clouded my vision and put me into a transient shock. Unwarranted images of my baby sister fighting for her life while being man-handled by five blokes twice her size appeared behind my closed eyes.

After dragging in a steady breath, I opened them again. "Last question, Haden," my voice wavered, and it took everything not to drive the blade into his eye, "are you sorry for what you did?"

"Sorry?" He laughed. "It was her or me. I chose *me*."

Three questions. It was all I needed to hear before sending Haden's arse to hell, but not the same hell he'd referred too. The monster controlled all my next actions as if I'd left my body and watched from the corner of the room—a bystander. I pulled out the needle and injected succinylcholine into the vein behind his ear. Then the only movements he could control were his eyes. This time, it was his body going limp in seconds. The terror in his dark eyes darted around, unable to move, unable to speak. Haden Charles finally understood the same fear Livy went through in her last moments: undeniably helpless with death on the horizon.

I hung him in his room and didn't stay around to watch his life slip away. He deserved to die alone, and if he managed to escape, the drug would suffocate him anyway. I'd seen the process before. I'd experimented with it because I didn't do anything half-arsed.

Automatically, my feet moved down the wing, one foot in front of the other, up the stairs, until I reached the bathroom. It wasn't until the door closed behind me when I collapsed to the ground. My entire body shook, and my lethal hands trembled out in front of me. I examined them, horrified and disgusted with myself. A sickness stirred as Haden's last moments replayed. I tried to climb the tiled wall, but my legs failed to move, and the queasiness pushed up my throat. Heaving and eyes burning, I lurched over and vomited over the bathroom tile.

Murder wasn't new to me. I'd slain before, and it never got easier.

The monster was quiet, full. However, it wouldn't be long until the bloody beast came back for more.

It was only a matter of time.

It took several minutes to break through the initial shock of my undoing. I scrubbed my hands until they turned raw, wanting to take off layers of my skin. I showered, brushed my teeth, and dressed back into my guard uniform, repeatedly going over the plan in my head.

I'd made plans for once I would leave Dolor, where to stay, money, passport, what ordinary criminals on the run would plan to avoid getting caught. I'd already told the Dean that after this job, I was leaving the country and never coming back. I made sure no one would come looking for me, and no one could pin these deaths on me either—no trace of Ethan Scott. But I'd never planned for the way I'd feel after taking a life.

Who was I to play God? Why did I feel remorse for those sick bastards? Why did it turn my stomach upside down instead of making me feel better?

That, I didn't plan.

Back on the second floor, the dinner rush blew past me. Time moved forward, and no one noticed Haden Charles never made it to the mess hall. I turned the corner and found myself face to face with Zeke.

Aside from Lynch, Zeke had been here the longest. Tommy's brother.

Zeke studied me from afar, his wild gaze roaming and trying to decipher me. "Zeke," I whispered, feeling caught in an act but knowing he couldn't have known what I'd done. But I was still afraid he'd be able to get inside my head and watch the memory of my crime play out. Each time his eyes locked on mine, I felt exposed. "Everything okay, my friend?"

Zeke held a sad look and let out a breath before nodding. The boy was capable of speaking but chose not to. He'd been mute since he was found on the steps of Dolor. His file mentioned selective mutism and sensory

14

processing disorder from severe separation anxiety as a kid. The only time he'd ever spoken was to Tommy. When I'd visited Tommy in jail, he had mentioned when they were kids, Zeke would use him like a barrier against the world around him. Tommy had always spoken on Zeke's behalf, and when the two were separated, Zeke's anxiety only worsened. Tommy had found Zeke after years of searching for him and planted himself inside Dolor to get his brother out. Tommy had failed Zeke.

Tommy and I were alike in a lot of ways.

Failing our siblings was one of them.

Murder was another.

I'd tried to get close with Zeke for Tommy's sake, but Zeke only allowed a few in. Mia and Masters being the only two aside from Tommy, and I never understood what it was Zeke found in them. But he saw something. Perhaps Mia eased his anxiety the same way Mia calmed my monster.

After dinner, I stayed at my post in the bathroom. Haden's last words echoed in my head, and I gripped my belt in an attempt to calm my nerves. Instinctively, my eyes found Mia across the room, looking for relief. I noticed the way she zoned out as her friend, Jake, talked to her. Mia did that often, and I wished I could see her thoughts when she got lost in her own head like this. Was she plotting out deaths like me? Was she sick too? Was she angry? What was her monster's name?

Lynch's voice vibrated over the intercom, breaking my stare on the girl my monster fancied. It didn't take long for someone to find Haden's body and the campus to go on lockdown. I looked at my watch. *Right on fucking time.*

When I'd thought the hardest part was over, it wasn't. Having to see the damage I'd done with my bare hands back in Haden's room, the sickness resurrected. When I'd thought there was no way I could ever hate myself more than I did after failing Livy, it had been a lie. Seeing Haden hanging in his room made me hate myself even more. Inevitably, the hate for myself would only grow because I wasn't finished yet.

I was only getting started.

By three in the morning, I was free to go back to my wing—back to Mia. I wanted to lie by her side and use her to smooth over the anger, shame, and guilt like she'd done so many times before. Mia was sound asleep upon entering her room. Finally, asleep in peace from her terrors. I wanted to drown myself in that same peace. I wanted it to wrap this fucking monster up in her soothing blanket and rock him to sleep.

One by one, I withdrew my belt and shirt and sank next to her ice-cold body to warm her. Mia was always cold, convinced she was born with half a soul.

"Ollie," Mia whispered, and though it hurt not to be the one she needed, I still selfishly needed her. It should make me feel guilty, my murderous hands straying over her silky chilled skin, but it didn't. Mia stirred awake and tried to get me to talk about whatever was bothering me, but I couldn't find it in me. I was a broken man with ill intentions. At this moment, all I needed was the silence of the night and her—almost naked—body against mine. All I needed was the façade of being needed in return, and for her storm to calm mine. Mia transformed my monster into a pet. Around her, he listened.

Like every other night since the first time she pulled me in bed with her, I waited until she fell back asleep and took. Running my fingers along the path of her silhouette, I absorbed what she had. Mia didn't mind, or at least she never mentioned anything. Deep down, I knew it was Masters she wanted, but Mia used me all the same. This is what we did. This was our relationship. We fed each other the only way we understood how.

In no time, Mia fell back asleep. Her soft breaths hypnotized me into a state of sweet serenity. My hands made their journey across her abdomen to her arse, pulling her close against my front to breathe in her natural flowery scent.

Regardless of what her file stated, Mia was nothing less than captivating.

Her shallow breaths hit my neck as my chest rose against her breasts. "Will you forgive me, Mia?" I asked, knowing one day I'd either abandon her, fuck her, or kill her.

16

"Mmhm," she hummed half-asleep.

I was a sick fool. A *murderous* sick fool.

Mia had what I needed, and each night, I took it.

I just didn't realize it would become an addiction until it was too late.

ONE

"This world needs more women with
spines bitten by fortitude,
and more men with
hearts kissed by a tender grace."

OLIVER MASTERS

Mia

S e v e n   M o n t h s   L a t e r   –   R e l e a s e   D a y

t should've been easy for the darkness to take over, so disturbingly easy considering I had all the elements necessary to drag me there. Why didn't I end up there this time? Why, after all this time, did I desire to outrun the murky black abyss when before I'd allowed myself to drown in it?

Thoughts of Ollie continued to give me hope. I knew he was there, standing in the light, waiting for me. I slammed my eyes closed and imagined us there, the sun hanging high, running through fields of poppy, the blush satin petals tickling our ankles. It was warm, safe, and better than this reality.

But it was a temporary haven, and God could dangle Ollie and the future we dreamt of right over my head all he wanted. It was a cruel torment, giving me everything I never knew I wanted only to take it all away. How dare he test my strength? Did he not know I wasn't reaching this time?

I was fucking taking it.

Over the last two years, I'd let all outside forces dictate my life, my feelings, my head. I had allowed everyone else control what my punishment should be for all my wrong-doings.

Thank you, God, for testing me. I'd learned my lesson.

I had suffered long enough. I'd paid my dues.

And in the end, even the *once-upon-a-damned* deserved to be happy, too.

The last thing I'd remembered before blacking out had been the black muddy shoes hanging from above when my vision transformed from blurry to black—pitch black.

A tear slipped down my cheek, and when my eyes snapped open, the darkness welcomed again. But I didn't let it in—not this time. My immediate response was to scream, but the tape stretching across my lips not only prevented it but rose panic where it became harder to breathe.

Oxygen turned scarce, and my nose burned. My wrists and ankles had been bound together, and I twisted in place, throwing my joined legs out only to have my knees hit the walls all around me. There was no way out. I squeezed my eyes shut, and another hot tear tumbled down as my chest burned from the lack of air and fear swimming through me, trying to pull me under the current.

Ethan. It had been him all along. But why didn't I see it before? Once, I'd confessed Ethan had the heart of a grim reaper, and for months I'd let this man I thought I knew into my bed, even on nights he'd taken lives. Ethan didn't only have the heart of a grim reaper. He had been the blasted Angel of Death all along. And I'd let him touch me, let him soothe me. I allowed him inside, and it pissed me off how wrong I'd been about him. Knowing human behavior was the only thing I was good at, and I'd gotten Ethan all wrong.

Ethan had led those guys to their deaths—stole lives—and he could have gotten away with all of it too if it hadn't been for me walking in on him. He'd looked at me back in the classroom on the third floor with utter shock in his electric blue eyes, mine carrying the same horror before he took me down to the ground. *"Sorry,"* went on repeat until it turned into the last thing I'd heard before the blackness took over.

It wasn't until the car came to a stop before I realized I'd been moving the entire time in this dark, small space. A door slammed, rattling the trunk I'd been confined in, and my tears stopped mid-stream. Remaining still, I awaited the inevitable.

This was it. Ethan would try to kill me, too.

I'd never been afraid of dying. As a matter of fact, Death feared *me*. For years, I'd danced on the tight ropes without a care in the world, taunting the ominous fate, whispering, "Take me, I dare you," with my arms high at my sides. Turns out, Death was a scared little bitch.

But that was before Ollie had come into my life.

The moment Ollie forced his way in, he became my center. My gravity. Ollie loved me enough for the both of us until I'd learned to love myself. And eventually, I had learned. I'd learned to love myself and the person I grew to be. Dolor, the pranks, nor the bullying could take that away from me.

Ethan wouldn't be able to either.

If Death wasn't a scared little bitch, then it should surely be now because there wasn't a fight I'd surrender to—not this time. I'd not only fight for myself, but for Ollie and a lifetime together.

The trunk opened, and a gust of crisp air blasted through the closed space I'd been trapped in. The bright sun forced my eyes closed, and I jerked my head away from the light for a moment until they could adjust.

"We're here," Ethan stated, but it was indifferent this time. Reluctantly, I blinked my eyes open, and Ethan's features came into view. Hollow eyes stared down at me, and I fought words against the tape. Curses, death threats, and screams came out as high-pitched hums. For a brief moment, Ethan turned away and scratched the back of his head as

20

his shoulders tensed against the plain black tee. Then he straightened his posture and turned back to face me. "This is your fault," he emphasized, sounding more like he was trying to convince himself instead of me. He shook his head, releasing a broken exhale before his two large hands grabbed me from the trunk and threw me over his shoulder.

I thrashed against his strong hold, but there was no escaping Ethan's tight grip at the back of my knees. Amid the struggle, I chanced a look around to see a dense forest surrounding us—a canvas of greens and browns. Not even the sky was visible from this angle, blocked by the betraying canopies of branches and leaves.

Trees went on for miles with no sign of civilization besides the two of us. No sign of Dolor, Ollie, or help for that matter. Only Ethan and me. The Angel of Death and the ex-sociopath.

A door creaked open, and Ethan pushed his way through and managed to kick it shut behind him, erasing the light from outside.

It was dark again, and the musty air smelled of mold and vacancy. Wooden planks covered every wall, and Ethan turned to deadlock the door, giving me views of the entire space, which was limited. A kitchen with a small window above the sink sat against the back wall. Beside it, a back door. *Another escape route.* To my right, a dusty floral couch lay against a wood planked wall facing an empty wall with an interior door. I didn't have much time before he whipped back around and silently walked across the creaky floors until we stepped through another doorway and descended a flight of stairs.

Fighting against him was useless, at least until I could be free of the restraints tied around my limbs. They were so tight, cutting into my flesh, and each move against them only burned deeper. Saving my energy became a priority. After the last step off the stairs, Ethan threw me backward until my back hit, then bounced off, a spring mattress.

He paced back and forth, tugging at his hair as I remained still, watching him. The room was tiny, with no other furniture aside from the mattress beneath me. My gaze steered from Ethan to a window. A slice of the sun's rays glared between the two of us, sending dust particles dancing in the space like weightless snow. The window was high, out of reach.

"Why, Jett?" Ethan turned to face me with his arms in the air, cheeks raging, and eyes straining. "You weren't a part of the plan!" he screamed as his face shook. A lone tear ran down his cheek as he pushed himself on top of me. Ethan tore the tape from my mouth, and a scream ripped through me, desperate for anyone to hear, for possibly the trees to send a message across the UK until it reached Ollie.

Ethan gripped my jaw in one hand, and his face came within inches of mine. "I don't want to hurt you," despair flowed through each word, his eyes heavy with regret, "Please, don't make me hurt you. If anyone could understand, it would be you. You just need to understand."

Ethan pinned me still with a plea in his eyes and hesitantly let go of his lock around my jaw. With a window of opportunity, I threw my head forward and slammed my skull into his. The intense pain sent me sideways with an unbearable ringing in my ears. Ethan cursed under his breath before he pushed against my shoulders to hold me still. "Let me go!" I screamed. My throat was dry and thick and caused my scream to fade into a tear-filled whisper. "Please, Ethan. I didn't see anything … I won't say anything! Just let me go."

It was true. I wouldn't say anything. He could let me walk out the door, and I could forget this ever happened. It was in my nature. Whether I wanted to forget or not, my brain had a history of abolishing moments that were too difficult to deal with.

For a fraction of a second, I thought he was going to let me go. But then something dawned on him, and his gaze went from apologetic to angry like a snap of the fingers.

"And where will you go? Back to Masters? Do you honestly believe Masters or Lynch is going to forget your disappearance and not ask questions? I'm not an idiot, Jett. I can't risk it … and I'm not finished yet."

"Finished with what? Haven't you done enough?" Four guys died of suicide in the last seven months. I'd only walked in on Lionel, but it didn't take a genius to put all the pieces together. Ethan had murdered all four of them. If he had been capable of that, what else was Ethan Scott capable of?

"Not yet," Ethan whispered. "I have to finish what I've started."

"You're a sick son-of-a-bitch," I screamed, then spit in his face.

Ethan slammed his eyes shut and wiped my spit from his face with the back of his hand. When his eyes opened again, a disturbing calmness swept through his black pupils. He launched forward and slapped the tape over my mouth again. "You just have to understand. I don't want to hurt you." Ethan's forehead dropped to my thumping one. "Please don't make me hurt you," he gravely whispered. I closed my eyes, refusing to look at him. "Behave, Jett," Ethan said to me in a soft tone. "Behave, and when the time comes, I'll let you go. But right now, you need to cool off."

He kissed my throbbing head and pushed himself off me, leaving me alone in the room.

Time elapsed. The sun died, and the moon moved passed the window out of sight. Heavy boots clipped the wooden planks above as Ethan continually paced the small cabin for hours. With every step, the floorboards creaked beneath, sending dust to fall from the ceiling and into the moon's light. He had to come down sooner or later, and I preferred sooner. My bladder burned, reminding me I was human.

I pushed myself against the back wall and forced my eyes to stay open. My eyelids felt as if they were being pushed down against my will, and each time I drifted, I shook my head to keep myself alert. Outside the window, the haunting trees swayed against the harsh wind. My own words taunted me, *"We'll never be out of the woods,"* and the irony made me chuckle.

But, I had been wrong before—a *glass-half-empty* pessimistic coward.

And there was no room left for pessimism in this world.

I was getting out of these damn woods, even if I had to cut down every tree.

Ethan's boots bounced off the stairs, and my head snapped forward. A mixture of anger and adrenaline washed over me and woke me up entirely. The door opened, and he appeared, still wearing a black shirt with black jeans. His red hair looked almost black in the dark as well, and his blue eyes glistened like the moon against an ocean. Each step closer made me want to become one with the wall, but I held my ground, lifted my chin, and looked him in the eyes, giving him no escape from my silent promise to kill him as soon as I'd get the chance.

Exhausted, Ethan stood over me and dipped his fingers into his pocket and flicked open a knife. I held back from flinching, but shook my head and mumbled against the tape.

"Relax," he muttered, placing one hand over both of my ankles before cutting them free from the bind. "You can use the loo, and I'll feed you."

Leaving my wrists still bound and the tape over my lips, Ethan led me up the stairs. The smell of sweet tomatoes wafted down the compressed stairway, and my feet moved slowly up each step, still heavy and numb from the lack of blood flow.

I thought about running and how stupid that idea would be, considering I couldn't open a door with my arms behind my back. For the time being, I'd comply with Ethan's demands and earn his trust until an opportunity arose.

The main floor was how I remembered. In the kitchen, a small pot set over a gas stove. I looked around and noticed there was no other bedroom, no other hallway, or upstairs. This was it. The only bedroom in this cabin was the one I'd been trapped in.

"Need to go?" Ethan asked as he pushed the bathroom door in the staircase open. My eyes flitted from his to the tiny bathroom. There was no cabinet, only a free-standing sink, a tub, and a toilet. You could tell there had been a mirror above the sink by the nail holes in the drywall, but it had been taken down. Ethan had removed it. *Smart.*

I had to pee but didn't want to. However, I didn't know how long until I had my next chance. I dropped my chin, and Ethan laid his hand on my shoulder to guide me in. "I want to trust you, I do," Ethan explained as he lifted my black POETIC hoodie and fumbled with the button on my jeans, "but I just can't take the risk." My eyes found the ceiling as he slid my bottoms down and sat me over the toilet.

After Ethan left the room and closed the door, tears slipped from my eyes and soaked the tape stuck to my mouth, and the tape fell off halfway. I sat on the cold seat, sucking in enough air to fill my lungs while relieving myself in record time. The oxygen I desperately craved only made my dry throat worse.

There was a tiny circular window above the shower stall with no way to open, only to bust through. This gave me more than two ways to get out of here, but my best chance was out one of the doors.

Ethan appeared less than a minute later. "All done?" he asked as if he was having a conversation with a three-year-old. He grabbed a roll of toilet paper from behind me, crouched down, and wrapped his hand a few times with the paper. "I'm going to take care of you, Jett."

"I hate you." My voice was low, almost a whisper, and I slammed my eyes closed as his covered hand swiped between my legs. They didn't open again until the toilet flushed. "Why are you doing this?"

Ethan stayed silent and pulled me up into a standing position between his crouched knees. One after the other, he slid up my panties, then jeans. He couldn't look at me in the eyes any longer. Instead, his hypnotized gaze was focused on the way his fingers dragged up my legs.

Separating the living area and the kitchen was a small wooden table with two chairs. Ethan pulled out a chair and sat me down, putting me back into the restraints. He turned to face the stove and switched off the burner. "What are your plans, Officer Scott?" I attempted again, distancing myself from our prior relationship. "You plan on keeping me as a pet for the rest of your life? What was it you used to call me?" I leaned over the table, yanking my arms against the chair to get his attention. "Oh, that's right," I laughed, "I'm a storm. And you should know by now you can't tame a storm."

He hung his head, and every muscle in his arm tensed.

"I will get out of here," I continued. "Maybe not today, maybe not tomorrow, but there will come a moment when you least expect it where I'll escape … And you know my past, Ethan. I have no problem killing you if it comes to that. I could bash in your pretty red head and never bat an eye. I'd be able to carry on without an ounce of empathy for it. But you? You'd walk around with regret every day, more than the load your carrying now. I couldn't imagine the daily pain you'd face if you ever hurt me."

A growl roared from him before he slammed his fist through a cabinet. Knowing I got a reaction out of him brought a menacing smile to my face. Everything I'd said had only been a half-lie. The truth was, I may feel empathy because it had found me before.

Ethan stormed toward me, grabbed my hair in his fist, and yanked my head back, his chest heaving. "You know what your problem is, Jett?" Despite every strand of hair ripping from my skull, I sucked in my lips and narrowed my eyes to match his strength. "You forget, you and me? We're one and the same." Ethan released his hold and returned to the kitchen counter, and my held breath returned in short, harsh shudders. "Don't underestimate me."

Afterward, dinner was silent.

Ethan spoon-fed me tomato soup he heated over the stove from a can. I'd thought about refusing to eat, but I needed strength. I needed to get out of here, and the only way was to take care of my health and eat the food he offered while planning my escape.

After the entire pot of tomato soup was gone, Ethan left me waiting at the table and returned to the kitchen counter. One by one, he hand-washed every spoon, spatula, and dish, drying and placing each item in their designated spot. He scrubbed counters, the table, and wiped down the stove before washing and drying his hands for the third time.

I never took Ethan to be so meticulous—a clean freak. But then again, I never really knew the man at all.

Once Ethan cleaned the kitchen area to perfection, he grabbed me by the arm and lifted me out of the chair. I walked in front of him down the stairs and back to the bedroom. Again, my ankles were bound, and I was left alone.

Hours passed, and the night only grew colder and crueler.

Without Ollie, my heart felt like December in the middle of spring.

26

A tear ran down my cheek, and it was warm and welcoming.

At some point, I must have fallen asleep because the next time my eyes opened, Ethan was lying next to me with a damp cloth to my forehead as he hushed melodically. My body trembled inside the only warmth of the hoodie, refusing to use him as a security blanket like I once had. Ethan would be warm, but I'd rather freeze.

TWO

"I have a **locked box** inside my heart.
It's filled to the **brim** with memories,
your **smile**, lovely scent, **stolen** touch;
they're all **mine**, the things I **love** so much.
My little **treasures** of all your **freckles**.
The sound of your **laugh**; your **stride**,
that **candid** look you get in your eyes.
I **relive** them whenever I want to,
My **heart** is a treasure box of *you*."

OLIVER MASTERS

Ollie

// 'm worried about you, man. They'll find her. Just come home,"
Travis rambled on for, what it seemed like, the hundredth time
into the mobile he had given me earlier. He'd mentioned I would
need it for work.

I didn't need a fucking phone.

I needed Mia and not this bloody picture, the polaroid picture I'd been holding in my jittery hands. The first picture we'd ever taken together.

Her. I needed her—all of her.

"I'm okay," I lied. "I'll ring you in the morning with an update." Another lie. And there was nothing to slam shut with the stupid mobile to ease my frustration. So, I pressed my finger into the red button harder than what was necessary before throwing it over the bed in the motel room.

I refused to walk into our home without her. I'd imagined the day we'd walk through the front door of our home so many times, and it wouldn't be the same if she weren't by my side.

I couldn't sit still, repeatedly pacing the motel room with a rented car waiting in the car park. Every precious second was wasted without looking for her, and though it was almost midnight, I still shoved a hoodie over my head, swiped the keys off the dresser, and walked out the door without a destination or solid clue as to where she could be.

The drive was pointless, but my mind couldn't stop replaying every interaction from today that lead me here: the smile Mia had on her face after waking, saying she was ready for a lifetime of mornings and coffee in bed. The lovemaking shortly after had been proof she couldn't imagine anything different than the two of us. Mia wasn't a liar. Her head may have played tricks on her, but her eyes and heart were honest. She'd promised to meet me. She wouldn't have left me. Something was wrong.

After she didn't show, I'd spent hours checking every room, looking over every floor, talking with Jake, Tyler, questioning every fucking person inside the walls of Dolor. Lynch had been pre-occupied with a suicide in a classroom, and a part of me believed Mia's disappearance and the suicide all happening on the same day wasn't a coincidence.

It had been fifteen hours since I'd seen her, ten hours since *anyone* had seen her.

Where are you, love?

I'd driven through the black night around the surrounding towns of Guildford before stopping the car on the side of the road. One second, I was sitting inside the vehicle, the next, I was standing over the wet pavement, unable to breathe. Headlights rushed past, people trying to get home, but I was lost without Mia, the only home I'd ever known. Each car that flew by couldn't see I was standing here suffocating, and I kicked the tire before crumbling to the ground with my back against the wet vehicle. "I don't know what to do. Tell me what to do," I shouted to no one. Zeke wasn't here to shove the broken pieces back at me.

It took less than five minutes to realize sitting out here in the cold rain wasn't going to get me closer to her, and less than five minutes to know I couldn't do this on my own.

I got back into the car and dialed Jinx, the security guard from Dolor, who had become a good mate over the two-year sentence. He answered on the third ring, music blaring in the background with a fog of conversation. "Who's this?"

"Masters. I need a favor."

"Whoa, Oliver Masters. I didn't think I'd hear from you so soon."

"I need Lynch's address." There was no time for chit chat. I'd seen him earlier at Dolor, and we'd exchanged numbers. For hours, he'd helped me turn Dolor upside down. How was the entire world able to move on with their lives knowing Mia was missing? How was he at a fucking party at this time?

"Yeah, okay. Been there once to deliver something. Foxenden Court off Chertsey. Flat 8. Don't tell him I—"

I hung up and steered back onto the road, making my next left over the slick street.

Ten minutes later, I pulled up to the red brick building and pushed the gear into park. Rain fell over me as I ran through the door and up the stairs. My body shivered from either the cold, impatience, or anger ... I couldn't tell anymore, only pounded my fist over the door of Lynch's flat, most likely waking the entire building.

Lynch opened the door in his plaid pajamas with a baseball bat in one hand. "Oliver." He gritted his teeth. "It's been a long day. I don't have the energy for this, and how did you find my address?"

"Your daughter is fucking missing!" I pushed my way through his door and into the flat. It was small and minimal, and I spun around as he dropped the bat beside the door frame and ran the back of his hands over his eyes. "Wake up, Lynch. I'm not leaving until I get answers."

"You have no business being in my home, let alone at this hour of the night," he grumbled as he strolled over to his kitchenette and flipped on the coffee maker. "I should call the police." But his actions went against his words. Deep down, Lynch cared about Mia. And he wouldn't call the police on me because I was the only other person who gave a damn about his daughter.

"Please! Call them," I challenged with my hands in the air. I'd called earlier, and they weren't much help. But if the dean of the reformatory school called, maybe they'd see the importance of a missing girl.

Lynch shoveled coffee grounds into his pot, mumbling incoherently to himself and ignoring my frustration. "I talked to Bruce. Mia has a history of running off, especially when things get too hard. Mia running away on release day seems to be in her character. I wouldn't be surprised if she happened to get cozy with someone other than you, took off, and now shacking up somewhere," he sighed, rubbing a hand over his balding head. "Don't beat yourself up over it."

Travis had said the same bloody thing, but I knew Mia. "If you'd taken the time to get to know your daughter, you'd see she isn't like that anymore." Mia was smart. She wouldn't have given up so quickly at the first chance of running away. Not on me, and not on herself. Not after everything she'd been through. She had court back in the states in a week. If she didn't show, where would they would send her next?

Lynch pulled a mug from the cupboard and turned to face me. "I knew her mother, and her mother ran off back to Pennsylvania without so much as an explanation. The apple doesn't fall far from the tree. Mia is just like her. She may have my eyes, but everything else is all her mum."

Mia never spoke much of her mum, but this didn't change anything. "You're wrong about her." I stood and leaned my elbows over the kitchen counter, separating us. "Somethings not right. I can't put my finger on it, but something went down at *your* school. I can feel her. I can't explain it, but she's in trouble."

"You don't look so good, Oliver. You look tired."

The wanker was deflecting.

My jaw clenched. "I'm fine," I gritted out.

The coffee pot beeped, and Lynch turned away from me. "If you want my advice, go home. She'll turn up eventually. Bruce said he'd call if he hears from her. Until then, there's nothing I can do."

"So, that's it? No missing person's report? You don't even care enough to notify authorities?"

Lynch laughed, pouring himself a cup, then sprinkled in sugar. His nonchalant behavior only set every irritated nerve on fire, and he brought the mug to his mouth before saying, "You honestly believe anyone is going to take Mia seriously with her history? The authorities won't give a missing person's report the time of day. Go home, Oliver. If a week passes and she doesn't show, I'll go to the police. Until then, move on with your life. I'm sure she's just fine. Do you have somewhere to go?"

My heart broke for Mia and how little she was cared about by the people surrounding her. How could they not see how much darker everyone's world was without her in it?

I looked off to the side, unable to lock eyes with the man who created Mia, brought her life, when there was so much anger in mine. "Ethan Scott. Where is he?"

"Probably home, sleeping. The same thing you should be doing at this hour."

Getting Scott's address out of Lynch would be like pulling teeth. Jinx would have no problem giving me the information if he had it.

I drove around Guildford, passed by Dolor, and by three in the morning, the car turned back into the car park of the motel. My thoughts twisted, believing my brother had, somehow, something to do with this. It had Oscar's name written all over it.

As I pulled into a parking space, I grabbed my mobile and looked up visiting hours for the prison. My eyes glazed over as I read the small text on the screen. An eight-day advanced notice was needed to arrange a meeting with a prisoner. Eight days was too long, but I rang High Down Prison anyway to book an appointment with Oscar. Office hours were closed, and I made a mental note to ring back at nine in the morning.

I never planned to see Oscar again, putting him in the past and keeping him there. But Oscar had always found a way to wedge himself in my life, time and time again. He might have been able to round up a few boys to take Mia in exchange for me. He wanted something from me that I would never give up before, but if Mia was on the line, he could bloody have it. I'd give anything in exchange for her freedom, including my life.

My phone rang, and I immediately answered with my heart in my throat.

"Find him?" Jinx's boom-box of a voice rumbled into the mobile against the beat of the bass in the background.

"Yeah, it was no use." I stared at the motel room door from the car. Sleep would be impossible and a waste. "Do you know where Ethan Scott lives?"

"Nah," he grumbled as a girl whined beside him, vibrating my eardrums. "We don't talk to Scott."

"What do you mean, *'We don't talk to Scott.'*" I wiped the exhaustion from my eyes. "Where are you?"

"I'll send over the address, and you can meet me. I'll tell you everything you need to know."

After Jinx sent the address over, the drive had only been twenty minutes before parking outside a gated property. With my arms crossed over my chest, I posted against the vehicle as music and bodies spilled from inside the house. Red cups and tea lights decorated the pristine lawn. Everyone was partying, laughing, and having a proper time, living life without a care in the world. But for me? My head spun, and panic surged with every passing second waiting out here in the cold for his arse. I shouldn't have come, but desperation pulled me under. If Jinx had information on Scott, I needed to know—anything that would lead me closer to Mia.

Jinx spotted me from the large doorway with a lazy, drunken smile plastered over his face, lights bouncing off his gold teeth. He walked toward me with a girl under his arm. She was tiny against his broad build. Instantly, she made me feel uneasy with her red lipstick smeared and a cigarette between her smoke-stained fingers, forcing me into a time I'd tried so hard to forget.

The window doesn't close all the way, leaving a small crack where the cold slips through. It's dark outside, and the buzz from traffic turns the city into a nightlife musical, slipping a lullaby through the window along with the chill. It drowns out O's snoring. He gets to sleep in the bed with mum. But, Mum isn't home yet.

I turn the page of the book the lady with kind brown eyes gave to me from the library. She said I should choose another from the children's section, but those bore me. The two clutched in my hands were thick, and the text on the back promised a mind-provoking change within my heart, which could possibly change the world. I wanted to be a part of that, and I'd fly through both books this week. She said I could only choose one and come back for the other, but only after I returned the first book—in the same condition as I took it. She didn't trust me, but I didn't blame her. I wouldn't trust a young kid with a piece of history either. Trust is earned.

I'll show her.

My eyes steer from the page to the clock in the kitchen with bright yellow numbers. It's four in the morning, and mum should be home any second now. Sometimes she's late. Sometimes she's early.

I return my eyes to the book and sink under the window sill, where I'm allowed to sleep. I like this spot because there's a small cushion over a bench, and it's cozier than the floor. Sometimes, when I get really cold, I use the curtain from the window. It's long enough to blanket around me.

The lock slides and Mum's giggles allow my heart rate to steady. She's back. A man mumbles through the doorframe, saying his goodbyes, and she drops her keys over the side table and closes the door behind her.

She's wearing a top which shows her belly and a small skirt. She has to be cold, which makes me feel bad, but it doesn't seem to bother her as she kicks off her heels and stumbles toward me with a cigarette between her red lips. She pulls the cigarette away and blows out smoke before leaning over to kiss me. "You worry too much," she reminds me when she sees I'm still awake, and my fingers reach out to touch the warm skin on her belly where the scars crawl up, but she slaps my hand away. "You like what you did to me?"

"They're different. Unique."

She calls them stretch marks, and they are my fault. She says Oscar gave her beauty, and I took it away. But I tell her she's beautiful, they're beautiful, even though she doesn't agree. The stretch marks are like the lines of a book, each one a sentence telling a story. I've caused this, proof of my existence written over her skin. And she hates them.

"No, Oliver. They're ugly. You completely ruined me. I could be making more money if I hadn't had you."

It should hurt me, but it doesn't. Not anymore. It did the first few times she said it, but I've realized she's in pain and uses me to release it, so I don't respond. I'm just glad she's home, and I take a second to remember my page number before closing the book and using it as a pillow. Mum puts her cigarette out in an ashtray over the floor, then falls beside Oscar, twisting her arms and legs around him, finding warmth.

"You made it," Jinx bellowed with a pat over my shoulder, pulling me from the memory. I flinched, and his expression twisted. "Come inside. You can meet my crew."

Laughter and conversations rang from all directions, filling the background noise and making my head spin and my palms sweat. It had been a while since I'd been around a crowd of this size. Panic doubled within me, and I couldn't find focus. Rap music thumped, a song I'd never heard before, and the hype from the party crawled over me, pushing my boundaries. "I'm not staying."

"You doing alright?"

"I'm fine. I'm okay."

A smile of scattered teeth stretched across Jinx's face as my brain pounded inside my head. "Get my mate a drink," Jinx ordered the girl. She nodded and twirled to head back inside the house.

"Is she your girl?" I asked, leaning against the car and propping up my foot to steady myself. Too much chaos moved around me, and the anxiety within only worsened the more I noticed the little control I had at the moment, attempting small talk to distract myself.

"Leslie? Lila, Leigh or some shit like that … No, only met her tonight." He pulled out cigarettes and packed the box into the palm of his hand with humor in his eyes. "You looking to smash?"

I glared at him, putting no energy into responding to the ridiculous question before my gaze made the journey over the packed crowd. Smoke swirled in the air between us, and Jinx went on about something that had nothing to do with Mia or Scott.

But I couldn't focus on a single thing. Many heads turned to face us, looking over to where we stood, judging, plotting, or admiring, I couldn't tell. There were too many eyes on me, and their noise was too fucking loud.

"Oliver," Jinx pulled me out, and I snapped my eyes forward where the girl whose name started with an L looked up at me with a cup in hand. Cheap vodka on ice. The burn hit the back of my throat as I drank it in one large gulp to drown out the noise around me. Setting the plastic cup on the hood of the car, I looked back over at Jinx who wore a pleasing grin. "You okay?" he asked, and I nodded in reflex. "Let's go inside. I'll tell you all about Scott."

After two drinks, I'd learned Scott kept to himself and made zero friends with the other security guards at Dolor. My nerves calmed a tad from the liquor, mind stuck in a trance, and my gaze hung on to the blur of bodies dancing before me. A new song I'd never heard of drifted, laughter and soft voices flowed, and the girl with the L name ended up at my side, the both of them feeding me drinks and information. None of which were of any use to me.

Everything he'd said about Scott wasn't new to me.

36

Scott was quiet, careful, and cautious.

The only person he fancied was Mia.

"I'd never heard anyone talk to Lynch the way Scott did." Jinx leaned over and flicked his cigarette, dropping ashes in a cup between us. "Scott just didn't give a shit, you know? Acted like he was doing Lynch a favor by being there, and Lynch never said otherwise. It was fucking weird, and it pissed off some of my mates. The whole situation was dodgy."

"So, you have nothing," I mumbled before bringing the rim of the cup to my lips. Sinking back into the couch, I stretched open my thighs as my heel tapped over the ground.

"The best I can do for you is to try and get his address tomorrow. My shift starts at one, but it's risky. I'm putting a lot on the line for you."

"I'll take care of you," I said, meaning every word. Usually, I wouldn't put anyone on the line for me, but Mia? There was no line.

Jinx stood and gripped my shoulder. "I know you will. You've never done me wrong."

After every sip, it became harder to hold it together. I clenched my teeth and fisted the plastic cup at the smiles surrounding me, couples rubbing against each other, and people pairing off. My eyes burned from the memories swirling inside me, reminding me how far apart Mia and me were.

"Jinx says you're a writer?" L asked with a hand over my stretched thigh and vodka in her breath. I climbed to my feet and snapped my eyes to where Jinx had been sitting moments before. "He's gone," she added, tugging on my arm.

"Where did he go?" The room spun as sweat, the beat, and the laughs infiltrated my useless fucking brain. The dizziness sent me back over the couch, and I dropped my head into my hands.

"C'mon, I'll take you to him." The girl with the L name lifted me off the couch and led me down a hall. We squeezed through sweaty bodies, and drinks spilled down the front of my shirt and pants until we pushed through a door. The room was bright, and all I wanted was to lay my head to stop the world from spinning. The last time liquor hit my tongue had been with Mia on New Year's, and my tolerance for it had since ceased. "You're wet." She giggled, her hands crawling over my chest.

We were in a small room, separating the kitchen from another door leading somewhere else. Disgusted by the touch, I gripped L's wrist and pushed her arm away. She had blonde hair, but brown seeped from her roots, and her black eyes looked up at me from below as she held my hips steady against the wall. Everything about her screamed my mum, and I wanted to curl inside a ball until she disappeared.

"I have to go. Tell Jinx I'm leaving for me?"

A curtain of blonde hair surrounded the faux innocence in L's black eyes. She was too close, and the air around me thickened. I laid my hands over her shoulders to keep her at a distance, but she was too drunk to take notice in my placid rejection.

"It's okay. We're alone in here." L's voice hit my skin, sounding like syrup pouring from sticky red lips. She gripped my bicep, and naturally, I jerked away from her.

The wall behind me was the only source to steady myself through the swaying fog. Time didn't pass normally in this black hole. "I need air … I need to find air. I need to find Mia."

"Is she your girlfriend?" L asked, and my head snapped forward at the sound of Mia's name coming from somewhere else other than my head.

She's my love. Why couldn't she meet me? We'd made a promise. Hell, we fucking made promises. Plural. "I can't feel her anymore." I scratched at my chest. The alcohol was poisoning me—my heart and mind. "Why can't I feel her? Something's not right. I don't feel right."

My back hit the wall again, and I dragged down until two hands gripped my hips to keep me upright. "Oliver." My name slithered into the space between us. "Are you okay?"

"Yes, I'm okay! I'm fine!" I pushed past her, stumbling through the other door, into a garage, until reaching the side of the house. My fist punched the stucco, breaking the skin, and I turned and slid down the rough siding until my bum hit the floor. Fist pounding and blood spilling, I was drunk in despair and stuck in the middle of nowhere.

I shoved my hands into my pocket for my mobile.

Ringing Travis, he picked up with a tired tone, and my fingers pinched the bridge of my nose. "I'm not okay, Trav," I finally admitted, dropping my forehead into my hand. My shoulders shook against the side of the house. "I'm not fucking okay. I'm a fucking mess right now."

"Where are you?"

"She's gone, man. Fucking gone," I slammed my eyes shut as the world spun around me, "What if she left me? What if she doesn't want me to find her? I don't know what to do anymore." I turned into a bloody drunken wreck. "I have to believe something happened, that she wouldn't leave me like this. She wouldn't turn her back on us—"

"That's it. I'm coming to get you."

THREE

"Don't mistake her calm,
for she's dangerous.
Copper skin wrapped in gunfire;
backbone sharpened by knives.
Silent but mind-altering;
the shiver up your spine.
You mistake her for a siren,
but she's the eerie black night,
devising to devour you whole."

OLIVER MASTERS

Mia

After counting three sunrises and three moons, the days smeared into a never-ending blur. Every day had been the same old routine, Ethan fed me breakfast, lunch, and dinner. Then he'd bathe me before rescuing me from the terrors in the middle of the night. Between all this, I'd stayed locked in this room and over this mattress. Dolor had prepared me for confinement, and Ethan wasn't forthcoming with words or reasoning.

A few hours a day, I'd overheard muffled sounds coming from upstairs as Ethan talked on his cellphone, or no sounds at all. He'd hardly left, and when he did, it was only for a short period. The times I didn't have tape around my mouth was when Ethan fed me. And the only times he didn't have my wrist bound was when he'd let me go to the bathroom on my own.

I didn't fight him or speak a word, even when the tape was gone.

A time would come when he'd slip or learn to trust me, and each day he was trusting me more and more. Regardless, I hadn't had an opportunity to get away yet, and each day that passed, I felt myself falling deeper into a dazed and paralyzed state. Every second spent here made the past seem like a dream, losing grip on what was and what could have been.

None of it actually happened.

Ollie never existed.

It was all in my head.

Because if he did exist, he would have come for me, and he didn't.

So, that was what I'd decided.

Ollie was a dream.

The large white tees were the only clothing to keep me warm. Ethan was kind enough to wash my clothes, but today was wash day, and my legs were left bare to the cold.

It was morning, and my eyes never left him as he cooked sausage over the griddle. Ethan had cracked the window above the sink open, allowing in the brisk morning air. I shivered inside the shirt, but my bare legs had nothing to hide behind.

Ethan wore jeans and a plain black shirt, his red hair in disarray.

He cut off the griddle and placed the sausage over a plate before turning to face me. His eyes roamed down to my chest to see my nipples responding to the cold. There was a longing in his deep blue eyes, but it was short-lived before he yanked the chair out and dropped the plate over the table for two.

He always looked at me with conflict. It wasn't a combination, more like flashes from one need to another. Flash. *I want her.* Flash. *I have to keep her safe.* Flash. *What have I done?* Flash. *I'm going to hell.* Flash. *Might as well drag her with me.*

Every single time.

"Ethan," I whispered, and the single word slowed his cutting of the sausage. His eyes didn't leave the plate in front of him. "I miss the way we used to be." It had only been half a lie. I did miss how we used to be. I missed being able to see him as nothing more than my security blanket. But I missed my fantasy of a man with green eyes, a warm heart, and a loving touch more. "Talk to me. Why are you doing this?"

The knife clanked against the plate, and Ethan adjusted in his chair. "I can't think right now, Jett,"—he stabbed the sausage with a fork and dropped his elbow over the table between us— "Eat."

I opened my mouth, and he slipped the sausage in before he took a bite for himself.

Swallowing, I locked my gaze on to a book of matches next to a candle over the counter. "Untie me. You can keep my ankles bound, Ethan. I'm not running anywhere. Just let me feed myself."

After a long pause of silence, Ethan stood and cleared the table free of silverware, dropping both knives and forks into the sink, then crouched behind me and undid the zip ties from around my wrists. Instant relief set into my arms, and they felt like Jell-O as I tried bringing them up to my plate. "Thank you."

He knew I wasn't going anywhere either. Not yet, anyway. With my ankles bound, I couldn't run. Ethan returned to his seat and picked up a piece of sausage with his fingers. A smile fought its way through, knowing he'd cleared the table of weapons I could stab him with, but it was just as easy to force the smile back down. I was a caged animal in these restraints, in this cabin, and my mind.

After breakfast, Ethan cleaned the mess, hand-washing each dishware and placing everything back where they belonged. He swiped the book of matches from the counter and dropped them into a drawer beside the small fridge. Once the kitchen was spotless, Ethan lifted me into his arms and proceeded to carry me down the flight of stairs. How long would he be able to keep this up?

He kept my arms free, and I laid over the mattress, ready for my morning nap.

This routine was my life now, but I refuse to let it be my forever.

"I'll grab you pants today," he offered, looking down at me.

I kept my eyes forward, glazed, unblinking.

Believe it or not, this was me fighting.

Each day was a struggle to not surrender to the fade. Instead, my body stayed in reserve. Comatose and utterly compliant on the outside, but on the inside, I never stopped planning my escape. Smart. I had to be smart.

Ethan stood over me, awaiting a response he'd never get. All I wanted was for him to go upstairs and make his call so I could fall asleep to the muffled sounds of his voice and dream of the angel who came to me when my eyes closed—my green-eyed angel with the voice of song and gentle, slow hands.

Ollie …

"Keep them closed," he whispers in my ear. I know he's beside me, his free and gentle spirit is radiating and raising every hair over my tingling skin.

We're lying over his bed, completely still. It's quiet now, aside from the air releasing through my nose and the shallow breaths coming from him. I don't know what his plans are yet, but everything Ollie does is not without purpose.

His sculpted yet slender body moves over me with ease, and my legs fall to the sides to let him in. He's holding himself up because I don't feel his weight, and his palms clasp around my ears. I no longer hear anything, only a soft and continuous beating from within. It's either his heartbeat or mine. I can't tell.

His minted breath hits my lips first, and it makes me dizzy. I'm trying to remain still, but when Ollie's mouth traces mine, the heartbeat in my ears slams harder and quickens with every sweep of his tender lips. Mine quiver, his breath shatters, and I taste him upon each inhale. We're not even kissing, but his mouth still has a way of exploring mine and my lips part, anticipating his every move.

His mere taste is nostalgic, a slice of heaven, and I long for more. Slowly, his lips stroke mine, unapologetically yet forgiving. And how is it possible? He nips at my bottom lip, and a flame lights as I crumble. Each time I lift my head for more, he pulls away, and the loss slices through me.

It's exhilarating. Almost too much to bear any longer. An ache forms inside my chest from the torture. Why can't he give me what I'm needing? But I trust him, and so I remain still as I'm breaking apart beneath him.

Suddenly, Ollie's tongue sweeps against mine, and every nerve bursts into flames. A fire flares behind my eyes. I don't know why, but I want to cry. He's inside my head, inside my chest, teasing my very heart, but he's barely touching me, and it's all too much.

A whimper escapes me, and Ollie surrenders, catching my mouth. My chest, it clenches with every stroke of his tongue, and we kiss as if emotions are bleeding out between the sheets. Tears roll down my face, and the salt mixes with his sweet taste. I don't understand what is happening to me. I'm shaking. The beating inside my ears is so loud now. Its fast pace doesn't match the slow and consuming rhythm of his kiss.

Finally, Ollie pulls away and grazes my wet cheek with his thumbs. Both his forearms and words shudder as he says, "Now, love. Now open your eyes." Speechless, I blink three times as glossy green eyes stare down under wet lashes. "What do you feel?" he asks nervously, and his eyes bounce between mine as the crease between his brows appears.

I suck in air then release a steadier breath. Ollie was able to show me a remnant of the way I made him feel. The constant dilemma to fight or let go, and this was only a kiss. But Ollie managed to by shutting off my other senses. I closed my eyes. He blocked out my sound. The only touch was his lips his hands, feeding me his bohemian heartbeat. "Everything. I feel everything, Ollie."

Ollie closes his eyes for a moment and licks his lips. "Do you understand now?"

I bring my palm to his face, nodding. "Yeah. I do."

Shaken awake, I blinked my eyes open to Ethan standing over me with a bag in his hand.

"Did you have a terror?" he asked with his brows bunched together. "You're crying."

I swiped the back of my hand across my cheek and shook my head.

44

"I'm sorry I left you alone." The mattress dipped as he sat beside me. "I have pants for you. A pair of jeans and these," he took a pair from the bag and examined them, "sweats. They'll probably be too big, but I grabbed the smallest size."

It was the most he'd said in days.

Ethan was trying to reverse the damage he'd done, but couldn't. We would never be the same, and all I wanted was to go back to sleep and be with the man in my dreams.

He would only come when the sun was out, never in the middle of the night. Never when Ethan slept beside me.

I wished there was a way I could stay locked inside the dream forever and never leave, but Ethan always woke me. Ethan always took me away from him.

"Let's take a walk," he offered with a single shoulder shrug. "You need exercise. You can't sleep your days away anymore."

The last time we went for a walk, I'd taken off running into the woods but didn't get far. He'd quickly caught up to me, wrestled me to the ground, and put me to sleep. Ethan was good at that. He knew just how much oxygen to cut off for me to lose consciousness. And the less I struggled, the quicker I was out and back in Ollie's arms. That day had been the first time I dreamt of Ollie, and since then, it was all I wanted to do.

"Okay," I mumbled through a sigh and sat up.

Victory laced his expression, and he broke the zip ties around my ankles. Once my feet would touch grass, it was game on. I would run, and he would catch me and put me back to sleep—back with Ollie. It would be a win-win for us both.

Ethan had been right, the sweatpants were loose, but didn't fall off my hipbones. Once my feet were securely inside my combat boots, he walked behind me up the stairs and toward the front door.

The same silver Nissan was parked in front of the cabin. The last time I'd seen it, I'd memorized the license plate number just in case, but I'd since forgotten the plate number, unable to contain information any longer. Even Ethan's expressions had become unreadable. His body language, too. I had no idea what his plans or intentions were. Simply, I'd become a ghost, moving along to every demand and adhering to what Ethan had expected of me. I was nothing more than a shadow with morbid thoughts of everything I wanted to do to him.

I thought about breaking the glass cup against the dining table and slicing his throat. I thought about suffocating him in his sleep with a pillow. More than a dozen murders played out inside my sick head. But there was a nagging voice stopping me. Ollie's voice. The angel.

Side by side, we walked the trails in silence until we came across a clearing in the middle of the forest. Ethan paused and turned to face me with curious eyes. "I wasn't always like this, you know," he began, and I pried my eyes away from him and toward the tree line. "I had my first kiss here,"—in my peripheral, he took a few steps to his right— "Actually, right here to be exact. Her name was Ashlyn. I was fifteen when she showed up one night on the doorstep of my family's cabin wrapped in a winter coat over her pajamas, asking if we had a bottle opener."

Ethan's chuckle should have made me feel lighter, but it didn't. I froze, catatonic and eyes fixed out before me, refusing to look at him and counting how many steps it would take before reaching the forest.

"I mean, what on earth could she need a bottle opener for? She was fourteen at the time, hardly of drinking age, especially at one o'clock in the morning. But later, I discovered it was for her father."

"I don't care," I finally whispered, but the frozen, lifeless parts of me slowly chipped away. The only thing it revealed was a rage. For some reason, Ethan's confession made me angry.

"No," he appeared before me, cutting off my direct line to the trees, "It's time you heard *my* story." His eager tone stirred the calm of the woods, causing birds to fly from their branches. I held my gaze, not moving an inch. "I walked her back, all the way to her cabin. It was a tad over a two-mile walk. Four thousand one hundred and forty steps. But it didn't take all of them for me to fall for her. It only took half. Right here, I stopped her rambling about how crazy it was that we found ourselves

46

walking in the middle of the night in the cold, two strangers. She joked that I could easily murder her and throw her body into the woods, but said she felt safe with me. And something came over me. If I didn't kiss her right then and there, I was so afraid I would never have the chance again. So, I kissed her," his voice faltered. "I'd never kissed before, and I'm sure she hadn't either, and it was sloppy and messy, but it was ours."

I'd kissed Ollie in my dreams. Over and over, we kissed, and it wasn't sloppy or messy. Every single time was earth-shattering, breathtaking, and painted an endless array of color in my black and white dreams.

"We walked the rest of the way after that, hand in hand until we reached her cabin. Her dad yelled from the inside once he heard us laughing, so we said our goodbyes after I kissed her again. It was the first and last time I ever saw her. The next morning, I woke up to helicopters flying over us, firetrucks, and alarms going off. Her cabin went up in flames because her drunk dad fell asleep with a cigarette in his hand. Ashlyn and her little sister never even made it out of their beds. They died in their fucking sleep, but her dad and his mate made it out alive. I punished myself every godforsaken day for not listening to my gut. I should've never let her back inside that house with those two drunks."

Ethan paused, and the only thing simmering in my mind was the fact the girl died in her sleep. If I died in my sleep, did it mean I could be with Ollie locked away in a dream forever? The idea washed a sense of peace over me.

"That's why I joined the police force," Ethan continued. "All I've ever wanted to do was protect those who couldn't protect themselves. I'm not going to hurt you, Jett. I'd never intentionally hurt you. Despite what you might be thinking right now, I do care about you. Maybe I'm not doing it right, and maybe I just don't know how, but … fuck … I don't know. Anytime I let someone I care about out of my grasp, death follows. I'm scared for a million damn reasons to let you go at this point."

I think a part of me could have felt for him at that moment or understand him at the very least, but this need to run had complete control of me.

47

As soon as Ethan turned his back and took a step in the opposite direction, I sprinted toward the trees.

One.

Two.

Three.

Three long strides were all it took before he brought me down.

"Are you fucking stupid?" Ethan breathed harshly in my ear as his chest pounded against my back, and I closed my eyes, waiting for him to put me to sleep. "How many times do I have to remind you? We're hundreds of miles from anything!"

He never did.

Ethan fed me dinner that night. In my zip-ties, unable to escape this abyss of nothingness. Worry etched his features with every spoonful of soup he brought to my mouth as I sat paralyzed. He pleaded for me to talk, to say anything, but I couldn't. All I could do was imagine breaking free from the restraints, snatching the silver spoon, and shoving it down his throat.

During my bath time, I laid immobile and locked inside my head as he washed me with his bare hands. They were strong and generous, but nothing like the man in my dreams. I concentrated on the lines on the wall, counting as his soapy palm roamed over every surface of my skin. Ethan washed me like the dishes in the sink—raw and to perfection until I was shiny and new again.

Ethan dressed me and carried me downstairs to the bedroom.

And that night, he laid beside me as my eyes stayed wide open. Ollie wouldn't come, not with Ethan beside me, so I'd save my rest for when Ethan was gone. There was no point when the terrors came at night, anyway.

Outside the window, the trees danced with the moon, and I watched them swaying for hours with Ethan's arm clasped around me in a tight hold. Even though his hands were on me, he couldn't touch me.

FOUR

"There's a melody to his madness,
and if you listen closely, you'll hear
the rain beat beneath his skin."

OLIVER MASTERS

Ollie

Oscar had transferred to High Down, which wasn't the worst prison in the surrounding area. Good for him. But, if I was honest, I liked the idea of knowing he was at the shit-hole Bronzefield, but at least High Down was closer.

The last time I'd seen Oscar was during sentencing. They'd allowed me to be there, and the smirk marring his mouth branded an unwanted memory ever since. It was a silent promise he'd find a way to get back at me for what I did—for what we both knew I'd taken from him.

But Oscar had it coming. For years, I'd watched him not only objectify women but brainwash them into submission to fuck them senseless. For years, he bullied and mentally-terrorized girls, grooming them into loving his sadistic nature. And for years, I'd become his project, wanting to turn me into his sidekick under his prostitution ring … What had the police called it? *Oh, yeah. White Fox.*

The cigarette between my two fingers burned, pulling me from the past. One last drag and the menthol slithered to my lungs before I flicked the nasty stick over the cracked pavement of the car park. Thanks to Travis, it only took two days for me to pick up the habit. The gum was useless at this point. Cigarettes kept my hands and grinding jaw occupied.

The sun peeked from the morning clouds, and I squinted toward the prison doors. Two minutes, and I would be face to face with my low-life brother again. I pushed off my newest purchase. An early 2000 station wagon. Black. I'd found it in a newspaper ad and negotiated my way down because the lady was eager to sell. Every day, the rental had taken a jab at Mia's and my bank account, and Travis mentioned I could pay cash for something newer. But I didn't need a fancy car. The bloody thing dropped in value every day, and I wasn't a fool when it came to money. And I especially wasn't foolish to waste a dollar to impress strangers. As long as it got me from point A to point B, the heap of junk would work the way I needed.

"When Hijack mentioned I had a visitor from no other than Oliver fucking Masters, I couldn't believe it until I saw it with my own eyes," Oscar scoffed, sarcasm dripping from his grin. "Please, tell me, little brother, what do I owe this pleasure?"

This visit wasn't like what you would see on the telly. There was no glass separating me from Oscar's vicious glare. Oscar's black hair had grown out, and the tips touched his cheeks, where his deceiving smile rested. His dark eyes traveled over my attire, judging me and my freedom.

But despite my new-found freedom from Dolor, I was still a slave to heartache. The guards took my beanie before I entered the room, and every day I still wore either sweats or the black jeans and basic shirts that screamed I'd never left the world Mia and I were in, wanting to stay there for as long as possible. Travis said it was time to shop for new clothes, especially since I had my first book signing coming up, but I didn't have time to go shopping when Mia had simply vanished.

My knee bounced under the circular table, reminding me of the one from the mess hall at Dolor as Oscar took a seat across from me, getting himself as comfortable as he could with chains around his ankles. "What have you done?" I tried to say, but it came out more like a cry for help. My chest heaved harshly to the point it hurt to breathe.

"You're going to have to be a tad more specific." Oscar chuckled and dropped his gaze to his arrested hands in his lap. "I've done a lot of things, including your precious Mia."

Oscar and Mia had sex, which had screwed with my head for a while. But I'd learned to look past it. He couldn't use that as a weapon any longer. "Where is she?" My voice raised, and I stopped and looked around to see correctional officers eyeing our exchange. I lowered my tone. "If I find her—when I find her—if one bloody hair is harmed on her body, I'll fucking kill you."

"Dolor did a number on you, yeah?" Oscar raised a brow and moved his chained hands over the table to lean in. "Do you hear yourself? Look at me,"—he dropped his eyes to the chains— "what could I possibly do?"

"Who have you been in contact with?"

"Oliver, you sound like you've gone mad. I think you need help."

I shook my head, my heart pounding out of my chest. "This isn't funny. We both know you took her and why. Tell me where she is."

"We're still talking about Mia, right?"

"For fuck's sake, yes. Mia." These games grew old fast, and he was already getting inside my head, using my desperation as entertainment. I should've known better.

"You know what I want. Give me what's mine, and I'll release her," Oscar said in a low tone. His fingers managed to scratch the back of his other hand, a habit he had his entire life. His brow raised, waiting for a response. But with that single scratch, he'd already told me what I needed to know. He didn't have her. "What's it going to be?"

If Oscar didn't have Mia, it only confirmed Ethan Scott's involvement, and Oscar couldn't help me. It was true, I'd do just about anything to get Mia back, including asking for my brother's assistance, but Oscar would be of no use to me. I needed someone on the outside—a person who had connections and more access than a phone call and an eight-day wait for visitation.

I stood and pushed in the chair as Oscar straightened in his when he noticed this conversation was over. "I'm not coming back, O. I hope this place changes you, I do. And for your health, I hope to God you had nothing to do with Mia's disappearance." I leaned in, leaving a challenging space between us. "Don't underestimate me. You have no idea how far I'm willing to go."

Fury swallowed his smile as he stood to match my height. "Are you threatening me?"

"Come on." I laughed. "You know me. I don't make threats." I tousled his greasy hair with a smirk. "Don't bend over, big brother."

"You stole from me, you bloody bastard!" His cuffs bounced off the table, and his shouts faded as I walked away. Guards rushed past me, and I swallowed the smile wanting to merge with my lips.

The mobile sitting on the dresser blew up, ring after ring, every call either Travis or Laurie, my contact with the publishing house. For days, I'd ignored everyone, and today was no different. My greedy eyes remained on the digital clock over the nightstand back at the hotel room, awaiting the proper time to ring Bruce, Mia's dad.

Pennsylvania was only five hours behind me, and it was a tad past noon. Not a day went by I didn't make that call, eight in the morning his time, to see if he'd heard from her. Today would be no different.

And for thirty more minutes, my fist clenched as I sat at the edge of the made-up bed, staring at the green letters until they blurred into an unrecognizable shape.

At exactly 1:00 pm my time, my alarm went off, and I swiped the mobile off the nightstand.

"Nothing," Bruce greeted me through a weary sigh. "You know you don't have to call every day. I'll call you if I hear something."

I appreciate it, Bruce, but I'm still calling. "Did you file a missing person's report yet?"

The hesitation in the silence lingered for a moment, and I already had my answer.

"Oli—"

"No, don't. I don't want to hear it."

"I'm sure she's fine."

"I want to believe that, but I know different."

"I'll call you if she turns up."

"I'll ring you tomorrow."

And that was how the conversation had usually gone. Mia had always said her relationship with her dad had been estranged from the moment her mum died. My faith in humanity was slowly dissolving with each passing day. It had always been Mia against the world, but now it was the two of us against them. She had me, and I hoped it would be enough to save her.

My resources were limited, coming straight from a reformatory school without many friends. Jinx had swiped Ethan's address from Lynch's office out of the goodness of his heart, but I still wired his mother funds to keep food in the fridge. He'd said it wasn't necessary, but I couldn't let his family go hungry either. Jinx was a good man. He worked hard and stayed away from trouble for the most part. But like every other bloke, his biggest weakness was girls. And Jinx liked to drink from a tall, white glass of milk. His words, not mine.

A few days ago, I'd driven past Ethan's house to find no one home. I'd even peeked through the windows and challenged every lock, but nothing. Only a nosy neighbor who wanted to know what I was doing loitering around Ethan's cookie-cutter home. After striking a conversation, the polished older lady had mentioned she hadn't seen him or his car in a week, which wasn't unusual for him. He'd always leave for weeks at a time. I'd also tried his mobile, but the number was disconnected.

During my last visit with Lynch, he'd informed me that Ethan resigned by email, and he'd taken off on release day, which also wasn't unusual. Lynch only had him in contract until that day. None of it made sense. It was all too easy—too clean.

The rap at the door grabbed my attention.

"It's Travis. Your mate. Remember me? Pretty blond hair. Irresistible blue eyes." I made no movements to get up, but then … Another knock. "C'mon, mate. It's cold out here, and I need to talk to you."

I stood and walked to the door to unlock it. Travis sauntered in and plopped over a navy armchair, making himself comfortable. Regarding my shirtless chest and joggers, he raised a brow. "You can't go to Thurrock like that." I paused and narrowed my eyes, waiting for him to drop a laugh or a line to indicate he was joking. For two and a half seconds, we had a stare-off. "I'm serious," he added.

"No, no, no, no …" I shook my head and dropped over the edge of the mattress with my head in my hands. My chin fastened between my fingers, and I peered up at him. "I left that place two years ago, Trav. I'm never going back." My main focus was on finding Mia. There was no reason good enough to go back to that shit-hole. None.

"Summer's receiving calls. Threats. The Links are looking to collect. I only need you there to back me up."

Except for that.

I groaned. "I thought you were past the Links and moved on from that life. What about Summer? The baby?" Guilt ate at his features as he ran the pad of his thumb over the flint wheel of the lighter, igniting and watching the flame fade away. Over and over. "What do they want?" I finally asked with my hands in the air.

The vein in his neck popped, making the angel wings tattoo come to life. Trav's eyes moved from where the flame disappeared to me. "They want me to finish the job I was arrested for."

"How much?" I'd rather pay them off and finally get him out of this mess. There wasn't an amount I wouldn't pay for Summer and their baby's safety. He'd finally got his life in order. How long had he been keeping this from me?

"I'm not asking you for money." The lighter disappeared inside his fist as he leaned closer. "I'm meeting them at Jack's. The pub in Ockendon. It's an hour from here—"

"I know where it is," I seethed.

"You can stay in the car. I just need someone there in case the conversation goes south."

"South …" I laughed incredulously, "South. You're walking in and saying what? *Thank you but no thanks, I'm out.* You can't be serious, Trav. What direction are you expecting this to go? East? They're not going to let you out until you get the job done. And even then, I'd be shocked it would ever be over." Travis had asked me because he knew I'd never say no. However, my main focus was on finding Mia.

Travis answered my turbulent thoughts, "You're right. I'm sorry for dragging you into this. I don't know what else to do. I can't let anything happen to Summer. To the baby. I'm desperate here. It's like no matter how hard I try, I can't escape the past … I. Can't. Run. Fast. Enough."

In the face of my boundless heart, Travis and I had piled into his banger. Though the hour drive was silent, my head, heart, and soul screamed for Mia. It was painful being this far from her. I understood Travis's fear, the reason I'd gotten into his car to begin with. No matter how hard I tried, it was as if the entire world was against the two of us being together, our love tested. I was desperate but had no direction on which way to go. Lost. I was fucking lost.

"You staying?" Travis asked from the driver's side once we pulled up to the white standalone building. We couldn't see in through the blacked-out windows of Jack's, but there were numerous cars out front. Expensive cars. The Links were here.

I shook my head, climbed out of the car, and stretched my legs. Travis was my friend, and the hour drive gave me time to think this through. His head popped from over the hood on the other side.

"I have a plan, but you have to follow my lead." I pulled my hood over my head and peered back over at him, resting two hands over the top of the car. "Do you trust me?"

"With my life."

My hands tapped the hood once, and we took off inside. The bell chimed, acknowledging our presence. Travis stepped around me and nodded over to the bar, where a group of three men huddled. I'd been around intimidating men my entire life between the business Oscar was in and the johns Mum used to bring home.

"Travis, you brought a friend." The smallest of the three greeted Trav with a grip on the shoulder and nodded in my direction. "How was your time?"

Patrons of the bar eyed our interaction before going back to their day drinking. This was the norm around here in Ockendon—at Jack's. Five men with tattoos in all black at this hour only meant dodgy business. I stood behind Travis with my arms crossed over my chest.

The Links were just that, links made up of petty crimes and drug deals to fund a more prominent trade at the top—a pyramid scheme. If a bottom link snapped, the organization still held strong.

"Have a seat," a voice stated from a stool behind the other two. "Doris, a round for my friends." The bartender dropped two glasses over the bar in my peripheral. My eyes stayed glued to the man who radiated arrogance, legs parted, posture relaxed. Most likely packing behind his excessively loose jeans and jacket. "Are you going to introduce me?"

Travis stepped to the side to reveal me, and that was when his eyes found mine.

Dex Sullivan.

He chuckled and ran a palm down his face. "Baby Oscar, is that you?" Dex stood, and the other two men backed up, giving the king room. He placed both hands on my shoulders and searched my eyes. "It *is* you." He grinned. "It's been a long time, Oliver."

"Not long enough."

Dex gripped my chin to get a better look, and I narrowed my eyes. Oscar and Dex were mates growing up, always in competition with one another, racing up the ladder of crime. Oscar put together *White Fox*, losing his best mate in the process. Because of envy and greed, the two had a falling out. It seemed Dex went to the competition. "I've been meaning to thank you for slamming your brother. Tosser deserved it, yeah?" Dex swiped the drink from the bar and shoved it into my chest. "To Oliver!"

"To Oliver!" The regulars shouted in unison.

"Drink up, mate." Dex flashed a menacing white smile. "Doris, let's do another. This is a celebration." He twirled his finger, and my hand gripped the glass before chugging it and slamming it over the bar face down. Travis's brows snapped together, and I shook my head. It wasn't the time to explain. Dex and me had more important things to discuss. "Oliver Masters, the boy who spits on fanny before he smashes." Dexter chuckled. "You know, we call it OJ'ing now. You're a fucking legend, baby O."

"Here's the deal." I didn't have time to schmooze. "I've come into a situation where I need services."

Dex pressed his lips together and dropped his head, then peered up at me through humorous eyes. "Just like your brother, Oliver." He gripped my shoulder, led me to a stool, and shoed the rest of his men away as Travis stayed quiet at my side.

"I'm taking the job for Travis. Show my commitment. But I need some things in return."

Dex grinned. "We don't pay in favors, little O."

"I don't need the money. I need services. One, Travis is off the hook infinitely. He's no longer doing the Links bidding. Free and clear, he's out."

"You're going to have to put more on the table if you're asking for two things and only completing one job."

"No, you're missing the point. Travis isn't working with the Links any longer, period. This job I'm doing is to show you my commitment. The deal is, you find me someone, and if you do, I can get you something you've always wanted." Making a deal with Dex Sullivan was a huge risk. If there was one person equally dirty and hungry for money as Oscar, it would be Dex, who happened to have the connections I needed. And, it seemed as if the dicey and cunning cards rose from Hell and fell at my feet. *Perfect timing.*

Dex tilted his head. "And what do I want?"

"*White Fox.*"

"Nice try, baby O. We both know there is no more *White Fox.*" Dex shook his head with the drink pulled to his mouth. His eyes slid over to his mates, who both stood in the corner of the pub watching us.

I took a step closer and cut off his line of vision to his entourage. My confession had to stay discreet, for Dex's ears only considering I had what he wanted, and the very thing he wouldn't want to share with anyone else, especially his boss. Greed and power and all. "I am *White Fox.*"

My comment captured his attention as I knew it would.

Dex lowered his drink, his brows pinching together. "I don't understand."

"You knew my brother. He was a bloody idiot, all jump first, ask questions later. He didn't try and force me all these years because we shared the same blood. No," I shook my head and leaned closer, "he wanted me because I didn't operate like everyone else. I think outside the box. I see lines before they're drawn. I feel intentions before they're stated. I'm always ten steps ahead."

"*You* are *White Fox.*"

I held my arms out to the sides. "In the flesh."

FIVE

"Her ravenous fire
lights a cigar
with her smile.
She was always
crazy like that."

OLIVER MASTERS

Ethan

Mia was acting strange.

Not your typical girl who'd been taken and held against her will. Although Miss Jett was anything but ordinary, so I wasn't sure what to expect with her. First, she'd been hell bound on killing me, which *was* expected. Now, it was as if she couldn't recite the alphabet.

She was confusing the hell out of me.

Our stay at the cabin lasted longer than I'd originally wanted. Mia, again, disrupted my plan, and I had to figure this shit out. For almost two years, the plan had been in motion. The cabin held all my resources before taking off to another country. By the time my mates from the academy put the pieces together at Dolor—if they ever put the pieces together—I would be long gone without a trace, living somewhere on some yacht, over some ocean, sipping on some drink in some warmer weather.

But what the fuck was I going to do with Mia? Not only had she corrupt my plans, but she cracked my common sense too. And she was right. I wouldn't lay a hand on her. Mia was the first girl I'd cared about since Livy died. It also didn't mean I was just going to let her walk out of here. Perhaps she could learn to spend the next sixty years or so running away with me. Maybe she could learn a thing or two about life on the water. Anchor a ship, sail through a storm, and learn to gut a fish—maybe even learn to love me.

Surprisingly, no one was looking for her anyway.

Dean Avery kept me updated. I'd met the twenty-something-year-old gypsy two years ago after a trip to Nova Scotia during a bidding war in Halifax on the *Carmen Olivia*. It seemed, no matter the cost, we'd both stopped at nothing to win the beautiful boat with the fated name of my sister. After a long day back and forth, both of us had been out fucking bidden and exchanged sob stories over aged whiskey at Durty Nelly's. Dean had been running away from something too. We'd connected. He'd disapproved of my plans to murder. But he'd understood my reasons and my fight for family, for justice. He'd gone on about being able to do things most couldn't and get me the documents I needed to help carry out my revenge.

It was then, two strangers in an Irish pub both far away from home, when justice became more than a dream. It became real—tangible. By the time we'd parted ways, it was as if we were two brothers from another lifetime. I'd never seen him again after that. Dean changed his number every month, along with his location. He'd call once a week, same time, and kept his promise on getting the documents and information I needed.

No one reported Mia as missing yet.

I only needed her to trust me enough to get her quietly on a plane out of the UK. Her passport and birth certificate were easy to retrieve, thanks to Dean. I'd left a few details out, the biggest one being I'd taken Mia against her will. Dean was under the impression she was my girl. He'd never go for kidnapping, especially if he knew she was in love with someone else. Dean could look past a lot, even me murdering killers, but not separating love. Hopefully, I could break the fucking umbilical cord tying Mia to Masters soon and get her on team Ethan before we had to board a plane.

Staying here another day wasn't an option.

We had to leave tomorrow.

"What's taking so long?" I asked after knocking a knuckle over the bathroom door. She'd been in there too long. Mia didn't answer. "I'm coming in." The bathroom door creaked open, and Mia had submerged herself in the tub with her head peeking above the waterline. "What are you doing?"

She looked straight ahead at the water dripping from the faucet.

"Mia?"

Drip.

Drip.

"Come on, let's get out of here, yeah?" I took a seat over the toilet and looked down at her. "You're going to freeze to death."

Mia didn't move. Mia didn't blink. I'd seen her naked too many times to count, but each time still sent a buzz to my cock. I couldn't remember the last time I'd been buried inside a female, using all my nights caring for the tease instead. Not like she owed me anything for it.

But there she was, ivory skin, perfectly proportioned tits, pink hardened nipples, and a soft velvety pussy. My fingers and tongue had been inside her. I'd tasted her. I'd pushed my dick through her slit, feeling her warmth, and she still wouldn't let me in. It was no secret, the girl got an A for pissing me off, but I fed off the challenge. Masters' hold had been stronger than I thought, but it wouldn't be much longer until I'd have her completely. Over the last few days, she'd turned into this emotionless puppet. I pulled every string, and she submitted.

I yanked the plug from the tub and gripped her arm and forced her out. Mia stood before me naked and wet as I took a seat over the toilet. She didn't even shiver. Just fucking stood there and stared ahead, her olive skin asking to be touched despite her refusal to talk to me. It creeped me out how out of touch she was with reality.

My palms wrapped around her sides, and I dragged my hands up until they rested below her breasts. Mia's muscles relaxed in my hands, and I brushed over her nipples with the pads of my fingers. She took a step forward between my opened thighs, and my gaze flicked up from her breasts to her face. Her expression was stone cold. *Was she testing me?*

"Jett, you're being ridiculous. You can't act like this forever," I sighed, dropped my hands, and stood, towering over her to yank the towel from the hook.

Mia didn't move.

I dried her off and slipped one of my shirts over her head. My puppet. Mia's hair was still wet. I wrung it out into the towel. Mia allowed me to care for her. It made her easy at first. The past three days, she'd been out of the zip ties. And maybe she trusted I wasn't going to hurt her. Perhaps she finally fucking realized I cared. I had only been doing what was best. But I missed her storm. I missed the bite in her words and the fury in her eyes. I missed the fucking challenge.

She followed my lead willingly down the stairs and stood beside the mattress—waiting for my next command. "Get some sleep. We're leaving in the morning. Somewhere warm." Like she fucking cared. Mia's eyes never left the window as she sprawled out over her side of the mattress. I shook my head and flipped the lights off, trusting she'd be in the same position when I'd get back like she was the night before.

I took two steps at a time up the stairs when my mobile rang.

"Something came up. We're already three hundred miles out," a reluctant voice pulsed through the phone.

Dean.

"Were you found?" The Avery's stayed low-key, survived off the minimum, and never lived in one place too long. He'd told me some story about their history, but at the time, I had to be either too drunk or exhausted to take it seriously.

"They killed him."

"Who? One of your brothers?" I fell back into the couch. He had two brothers, Luke and Ash, and talked about them often. The three of them were close, and I envied their brotherly bond. If anything happened to one of his brothers there was no telling what Dean would do. Apart from murder. The Avery's didn't kill. He'd reminded me too many times to count.

"Our pops. Long fucking story. But I can't help anymore. There's shit I have to take care of. Luke's on a mission of his own. Everything's set up for you. Keys are in the office. Ask for Mandy. I left her with the bag."

Fuck. Their dad. I leaned my elbows over my knees and brought my hand to my forehead to squeeze my temples. "I'm so sorry, mate." I'd never met Dean's dad, mum, or brothers, only him. But Dean and I were close. Friends were hard to come by for the two of us. He'd spent his life on the run with his family for reasons I couldn't comprehend. Now his dad was dead, which only meant one thing. The other three were completely dependent on Dean's direction. He had to step up for his family.

I waited until he was able to fight out more words. His silence screamed emotion. "Thanks, E."

"Is there something I can do?"

"Nah, man. This is something you don't want to get involved with. You *can't* get involved with. You wouldn't understand. But I appreciate it. I do."

"There may come a time when you need someone to do your dirty work. Just ring, and I'll be there." I would. Just because they didn't believe in taking matters into their own hands—just because they couldn't kill for whatever reason—didn't mean I couldn't. I'd do it for him and for everything he'd done for me these last few years.

Dean chuckled through the phone, but it was empty and forced. "I'll keep that in mind. Listen. Stay safe, E. I'll give you a call when I can."

"You too." The call disconnected, and I spent the next few hours packing the car and scrubbing the house of evidence—of any indication Mia was here. Nothing to trace her back to me. By three in the morning, I slipped downstairs to find Mia exactly where I left her.

Her brown eyes were still open and gazing through the window into the night. I'd already tried talking to her. I'd tried to explain myself. She wouldn't listen. I wanted to scream no one cared about her. I was the only fucking one. For her entire life, everyone had done nothing but lie and toss her to the side as if she were rubbish.

My clothes smelled of bleach. I stripped down to my boxers and laid in my spot beside her. She had to have been cold. The heater didn't work down here. Whether she liked it or not, I pulled her on top of me inside my arms. She didn't say anything or fight me on it. She obeyed like a puppet. My puppet. Which only made it harder not to please her the way I wanted to. A constant war against my head and my ... well ... head.

I could fuck her so easily and sleep even easier.

But I wouldn't do that, not unless she wanted me to.

Swallowing the temptation, I kept my dick in my boxers and let my hands stray over her cold skin to warm her, up her thighs, over her arse, across her back. She'd never flinched, and each night I took it further, testing her, breaking her. One day she'd realize Masters had never cared about her, and until then, I'd remind her how much I did. I could make her feel good, ease her mind, and bring back the spark within her.

The struggle to breathe woke me as I fought for air. A cloud of smoke tumbled down the stairs and seeped into the room. My eyes burned. "Mia!" She wasn't at my side. My pulse hammered in my chest. Coughing, I sat up to bright fiery lights bouncing against the walls from the top of the stairs. The smell of burning. Panic. "Mia!" I couldn't get my pants on fast enough. No time for a shirt or shoes, but the heat from the fire was too much. I ran back for my shirt to cover my head and ran back up the stairs. There wasn't time to think—to plan. The fire roared in the kitchen. Orange, red, and yellow flames danced over the stove and crawled up the wall, the curtain's being eaten away by the rage of the heat. It was spreading fast. My burning eyes darted around the thick smoke. Mia was laying over the couch, bright white tee against the black fog with her eyes closed. An angel wrapped in hell. Had she lost her bloody mind?

The car keys were laying on top of the fridge. There was no way I could get to them. Thank God for a spare inside the car. It was all I needed.

I scooped up Mia and flung her over my shoulder.

"Stop it!" she screamed against the sound of the cabin burning down. "Let me go!" I hadn't heard her voice in so long. In that moment, she had more fire in those five words than my childhood cabin. Her screams had the power to slice through the smoke as she fought against my tight grip. Each cry stole another breath I couldn't afford. Another punch to the gut.

My knees hit the floor, and she fell from my arms.

Flames and smoke surrounded us, and I couldn't see anymore.

Her cries turned into coughs, and both of us gasped for air, crawling across the wooden floors, searching for clean oxygen like deprived junkies.

Mia wanted to die—to burn both of us alive.

We were going to die.

"Shhh …" Ashlyn giggles. "My dad will hear us."

"I want to see you again." I've never been this real with anyone, this raw. Ashlyn has the power to make me say things I would never say out loud. She's some sort of enchantress. "I like you. Like a lot. Already. Have I gone mad?"

It's dark, and the single light buzzing above reveals the blush crawling up her neck. "Tomorrow," she whispers, answering my first question. Her blush answered the second.

"Okay. Tomorrow." We have tomorrow. We have this entire holiday.

"Goodnight, Ethan." Ashlyn steps forward. It's small but enough. She wants me to kiss her again. I smile because I can't help it. Our first time was messy. I didn't know what I was doing before. But this is my chance to make it right. I close the distance between us and pull the glove from my hand. My touch is warm against her cold cheek.

I don't hesitate and lower my head and kiss her. The force causes her to take a step back, and I sneak my arm around her waist and pull her against me. Chest to chest. Heart to heart.

And this time, it's perfect.

SIX

"We're all born without
mercy and half a soul.
And we'll spend the rest
of our lives starved
and searching."

OLIVER MASTERS

Ollie

wasn't perfect.

I'd never claimed to be better than the next person. I'd made mistakes, continually throwing my own spanner in the works to save my arse when the time came. This was that time.

And suddenly, I was thankful for my grudge against Oscar.

Once Oscar had pinned the attempted murder of Brad on me, I'd stolen *White Fox* out from under him. The money, assets, accounts, I'd drained and hidden the cash in a secure location no one would be able to find or trace back to me—cash I had fully intended to give to Brad's wife and two kids. Though their dad had a taste for prostitutes, preferably Mum, his family was innocent.

After they'd confirmed me as a suspect, I had tattooed a hint of the location beside the scissors on my arm before turning myself in. It had been a daily reminder, my strength to make it through my false punishment so one day I could, at the very least, give back a morsel of what had been taken from the family, though it would never be enough.

I'd become White Fox, and my brother had been chasing me ever since.

Oscar should've known never to trust a fox.

Dex wasn't any better of a man than Oscar, but Dex had resources. And desperation called for making deals with the devil and bathing in sin. But the devil would be foolish to underestimate a broken man with nothing left to lose.

It made me nervous to mention Mia's name to Dex, so I gave Scott's name instead, sure wherever Scott was, so was Mia. The last thing I needed was for Dex to find out about Mia, for him to use her as a pawn and hang her life over my head as some sort of sick threat in the future.

It had been two days since the meeting with Dex. Travis and I were back in Surrey, sitting at a bar in the village and waiting on orders for my first assignment from the Links, and for Laurie, my agent, to meet us.

The Green Lion's atmosphere was very different from Jack's. On the outside, the building had welcoming white brick, green trim, and brown shingles, straight out of a fairy tale. The inside was warm and inviting, with a fire going in the curved-brick indoor fireplace.

"I don't like it." Travis groaned beside me with a shake of his head.

We'd found a booth in the far corner of the restaurant, and the constant tapping of his fork against the wooden table beside his uneaten burger wasn't helping my headache. "It is what it is."

"I can't let you keep fixing my past."

"Trust me, mate. I need this more than you. I need to find Mia, and Dex is my only option." The barkeep turned up the volume on the telly

68

hanging on the wall above the bar, and it displayed news of a cabin fire in Cheshire last night. I returned my attention to Travis. "Eat your burger before she gets here."

"Two fatalities in a cabin fire," the news reporter stated on the television, pulling my gaze from Travis to the images from the night before flashing over the screen. "Investigation continues to the cause of the fire, and the identities of the bodies are still underway."

The news lit an ache in my chest. I stood, emotions kicking into high gear. Something wasn't sitting right with me. My gaze locked on the screen as a drone flew over the destruction, capturing images of smoke and the cabin burnt to a crisp. My mind was in chaos as it tried to put together what I was seeing and feeling inside my chest.

"What is it?" Travis asked with a mouthful.

"I don't know." I shoved my hand into my pocket to retrieve my phone and dialed Dex. He didn't answer. "It's Oliver. The cabin fire in Cheshire. Find out who owns it and give me a ring."

Travis spoke up behind me, "You think Scott had something to do with it?"

"I'm just following my gut." Usually, I was right. And for once, I didn't want to be. I'd put all my cards into one basket with Dex. No, I didn't trust him, but sometimes you had to play nice with your enemies as long as you didn't lose yourself in the process. And the only way I could lose myself was if I'd lost Mia.

"You're Oliver Masters," the voice was mixed with a question and statement. I pried my eyes from the television screen above the bar to a lady in her mid-thirties looking up at me, a satchel over her shoulder. Her blonde hair twisted behind her head as strands fell from the tight hold, wearing a navy suit with black heels, which only increased the agitation I'd already been facing. Big hazel eyes peered up at me behind large black-rimmed glasses, and her mouth parted. "Oh, this is great," she continued, taking in my appearance. "You're—"

I lifted my chin. "I'm what?"

"Unexpected." She slid into the booth beside Travis after a quick *"how-do-you-do"* and pulled out a laptop from her satchel. The MAC powered up, and I took a seat across from her. Travis had talked me into this meeting, but he was right. If I gave up on the future I'd worked so hard on building for Mia and me, there would be nothing left once she was back in my arms. I had to maintain my job, Dex, Laurie, and my heartache and pain. I had to do it all.

"Congratulations are in order. Your first book was a success. But it's the second book that could make or break you, and I'm sure you're already working on it."

I didn't answer, and she peered up at me from behind her round glasses.

"Of course." *Not.*

"Good." Laurie went back to typing over her laptop. Travis and I exchanged glances. "So, are you ready for your first signing this weekend? I know it can be a bit much at first, but I'll be there with you every step of the way. We'll have to get you out of those clothes and into something more—" her head tilted to the side, and she pushed the glasses up the bridge of her nose "—proper."

My mobile rang.

"Go on, answer it," Laurie stated without looking up from her computer.

I didn't recognize the number, but it could be Dex.

"Yeah?" I answered.

"I checked out the cabin. The title was transferred over to an Ethan Scott a few years back …" Dex continued, but I couldn't hear anything else.

Two fatalities.

Everything stopped—the blood in my veins, the pleads at the tip of my tongue, even my lungs stopped working. I couldn't breathe. Travis snatched the phone from my fist and jumped from behind the booth to take over the conversation. But for me? I was frozen as the world continued to spin on its axis.

Thoughts even froze inside my head.

I closed my eyes.

Mia Rose is walking closer as Alicia, Jake, and I loiter in the hall between classes. I straighten my back against the wall and hold my breath as my fingers comb my hair back. Is she coming to talk to me? The heart in my chest is beating at an impossible rate. I'm trying to keep my cool, and hope it shows, but then her eyes lock on mine, and suddenly, I've lost it. Words are lost, my grip is lost, and she walks past me.

"Breathe, Ollie," Jake whispers at my side, and that's when I realize how obvious my affections are for her. "Way to stay subtle."

"Shut up."

She disappears around a corner, and I can already feel my heart breaking with the distance. Last night she came to my room for the first time. To say I was surprised to see her was an understatement. The few hours with her were spent in crisis mode. I've never felt so calm and nervous at once. I only wanted to be myself, but it was hard when she was turning me into this new man whenever she was around. Because around her, I wasn't afraid of reality anymore. Around her, I wanted to keep my eyes open.

Jake chuckles. "She's going to break your heart."

"I can see it already," Alicia waves her arm out in front of her, mimicking an invisible headline across the air, "Sociopath stomps on dreamer's heart, death by ignorance."

Instead of fueling their amusement, I stay quiet and smile to myself. Loving her until it kills me seems like a wondrous way to go.

A sting to my cheek snapped me out of it, and I opened my eyes to see Travis staring back at me. "I'm sorry, brother," he whispered, and I looked to my left to see my agent had left. Travis grabbed my chin and redirected my gaze. "I'm so sorry."

My head shook. "No," I gritted out, and Travis dropped his head. "She can't be…I'd know if she was…I'd feel it," I slapped my chest, "right here. I'd know. She can't be."

"There were two fatalities, Oliver. Two—"

"Don't." I pushed him off me, looking for a way out.

71

Travis rushed to my side and yanked my shoulder back. "Scott owned that bloody cabin. You said so yourself. He had to have had something to do with her being gone."

My palms flew over my ears. "Stop it!" I screamed.

"Listen to me! She left you! She ran off with the wanker to a fucking cabin for crying out loud! Don't you see?" Travis's voice broke, "She's dead, Oliver. I'm so sorry, but she's gone."

I gripped Travis's shirt collar and slammed him over the bar. People jumped out of the way. "You don't fucking know her!" Spit and agony flew between us. "I would know if she was gone! She's not gone! She's not!" My fingers released from his shirt, and I darted my gaze to the crowd surrounding us. All eyes were on me. A mother held her little girl behind her. They were scared of me. I was scared of me. It was quiet. My chest ached, unimaginable pain. A fire burned in my eyes because I'd refused to cry. Because she wasn't gone.

Travis reluctantly placed his hand on my shoulder. "Okay, mate. Let's get you home."

"No." I pushed him off me, knowing what he was implying. He didn't know how I'd already made a home within Mia. She was my home, and I'd been trying this entire time to get back to her. I lost my footing, trying to push my way through the waves of gazes to find air.

My cellphone had been ringing non-stop since I'd left the bar I'd forgotten the name of. Hours had passed, I knew because it was dark outside. The reflection of the opened window stared back at me through the mirror. I'd been sitting on the bathroom floor, listening to the drainpipe leak from inside the motel walls. The occupant next door had flushed the loo numerous times over the last few hours. Poor chap must've not been feeling well, and I'd made a game of his misery.

With every flush, I'd grab a new beer bottle from the grocery bag beside me.

72

No matter how many bottles stacked to my left, the ringing from the mobile wouldn't bloody quiet. Over and over, I banged the back of my head against the opened bathroom door I'd sat against until the pain lessened inside my chest.

It never did. The ache only worsened.

"Ollie."

I looked up.

Travis stared down at me, terror in his features. From this angle, he could've passed for James Franco in the movie *Spring Breakers*. I only knew of this movie because it had played in the tattoo parlor one time when I'd gotten my ink done, though Travis's hair was blonder. Perhaps Marshall Mathers, if the talented rapper had blond braids, facial hair, and angel wings tattooed on his neck.

"You can't throw it all away," Travis stated, taking a seat on the floor across from me against the sink cabinet. "You worked too hard."

"I'm not throwing anything away. Momentary relapse," I grabbed a bottle from the bag and tossed it over Travis's lap, "Mia's alive. I'm going to find her."

"You're in denial."

I ignored his nonsense and took another sip.

He wasn't listening. No one was listening.

Even the alcohol wasn't fucking listening.

"You know, you never did tell me about her." My blurry vision settled on him, and he continued, "Who was the girl who stole Oliver Masters heart?"

"Is," I corrected, pointing at him with the bottle.

"What?"

"You're talking as if she isn't here. As if she's …" I couldn't say the word, so I just let the sentence stall like my life had. Travis turned his eyes away from me into the space between us. The person in the next room flushed the toilet, so I finished off the bottle and grabbed for another. "It's pointless because no matter what significant words I could come up with to describe what we have, it would never sound as amazing as the way

we're connected. And right now, we're connected. That, my friend, is how
I know her heart is still beating. I've memorized that sound. I could pick
her heartbeat out in a line-up. But just as much as I know the sound, I feel
the hard and steady beat inside my chest. It mirrors my own." I dropped
my head back against the door and allowed the beer to slide down my
throat. "No matter how far apart we are, I can still feel her."

"You and your words," Travis sighed, "And what happens if Mia's
gone? What then?"

"I'd die." It was as simple as that.

"From?"

"The disconnection."

Travis smacked my leg with the back of his hand. "I think you've had
too much to drink, wouldn't you say?"

I pointed the mouth of the bottle at him. "Ah, you think I'm joshing,
yeah? Read a book. You may learn a thing or two." I'd read about it
before. Dying from a broken heart was a scientific fact—death of the
desperate and lonely.

"Alright, brother. Let's get you into bed." Travis jumped to his feet
and pulled me up from the bathroom floor.

And that was the last thing I recalled.

SEVEN

"She walked through the
valley of the shadow of death,
looked fear in the eye, and fell in love."

OLIVER MASTERS

Ollie

There was a split second upon waking when everything seemed all right in the world. Mia wasn't missing. I wasn't experiencing a gruesome hangover. I hadn't made a deal with Satan. I was an honest man, living an honest life. A poet in love. For a fleeting second, my heart didn't ache and my head didn't spin.

But only for a mere second until everything had come crashing down.

Groaning, I rolled over and opened my eyes to see Travis's cheery face with a trash bag in hand, cleaning bottles from around the motel room. "What are you still doing here?" I sat up and swung my feet over the edge of the bed until they met the stiff carpet.

The bloody headache returned.

"Here, drink this." Travis threw a water bottle at me, and I caught it mid-air. "You're going to need it." I fed my thirsty soul from the poison of last night. After downing the entire bottle, Travis held up the bag, and I tossed the empty bottle into the rubbish. "It's half-past three. Dex rang."

"Why didn't you wake me?"

Travis shrugged, focusing on tying the bag and avoiding my hard glare. "You needed your beauty sleep."

I tilted my head, my eyes following his every move. Travis was nervous about something. "Well, did you answer?"

He tossed the bag outside the door, still not looking at me. "Yeah."

I stood and threw my arms up at my sides. "And?"

Travis turned and peered around the room, still not looking at me. "The plan is to meet at nine back in Ockendon."

"What are you worried about?"

"Are you sure you still want to do this? Mia's—"

"Mia's what?"

"I'm not going to be that mate who's going to tell you everything will be fine. Mia's dead, and there's no reason to continue with the Links. You should follow up with the remains for confirmation. I'll do this job, but it's not healthy to live in denial like this. I'm not going to watch you fall down that hole. I've seen it before, it's not pretty, and it's impossible to climb your way out. Trust me on this one. I'm doing you a favor. You should be grieving her, mate. Not doing a job to find a ghost. Concentrate on you. Better your life. You did it for me once, and it's time I do the same for you."

My teeth clench, and muscles twitched. "Get out."

"Oliver—"

"No, get the fuck out." I pulled a shirt over my head and walked to the door and opened it. "Go on. I'll do the job. You go back to Summer. Give her a fucking kiss, mate. Hold her close. Make love to her. Trust *me* on this, don't waste a God-given second."

Travis hung his head and walked toward me. "I didn't mean to—"

"It's taking a lot not to hit you right now. Take one for the team and fuck off."

He left. I slammed the door.

There were four of us standing in the car park at Jack's, going over the plan one last time. These boys were fresh recruits, new to the gang scene. I could tell by the way Adrian was unable to stand still. He was nervous, and I didn't blame him. But nerves could only get him arrested or worse, killed. I pulled him off to the side.

"You okay?" I needed him to pull it together if this was going to work. I couldn't have his tension spread over the other two. Adrian wouldn't look at me directly. He scratched behind his head, neck, and ran a palm down his face as his eyes wandered over the streets of Ockendon. "Hey, it's going to be alright. You have to have faith in me."

"Faith in you?" He threw his arm in the air. "I don't fucking know you, man."

Adrian was right. He didn't know me. None of them knew me, but we didn't have time to exchange stories of our past. "Look. The only thing you need to know about me is that I'm not leaving anyone behind. No one is going to jail tonight. No one is dying. All I ask in return is to trust me blindly." I gripped the back of his neck. "Can you do that?"

Standing at the same height as me, Adrian had young features, untainted by power, money, and murder, and his vibrant eyes arrested an old, determined soul. With black buzzed hair and fresh, unmarked skin, he should be fancying a nice girl at this hour, not preparing for a robbery. I would ask him how he got himself involved with the Links, but he was here now, and there wasn't time for any of us to back out. If the job didn't get done, then Dex wouldn't help me find Scott.

Mia was still alive. I had to believe in that.

"Yeah, mate. I can do that," Adrian said through a sigh.

I gripped his shoulder and pulled him back with Reggi and James, the other two boys Dex assigned to me. "Unload all your guns," I ordered, and three scared eyes shot up at me as if I'd gone mad. "I'm serious. No bullets. Make sure there isn't one in the chamber either."

"What's the point in carrying a gun with no bullets?" James, the biggest of the three, asked. He reminded me of a younger version of Travis, with blond hair and navy eyes, but James was built whereas Travis now sported a proper gut from Summer's fabulous cooking, or so I was told.

I arched a brow and lifted my chin. "Are you going to shoot it?"

"Well, no." James shook his head and raised his palm. "Only to frighten them. But things could take a turn for the worst, and we have to be ready."

"You three carry these guns around as if it gives you power. It doesn't. Your guns aren't going to save you, especially since none of you have shot a gun before." I paused and glanced around at the blokes, and neither of them corrected me. "One, you don't pull one out unless you're going to shoot it. Two, we can't draw attention to the police. And three, what if the owner of the shop has a gun? If you pull yours out, he won't hesitate to fire back. And like I told my mate, Adrian. No one is going to jail or dying tonight. If you need to take your ego with you, I suggest you keep it in your waistband, unloaded. There are other ways to get what you want."

They exchanged looks. Adrian tossed his unloaded gun into the trunk, while the other two pushed the muzzle of their weapons into their waistband behind their backs—unloaded. I closed the trunk, and the four of us piled into a prepared car with a false license plate.

The robbery hits from the bottom were in run-down places, small, and the cash was even smaller, which had been Travis's first mistake. Just because the job was small, didn't mean to treat it any differently, or be careless.

We pulled into the car park where only a single working street lamp shone over a few scattered cars. There was a clear view inside, customers sprinkled throughout, and I turned back from the driver's seat to face the recruits. Their nervous faces glowered back at me as the rain beat against the roof of the car, matching our heartbeats. "Here's the deal, this is your first run and initiation into the Links. If you can't follow my instructions or want to back out, now is the time." No one moved. "Adrian, you pull the car around to the back door. The rest of us are going in."

"We're running out the back?" Reggi, the smallest one, asked.

"We're not running out of there. We're walking." I cut the engine and exited the car, and the other two followed as Adrian moved to the driver seat. Behind me, the two boys whispered back and forth as we walked casually through the rain toward the entrance.

The bell chimed as soon as the door opened, and the customers' eyes flitted over us briefly before going back to their laundry needs. This wasn't the best side of town, and the residents of Ockendon knew to keep their noses out of everyone's business.

An older man worked the cash register, reading the newspaper and completely taken off guard. The three of us approached, and I took a step forward as the other two fell back, I'm sure wondering how this was going to play out.

"Do you know why I'm here?" I asked as the old man locked eyes on me over the newspaper. Nodding, he slowly rose from his chair, reaching for something under the counter. I leaned forward and planted both palms over the counter. "You don't want to do that." The old man paused. "I know you have video surveillance, and we're not wearing masks. I know you have a weapon under there because why wouldn't you when your shop is twenty-four-hour service. And I also know, once we leave here, you won't ring the police because this laundromat only pays for your … repulsive fetishes."

His bushy brows snapped together. "Who are you?" he asked, and I wasn't so sure I knew anymore.

"There is a car waiting at the back entrance, and you'll fill it with the contents from the safe in the back room. You can keep the money from the register. It isn't but a hundred quid, anyway—plus, your wife deserves something pretty after the shit you've put her through—and we'll leave without disturbing your customers."

The older man looked past me to James standing behind me to my left before he nodded, having more to lose if this entire ordeal went bad. The three of us followed him back to the safe, and I ordered Reggi to get back in the car as James and I helped the chap fill two laundry bags to the brink with cash.

We tossed the bags into the truck, and I slammed it shut. "You have a nice night, Mr. Taylor."

The old chap, eyes fuming in a blind rage, shook as I got into the, now empty, driver seat before driving away.

Before I'd shown up at Jack's Pub, I'd learned the laundromat we were jacking was owned by Mr. Taylor, who wasn't as innocent as he claimed to be. Even though he had more than enough money to take care of his family, his pounds went toward thirteen and fourteen-year-old girls Oscar had previously groomed for him. Oscar was gone, but I wasn't naïve to believe his taste dissipated in Oscar's absence.

"What the fuck just happened?" Adrian stated at my side from the passenger seat.

"Know your target, my friend. You always have to be ten steps ahead."

Laurie, Travis, and I arrived in London for my first book signing, and I'd escaped from their tight leash in search of the toilet room as they set up the booth. Daunt Books was a three-story wonder in the eyes of a dreamer, with mahogany shelving and railings, wooden staircases, and leather seating. The details were rich and masculine, showcasing books lined on both walls from one end to the other. The ceiling opened up to the sky, and vibrant green light pendants dropped from above, matching the same color as the paint surrounding the arched window at the end of the building. It smelled of aged paper and coffee, and the serene silence rooted itself in every nook and cranny of the bookstore, wrapping me in temporary peace.

No matter how badly I wanted to enjoy this moment, to celebrate this stepping stone in my career, I couldn't. Not without Mia here to celebrate with me. What should have been a marvelous moment, ended up being a chore I'd been forced to take part in. It seemed pointless to be here when I could be doing something, anything, to find her. She should be here with me, calming my nerves and telling me she was proud, but she wasn't.

"There's no reason to be nervous. You'll do just fine," Travis stated, appearing at my side and flipping on the faucet to wash his hands. He never used the loo, and it was just an excuse to talk me down from the cliff my emotions were hanging on. We both knew it, and we never did discuss what happened the other morning. He had his beliefs, I had mine, and there wasn't anything he could have said for me to change my mind or convince me to stop looking for her.

"I'm not nervous." I continued to roll the sleeves of my black dress shirt up until it reached my elbows before moving on to my other arm, showing my tattoos. Anything to bring forth the real me under these masked clothes that screamed I was an imposter. "I just don't do well around crowds."

I turned to face him, and he looked ridiculous in a white button-up and blazer, though Travis exuded poise and control.

"Everything is set up. There's a line out the door waiting for you. Laurie wanted to have a pep talk with you before going in, but I told her I had it under control." Travis forced a reassuring smile. "Your pretty face is on your cover, but I think it's time to show these people who the real Oliver Masters is."

"Yeah, whose idea was that anyway?"

"You're a good-looking chap," Travis adjusted my collar, "the ladies fancy you and your face sells." He patted my cheek. "Let's go, lover boy."

The event had lasted four hours long. Men and women gushed over my words, talking a million miles a minute, and I couldn't keep up. Some wanted pictures, and others simply wanted my signature inside a book they either brought with them or purchased from the table. With every passing body, my energy gradually decreased from their emotions, tears, smiles, and life stories they felt compelled to tell me about. My hyper-sensitivity made the entire event worse, mentally and physically drained from absorbing whatever they were putting off.

"Oliver?" a familiar voice stated, and I turned from the table Laurie and Travis were packing up to see the girl with the L name staring up at me with my book clutched to her chest. She looked different than when I'd first seen her at Jinx's party, no lipstick, roots touched up, and wearing a pastel floral dress despite the cold temperatures outside. L no longer looked like my mum. Did she make the hour trip to London just to see me?

"You two know each other?" Travis asked, his palm smacking my tense back.

I tilted my head toward him. "A friend of a friend."

"Well, in that case," he held out his hand, and his gaze slid over her bare legs, "Travis Lehman."

"Leigh," she introduced herself, shaking his hand with eyes locked on me. It made me uncomfortable. "Looks like I missed the event."

"It's okay, would you like for me to sign the book? I didn't know you were into poetry." I couldn't recall her mentioning it back at the party I'd met her at, though I was drunk and could have missed the entire conversation. Leigh held out my book with my face on it, and I grabbed it, leaned over the empty table, and retrieved a pen from the back pocket of my jeans.

As I signed, she added, "Can I get a picture, too? If that's all right, of course."

"Absolutely," Travis answered for me. Turning back around, I waved Leigh over and held the book up for the camera. Her arm slipped around my waist as she pulled me close, and her body trembled at my side. Travis snapped the picture. "You know, we're going to the Green Lion afterward to celebrate. You're more than welcome to join us."

My jaw flexed, and I shot Travis a knowing look. This gathering was news to me, and I especially didn't have the energy to entertain Leigh.

Leigh's eyes and voice lit up. "Oh, that sounds like fun!" She released me and took her mobile from Travis. "I'd love to come."

After everything was packed up and ready to go, I helped carry the boxes to Laurie's car before we said our goodbyes. I got on to Travis for putting this last-minute outing together without talking to me about it first. *"This is a good reason to celebrate,"* he had said, but there was nothing to celebrate. The only true measurement of success was happiness, and my number was in the negative.

The drive back to Surrey was a tad over an hour, and I'd advised Travis I'd meet him in the beer garden after ringing Dex to check on the progress with finding Scott. I'd dropped the money off from the laundromat run the night before, and he seemed pleased with how smoothly the run went. In return, Dex had confirmed he'd take a closer look into the cabin fire, get more details, and if Scott had any other properties or vehicles in his name. As always, he didn't answer, and I left an urgent message.

The rain had stopped, and the temperature decreased as the sun descended behind the arbor. I didn't want to be here, but Travis had invited his fiancé, Summer, and it was important to him for me to finally meet her. I spotted him in the garden at a secluded table in the corner with, I assumed, Summer at his side.

I made my way toward the two as they faced a band playing laid back acoustic music. A few people danced in the garden, chilled beer mugs in hand, as children ran carelessly about the swaying bodies.

After an hour, I'd learned Summer was older than I'd presumed, with golden hair, blue eyes, and soft features. At only four months pregnant, her loose blouse hid her tiny belly as she sipped on ginger ale. She was forthcoming, witty, and cursed like a sailor, but able to quiet Travis when no one else could. I liked her immediately and knew Mia would too.

Leigh showed, and I introduced her to Summer like the respectable gentleman I was, but I couldn't help the way my crestfallen heart pounded to a somber beat as they shook hands. This entire day was meant for Mia and me. She should be here. Mia should've been the first girl I'd introduce to Summer, to Travis, to everyone.

I needed another fucking drink.

The girls took off to the loo—Summer's third time—and Travis leaned into me with the cup brought to his lips. "The girl wants to fuck you," he whispered now that Summer was not around. I didn't bother meeting his eyes, keeping my gaze on the band and my hand steadying my bouncing knee. "She's not bad to look at either. She seems young but legal. Maybe some fanny would be good for you, nothing serious. You're on edge."

"Grow up, Trav. My dick doesn't get hard whenever a female is in proximity." Not anymore. That was the *medicated* Ollie, the one polluted with pills and morality stripped.

Back at Dolor, I'd discovered a lot about myself—the hypersensitivity. For me, a whisper seemed like a scream—a touch, a violation—and the energy others produced, consumed me. I'd rather be back at the motel, but I had responsibilities now and people to please—a job to do. And Travis regularly reminded me. He was only trying to be a friend.

The girls returned as soon as my phone rang. It was Dex, and I excused myself and walked off from the crowd to answer.

"Scott has no other properties besides the two you're already aware of," Dex confirmed, which was what I'd been worried about. "It can take over eight weeks to identify the bodies from the fire, but they are confident one of them is him. We just won't know for sure until after they complete their investigation." A silence played out between us. "Look, Oliver. I'll continue to look into this for you, but we have a dodgy cop who mentioned Scott is a member of the force, which you failed to tell me about. Now, I don't exactly know what you got yourself into, but if I continue digging, I want you officially on my payroll. You work for me now."

"The body in the cabin isn't Scott's. It can't be. Keep digging. I'll continue to work for you until Scott's found, but I'm giving you one week to get me a lead—something. Check the airports, street-cams, all of

Cheshire and Liverpool. If a week passes and you don't have shit, consider this deal voided."

"You'll have to give me more. Why are you looking for him?"

"That's none of your concern. Just find me Ethan Scott."

"I'll call back with your next assignment."

The call disconnected, and helplessness crept along my veins until it reached my aching heart. My fingers clenched around the mobile, wanting to drive my fist into the first object my eyes came across, and before I knew it, I was inside the bar, ordering a shot of whiskey to dull the pain. For one night, I didn't want to remember how bad it hurt. I was tired of waiting for Dex to find her for me. I was tired of waiting for her to come back to me. I was so fucking tired of feeling like this. I just wanted to get past midnight for once without the cold inside my chest, without the thoughts of our last moments replaying over and over in my head. I couldn't accept she was dead. I couldn't accept she left me. The only thing I could accept tonight was a shot of whiskey—or three.

Travis ushered me away from the bar and back into the garden where the music was pumping and the crowd was increasingly rowdy. The hours passed as the rest of them laughed and danced, and I fueled up on liquor as I slowly burned in this miserable hell, invisible to the world around me.

Leigh tried to pull me up from my seat, but the only girl I'd ever dance with was Mia.

"His girl left him," Travis incorrectly informed her. "He's a bloody wreck."

"She didn't leave me," I stated, but my voice choked on annoyance.

"What happened?" Leigh asked, taking a seat beside me and moving her hand to my thigh.

I should've moved it away, but my arm wouldn't work properly. "She just…" I lazily snapped my finger, "vanished. Into thin air."

"Well, she's stupid for ever leaving you."

I tilted my head and narrowed my eyes at Leigh. "She didn't leave me."

"She died," Travis whispered, thinking I couldn't hear him, but I did.

85

Leigh's features changed, and she scooted her chair closer to me, too close, and moved her clammy hand over my tattooed arm. "Do you want to talk about it?" It was kind of her to ask. On any given day, I'd fancy any conversation pertaining to Mia. I could write an entire book on her eyes, her smile, her kiss, her lips, the way she made me feel, and how all the men in the world combined couldn't compare to her strength. I admired Mia and what she was capable of.

A tear slipped from my eye, and I rolled my head back and pushed a palm down my face. The alcohol wasn't helping, and Leigh was too fucking close for my liking.

"I'm taking you home." She stood and attempted to pull me up along with her. "It's getting late, and you shouldn't drive like this."

"I'm fine. I can walk back. It's not far."

"She's right, mate. Let the girl take you back to the motel," Travis agreed.

Could no one hear me?

The four of us walked to the car park, and before I knew it, I was inside the cabin of someone else's vehicle as Leigh's voice became a backdrop, asking questions, answering them herself, and going on about my poetry bringing the two of us together. I chuckled at her nonsense. Leigh was wrong. My poetry rested in the hands of a girl with a candid spirit and guarded heart.

"I feel like I'm talking too much," she said through a sigh. Funny enough, I hadn't been listening. Not really. Instead, my focus stayed out the passenger window, counting cars to make sure I didn't pass out. The headlights and streetlights zoomed by, and I closed my eyes. I could pretend I was in a space shuttle on my way to the stars. Perhaps Mia was there, hanging between the sun and moon—the only threesome I'd fancy. "We're here, anyway."

Leigh made a turn into the motel lot, and it was odd she never did ask me where I was staying. Or perhaps she did, and I just didn't hear. Either way, we made it, and the car came to a stop right in front of my motel room beside my station wagon. "Thanks," I said, pulling the door handle.

I made it out of the car and in front of the door, clumsily searching for the motel key as Leigh walked up behind me. When I turned, a bottle of Hennessey magically appeared in her right hand, and she held it up at her side and shook it with a shy smile. "Thought maybe we could get to know each other a little better. What do ya say?"

"I say you have the wrong idea about me." Already drunk on alcohol, I hoped my point made it across without sounding like a world-class wanker. "I'm not looking for a quick smash. I'm engaged and in love with someone, happily."

She considered my words for a moment, too long, and I felt my world spinning, maybe from the booze, so I went back to trying to get through the door with the key.

"I'm only here to talk, Oliver. Just a friend." Her cold hand landed on mine, and she took the key from my fingers. "Let me at least get you inside."

Quickly, I brainstormed every scenario, none of them ending in a way Mia would be proud of. I could let her inside, share a bottle of Hennessey, and exchange our favorite colors and explain what my tattoos meant. Eventually, she'd be too drunk to drive and would have to stay, and there was no room for her to sleep that wasn't beside me, which was the best-case scenario. Every other ended in sex, and I refuse to have a girl take any part of me that didn't belong to me in the first place.

That would be stealing.

The world spun with me as I turned to face her. "I have this. It's late. You should be heading home. I appreciate the ride, truly," I stretched out my palm for the key, "I'm sure you're lovely, but I'm not allowing it to go any further than this."

EIGHT

"He was always too busy
dreaming and gazing at the stars,
but unlike all the others,
the stars loved him back."

OLIVER MASTERS

Mia

Three days had passed since Ethan rescued me from the fire I'd caused. I'd wanted to burn down with it, to die in my sleep so I could be with the man in my dreams, Ollie, forever. But once again, Ethan had taken him away from me.

My plan to remain compliant backfired. I'd tried to run away, but what people never seemed to realize was you never had to run to escape from something. The man in my dreams had taught me that. Ollie continuously closed his eyes if he ever needed to escape from the cruel world around him, often bringing me there with him. Then I'd realized people ran away every day, getting lost in work, hobbies, habits, or in my case, my head.

The fire was my way of running away from Ethan.

It was the only way my complex brain understood how to run away.

Ethan and I had barely spoken since. He'd taken me to an abandoned apartment and locked me away in a room. The room seemed commercial, and nothing to announce it had been lived in or cared for in a while. The only window in this room had been boarded up, leaving me with no landmarks to look at to know where we were, not that I would've known anyway. The only place I was familiar with was Dolor since arriving in the UK.

The bed here was larger with burn holes in the mattress, and the ceiling was stained yellow above. It reeked of cigarette smoke, and I'd never seen Ethan smoke. I'd been tied to this chair, waiting patiently for Ethan to return.

It had been three days since I'd seen the sun, and I'd forgotten how it felt on my skin. I wondered if I'd ever see or feel it again, but if it burned my skin as the fire had, I never wanted to be in it. Perhaps I was better off inside.

I didn't know what time it was, either.

Ethan pushed through the door with bags lining his arms, rain dripping from his hair and leather jacket, and he paused as soon as our eyes locked. "This is only temporary," he said, reading my thoughts and looking at me as if I was a huge mistake. A regret. Did he regret saving me too?

He placed the bags over the dresser, and I tilted my head to see them filled with snacks for us to get through the evening. I snapped my head forward again as he walked toward me, crouched down between my thighs, and leaned forward to peel the tape from my mouth. "I'm not hungry," I whispered low, and the muscles in his neck flexed in response.

Ethan lifted his head, and his face was within inches of mine. His eyes darted back and forth, and he dragged in a breath. "You need to eat," he said slowly with a delicate sincerity in his eyes, the kind mixed with longing. I had to remind myself he'd forced me in this position, and my heart was with someone I'd clearly imagined—so entirely stupid. How did I fall in love with a person who wasn't even real? How on earth did I give a fictional character my heart?

He stood, removed his leather jacket, and hung it on a hook beside the bedroom door before switching on the heater. "Listen, Mia. I know this past week hasn't been easy, but you have to know I won't let anything happen to you," he turned to face me and placed a hand over his heart, "I'm not your enemy."

"Then let me go." It was easy to say, and I already knew the answer, but I didn't want him to think I wanted to be here with him, that I liked being held against my will—just in case the fire wasn't proof enough.

"You know I can't do that."

The tone in his voice sounded as if he was talking down to me. We were back to the big brother and little sister. Out of all the roles we'd played, brother and sister was the worst. I didn't like being told what to do. I didn't like being talked down to as if I didn't know any better. "And why not?" I leaned forward, and the ties dug into my flesh, but I didn't care anymore. "I wanted to die! You took that away from me. All I wanted was to be with him!"

Ethan stood over me, raising a brow. "With who?"

Telling him would be stupid, but I had nothing left to lose at this point. He already believed I was crazy. "Ollie."

Ethan dropped to his knees before me and clutched my shoulders, his face red. "Masters doesn't care about you. You want to know the truth, Jett?" he pulled his cellphone from the pocket of his jeans, and his fingers typed over the keypad. The light from the screen bounced off his dilated and infuriated pupils. "Look! Tell me what you see! Because from the looks of it, your prince fucking charming looks like he's having a grand ole time *not* looking for you."

He pressed a button, and the phone clicked to a black screen, but the image had already burned into my brain. *Oliver Masters first book signing in London at Daunt Books.* It was the man from my dreams, only different. He

90

was the same yesterday's child with the wayward brown hair and fierce green eyes, but he was dressed in a black button-up and tailored jeans with a forced smile. His height towered over two other women as he held up a book with his face on the cover. "He's real."

"Yeah, a real liar if you ask me." Ethan pocketed the cellphone and returned his eyes to mine. "Listen to me, Jett. He's been lying to you and everyone else this entire time, making moves to build a life without you. I didn't want to tell you this, especially now. But you needed to know."

I didn't imagine him. He was real. He was mine.

They weren't dreams I was having. They were memories.

"My mum once told me that people come into your life for a reason, a season, or a lifetime. Masters was only a season, a way to pass the time to make his bearable. You're with me for a reason."

"No, you're wrong."

"Did that look like someone who fucking loves you?" Ethan shook his head and wrapped his fingers around the sides of my thighs. "I'm sorry, Jett. No one is looking for you. No one else gives a fuck about you. To everyone else, you. Are. No. One. Rubbish. It's you and me now. We need to stick together. I'll take care of you."

Each word was a knife to the chest. I dug my teeth into my bottom lip to rob the pain from inside and stop my lip from trembling. I'd heard Ethan, loud and clear. The words registered, but I still couldn't understand. Ollie wasn't looking for me. No one cared I was gone. "My dad isn't looking for me?"

Ethan let out a disheartened chuckle. "Which one?"

I dipped my head back and blinked the tears from my eyes. "What do you mean?"

"Lynch or Bruce? Your biological dad or your fake one? And no, neither one of them are looking for you."

"You're lying."

Ethan raised a brow. "You didn't know?"

"This is too much." I pulled on the restraints again, begging to be out of them. The chair wobbled, and Ethan held down my arms to keep me still. Narrowing my eyes, I looked straight into his and screamed through the uncontrollable tears. "You mean to tell me you knew this entire time Lynch was my dad, and you didn't say anything? You're just as much of a liar as everyone else!" The chair rocked back and forth as I thrashed.

"You need to calm down, Jett! You're going to hurt yourself." His grip tightened, trying to keep me still until finally, he leaned over and cut my hands loose, then my ankles. "It wasn't my place! I thought Masters told you, he said he should be the one, and that Lynch lost his chance."

I froze, and a lump made of deceit lodged in my throat. "Ollie knew?"

"I'm sorry." Ethan's strong hands moved up and down my heavy arms, and he shook his head. "God, I'm so fucking sorry. I thought you knew."

Nausea churned in my stomach, and my heart felt as if it were trying to claw its way out of my chest. A fury came over me, controlling my next moves, and I punched him in the chest. "You're the liar!" I screamed. "You're the one filling my head! Get out of my head!" Over and over, my fist landed into his hard chest, releasing wrath far overdue. "I hate you," I cried.

Something came over me at that moment, like an atomic bomb went off inside my head, reminding me of my circumstances. Ollie and I were engaged. I was supposed to meet him. We were going to take off together and get married. I had a court date, did it pass? Were the last two years for nothing? Too many thoughts, each one driving my hand into his chest, shoulders, stomach, anything I could get my hands on, and Ethan hadn't moved or stopped me.

The beating went on until I crumbled in his arms, and he cradled me on the floor of the dark room, tasting my own salty tears and smelling his cologne mixed with the cigarette smoke. For a second, I wished the entire world would stop so I could have longer than a heartbeat to put these pieces back together inside my head.

"I missed us, Jett," he whispered. "We need each other."

"Everyone's a liar," I cried. "Even I've been lying to myself this entire time, believing he couldn't be real. That if he was, he would have rescued me."

"Rescued you from what? I told you, I'm never letting anything happen to you. You're safe with me. I promise. The only reason I kept you tied up, kept putting you out every time you ran away was because you're a little fucked up in the head if you haven't noticed, but you're my kind of fucked up. I'm afraid without me, you're going to get yourself killed, or worse."

"What's worse than death?" I cried out, looking up at him.

Ethan's chest caved beneath my head, and his fingers pushed wet strands from my face. "I'll show you tomorrow," he said, then removed his shirt, exposing his carved chest. "Tonight, I'm here, Mia. I'm the only one here for you." He grabbed a quilt he'd brought in earlier along with our bags, wrapped it around us, laid me over his chest, and took us across the floor.

I cried myself to sleep, wrapped inside the arms of my security blanket.

The next morning, I quickly showered in the bathroom connected to the bedroom. In the mirror, my puffy eyes showed proof of my long night of crying, but I didn't have the space to care. I stood, water dripping over the tile, waiting for Ethan to bring me my clothes he'd washed.

Ethan pushed open the door and rested a neatly folded stack of clothes and a towel over the bathroom counter before he looked up at me. "You have five minutes. There's one last stop before we head to the airport."

"The airport?" I asked, taking the towel to dry off. Where were we going? This news was bitter but sweet. It meant flying possibly farther than wherever Ollie was, but also farther from a place without lies and deception.

"I have a plan. There's a boat waiting for us back in the states," he explained, eyes following my every move.

I slipped on my panties. "A boat?"

"Yeah, now come on. We haven't got much time."

After getting dressed and towel drying my hair, I helped Ethan pack the car and waited in the passenger seat as he went back inside the apartment to finish up some last-minute things. The sun was out, penetrating through the car window and caressing over my sensitive skin. If I wanted to run, now would be the time. Ethan fully trusted me, leaving me abandoned with opportunity. But I had nowhere to go, and no one to go home to. Ollie was doing just fine without me, living out his dream as a poet, meeting people, taking pictures, and signing books. Bruce, my fake father, had Diane, my stepmother, and I was nothing but a burden in their life. A complication. Lynch had never bothered to tell me. It made sense now, why Bruce had sent me overseas into the hands of my real dad, thinking I was Lynch's problem to deal with and not his problem anymore.

Though I'd caught Ethan murdering the boy back at Dolor, I was a murderer too.

Maybe he had a good reason—a reason I was determined to learn more about.

Ethan was my safest bet for now until I could figure all this out.

He got into the car, not the least bit surprised I was still sitting here, waiting for him, and cranked the heat. "Are you cold?" he asked, leaning behind the backseat. "Here."

My hoodie dropped into my lap—my POETIC hoodie. "Where are we going?" I asked, slipping it over my head.

"There's someone I want you to meet."

The ride to Wirral was about forty-minutes. Ethan had spilled all his truths, starting with Livy being his sister and ending with the answer to my last question: *what day was it?*

"April seventeenth. Release day was two weeks ago."

Two weeks. I'd officially missed my court date and couldn't go back home now even if I wanted to.

Two weeks. It seemed like decades ago when I'd made love to Ollie, feeling his touch, hearing his voice, smelling his scent.

Two weeks since anyone had lied to me, too. *Had I crossed Ollie's mind since? Was he thinking about me? Did he worry something terrible happened to me?* I forced out those thoughts. Of course, he wasn't thinking about me. Oliver Masters was too busy enjoying his new life. One he never mentioned before because he never planned to share it.

Ethan lied to me too, but for a good reason. He'd told me what happened to his sister, Livy. The four guys at Dolor had murdered her, and he was carrying out justice in her name, taking matters into his own hands. On some sadistic level, I understood Ethan.

"Do you remember when you and I sat under that tree, and we swore we'd always be there for one another even though I was leaving the country? A pinky promise?" Ethan turned to face me, a small smile lighting up his face at the memory. I nodded, pulling the sleeves over my hands for warmth. "These are the circumstances we're in, Jett, whether you like them or not. I never planned to take you with me, but we're going to make the most of it. I can make you happy. I know it. You just have to meet me halfway. You're my family, remember?"

I looked out the window. It was foggy, the heat from inside the car competing against the cold rain pressing from the outside. "Just don't lie to me. I can't take any more lies."

Ethan pulled into a parking lot, passing a brown curved sign, reading, "Birch Tree Manor." The large brick building reminded me of a school back in the states, yellow brick on the top, orange on the bottom, with white windows. The car came to a stop, and Ethan turned to face me. "From this point on, no more lies. I'll tell you everything you want to know, and it's going to be a lot to take in, but all you have to do is ask." He held out his pinky. "I swear, Jett. And you swear to meet me halfway."

Our pinky's linked, but I didn't like it. Not like I did before.

Side by side, we walked through the doors of Birch Tree Manor, unsure of what was waiting for us. The inside smelled like a daycare dipped in mothballs, and the lady working the front desk greeted the two of us with a skeptical smile, her brown hair neatly parted down the middle and flattened behind her shoulders. "I wondered if I'd ever see you in here again," she said to Ethan, eyes moving from him to me, deciding whether I was a threat or not. "And who is this?"

"This is my girlfriend, Rebecca," Ethan introduced me, throwing an arm around my shoulder and looking down at me with a proud smile, "How has my mum been?"

The girl frowned, pushing a clipboard forward. "Oh, you know …" She waved her hand in front of her, trying to mask the disappointment over her face. It had been a long time since I was around strangers, and luckily, I hadn't lost my ability to read body language entirely. "Not much has changed since you were last here. But, I suppose a lot has changed for *you* this past year."

I idled in my spot, looking over the colorful interior as the two continued with small talk, then Ethan grabbed my hand as the receptionist lead us down a hall. "Your mum has taken a liking to the media room lately," she continued to say, and each hall we passed through had different colored walls, doors, and themes. Finally, we entered a room with yellow sunflower wallpaper, matching yellow curtains, and a collection of elderly people. A large window brightened the entire room, where the sun shone after the rain, casting rays over the souls who were on the brink of death.

"Ah, there she is," the receptionist gestured over to a red-headed lady sitting with a group, playing a game of checkers, "she'll be so happy to see you."

Ethan's hand squeezed mine. "Really?"

"Well, we've had some good days this past year. She's asked about you a time or two. Let's see if we caught her on a good day."

It dawned on me the redhead was Ethan's mom, which he hasn't seen in over a year, and the entire situation seemed too personal for me to be involved with. I was intruding and shouldn't be here. Ethan's palm sweat in mine as he walked toward her, and I turned to stop him. "I can wait in the car. You need this time alone with her."

"I need you, Jett," he whispered, eyes forward, admiring the woman who gave him life. We walked closer until we stopped before the table. No one looked up from the table to acknowledge us.

The receptionist tapped the older woman on the shoulder and pointed toward Ethan and me. "Mary, look who came to visit you," she said gingerly with an even amount of excitement as if talking to a young child. "It's Ethan, your son."

Mary had the same red hair as Ethan, though hers was wispy and dulled. Her eyes were a pale blue against her even paler skin, and her thin lips opened into a big smile, the corners of her eyes crinkling as she admired the man standing beside me. "Ethan?" Mary's voice came out tired and ragged, and Ethan clutched my hand tighter. "I have a son?"

"Hi, Mum."

I'd never seen Ethan so nervous. He was usually put together, composed and unbreakable. But as his eyes hit his mum, he instantly became vulnerable to the woman sitting before him.

"Would you look at that, Ellen," Mary clapped her hands together, "I have a son, and he's so handsome."

"I'll be back at the desk if you need me," the receptionist stated as the older ladies around the table agreed before she slipped away.

Ethan let go of my hand, and I awkwardly stood as he took an empty chair beside Mary. "How have you been?" His eyes beamed at the woman as he rubbed his palms down the front of his jeans. "Is this place treating you well?"

"Yes, sir. It's like one big holiday here, though George is probably somewhere sleeping. Have you met George, my husband? I can go wake him up. He should meet you and your beautiful—"

"Mia," Ethan quickly said, waving me over. "This is Mia, Mum."

I walked closer, and Mary held out her hand. "Well, nice to meet you, dear. Aren't you just the prettiest girl I've ever seen." Her cold hand patted the top of mine. "Ellen, would you look at her. Natural beauty right there, I'll tell ya. Nowadays, girls cover their beauty with makeup and nonsense. However, you should visit the salon we have here. They could doll-up that hair of yours, make it look posh."

"Yeah, real posh." Ellen nodded with a trembling hand, reaching for a black checker on the table.

Mary smacked Ellen's hand. "Don't think I'm not watching you, this boy may be blinding my vision, but not my senses. You can't pass one by me."

I laughed, something I haven't been able to do in a long time.

Mary pointed a shaky finger at Ellen. "That Ellen, I'll tell you what. You have to look out for that one. Never played an honest game in her life."

I glanced over at Ellen, who continued to nod and agree with her friend.

"Mum, let's take a walk in the garden. Get you outside for a little bit, yeah?"

"Yeah, all right, handsome. And, Donald." Mary tossed a checker over at a gentleman staring out the window in a daze to grab his attention. It hit him in the chest. "Watch Ellen while I'm gone, will ya?"

"All right." Donald nodded, munching on his veneers, his big brown rimmed glasses covering his face.

Ethan pushed his mom in a wheelchair across the grass until we parked by a concrete table surrounded by benches. His foot pushed down the brakes of the wheelchair, making sure it didn't wander off, and I took a seat over the bench, following Ethan's lead. He pulled a large coat tightly around Mary's small frame as white clouds appeared with every breath he took between them.

"Did ya hear about that cabin fire in Cheshire? Two dead, they say," Mary shook her head, "such a shame."

Two dead? My eyes snapped to Ethan, and he didn't look shocked by the same news I was hearing.

"You shouldn't be watching the news, Mum," Ethan pointed out, ignoring my blatant stare and taking a seat beside her, straddling the bench. "You should be enjoying yourself."

98

"How else am I supposed to know what's going on in the world?"

"You're not, you've done that for far too long. It's perfectly okay not to have to worry about everyone else. Enjoy your days. Every single one of them. For me."

"Then tell me about yourself, would ya? Put me at ease with some good news for once." Mary kept her eyes out in the distance, her hand in Ethan's and my heart clenched inside my chest.

"Mia and I are taking off to the states after we leave here. We're going on a boat, how's that for good news?"

"Are you taking your sister? You can't leave her behind, Ethan. Olivia needs you right now. She's not doing so well. I always said that's why I had two kids. In case anything ever happened to me and George, you and my Livy would have each other. You have to push her through it, the darkness took her under, but you can lead her out. I know you can." She sighed, shaking her head before turning to face Ethan. "Depression isn't funny business. Not something to treat lightly. And it's not that she doesn't care about you either, you have to remember that. Depression isn't about not caring anymore. It's about caring too much for too long. It's the ones with the biggest hearts, giving too much away to too many who end up in the dark." She turned to look at Ethan. "Be her beacon."

The tears falling were like fire against my icy cheeks, and my clouded vision trailed toward Ethan, whose cheeks were red. He briefly glanced toward me and quickly wiped a tear before it had a chance to fall. His mom had no idea she'd been dead for over two years now.

"I know, Mum. I know." Ethan paused to gather himself. "She'll always be with me, wherever I go, you can rest easy knowing that."

"Good." She patted the top of his hand again. "Now tell me about this trip. Will there be a wedding in the future?" Ethan laughed through a sniffle and looked over at me when Mary continued, "You know, they say love at first sight isn't real. But that's a bloody lie if you ask me. And let me tell ya something, Mary—"

"Mia," Ethan corrected her with a chuckle. "Mary is *your* name."

"Right, well, in any case, people come into your life for a reason, a season, or a lifetime. It only takes a woman five seconds to know she's staring at her lifetime. Now, tell me, dear. How long did it take you to realize you were looking into the eyes of your forever?"

The dead of silence landed in the space between the three of us. A matching pair of blue eyes stared at me as I contemplated my answer. Ethan couldn't lie to her, and either could I. "Three seconds," I whispered, remembering the moment I'd locked eyes with Ollie in the mess hall on my first day at Dolor. "It only took three seconds."

NINE

"You smile,
making sweet love
to my dry and demented soul,
and it's killing me soft and slow."

OLIVER MASTERS

Ethan

Seeing Mum was so much harder than I'd expected, especially since it was goodbye. She would forget about our visit by the morning, which gave me a sense of peace as Mia and I walked out of Birch Tree Manor to the car.

"Your mom seems like a good person," Mia threw into the air once we were back on the main road toward the airport, and I nodded. She hadn't spoken in twenty minutes, and this small compliment about the woman who raised me was only a gateway into more questions about the cabin fire, and the two bodies my mum mentioned.

I'd feared Mia would bring up the fact that it was my mum's cabin she'd lit on fire. The cabin where my mum and dad had spent memories during the holidays. At least she spared the poor woman of that news, if my mum would've even remembered. Still, Mia had held her tongue, but her heavy stare had been hard to ignore. Thankfully, Mum quickly changed the subject, lifting the tension.

Mum had that effect on people. I was going to miss her.

At the corner of my eye, Mia shook her head, unable to sit still. "How could there have been two deaths, Ethan? I don't understand. Do they think we're dead? That doesn't make sense. If we're here, then whose bodies did they find?"

There it is. The pressure of Mia's questions was as if she were a thousand pounds and sitting in my lap, pouring cement down my throat. It was in the fifties outside, but I still rolled down the window, needing more air in the stifling space.

"Don't ignore me. No more secrets, remember?"

It seemed my puppet cut another string, and I was losing control of her. She was turned in her seat, facing me with her hands waving out in front of her as I kept my attention on the road. The questions kept coming, and I couldn't piece together an explanation that didn't make me sound any less of a monster. Only twenty minutes left until we were at Liverpool airport, and if I couldn't contain this problem, I didn't know how I'd be able to get her on the plane compliantly.

A *Frankie & Benny's* was up ahead, and I pulled into the car park and cut the engine. My eyes landed on her two hands resting on her thigh, and I took them, heating them between mine, thinking about what I would say. I couldn't lose her. I'd read her psych file back at Dolor to understand her better. Mia responded positively to touch. I'd invested too much time into this girl. I'd studied this girl. I'd consoled this girl. I'd bent over backward and disrupted my plan for this girl. Then Masters had come back and intervened. If it weren't for him, Mia and I would probably be together romantically this very moment. But I'd settle for whatever she would give me right now, and the rest would come with time.

I closed my eyes, taking in as much oxygen as my lungs would allow before looking into her daunting brown eyes. Then I released it, slow and steady. "Do you remember the story I told you about with Ashlyn?"

Mia impatiently nodded. "How does she have anything to do with this?"

"Everything. I couldn't let them live, not after what they did. The two bodies they found in the fire were Ashlyn's father and his mate. I killed them both. For a number of reasons." An abrupt pause played out between the two of us. Her eyes froze, locked on mine. I waited for a reaction, more than the drawn-out stare. Possibly for her to scream for help or try to escape from the car. If Mia wanted complete honesty, I should've also told her the apartment we slept in the past couple of nights was Ashlyn's dead father's too, but that would have taken it too far, and she hadn't specifically asked.

Mia pulled her hand from my grasp and looked at me as if she were seeing me for the first time.

"Mia," I reached for her hand, and she jerked it away. My fingers pushed through my hair. I needed to pull us back to where we were thirty seconds before. "Talk to me."

Her chin lifted, studying my every move, which was disappointing. She was losing the little faith she had left in me. "What were your reasons?"

I exhaled. Perhaps not. Mia wanted to hear me out. This was good. Taking a dive, I reached for her lap, and she didn't move. My palm landed between her legs, and I gripped her tiny thigh in one hand, giving her the touch she needed to get her through my next confession. Her muscles relaxed, and I continued, "The most important reason was for Ashlyn. They left her there to die to save themselves. What kind of father does that, Jett?" A sore spot Mia had understood well, and she shook her head, processing. I saw it in her eyes, the way she was trying to work the problem in her head. "Second, I needed to test the drug to carry out my revenge at Dolor. But they deserved it. They all fucking deserved it."

My hand was practically begging at this point, having a mind of its own and moving underneath hoodie to find skin. She just needed to let me in. Then we would be fine. My palm rested over her hip, and I gave her a gentle squeeze.

Mia released a shallow breath. "How many people have you killed?"

It was a simple question, one with a number for an answer. "You have to believe me when I say I don't take the lives of people who don't deserve it."

"Ethan," her voice scattered. "How many?"

I sucked in a breath and brushed my thumb across her stomach. "Six." I'd be able to name them all too, and every person in their immediate family, their addresses, how they preferred their tea …

"Six?" she laughed, but it was empty. I'd lost her. "You're a certified serial killer, you do know that, right?" She looked around the cabin of the car, eyes bugging out. "I don't know why the extent of this situation didn't hit me before, but you're a serial killer. I'm actually on the run with you, a serial killer. You're a *serial* killer, Ethan! You kill *people*. People! More than one! You've *murdered* people."

No matter how many times she'd said it, it didn't change anything. "Six," I confirmed. "Six lives who deserved it."

"So, that makes it okay?"

"I didn't say that." I'd never asked for this. Livy's murder had taught me a lot. Anyone could be capable of anything when grief mixed with anger. In my case, a ruthless monster was born. Mia side-eyed me almost as if she couldn't look at me, but wanted to make sure she knew where my other hand was at. I still had one latched to her hip to keep us connected, to keep her with me. "I'm not going to hurt you, Jett. I. Love. You. Don't you see that by now? If the roles reversed, and you were in fact missing, I'd be filing every fucking report, knocking on every door, stopping at nothing to find you. Yes, I'd even fucking kill for you. That's how much I care about you. Not Masters, not your fucking dad, Not Lynch. Me!"

104

"This is a lot." A tear slipped from her eye, and I leaned over to catch it with my thumb.

"I know." Two steps forward, ten steps back. I scratched my jaw, a nervous habit, wishing I could use my hands to untangle all her worries.

Then she quietly added, "Did you feel it? The silence?"

My brows pinched together. "What do you mean?"

"Never mind," she muttered, looking off into the car park.

"Let's have breakfast, all right? Take this slow. You can ask me anything you want."

Mia had ordered the pancakes with chocolate and banana. She'd moaned with every bite, eyelids fluttering, and I decided her psych file was incorrect. It wasn't touching that calmed her. It was food. In seconds, she cleared her plate as if she hadn't eaten in two years.

When I'd told her she could ask me anything, I didn't mean about fucking Masters. Question after question, and each one revolved around the tosser, a few about Lynch. She was so interested in seeing Masters' poetry book, the cover, the news articles, and scrolling through my mobile, reading every review. Masters fucking lied to her, and her face lit up at the screen like a proud girlfriend. She'd never looked at me like that before. *Would she ever?* Masters made something of himself, and the only thing I'd accomplished over the last year was murder.

At the airport, Mia stayed silent at my side as we checked into customs. Every step closer to the terminal, my conscience weighed heavier and heavier. Something inside me changed. Maybe it was seeing my mum today, or perhaps it was because I loved Mia enough, I'd be willing to let her go. Either way, once we would board the plane, there was no turning back. She knew it too.

People pushed past us, rushing to catch their flight as Mia and I stood awkwardly in the waiting area to board the plane. My fist tightened around the handle of our duffle. We had no other luggage, but this was all that was needed. There wasn't a passing second wasted, each one of them spent contemplating the next words I'd say.

Over the last two weeks, I'd made sure to gather all evidence to show Mia what a piece of shit Masters and Lynch both were, giving every reason to despise them to get her here, at this airport, under her own free will. But I'd been an idiot all along. Their bond was too strong. Stronger than hers and mine could ever be. I'd realized there was nothing I could say to keep her from loving him. No matter how long Mia and I were together, one year, five years, twenty years, he would never go away. Oliver Masters permanently stained her.

To be the good guy for once, I needed to let her know she had this single opportunity to leave. I'd give her the option now, and if she didn't take it, it was possible I'd keep her forever.

"Mia—"

"It's fine, Ethan."

"You can have my car. You should go to him."

She looked up at me under heavy lashes. "No, you were right. Ollie is a liar. He never loved me. Never even bothered looking for me."

"But—"

She placed her hand over my arm to stop me. "I'm going with you."

My heart jumped, the Monster cheered, and our destination and flight number rang over the intercom, notifying passengers it was time to board. Mia pulled her hand away, and though I was pleased with her decision, I was also worried I'd be looking into those disheartened eyes for the rest of my life.

Thirteen hours later, we made it to JFK airport in New York City, but we gained five hours back due to the time change, making it six at night. About a week ago, Dean mailed me the location of my new car, which was waiting in the car park at the airport with our new identities located inside the glove box. I'd never questioned or doubted Dean, but I was still dumbfounded by him and the things he was able to do. He'd got the job done, and I owed him a lot.

Mia hadn't questioned it either. For the most part, she'd been quiet during the entire trip. Utterly spent, I looked over at Mia from inside the cabin of the brand new black Supra. Her eyes matched the same red color and heaviness mine surely had. "Do you want me to drive?" she asked with soft humor in her tone. I would be able to figure it out, the different sides of the road, but tonight wasn't a night to take chances considering our exhaustion and unfamiliar territory.

Under a silent agreement, we both exited the car and switched places.

Mia pulled into the nearest hotel. It was posh and pricey, but the cash planted in the glovebox gave us enough to get by until we made it down to Louisiana to fetch the yacht.

Our travels finally caught up with us, and as soon as we entered the hotel room, I plugged my phone into the charger and took one of the beds, sinking into the soft white duvet, and closed my eyes. Mia's breathing sounded above me, and I opened one eye to see her standing with her hands clasped in front of her. "I … um …"

I lifted the sheet, motioning for her to curl up at my side. I didn't ask her, it was her choice, and she didn't hesitate. After the long day, the truths I'd admitted, the heartbreak she was enduring because of Masters, it was me she needed. And I'd be here for her every step of the way. My palm gripped her bare thigh, and I wrapped her leg around mine to pin her against my front. She was tiny in my arms and looked up at me through wet lashes. I hadn't known she was crying.

"You're right," she whispered. "We're the same, and I'm going to try."

Her lips brushed my neck, and my eyes pinched closed, my monster inside smiled, but my nerves shook at her confession. I didn't want her to try to love me, I just wanted her to, and the warm tears trailing over my skin from her eyes reminded me she was lying.

Mia would never be unconditionally mine. Mia Rose Jett would forever be his.

She'd always belong to Masters, and there was not a bloody thing more I could do to change that.

TEN

"One day you'll look back and realize
it wasn't all for nothing."

OLIVER MASTERS

Ollie

Each time I'd driven back to Ockendon, I'd lost a piece of myself. This triple life I'd been living had taken a toll on me. Not a double life. A triple life. The poet, doing book signings and adhering to a schedule Laurie laid out. The criminal, partaking in illegal and immoral wrongdoings. And the fiancé, making sure every action I took, and every mask I put on, only brought me one step closer to finding her while protecting the life I'd set up for us.

The address sent over brought me to a street in Grays South with chain-linked fences and rundown properties littered with rubbish. It was almost ten at night, and the buzzing street lamp shone a spotlight over the neighborhood kids playing basketball in the middle of the street.

I walked into the questionably stable house, and Adrian, Reggi, and James were already here. The three of them arguing, but still passing a blunt around. Adrian and James were sitting comfortably over a torn plaid couch as Reggi stood with his hand flying back and forth between the two of them. Dex appeared from a hallway, dark attire, hair slicked back, with his phone attached to his ear, and as soon as his gaze hit mine, he lowered his voice and pulled a cigarette to his mouth. I walked closer, and he turned his back to me, quickly ending the call. Facing me again, he pocketed the phone in his jeans.

"You're late." He approached the kitchen counter and rolled the tip of the fag into an ashtray to put it out enough to save for later. "You need to get a handle on this situation, Oliver." He nodded over to the other three arguing. He was hiding something from me, and I eyed him suspiciously.

Was he deflecting? I pointed to the phone in his pocket. "Was that about Scott?"

"Not that it's any of your business, but no. It had nothing to do with you."

"You know damn well it's my business, or did you forget our deal?"

The yelling match behind me became background noise as Dex stepped closer and puffed out his chest. "Remember your place. You work for me now. When and if I find Scott, I'll let you know," his tone was smooth and collected, and I fisted my sides to hide my agitation. "But until then, you don't get to ask questions." He punctuated his sentence with his pointer finger bouncing off my forehead. The ability to control myself from driving my fist into his face was unheard of, supernatural almost. But it didn't stop my fists from clenching or my teeth from grinding, mustering restraint from places I'd never visited before.

The fear of never finding Mia was what kept me back. I was already in too deep with Dex. I'd given him a week, and he had two days left.

Dex patted my cheek and flashed a smirk. "Now, round up the boys."

Nerves ran wild inside the cabin of the car toward the rivalry's drug house on the opposite side of town. Reggi drove, and I took notice in the way his hostile gaze drifted to James sitting behind him in the rearview mirror.

"We're not doing this until you guys hash out whatever has both of your knickers in a twist." It was none of my business what the two were arguing about, but we needed to bust through the rival's door as a team, so I made their business mine.

"James is fucking my girl," Reggi gritted out. "Caught the two of them. In my bed."

James chuckled. "We were just having a little fun."

Reggi slammed his palm against the steering wheel, jaw flexing.

"Is this a girl worth losing a mate over, or is this mate worth losing the one over?" It wasn't a question meant to be answered here and now, but something for them to think about. "We all have complications in our lives, but once the four of us pile into this car, nothing else matters but the job. James, Adrian, and me, we're your safety net and priority, and vice versa. We're going in together, and coming out together. This time, guns loaded."

The drug house we were busting belonged to the rivalry gang, BOGs, or Blood of Grays, controlling most of the drug trafficking in the surrounding cities east of London. Recently, the BOGs clientele had decreased in numbers, so their new drug had been spreading into the outside areas, rolling into Links territory. Fentanyl and heroin was a lethal concoction, taking the form of a Pez candy. The ideal packaging had become popular among the youth. The delivery was good marketing, but the only reason their numbers were decreasing was because the BOGs were killing their customers with overdosing amounts of fentanyl, and that was bad business on their part.

Links only cared about taking back what was theirs, and though this operation was forced upon me because of the deal Dex and I made, at least I could do some good in the process and possibly save lives.

We turned onto the street of our target location and parked out of sight a few houses down to go over the plan one last time. I had checked out the property the day before and walked the perimeter. The drug house was on a quiet street in an upscale neighborhood, a house no one would suspect. If they were smart, they would only have two—maybe three— blokes preparing and guarding the lab so not to raise suspicion, giving us the numbers and upper hand.

There were three exit doors. I advised James and Adrian to barge through the front as I came through the end, Reggi guarding the side door in the garden leading to the detached garage space just in case. "There are no customers, and these blokes will have guns fully loaded," I reminded them. "But this time, so will you." Before, we were in a public setting with innocent lives on the line. I'd spent the last forty-eight hours teaching these boys everything they needed to know about a gun, down to taking the bloody thing apart and piecing it back together.

When I was thirteen, a punter by the name of Gauge taught me one night after my mum passed out on the living room floor. I hadn't shot it at the time, but he said since I was living this life, it was time I learned a thing or two about the weapon, and when I would grow up, I should invest in one to protect myself and my mum. Guns were illegal and hard to come by, but they weren't extinct within gangs. I never did get one and learned to fight instead. Firing a weapon was clipped, distant, and easier than bloodshed caused by your hands. I knew from experience. Maddie was the only life I'd ever taken, and I planned to keep it that way until I was face to face with Ethan Scott.

James and Adrian took the front as Reggi and I crossed the garden. He took the side door, and I waited at the back. The night was in the forties, clear open skies and dotted with stars with fierce winds. I lifted my head and pinned my gaze on the moon, and the thought of Mia breathing under that same moon washed away my nerves as voices boomed from inside the house.

Swiftly and quietly, I picked the lock and entered the home. My shoes made little if any noise against the tile leading to the chaos. James and

Adrian stood facing me with guns drawn, pointing to the two BOGs, who also had their weapons drawn in return. James and Adrian didn't acknowledge me as I crept behind a BOG who had his back to me.

He didn't see me coming, and I gripped the wrist of his gun-holding arm, aiming the barrel downward, and jabbed my palm up against his elbow, breaking it.

In seconds, the BOG was on the ground with a broken arm with his gun in my hand before the other BOG had a chance to turn. Now it was three against two, and painful memories surfaced when Mia had a knife against her throat. At that time, I had a disadvantage. Maddie had us fooled, and I had everything to lose.

"Drop your gun," I demanded to the other man who couldn't decide on where to point the barrel, waving it back and forth. He knew it was over, but it seemed as if something else was holding him back. "Drop it!"

"I can't let you walk out of here with everything. They'll kill us. Either way, we're dead. I'd rather take a bullet from you than find out what they'd do to us." The young BOG was scared. He'd rather die a quick and painless death than suffer the consequences of their failure from their boss.

The gun in my hand was pointing at the young Blood curled up on the floor. James and Adrian had theirs aimed at the only one left standing, shaking with a pistol in his hand. The BOG wouldn't pull the trigger or draw attention to the house. The last thing the gang needed was the police to know one of their locations. "James, tie him up." I nudged my head to get him to start moving. Time wasn't in our favor.

James walked toward him and pressed the tip of the barrel against his temple as Adrian pushed his gun into his waistband before snatching a nearby wooden chair. I used my free hand to retrieve my mobile from my front pocket to send a quick text to Reggi, advising him to pull the car into the garage.

After my men cleared the house and James confiscated all weapons, drugs, and money, I approached the two BOGs tied to the chairs. "Get out of this life," I advised, throwing my fist into one's jaw to show he took one for the team. The one with the broken arm growled as Adrian secured his ties. "You both are still young. You have a whole life ahead of you." I left him with a swollen eye and a mouthful of blood.

Before we made it back to Dex and his crew, I'd driven us down an abandoned alleyway. Neither of them questioned my motives for taking them here. At this point, all three of them already looked up to me, putting their lives in my hands, which was a hefty burden to carry.

The car stopped behind the factory.

We'd lived a few blocks from here, and on nights my mum brought a punter home, and Oscar was gone, I'd collect pebbles, climbed the scaffold, and threw them into the barrels below. On other nights, when my emotions got the best of me, I'd climb to the top until I'd made it to the roof with a book folded into the waistband of my pants. I'd spent many nights in the sky reading until reading turned in to writing. *"One day you'll look back and realize it wasn't all for nothing,"* had been my first entry. At the age of twelve, I still had hope.

"What are we doing here?" Adrian asked beside me.

"Stay in the car." I exited the driver's side and walked around to the back and popped open the trunk. One by one, I threw the bags of drugs into a rusty barrel.

Despite my instruction, Reggi, Adrian, and James retreated from the car and stood off to the side, watching in an uneasy silence.

"Dex isn't going to like this," James pointed out.

The order was to bring everything back to him tonight, but I had other plans. These drugs were mixed incorrectly—deadly. Kids were overdosing on a single candy. I had to make sure to dispose of them.

I searched for my pack of cigarettes in my pocket and pulled one to my mouth, lighting it before throwing the match into the barrel. I didn't have gasoline to speed up the process. The burn was slow, consuming, and together we waited until the fire died, and drugs turned to ash before we got back inside the car.

"You burned all of it? The fucking money too?" Dex pounded his clenched fist over the counter before running his hands through his hair. It was no longer slicked back and stiff, but now falling off to the sides. "Do you realize what you've done?"

Dex wasn't alone when we arrived. The two men I'd seen the first night at Jack's were here with him but had walked off into another room under Dex's orders. He didn't want them to witness this conversation until he understood how to handle it.

"Yes, I saved your arse. Tell your boss you ordered me to destroy it. The drugs were bad, literally killing business. It was the Bloods mistake in the first place. The Links have something better. A reason to come back for more." Still drugs, but change didn't happen in one night. "As for the money, it was more of a bitch slap. The Links made a statement. We don't need their fucking money."

"How do I know you didn't keep it for yourself?"

"I have three witnesses. Go check the fucking car. It's gone. I'll escort you to the barrel where we watched it burn to nothing." I did the right thing.

"I have to make a call," Dex gritted out before disappearing behind the back door out to the garden.

James, Adrian, and Reggi took to the couch, already celebrating with a cheap bottle of vodka. Too bothered to sit, I waited in the kitchen, my elbows digging into the island, separating me from the three I grew a liking to. The night had started with Reggi and James arguing over a girl, and ended with smiles stretched across their faces as Reggi slapped his hand over his knee, laughing over, I'm sure to be, a terrible joke.

Minutes passed, and Dex returned from his phone call in a lighter mood as well. A hand landed on my shoulder and squeezed. "Bossman likes your crazy arse," he said through a chuckle with a cigarette between his lips. "And since you are making decisions of your own around here, needs you to approve this," he held up a white pill between us, "the future."

Our eyes locked. "Hard pass."

Dex's two other mates walked in from a room in the back and joined us in the kitchen.

"Did you hear that, mate?" Dex laughed. "Baby Oscar believes he's in control." The men cackled. The pressure rose. And my eyes bounced between the three of them. Laughter rolled in from my boys in the living room behind us. "Take the fucking candy, so we can get this party started. You raided the BOGs, mate. Time to celebrate," Dex pressed. His entourage popped the pill into their mouths and chased it with a beer. "See? Nothing dodgy here."

I took the pill from his fingers and said a silent prayer before putting it over my tongue. One of the men slid a beer across the counter. It stopped in front of me. I pulled it to my lips and swallowed the pill. "I'll make a few calls," Dex slapped his palm against my back, "Let's have some music going."

More bodies crammed into the small space of the house. Someone had moved the plastic outside chairs indoors. I was sitting in one of them, my limbs heavy and hanging over the arms of the chair with a cup in my hand. Music thumped in my ears, an eccentric yet hypnotic beat, as girls danced in tight skirts in the middle of the floor. Although it took vast effort, I turned my head to face the boys who counted on me. Adrian's gaze slammed into mine, and he leaned over and flicked ash from his cigarette into the tray sitting on the coffee table. Reggi sat beside him with his eyes glued to a girl's arse as James enjoyed a lap dance from a pretty little brunette. Dex had already taken one of them into another room, I was sure to smash, and his two men were in the kitchen drinking.

I'd managed to climb to my feet, but the living room swayed, and the crowd tripled. I needed to get out of here. I needed to make it to my car and pass out there. I needed to breathe.

My mobile was no longer in my pocket, but my keys were.

"Where are you going?" a girl at my side asked.

I turned my head to see a familiar face. Blonde hair. Black eyes. A girl who reminded me of my mum. "What are you doing here?" She was an hour away from Surrey. Come to think of it, I had no idea where she actually lived. "You shouldn't be here." I knew what I was trying to say, but I didn't know if the words were coming out correctly. On the tip of my tongue, they felt right, but she looked into my eyes as if I'd spoken a different language.

With eyes glazed over and lips painted red, she transformed back to the drunken girl I'd met the first night with Jinx.

Leigh grabbed my hand and led me out the front door. As soon as we stepped into the night, wind blew between us, sweeping her little skirt up to reveal her bare naked arse. It was then when I noticed her attire, miniskirt and cropped shirt as her blonde hair flowed around her shoulders and down her back. She turned to face me before falling over the grass, giggling, and taking me down with her.

"Your dick is hard," she pointed out. I hadn't noticed and didn't know why. It must have been the drug. It was doing things to me I didn't ask for.

"Yeah," was the only reply I could think to say because I had no control over anything else. Not moving my arms. Not getting back to my feet. I looked up into the stars and focused on the moon, wishing it could talk back to me. *Where's Mia?* It was the only question I'd ever asked the round faceless circle in the sky. It only taunted me in return.

Leigh straddled my hips, planting her bare feet on both sides. "Warm me up then."

My eyes dragged from the sky to her as she ground out a desperate rhythm against my pants. Another wind twisted her hair into its breeze, and my eyes followed the direction back to the sky. "We can't," I gritted out, arms heavy at my side.

Her cold finger hit my lips. "She's not here, Oliver. She's gone, remember?" The same finger trailed down my chest until it hit the button on my jeans.

My gaze stayed on the moon as I drifted in and out of consciousness. With my body sedated, emotions charged through me at her words, bringing tears to my eyes. I felt one slip from the corner, and it slid down the side of my face before it met the dying grass. I was fucked up and crying as Leigh relentlessly tried to dry hump me into submission, and I never felt so alone.

"You're just like your father," mum seethed earlier with a stick between her lips. "I can't even look at you. Eat your food." She turned from the table, and I went back to spooning the porridge into my mouth, quietly. I didn't mean to upset her. She was upset about the money spent on food this week, which I couldn't understand because Oscar was gone, and it was just mum and me. But I told her everything would be okay, and she didn't like that.

But as I lay here under the windowsill, all I can think about now is my dad. Who is he, and why isn't he here? Did I have his eyes, and does he like to read? I'm the only one with green eyes, so they have to be my dad's, right? Why does mum hate him so much?

There are no numbers in the kitchen. No clock. The electricity is out, and it's dark. I use the street light coming through the window to read a few more chapters until mum finally comes through the door. Her heel broke, and she's stumbling into the kitchen. The cupboards bang, drawers slam, and I know it's going to be one of those nights.

"Where are my fucking cigarettes," she mumbles, and a dish shatters against the linoleum. I sit upright, shove my book under my arse, and pin my back against the wall. She ripped up the last book when she was like this, and the lady with the brown eyes at the library gave me one more chance. "Did you hide my shit?"

Mum's in my face, her eyes look weird, cross-eyed, and her jumbled blonde hair smells horrid. I shake my head violently, afraid of what she will do next. I didn't hide her cigarettes. She ran out. I make sure to count them. It's the only way to prepare, but I've never seen her like this before—this angry. She's leaning to one side, and her eyes grow bigger. Mum yanks me from the sill and throws me over the bed. Maybe I get to sleep with her finally. Perhaps she'll finally hold me, keep me warm.

"You worthless piece of shit," she straddles me and shoves a pillow over my face. With her entire weight pressed against my chest, my stomach, my lungs, I can't breathe. "I wish I never had you!" A force digs against the pillow and tears burn in my eyes, but they can't fall. The pressure is too much, and I want to close my eyes, but I can't. The pillow is preventing me. I can't close my eyes. I can't breathe. I try to move my arms, but they're pinned to my sides between her legs. I try to turn my head. If only I could close my eyes.

Minutes past, and she's screaming at me as my body is jerking for air, my chest begging for relief. My eyes can't close, but it's still dark. I don't know what's real anymore. My chest is burning. My lungs are burning. My brain is burning. I'm on fire.

And then it all stops.

It's not dark anymore.

There's a light, but it's brief before Mum's terrified features replace it.

"Come back! Oliver, come back!" Mum cries, jerking her head from side to side as she's pulling back from my face. I gasp for air, and tears finally waterfall down my cheeks as I blink rapidly. "I'm so sorry," she splutters through sobs. Mum lifts me from the bed and holds me in her arms. "I'm so sorry."

The sound of my zipper pulled me out and gave me a burst of energy, and before Leigh managed to have her way with me, I rolled out from under her until my chest met the ground.

A slap against my bare arse woke me. "Rise and shine, Oliver," a voice called out, and I opened one eye to see Adrian with a big white smile. "Pull up your pants. You're frightening the kids."

The blinding sun glared from above. Groaning, I lifted myself onto my forearm and pulled up my pants before rolling on to my back. Despite the morning chill, the poison from last night drained from my pores. "James and Reggi, are they all right?"

"Oh, they're all right, alright," Adrian laughed as we clasped each other's forearms, and he pulled me into a sitting position over the front lawn. My cigarettes were tossed in my lap as he slapped my back with his other hand.

I lit the match and pulled the cigarette to my mouth. The crisp menthol oozed down my throat and filled my lungs, and my eyes closed once the wicked high from the nicotine soothed me. "Last night was fucked up," I stated as the cigarette smoke mixed with the cold air. My arms draped over my bent knees, and I hung my head. "This isn't me. This isn't who I am or what I stand for."

"Is this any of us, really?" Adrian blew out a long and hesitant sigh. "Listen, there's something I've been meaning to tell ya." I tilted my head, eyes squinting from the sun. Adrian rolled his head back and cracked his knuckles. "Last night, I overheard Dex talking to those two wankers about you."

"Yeah? What about me?"

"About a lead or some shit."

My heart jumped into my throat. I tried to swallow it back down.

Adrian rubbed his palms together. "They didn't want to tell you. They knew you wouldn't have completed the rival raid last night if you knew."

It was all I needed to hear before I was already on my feet and storming through the door. The small house smelled of sex and liquor, and a gust of smoke from the blunt James and Reggi were sharing engulfed me before the two jumped from the couch. Dex's two bodyguards laid passed out in the plastic chairs, and naked women scattered the floor at my feet. I walked around them and turned down the hallway before I pushed open the door of the back room. The boom of the door bouncing off the wall echoed, awaking Dex and his one night stand. "Get the fuck out," I ordered the black-headed slapper through clenched teeth. She scurried from the bed, collected her clothing from the floor, and breezed past me.

"Awe, you didn't have to go and make her leave, Oliver. She could have stayed." Dex smirked, and my rage pushed me forward until I had him lifted out of the bed and slammed against the wall. "You have a lot of nerve," he was able to get out before my fist swiped his jaw, whipping his head to the side.

"What I am is impatient." I pulled him back up by his biceps and pinned his arms to the wall. "What are you not telling me?"

Dex Sullivan was many things, but a fighter wasn't one of them. The only time he held true power was when a pistol was in his hand. Aside from his threats, a weapon was his source of intimidation. And at the moment, he didn't have a chance to grab one. He may have been powerless, but I wasn't. Something I'd tried to teach the other three boys these past few days. It was no coincidence the way humans were created, and by learning how to fight, I'd become my most valuable weapon.

I slammed another fist into his grin, knocking his tooth out, and it embedded into my knuckle.

"Scott bought two tickets to the states and boarded a plane in Liverpool yesterday," Dex rushed out with a mouthful of blood.

A burn crept behind my eyes as relief set into my soul. "Where in the states?" My voice cracked from emotion.

"You can't leave, baby O."

My hand moved over his neck, and Dex, like the pussy boy he was without his backup, withered in my hold. "Where did he go?" I screamed, my cheeks shaking and spit flying.

Dex's eyes widened, and he croaked something out, but I couldn't understand, so I loosened my grip from around his neck.

"New York," he finally said in a gathered breath. "He flew into JFK."

I let him go, and he collapsed to the floor. "He traveled with a companion," he croaked out as I walked away. "Mia Rose Jett." And the mention of my love's name managed to crack me open and spin me around to face him. A cackle slipped from his bloody lips. "You're not done, White Fox. This isn't over, not until you hold up your end of the deal."

ELEVEN

"We are ruled every day by
the choices we made
and did not make."

OLIVER MASTERS

Mia

I pried my eyelids apart to see the Hilton logo plastered over the ice bucket and plastic cups in the small kitchen, reminding me of where we were. Finally, back in the states. I was so close to my dad's house, a little over two hours to be exact, but my dad didn't care to see me. Ethan's constant reminders told me so.

A strong arm draped over my side. I inched away from Ethan's hold for a quick shower before he would wake and searched inside the duffle for a pair of sweats, clean panties, and one of Ethan's plain tees he wouldn't need. All my clothes were left at Dolor. I had close to nothing aside from the clothes I wore when he captured me and the few he'd purchased.

The night before, I'd told Ethan that I could try. I'd left it open-ended intentionally, allowing him room to fill in whatever missing pieces he needed. *Try to get through this, try not to kill him, try to trust him.* Over and over, Ethan drilled into my head how he was the only one who ever cared about me. The evidence laid out before my eyes, and my mind agreed, but my heart refused to listen. No one was looking for me. No one else cared. The only reason I'd gotten on that plane was because if Ollie was looking out for himself, I had to do the same.

I had to start thinking about me. I had to put myself first. I had to learn to live without Ollie though it hurt like hell.

Despite what Ollie had done, it still brought me peace to know he was living the dream he deserved. He gave me a sense of myself over the last two years, pulled me out from a dark hole, was the first to show me who I was, and what I was capable of. Oliver Masters, regardless if he tossed me to the side to go after his dream, gave me something I needed during one of the most challenging times of my life. Oliver Masters gave me something to hold on to for a lifetime.

But the distance didn't make it hurt any less.

If Ollie was able to do it, maybe I could too.

And Ethan was the answer.

Ethan killed people—numerous people, which I found intriguing. I had so many questions for him. *Did it bring him a sense of serenity like it had brought me when I'd killed my uncle? Did he have monstrous thoughts too, punishing those who'd destroyed him? Did he feel empowered, being the one in control? Did the void in their eyes give him the same high as it did me?* So many questions, and maybe Ethan was right, and we were the same.

The shower was hot against my back. The little Hilton travel-sized shampoo and conditioner smelled of rain in the spring, feminine. Very different from the coconut smell at Dolor, and the masculine scent I'd been using of Ethan's lately.

The clothes hung off my tiny frame, but I didn't care, assuming we'd spend the day in the car anyway. Ethan had planned everything out, and by the looks of the vehicle, new identities, and cash found in the glovebox, we weren't flying anywhere else. At least for a while.

My hair was still damp, but I couldn't pull it up off my back because I had no hair tie. When I walked back toward the bed, Ethan sat awake on the edge of the bed staring at me.

"How did you sleep?" he asked, still wearing the same clothes from yesterday. We were too tired to change, and apparently, he was too tired to take anything off. Ethan rarely slept in his clothes.

"Okay." I dropped the wet towel in the corner of the room. "I need to borrow a pair of your socks."

"You can take whatever you want from the bag, Jett. I see you're already wearing my shirt." He raised a brow and stood to his feet. "Anyway, I'm taking a quick shower then we have to head out. We'll get breakfast on the way."

"Where are we going?"

He paused halfway to the bathroom at my side and looked down at me. "It's best if you don't know."

Ethan

While Mia was in the shower, I'd rang Dean. Thankfully, he had picked up because I needed someone I looked up to for answers. I needed direction. The last thing I wanted to admit to my friend was that I'd tore Mia away, and she'd never agreed to any of this until last night. Dean hadn't held back and chewed my arse out. I'd never heard him so angry. When it came to love and relationships, the man reminded me of Masters. A few minutes into the call, I'd grown frustrated with how the conversation was going and hung up. *Fuck him.* But Dean was right. Regardless of whether I liked it or not, it was what I needed to hear.

Mia stood at my side as we checked out of the hotel. I'd promised to keep her safe, but all I'd done was break her down entirely only to build her into my version of perfection. I wanted her mine. All of her. Both the

124

storm and the compliant little puppet. I was almost there too, feeding on how fucked up she was. I'd turned her against the entire world for my benefit. Most of it had been true, though. In all honesty, I had no idea why Lynch, Bruce, nor Masters were out looking for her. But I'd used it to my advantage.

Dean had reminded me of the man I was turning into, and what I'd needed to do to.

Mia and I couldn't move forward, not like this. I'd told her that everyone had been lying to her, but if we didn't stop now, she'd be living a lie for the rest of her life. Mia would never love me the way she loved him. Even now, as we walked together toward the car, it was a fucking lie. The air between us reeked of a frontage, an act she was forcing herself to be a part of while her mind was elsewhere. We both knew it. Neither of us had to say the words out loud. Love turned us all into fools.

I unlocked the car and opened the passenger door for her after throwing the duffle in the backseat. She paused before getting into the car.

"I just want you to know that I understand," she quietly said and sucked in a breath. "I get why you did it. There was no way I would've been able to sleep at night if I knew my rapist was still living. I had a lot of time to think about it, and I agree. You and me are the same. I get that now."

"Jett—"

 Mia wrapped her arms around my waist, and I'd suddenly forgotten what I was going to say, but it would probably be something I would have regretted. I held her close, and we stayed like that for a while. I didn't want to let the moment pass, but all things that were only here for a season needed to come to an end at some point. The day with my mum reminded me of that. This entire time, I'd thought Masters was the season, but I couldn't have been more wrong.

I was Mia's season. A harsh fucking winter, nonetheless.

"Come on, let's get inside. You're shaking," I stripped off my jacket and wrapped it around Mia before we got into the car.

The heat cranked on high as I drove around the car park for a few minutes to get acquainted with driving on the opposite side. Mia laughed, and it was the first time I'd heard her laugh in a while. Possibly Dean was all wrong. Maybe he didn't have it all figured out, and Mia and I could stay exactly like this for the rest of our lives.

"You got this!" Mia praised at my side, I took her hand and drove out of the lot and onto a busy street.

I don't got this, and you have no idea why.

After going through a drive-thru, I entered the highway to our next destination. Mia ordered assorted pastries and a hazelnut coffee, eating every single one before passing out beside me. Last night, I'd heard her soft cries all hours of the night. She had to be exhausted, and I was too.

The entire ride, she'd slept in a curled ball to my right with my arm hanging over her leg, my large hand snug between her thighs. I didn't want to let go as she murmured in her sleep, and my lips twitched to smile.

We made it four hours later, thanks to traffic, and I pulled the car against the curb and put the gear into park. Mia was still sleeping at my side, drooling into my jacket. I had no clue how she was going to react to this, and I unbuckled my seatbelt, leaned over the console, and pushed the hair from her face. "Jett," I whispered.

Her eyes blinked open. "Where are we?"

"There's something you have to know." I didn't know how to string the words together for her to understand. I'd never been good with words, that was Master's territory—the overnight poet, who was probably pounding into random pussy as we speak. At this very moment, Masters was probably making girls fall in love with him with his fucking words, partying, drinking, smiling, and laughing at the rest of us. I bit the inside of my cheek, knowing I was about to destroy the rest of her too. "I'd made a mistake. I should've never taken you. It was cruel, selfish even."

Mia sat up, her stringy brown hair whipped against her sticky face as she turned her head and looked at the surroundings. "My dad's?" she whispered, recognizing the street we were on. "You took me back to my dad's?" Her glossy brown eyes narrowed at me. "Start the car, Ethan! I'm never going back there. I'm not getting out of this car!"

Her dad, the only man she'd trusted for over ten years, had dropped her off at Dolor two years ago. Here I was, the man she'd finally trusted again since I'd taken her from that place, dropping her arse right back off at her dad's. Full fucking circle. "Yes, you are."

"No!" Tears puddled in her eyes. "Drive!" her fist pounded on the dashboard, and her movements became frantic. "Drive the fucking car!"

I rubbed my hands up and down my face, trying to pull it together. I couldn't stop now. I had to see this through. "You're getting out whether you like it or not. I'll drag your arse up that driveway by your fucking hair, do you understand me?" My voice broke, and I swallowed the tears back down. "I don't want you anymore. I made a colossal mistake. You were a big *fucking* mistake."

Mia's eyes locked on mine, and she tilted her head as if she was seeing right through me. "You don't mean that."

Of course, I didn't. But if Mia didn't get out of the car within the next two seconds, I'd be afraid I would never have the strength to do right by her again. "Oh, I'm very certain, Jett. You will only drag me down."

Her fist connected with my face, sending my head back.

For a moment, I couldn't breathe. A ringing blasted inside my ears and I shook my head until my vision righted again. She busted my lip, and the warm copper taste slipped past my gums. I wiped my lip with the back of my hand, accessing the damage. I didn't expect that. Perhaps a slap, but not a punch.

I forced a laugh. "You hit like a fucking girl."

"Really? Because you're the only pussy in this car," she seethed. "Every day we've been together, you've done nothing but remind me how no one gives a shit about me. How everyone lied, but you're the biggest liar of them all. You can't even be honest with yourself! Look at you, Ethan! You're fucking pathetic. I'll keep your secret. I'll take it to my grave, but I'll never let you fuck with my head again."

"I never fucked with your head, Jett," I laughed, "That was all you. You were always fucked up to begin with." I knew what would hurt her the most, and I had to say it. "No wonder Masters left your arse the first chance he got. I'm not making the same mistake."

Mia's hand clenched into a fist as her chin trembled. If she was about to hit me again, I was more prepared this time. But she never did. Instead, she drew in a shaky breath, wiped her eyes, and got out of the car, barefoot in homeless attire. She didn't even turn back for a second glace, and it took all restraint to not get out of the car and run after her, to apologize for everything I'd said because I didn't mean any of it. *This is the right thing*, I repeated over and over in my head. *One day she'll forgive you for this.*

I peeled off the street, driving my foot into the gas before I'd have a chance to change my mind. Nausea hit me like a tsunami, colliding with an angry coastline, and I slammed my palms against the steering wheel over and over. My vision darkened from the maddening monster inside me, and a scream ripped through my throat as my cheeks shook.

"I love you, Mia," I screamed inside the car to absolutely no one. "I'm letting you go because it's the right thing to do. Because I won't let the monster fucking win!" The words meant for Mia's ears flew out of me until my throat went hoarse, crying for the first time since I'd killed Haden Charles.

Goodbye, Mia.

TWELVE

"This was her war cry in desperate times,
screaming because it hurt inside.
It shook the moon and lit the sky,
the wild one with the war cry.
All on her own, she called out her foe,
Screaming so they would know.
Shaking their bones to her lullaby,
my wild one with the war cry."

OLIVER MASTERS

Ollie

fucking knew it, and my mind has been spinning since I'd left Thurrock. I'd returned to Surrey two hours later because, at first, I'd headed straight for an airport, then realized after approaching the ticket counter, I had absolutely nothing on me. Both my passport and identification weren't with me, but back here at the motel.

There was no time for a shower, but I smelled like I'd come from a strip joint. I was in and out within two minutes and changed into something more presentable, something Mia could recognize, grey joggers, a basic white shirt, and a black hoodie. With my mind elsewhere, my hands grabbed clothes from Mia's suitcase, stuffing them into a backpack. *Did she have clothes? What has she been wearing this entire time?*

When I'd called Bruce a few hours ago, he had said she wasn't there, that he hadn't heard from her. But there was no other reason I could think of for Scott to fly into New York, a little under three hours away from Mia's dad's house.

The last two weeks felt like a never-ending chase after her, but if it meant spending the rest of my life looking, I would do it.

The flight had been fifteen hours long, and I arrived in New York at three in the morning. After my first step out of the airport and into the city that never slept, a repulsive stench of pollution, stagnant water, and rude and tired faces greeted me. I waited patiently on the curb, holding my arm out in the air to call a taxi, and when the yellow car pulled up, a lady in a black business suit shouldered past me and slid into the backseat.

By five, I was on the road in a small silver hatchback rented at Alamo, en route to Bushkill, Pennsylvania. It had been the only place open at that hour, and I'd taken whatever was available.

By six-thirty, I parked in the driveway of the Jett residence.

The house was a two-story home with a partial front porch. Was this the same house Mia lived where all the evil moments of her past had happened? Had Bruce moved her into a new home to shield her from the memories as much as he could? The house backed into woods, secluded, with a steep driveway. For the last hour, I'd debated on finding a coffee shop. If Mia were inside, she'd appreciate her croissants. But I was too afraid to leave the premises.

And by eight, I was standing in front of the door, knocking. My heart beat out of my chest, and my adrenaline punched through impossible levels. Unable to stay in place, I paced the front porch, hoping someone would answer.

The door opened, and Bruce stared back at me from inside the house. He wasn't like anything I'd expected, a balding head, years of guilt stacked in layers under his sunken eyes, wearing sweatpants and a Steelers football shirt with a coffee mug in hand. "You must be Oliver."

I wet my frozen lips. "Is … please … tell me—"

"She's here," he confirmed with a nod.

My palm fell against the door frame, and I hung my head, pinching the bridge of my nose to fight back the emotions threatening to spill onto the Jett's front porch. I'd found her. My vision glossed over, and I wiped my face into the sleeve of my hoodie before lifting my head to see the man I'd spoken to every day since release day. "Is she all right? Is she hurt?"

"Why don't you come inside. I have an hour before work. Let's talk." Bruce lead me into the kitchen, but my eyes couldn't help wandering around and up the stairs, looking for Mia. "Would you like a cup of coffee? You look like you just came back from a hundred-year expedition." He chuckled.

"It sure feels that way," he had no idea, "and yes, please. Black." I took a seat in the breakfast nook where a bay window overlooked the garden bleeding into the forest. My knee bounced under the table, itching to run up the stairs to find her. But this was his home. "When did she arrive?"

"Yesterday morning after I'd left for work. Mia hasn't spoken much. Barely left her room. I have no idea how she got here or where she came from, but she's been locked up in the guest bedroom ever since. Diane, my wife, isn't too happy with her being here," he pointed out, setting a mug in front of me over a wicker placemat. "Especially since we have to pay more lawyer fees to reschedule the court date she missed."

I pulled the mug from my mouth. "It wasn't Mia's fault. I'm sure she feels bad about it. And you don't need to worry about the cost. I can take care of a lawyer."

Bruce's brows peaked as he dropped into a dining chair with his mug in hand. "You?"

I leaned back in the chair and pressed my hand into my knee. "Yeah. I love her, sir. I'm in love with her, and Mia loves me too."

The deserted smile on his lips fed my anxiety. "Mia's not capable of love."

He'd said it as if I didn't know her—as if he knew her better than me. "You're wrong." I cocked my head to the side, averting my gaze briefly to contain myself. The words were there, hanging on the tip of my tongue. I wanted to tell Bruce how Mia had always been capable of love. That I'd felt her wistful heart beat furiously at her absolute worst, proving passion stirred in the midst of nothingness. Mia Rose Jett had always been desperate to love. She only had to wake up first. "Mia's been through hell and back, and not only has she survived, but she bloomed. Mia is nothing short of a wonder. If you took the time to get to know her, you'd see it too."

Bruce leaned back and folded a leg over the other. "Are we talking about the same Mia?"

"Would you let me go upstairs so I could make sure?" I tried, and he laughed. I hid my smile behind the rim of the coffee mug before taking a sip. I was serious. My veins shook from being this close and not seeing her. Setting the coffee back down, the laughter settled between us, and I let out a helpless sigh. "Please, let me see her. Let me go wake her up."

"Will she leave with you? What are your plans?" Bruce asked, straight and to the point.

His first question threw me off guard, almost as if he didn't want Mia here. Almost as if Mia was a burden. Bruce didn't say it, but he didn't have to. A vacancy loomed in his eyes, and it was apparent when it came to Mia, Bruce had checked out a long time ago. "For two years, I'd done nothing but make plans, and I stopped making them two weeks ago when Mia went missing. I'm done making plans, sir. I used to believe if I did everything I could to map out our future, it would happen because it was planned—because I thought I'd prepared us for the unknown. But that's not the case, and I see it now. The only plan I have right now is sitting right here in this chair until you give me the okay to run up those stairs to see her. I can't see past that right now."

"I like you," Bruce admitted.

"People usually do."

"When you get up the stairs, her room is on the left. Don't wake my wife."

I abandoned the chair and took off. My feet couldn't move fast enough, and when I'd approached the door, I drew in a deep breath and turned the knob.

It was locked, and my forehead fell over the door as I knocked lightly. "Mia," I pleaded. "It's me." The silence and barrier between us were terrifying. What condition would I find her in? What on earth could she have possibly faced over the last few weeks? What did Ethan do to her? Why did he let her go? Questions swam and my head spun. "Please, open the door."

"There's a key over the frame on top," Bruce stated from below.

I reached my hand up over the ledge until my fingertips touched the cold metal.

It was gold, and I pushed it through the hole and turned the knob.

The door opened.

But the room was empty.

Desperately, I checked the closet and the bathroom. The bed had been slept in, sheets bunched at the foot of the mattress. My eyes darted around the bedroom until they settled on an open window where a breeze came through, blowing the thin curtain carelessly. I stepped forward and swiped the curtain out of the way to find a ledge someone could easily jump from. A ledge she had jumped from.

Mia was gone.

I'd driven up and down mountains, gotten lost in the valley, and lost cell reception along with it. With no idea as to where Mia would run off to, I continued to drive around, afraid I'd end up off a cliff. Every driver I'd passed whipped by me, rudely honking their horn.

By three in the afternoon, I'd finally gotten service and tapped the nearest petrol station into the GPS. She had to be around here, she was inside my chest, inside my bones. My soul hummed, recognizing hers close by. A few more hours of searching passed by and on my way back to their house to see if she'd returned to her dad's, twisted brown hair, a tiny frame, and a black hoodie caught my eye and stole my breath. It was Mia, and she was sitting on a bench off in the distance, overlooking the mountain view.

I pulled the hatchback into the dip in the road and turned off the engine. Mia's back was to me, but I knew it was her. The pounding of my heart was all too familiar, and my nerves drifted, turning into relief as she sat there in numerous layers of clothes, engine-red rain boots covering her feet. She didn't bother turning around when she heard the car come up behind her. Or did she hear?

Exiting the car, I thought about what I'd say or do. And with each step closer, I had to refrain myself from pulling her into my arms. I took a seat beside her on the corner of the bench and released a shaky breath, my gaze never drifting from her. Under wet lashes, her lips were chapped, and she shook inside her clothes. But even when she was crying, she was beautiful. I couldn't take my eyes off her as she kept hers on the horizon.

We sat there for a while, neither one of us saying anything. Mia's silence called upon a panic teetering inside me, pushing it over the edge. I'd never been so nervous. The wind from up here blew violently, but Mia never faltered. The thoughts inside her head were so loud it clenched my entire being in a tight grip. She was confused, and I wished I knew the reasons why.

"Why didn't you look for me?" she finally asked.

Her words shocked me and broke open my chest, and I had to turn my head away to blink away the water gathering in my eyes. When I turned back to face her, I reached out for her hand in her lap, but she pulled away. "Mia, look at me."

Her eyes slammed closed, and she shook her head.

In seconds, I crouched down in front of her, refusing to allow her to accept the bloody lie. "I've been looking for you my entire life, Mia. I've never fucking stopped. I look for you in every room I'm in, in every face I see, and for the last few weeks, I've done nothing but do everything I possibly could to find you." Mia's eye's clenched together harder, tears escaping. "I'll never stop, Mia."

Mia's eyes opened. She looked at me, and I froze.

Despite the last few weeks, the single look in her eyes proved she was the same strong Mia I fell for all over again with every passing day. She stayed with me, and I blew out a long unsteady breath.

"You lied to me. For two years, you lied to me," she said, and her hand touched my cheek. Perhaps she wanted to make sure I was real. "You're a poet now—"

"I've always been a poet, love."

"You never told me you published your work. You never once told me the hoodie I wore almost every day was in your name. You kept so much from me."

Though she was speaking, I was too hypnotized by her touch. My face sank into her palm before she raked her fingers through my hair. I leaned in closer, needing more. "Everything I did was for you and Zeke. That's the truth. I was afraid to tell you because I was afraid to fail you. I didn't want you to be disappointed in me. When I found the first book was a success, I wanted to surprise you, but never got the chance."

"Why didn't you file a police report?"

"*God*, Mia. I tried. Lord knows, I tried. The police never gave me the time of day. I've talked to every goddamn officer and resident in all of Guildford and Surrey, visited Oscar in prison, showed up at Lynch's, bothering his arse every fucking day. I called Bruce. Every. Bloody. Day."

"You have an answer for everything."

"Because I've *done* everything."

And we went back and forth like that for over an hour, me on my knees before her with her hands on me. She'd told me what happened with Scott, how he was responsible for the suicides, and she had walked in on him, how Scott took her and held her captive in a cabin. How Mia set the cabin on fire, and Scott saved her. How it was her decision to get on the plane. How Mia didn't want to leave him, but Scott dropped her off. I told her I wanted to kill him, and she said no. I told her I loved her, and that would never change.

Communication had always been easy for us because we laid everything on the table and rarely held back from one another, but I did hold back. I should've told her that I'd gotten involved with the Links. I'd made a deal with the devil to find her, but telling her would only put more on her plate. Instead, I reminded her I'd wait however long she needed. That I'd stay with her for however long it took.

Temperatures dropped, and she still hadn't moved from the chair, not letting me touch her—not letting me hold her. It hurt, but Scott had done damage. It pained me to see her like this, so distant and on edge. Though her eyes remained on me, making sure I didn't disappear. I wanted to ask if he'd touched her in places my hands have been and if she'd touched him the way she touched me, but now wasn't the time. It wouldn't have made a difference, anyway.

"I'm so mad," she whispered, her hands still in my hair as if they'd keep me real as mine held onto the bench on both sides of her.

Her anger tore my soul to pieces and made me feel whole—a masochist. My legs were numb from crouching for so long, but I couldn't see straight from being in her space, too afraid to move—afraid of her hands pulling away from me. "Mia…"

She shook her head as her hands dropped from me and shook at her sides. "I never needed anyone. I didn't need anyone else to make me feel safe, to make me happy. I was fine and able to take care of myself … Because I didn't fucking care. Now I care, and suddenly, it's as if I'm relying on everyone else. On Ethan, on you. I hate not being able to defend myself. I hate how every time you're away from me, the pain eats me from the inside out like I'm dying a slow and excruciating death. I hate it," her voice increased, and I was scared of where she was heading and what her confession was doing to her. "I don't want my entire world to depend on anyone else but me. I want to start making choices. I want to make something of myself, to fight my own battles, to earn my own victories. I don't want to be weak anymore." Air escaped her lips, a puff of white chill. "I don't know anymore. I can't think at all. I'm so mad, I want to punch someone. I want to hurt someone. I'm so angry, and I want to scream. Yeah ..." she looked at me, gasping for a breath through furious sobs, "I want to fucking scream."

So badly, I wanted to kiss her to quiet the chaos swirling inside her mind. Mia was hyperventilating, words all over the place. Ethan had broken her down and filled her head with so much doubt and uncertainty, I wanted to take a knife to his throat for the pain and damage it caused her. In a hurricane of hysteria, she tried filling her lungs and looked up at me through heavy and desperate eyes. For the first time, I didn't know how to help her. But the words just fell out of my mouth as if it were a reflex. "Scream, Mia."

"What?"

"Scream. It's just you and me here, let your worst out." I nodded, hoping this would work. Mia's head snapped up, and she pinched her brows together as the wind tossed her strands against her face. I took her hand and lifted her from the bench toward the railing. It made me nervous how close to the cliff she was, and I stood behind her as she continued to search for air. Looking out into the sun setting behind the rigid mountains, I dipped my head close to her ear and closed my eyes. "Let go."

I wanted her to fall apart.

I wanted her to fall on me.

With every struggling piece of her, I was ready.

I wanted my *too much* heart and soul to be the filter for her.

Then Mia's fists clutched the railing, knuckles white, and a scream pierced through the evening air. A battle cry, echoing in the valley, the entire world her audience, the mountain her stage. It penetrated my soul, passing through every part of me. Her scream entered my bloodstream, crawled through my veins, and brought tears to my eyes. My chest ripped open as I held on to her, believing she had the power to move planets and stop time. It was that powerful. Mia screamed because it hurt, and for once, she wanted everyone to feel the same pain she felt—and I fucking felt it. She screamed because she thought she was broken, but her broken would never make me run. She screamed until the scream turned into a cry, and she collapsed into my arms, and I rocked her against the wind.

"You can lose your mind, Mia, but you're never losing me."

THIRTEEN

"The easiest way to lose yourself is within another.
The easiest way to find yourself is within another."

OLIVER MASTERS

Mia

Oliver Masters was in America, his rented hatchback parked in my dad's driveway.

Neither one of us had spoken a word on the way here after I'd screamed, which made me feel lighter. In less than sixty seconds, the rage, pain, and hurt hoarded over two weeks had escaped through my throat, and it never felt so good. Ollie always knew what I needed.

Ollie had pulled behind my dad's parked car, and we sat in comfortable silence for a few minutes. Before we'd left Dolor, we made plans to run off and get married, our futures open and free, and for the taking, together.

But two weeks could change a lot.

Ethan made me question Ollie's devotion to me. His love for me. Ethan made me believe I was weak and needed him to survive, but that was before he discarded me—a useless card in a losing game of poker. A joker. My brain was a jumbled mess, and I wasn't sure what to believe anymore. I couldn't even trust my own thoughts. One second, I wanted to throw myself onto Ollie and beg him to erase the last two weeks and take me back to Guildford, where we danced inside his dorm room and laughed under the thin sheet all night long, talking about everything we'd do and the places we'd go. The next, I wanted to run inside my dad's house and devise a plan to live out the rest of my life alone, possibly singing in the streets for money, so no one could ever have the chance to betray me again.

Ollie sat in the driver seat wearing the black hoodie and grey joggers I'd seen him in so many times before. Exhaustion consumed his features, he looked even skinnier, and his hair was cut differently, shorter on the sides, but still long on top. Yet, his green eyes were still the same, only now a hint of relief shown through all the ways they'd always spoken to me.

"I'm getting a hotel close by," he finally said. "I'd really like it if you stayed with me." Words stuck in my windpipe, and I needed longer than a breath to think this through. "I understand if you don't," he continued. "I know you need time, but I'll be here in the morning, and I'll show up every morning on that doorstep until you realize I'm not going anywhere."

"Okay," was all I could gather. Ollie pinched the bridge of his nose, and my heart collapsed into the pit of my stomach. He was trying to be strong, and it tore him up inside. Instead of finding his fiancé, he'd found a girl with a broken spirit. And I didn't want him to bring me back this time. I needed to find the strength to bring myself back for once, to know I could.

"I'm in love with you, Mia." His feelings compromised his voice. "I'll always be in love with you. Forever, madly in that place you never have to question, no matter what happens. Wedding or no wedding, it's you

140

and I evermore. Do you understand me?" Nodding, my bottom lip trembled and my eyes burned as I watched my broken spirit only strengthen his. His faith shook, but he still believed in the two of us—enough for the both of us. He forced a small smile and released a breath. "Good, now go get some sleep. I'll see you bright and early."

I didn't say it back. I didn't kiss Ollie goodbye.

I was too afraid. If our lips met, I'd be on my way back to the hotel with him. And if I'd gone back, I'd never find out the truth. Was I the dependent girl whose happiness and strength relied on someone else, or could I find the strength within?

After Ethan drove off, I'd officially hit the bottom of what was supposed to be a bottomless pit. The joke was on me when I'd crashed into the hard surface.

Three things I'd learned about myself. First, I was definitely not a sociopath—never was. Two, I would forever be in love with Oliver Masters. And three, I didn't know who I was without him.

Number three was the punch to the gut, and the main reason I needed this time. With or without me, Ollie had a future, a life, dreams, a career…Everything I didn't have and never knew I wanted until now. A part of me was jealous, another part incredibly proud. I couldn't be angry with Ollie for going after it, but it only reminded me of how less of a person I was. At least with Ethan, on the run, it could have distracted me with a false sense of purpose. At least with Ethan, I wouldn't have been the only one hiding, pretending, and lying to myself.

Ollie waited in the driveway as I climbed the porch steps and pushed through the door of my dad's house, where Dad sat over the beige microfiber couch in front of the TV, watching the Steelers play, his hand clasped around a glass set on the side table. His head scooped to the side to see I'd come through the door.

Diane poked her blonde head through the kitchen opening with a rag in her hands. "We already ate. I'm not used to making dinner for three, so you'll have to figure it out." She threw the rag over her shoulder.

"You're an adult now, Mia. Time to take care of yourself." Her head disappeared, and I hadn't expected anything different from her.

"It's okay." I stepped toward the living room, passing her on the way. "I wasn't hungry, anyway."

"Starving yourself or too lazy?" I heard behind me from the kitchen.

I paused mid-step, my fists clenched at my sides. "Just tired," I forced out. It was already close to six-thirty at night, which would've made it almost eleven-thirty in the United Kingdom, but as tired as I was, a conversation between my dad and I needed to happen. We hadn't spoken since I'd returned, avoiding both of them until I could figure out what to say.

Our sectional was L-shaped, and I dropped into the plush fabric on the opposite side of my dad. He looked over at me, and I felt exposed. I shoved my hand beneath my thighs to refrain from fidgeting. "I'm sorry."

My dad grabbed the remote from the arm of the chair and turned the volume down on the TV. I wished he hadn't. I didn't want Diane overhearing our conversation or jumping into it. His bushy brow shot into the air, and he crossed his ankle over his opposite knee. "What are you sorry for?"

I didn't exactly know what to be sorry for, only that we had to make amends if I was staying under his roof. He was already dealing with the strain it put on their marriage, and I hadn't noticed it until now—until my heart thawed out since Dolor got ahold of me. Or Ollie. Or both. "That all this happened. That it got to this point."

"I appreciate that, Mia."

Diane laughed from inside the kitchen and my stomach knotted at the sound.

"Bruce, don't fall for it. Mia manipulates, it's what she does. The only reason she's apologizing is because she has no place else to go. Twenty-years-old and nothing to show for it." Her laughter continued, bouncing off the lifeless white walls inside the house. Perhaps I deserved it. For over ten years, I'd put them both through hell for my amusement.

Before, I'd say something smart in return. Probably comment on how Diane never worked a day in her life and lived off my mother's life insurance to pay for her manicured nails and yoga classes, which was what the two of them most likely expected from me. The anticipation in my dad's eyes zeroed in on me, and a huffing and puffing song drifted into the living room from the kitchen as dishes clanked inside the sink.

Deserted in the desert. Hands behind my back. A hundred rifles aiming at me.

"I just wanted to say I'm sorry," I repeated, standing. "Thank you for letting me stay here until my court date." There was an unsaid awkwardness in the air, and I walked toward the stairs to head back to my room without a second glance back to acknowledge Diane's mutters under her breath. The thought of staying with Ollie at the hotel seemed like a better idea, but if I had done that, it only meant running away from my problems.

As I walked back up the stairs, the TV's volume increased, proving I was some sort of temporary fixture that could be easily ignored and soon removed if the wiring got faulty.

My old room was no longer my old room. It had since transformed into a guest bedroom, complete with wall-papered floral walls, white wicker furniture, and a sign over the headboard, reading "Be Our Guest." A crisp white quilt laid over the bed with over a dozen throw pillows. White, plush, and completely useless. And in the corner, where my desk used to be, sat a luggage rack for guests whom, I was sure, never visited.

I stood on my toes, grabbing a box of my old clothes from the top of the closet. Diane had thrown most out, but these had made the cut.

After a hot shower, I climbed into bed and flipped on Netflix to fall asleep to shows about unsolved murder cases and fell asleep wondering if the murderers were anything like Ethan and if the victims deserved it.

The next morning, I woke to the sound of Diane knocking at the guest bedroom door. She entered, unannounced, but there wasn't much I could say. This was her room now, her house. "There's a guy outside asking for you."

Ollie. He was here, and my heart did a round-off backhand spring inside my chest, ending with a backward free-fall, landing over on an invisible mat. I shouldn't have been this shocked he'd come, but he could decide to up and leave at any point just like everyone else. I sucked in a breath, remembering what I needed to do. "Okay."

"He's not allowed in this house."

"Okay ... I understand."

"Good." She left, and as soon as she disappeared around the corner, I hurried toward the closet and slipped a sweatshirt over my head and pulled up a pair of sweats. I didn't really own anything aside from jeans and sweats, believing life was too short to be uncomfortable. Each step down the stairs scratched at my nerves, and I paused before the door.

If I saw him, I'd go with him.

If I'd let him talk, I'd listen.

I opened the door. Ollie turned to face me. And all my feelings drowned out the words I wanted to say.

"Hi, love." He smiled his heart-stopping smile, looking at me in the way all girls, at least once in their lifetime, craved to be looked at. With admiration and without judgment. Three seconds, and that single look had always been what it took to remind me Oliver Masters was my forever. He looked away for a moment like he always did to hide the effect I had on him—the blush shading his cheeks and the smile he could never do away with. "How did you sleep?"

"Horrible." I missed lying next to him.

He seemed relieved. "Me too."

Silence invaded the air between us, but it wasn't awkward—it was never awkward. Being in Ollie's space brought back a sense of self-awareness. I knew who I was around him. The girl capable of defeating the darkness that had taken over, and if I was capable of that, I could do anything. Around Ollie, I could fight monsters, have a future, and be the best version of myself. But I wanted to do all these things without him too.

144

"Can I take you to breakfast?"

My gaze roamed over him, finally taking all of him in. The tattered black jeans were familiar, the ones he'd always wear at Dolor. I'd pulled the stray threads from the holes over his knees in the mess hall whenever his leg bounced from the nerves of the crowd, and took a pen and wrote our names over the parts around his thighs when I was bored, and he'd let me because he knew I always had a hard time keeping still. But the gray hoodie under the jean jacket and fresh white shoes were all new. While I'd been held captive by Ethan, he had time to go shopping.

"Mia …"

My eyes snapped up. "I need more time than a night."

"Can I come back later?"

I shook my head.

"This is killing me," he admitted, shifting in place.

"Come back tomorrow." It may not have made sense to him, but it made sense to me.

"I'll be here. Tomorrow," Ollie confirmed, and when I went to close the door, his palm came up and pressed against it to stop me. "I will be here, Mia. Every single morning, I'm going to be here until you find whatever it is you're looking for."

The following morning

For most of my life, I'd been both a morning and night person. I would be up all hours of the night, talking to the night sky, my best friend. Before Dolor, I'd jump out the window during the sticky summer nights and lay under the stars over the rough and itchy shingles, asking questions google or a textbook couldn't answer, like was Earth God's ninth draft because Venus was too hot, and Mars too cold? Maybe God never got it right the first time around. And was there an alternate universe with another Mia under different circumstances, never taken advantage of by her uncle,

Mom still alive, with loads of friends, and partying in her senior year? And why and how was the word *moist* made-up?

The night never talked back, only listened, which was the reason we'd gotten along so well.

I'd never found someone I could stand to talk to until I heard Ollie's voice. He'd quickly stolen best friend status right out from under the night sky, staying up all hours of the night with me after flying through the vent in the ceiling to be with each other. *"Is Earth Gods ninth draft?"*, I'd asked him. *"No one is perfect, Mia, but God is. God does nothing without purpose. Perhaps the other eight are there for balance." "Is there an alternate universe?"* I'd drilled him under the fort of the sheet we'd held up with our heads. *"If there is, I'm with you there too. We're together in every universe." "And what's up with the word moist?" "Phlegm was already taken."*

It had been easy to fall asleep at night when you had no more questions. With Ollie, everything was going to be okay, even if I didn't have the answer to everything. Next to Ollie, space and time were non-existent, and I'd slip into a coma of warmth without worry.

And though he wasn't sleeping with me now, the dreams of our time together held me over.

I woke up before Diane entered this time and looked out the window.

Ollie was there, standing against the silver hatchback on the curb with a *Dunkin* cup in one hand, the other shoved into the pocket of his hoodie. He must have felt my eyes on him, and his head tilted to catch me staring. *What time did he get here?* There was at least fifty feet, a window, and a tree branch between us, but his eyes found mine against the obstacles. Straightening his posture, he smiled, and his hand withdrew from the pocket and lifted in a small wave.

I waved back.

He held up a finger, sat his coffee over the top of the car, and opened the driver-side door.

His back was to me, and I took the opportunity to fix my hair. My pillow-head only made my left side decent, and a large *Champion* sweatshirt hung from my shoulders. My arms dropped to my sides as Ollie faced me again, holding up a second coffee cup in the air as an offering.

I shook my head.

He held up a finger again.

Then a white paper bag appeared from behind his back, and he gave it a little shake in front of him.

I laughed lightly, hoping the distance, tree, and glass of the window gave the illusion I wasn't blushing or completely taken by his determination.

Ollie held up his palm in the air as in to say, *give-me-something-here.*

I shook my head, and he hung his.

A few beats later, he'd sat my coffee beside his and disappeared inside the car again, grabbing a backpack. I'd watched from the window as he balanced the backpack over his knee, unzipped, and dropped the white paper bag inside, I'm sure filled with croissants and pastries, before closing it back up. Ollie grabbed my coffee off the car and walked under the window and toward the front door, disappearing from my view.

When he walked back to the car, his hands were empty.

He'd left it all waiting for me.

Ollie paused before he got back inside the hatchback, car door half-ajar, shielding half his body. He looked up once more, his eyes saying everything I needed to know: *I'll be here tomorrow, I'll do this forever, but hurry up because you're killing me.* And before he got inside and closed the door, the last look in his eyes said the very thing I needed to hear, taste, and feel instead. *I love you, Mia.*

The morning after that ...

I'd spent yesterday's brisk morning walking up and down the hills of Bushkill with the camera Ollie left me from the backpack, which also held some old clothes, a new pair of Converse, and a few simple shirts he'd purchased.

Bushkill, Pennsylvania was picture perfect during the changing seasons, and dead the rest of the year, known for the waterfalls and Pocono mountains. There wasn't nightlife here, secluded with reserves, hiking trails, parks, and museums. We'd moved here after my mom died from Allentown, which was busier, noisier, and suffocating for my dad. I didn't remember Allentown much, only the ice skating rink I used to visit on Saturdays with Miley and Charlotte.

I'd went through two rolls of film, and remembered the way I felt behind a camera. Powerful and in control. I could give any illusion I wanted. Make anything beautiful. Even a gum wrapper carried by the wind amongst the leaves, I'd clicked and captured trash, a mint blue star dancing across brown hues.

From the busy day before, Ollie had beat me to the front door.

We stood on opposite sides, completely still and staring at one another, and I shivered from the cold-front seeping through the breezeway and into the house. Ollie had more layers on this morning with a beanie, the temperature in the high thirties or low forties. Though his feet were rooted in place, the rest of him was alive, ready to pounce if I'd let him. "You all right?"

He stood in front of me, him on the doormat and me inside the entryway of the house, and I forced my head to nod to keep myself from caving. Here, I felt more in control of the situation. Here, I trusted myself. But with Ollie here, no distance was safe.

Ollie's chin dropped to his chest. "I won't keep you, but I went into town yesterday and got you a phone with international service. I want to make sure you have a way to reach me." He pulled out a phone from his front pocket and held it between us. "The young chap said the camera is the best feature, and I set it up for you last night, programmed my number. I also downloaded a few apps I think you'll like. Mostly picture apps where you can choose filters and distort images ..."

Ollie continued to ramble nervously, and I reached for the phone.

"Nah-uh-uh." He pulled the iPhone away and held it over our heads, clouds from our breaths pillowing between us. "I want something from you in return."

I shifted, leaning my hip against the doorframe in a pair of his joggers he'd packed me and his shirt that read, MAKE LOVE NOT WAR. He knew I loved this shirt, not because of the saying, but because it was his favorite. "What do you want?"

"If I give you this phone, you have to message me. And I'm going to watch you send me that first message now so I know you know how to use it."

The phone lowered between us, and I held out my palm for him to drop it in. "I know how to use a phone, Ollie."

"You'd be surprised how much has changed in two years."

Shaking my head, I fumbled with the buttons to change the black screen to something different. The home button was gone. Ollie smirked but offered no assistance.

Finally, I figured it out tapped the green icon. "What's your number?"

"It's already in your contacts," his hand jolted inside his pocket, "the only number in there, love."

I backed out of the messages and went to contacts. "Ollie" was listed, something so simple, but seeing his name across a screen made my heart grow wings and fly. I smiled, texting him.

Ollie's phone pinged in his other pocket. He took out his phone and dropped his head, his fingers working the screen to open the message, which simply read, "*I love you.*" His shoulders visibly relaxed, an exhale left him, and his gaze dragged from the screen until green eyes met mine. "I needed that."

and the morning after that ...

The late morning sun filtered through the lace curtains, heating the side of my face. All night, I'd tossed and turned, unable to get warm or comfortable. My throat burned, and my insides felt as if I'd been thrown into an inferno. An annoyed Diane pounded on the door, announcing Ollie's arrival, but there was no way I could get out of bed.

For the first time, in a long time, I was sick.

Groaning, I blindly patted for the phone inside the covers to text him. The phone was dead.

"Diane?" I desperately called out, hoping she'd understand me through the animalistic sound that came out. My voice was gone. "Diane!" I tried again, this time pushing through the lodge inside my throat.

Fully dressed in yoga pants, *Nikes*, and *Michael Kors* black puffer jacket, hair and make-up perfectly in place, Diane entered the guest bedroom with her bag slung over her shoulder, pink yoga mat peeking out.

"I'm sick. I can't get out of bed."

"Well, what do you want me to do? I'm on my way to meet Lisa at Barre."

"Can you tell Ollie I can't come down? And I need medicine. Do we have medicine somewhere?"

"There's Tylenol in the medicine cabinet in the bathroom."

"And Ollie?"

"I'll tell him." She adjusted the bag. "He's not allowed in the house, Mia. I don't feel comfortable with someone I don't know here."

"I know. He won't come inside the house."

She sighed and reached for the doorknob. "I'll stop to grab soup on my way back."

That single gesture was both a shocking revelation and the very thing we both needed to put us in the right direction. Since I'd arrived, I'd followed by her rules, kept to myself, and not once made this time difficult for her, or at least I'd tried. Was this her way of giving a little back in return? "Thank you," I tried to say, but it came out as a hoarse whisper.

After Diane left, I'd fumbled with the new charger, trying to stick the end into the phone, and waited impatiently for the phone to drink enough energy to light up. The Apple logo appeared, and I sat up in the bed, both sweating and shivering as my head pounded.

I immediately texted Ollie.

Me: I'm sorry.

His response was instant.

Ollie: Don't be. It's not your fault. Let me take care of you.

Little did he know, it was my fault. I hadn't dressed for the weather yesterday, walking around without a jacket, taking pictures.

Me: You're not allowed inside the house.
Ollie: Then come out here, and I'll take you back to the inn.

Even if I could get out of bed, Diane was bringing me back soup. As much as I wanted to be with Ollie, I needed to see where this would go with Diane and me. Perhaps this was part of me finding myself again, believing I could right my wrongs.

Me: I don't want to.

Little bubbles appeared, disappeared, and appeared again at the bottom of the feed. Then the phone rang in my palm, Ollie's name jumping across the screen.

I answered, and Ollie rushed out and said, "I don't like text anymore."

"Diane's bringing me back soup," I explained. "This is huge, Ollie. I think she's coming around."

"The ice queen is defrosting? That's good, love. I want this for you."

I forced my feet over the bed and onto the floor, then walked toward the bathroom to find medicine. "Yeah, it's weird. I guess we'll see how it goes."

"You sound terrible."

My eyes landed on a bottle of *Tylenol*, and I snatched it. "I feel worse."

His heavy sigh vibrated through the phone. "I hate this. I hate that you're sick and there's nothing I can do,"—his car engine roared— "Each time I drive away from you, it feels so wrong."

"Where are you?"

"Sitting outside the house in the car. Had to turn on the heat."

"I've been taking pictures."

"You have?" I could hear the smile in his voice.

"Yeah, I missed it. Thank you for leaving me my camera," I said, then popped a few pills and ran my mouth under the water from the sink to wash them down.

"You need more film?"

Shaking my head, I said, "I have a roll left."

"I'll get you more today. I need something to do."

"This is weird."

"What is?"

"Talking to you through a phone," I rolled back into bed and pulled the sheets up over my shoulders, "we've never done this before."

"I don't like it, but I'll take what I can get." Then he paused, and a drawn-out pause played out between us. "Have you found what you're looking for?"

"Not yet."

"You don't have to look alone, love…"

FOURTEEN

"Each girl is delicately designed in strength and beauty,
capable of conquering the world all on her own.
And it takes one special man to remind her
she can, but doesn't have to alone."

OLIVER MASTERS

Ollie

A week had passed since I'd arrived in the states. It was everything I'd imagined. Thankfully, Mia's dad lived in a rural area, and I hadn't crossed many people.

During the last few days, Mia has been sick, and I hadn't been able to see her. The phone had been a brilliant idea, giving me a way to at least talk to her during this time. Her court date was in one week. After everything she'd endured, regardless if she decided to mention she was kidnapped or not, the judge should approve the expunging of her record. If not, that was what a lawyer was for. I'd found a reputable one in the states thanks to my agent, Laurie. Mia completed her sentencing. Roger Richardson, the lawyer, stated the worst that could happen was to pay a fine for missing her court date. The check was pretty much already written out.

"Today is the day. I can feel it in my bones, boy," the old bell-hopper shimmied in his spot with a grin on his face. For the most part, I'd been keeping to myself, but Bud was here from ten at night until seven in the morning with the spirit of old St. Nick and the looks of Beetlejuice, with an extra kick in his step. He was a chipper fella, taking pride in managing holding the door open for guests and offering to carry bags.

Last week, the first morning Mia pushed me away, I'd walked across the main road and into a corner store that evening. Being in a foreign place, and my only home within Mia threatened, my once high, durable belief had cracked. I'd purchased a six-pack and had started on it on the walk back. The chilled temperatures couldn't touch me at the time, and I'd sat over a bench when Bud appeared, whistling an old tune I didn't recognize at a quarter before midnight. He'd mentioned I looked lost. At first, I hadn't said anything, until he went on, speaking about the many people who go through the doors lost and come out rejuvenated. That the Old Mill Inn was an R&R, and he'd seen the healing properties with his own eyes, which was comical because Bud was blind in one eye.

"I better meet Mia before you head back to Dublin."

"Surrey," I correct with a shake of the head. "I'm not Irish, Bud."

Bud leaned forward with his hands clasped behind his back. "What's that?"

"I'm. Not. Irish!" I repeated loud and slow through a laugh, then pulled an Irish accent from thin air. "Ah, feck it."

"You look like you're going for a run. I like this look better. You don't look like a hood rat for once. I don't know what is the fashion these days. Since when did wearing rags become a thing?" Bud pointed out, eyes addressing my attire. I wore new trainers, athletic shorts, and a hoodie with my hair stuffed inside a cap. "You getting the girl out of the house?"

154

"That's the plan." Mia had finally come down from her room yesterday morning but stayed behind the invisible barrier at the door. Her fever was gone, but her hesitant demeanor indicated she wasn't ready just yet. "I'm nervous," I finally admitted, keeping my eyes past Bud and on the turning mill behind him.

"Ah, a woman will do that to you."

"Well, wish me luck."

"Luck for the Irish?" His eyes twinkled, and my head fell back. "I know. I heard ya. Surrey. English, boy. But luck is for fools who live inside limits. And you're a dreamer, and dreamers are worthy of anything but the ordinary. Wish for magic. Love should be nothing less than magical."

Grinning, I called out loud so he and the world would hear, "Than wish me this magic you speak of, and that I never go a day without it."

"Thatta boy. Now, go get your girl."

The smile on my face never faded as I drove up and down the rolling hills of Bushkill. I wasn't used to the steep mountains with fast, disappearing ledges, and inside my smile was a breath held. What it would generally take the locals fifteen minutes, it took me almost thirty. Cars honked behind me at my slow and cautious speed, and I veered off the road when a hook appeared to let them pass. Mia's dad lived in a death trap, but nothing could stop me from making it there. And I made it by eight.

After knocking, the sound of Diane's voice echoed from inside the home, calling out for Mia as I clutched the bag in my hand. I couldn't think of the possibility of her saying no to me. Instead, I hung on optimism—*and magic.*

The door opened. I lifted my gaze.

"Hi," she whispered.

And I got drunk on that one word. It took me to places a six-pack or bottle of whiskey could never dream of. "Hi."

"What's that?" Mia's gaze assaulted the bag in my hand, and her fingers curved around the edge of the door as if she were holding herself back from me, keeping her feet glued to the laminate flooring beneath her feet.

"Mia, you're getting out of that fucking house today. You're putting this on, and you're coming with me. I refuse to take anything but a yes." I held the bag up, internally begging for her to take it. *Just take it, Mia.*

"Where are—"

I took a step forward, and her sentence caught inside her throat. My foot was treading dangerous territory, lodged inside the doorway. I laid my palm over the frame to keep *myself* back, not having been this close to her since the day she screamed into the mountain air, pulling at every string to prevent myself from grabbing her and throwing her into my car. Mia's eyes momentarily closed before she looked up at me through long lashes. I wanted to kiss her, and I think she wanted me to. As hard as it was, I took a step back because if I didn't, I would have. And I wanted it to be her choice. "Put this on, love. I'll wait for you by the car."

Mia grabbed the bag from my hand and closed the door.

And I couldn't wipe the stupid smile off my face.

Ten minutes later, Mia walked out of the house wearing the items I bought her. The Adidas shoes were simple and black and white. She couldn't learn to defend herself in a pair of Chuck Taylor's or combat boots. Mia never wore color, and I knew she'd like them and the matching joggers, tee, and hoodie I'd found in the woman's section of a Dillards. Her hair was up in a tight ponytail, showing off her flawless features.

Together we looked like we were on the same team, and my smile returned as I pushed off the car and straightened my posture.

Mia pointed a finger at me. "Couples who match are stupid and cheesy," she said, walking in my direction.

I cocked my head. "Then I suppose we're stupid and cheesy."

She blew past me toward the passenger side, not giving me a chance to open the door. If today went well, then perhaps tonight could happen. The possibilities were so close, we could reach out, take it, and mold it into any shape we wanted. But today had to go by Mia's terms.

The entire way to the restaurant, Mia had yelled at me from the passenger side. *"Go faster, Ollie!" "You drive like an old man." "That lady just flipped you off." "God forbid I die before we get there." "That's it. I'm never letting you behind the wheel again. Ever."*

But we'd made it to Perkins, and Mia finally seemed at ease once the waitress dropped the large plate of strawberry croissant French toast platter in front of her, complete with whipped cream and powdered sugar. "Tell me about your first book signing," she said before shoving a forkful of French toast into her mouth.

"You knew about that?"

"Ethan told me about it."

"It wasn't the same without you there. You were missing, and there wasn't much to celebrate."

Mia laid her hand over my wrist. "I'm in awe of you. No matter how mad or angry I was, I couldn't help but smile, knowing you did it. You deserve this, and people are listening."

"Was?" I smirked. "You're not mad anymore?"

"It's fading." She covered her mouth, certainly not hiding food. Probably her smile. "But I'm mad at some of the reviews though. Some people are rude."

I laughed. "Rude, yeah?"

"Have you looked?"

"No, I've been too busy looking for your arse." Laurie had mentioned not to look, too, that people could be hateful, and there would always be criticism. It came with the territory. Unfortunately, you couldn't write for everyone.

"I'm proud of you," she finally said, holding her fork to her mouth.

"I'm proud of you too."

Mia smiled. I grinned. And we'd finished our breakfast in serene silence.

I took her to Bushkill falls afterward. The cold front still stirred in the late April air, but the trees were slowly coming back to life after the harsh winter, painting the canopies green. It was early Sunday morning, and we walked the wooden, manmade decks, and I saw the regret in Mia's eyes for not bringing her camera.

"We can always come back," I reminded her with her gaze fixed on the waterfall.

It was quiet out here in the open woods aside from the water crashing at the bottom. The only sound within miles was nature. Mist from the falls dusted our faces, and Mia closed her eyes to drink it in. "We are definitely coming back."

Taking a chance, I stepped behind her and leaned my hands over the railing, caging her in. I needed to be close to her. "You lived here for how long? And you've never been to the waterfalls?"

"Ten years and not once." Mia backed into me and let the back of her head rest against my chest. The single gesture permitted me to breathe normally again.

Passed the falls and hiking trails laid a clearing in the woods. We'd been here for over an hour now, and I had to bring up the main reason why we'd come, dressed in comfortable gym attire. She looked at me curiously as I spun in place with my palms raised at my sides. There was no one around. We were way off the beaten path of the hiking trails, needing privacy for what we were about to do. "I'd say here is perfect."

Her brow arched high in the air. "Perfect for what?"

"Teaching you how to defend yourself."

"Ollie ..."

"I debated on taking you to a gym this morning, have some other bloke teach you because I'm not a fighter—"

"Bullshit."

I chuckled. "You think I'm a fighter?"

"You've been fighting for me for two years. You're a fighter, Ollie."

The truth was, I could fight, but never wanted to be the one to fight her. I had no idea if I could actually go through with this, putting my hands on her in ways I never wanted. "Yeah, I suppose when I have the right motivation. Anyway, are you willing to learn?"

"No."

158

Her reaction set me off, and I stepped forward. "I've promised you over and over again that I'd protect you, but I've been doing it all wrong. You have to start fighting back, Mia. You said a week ago, cried in my arms how you hated how weak you were, how angry you were, and how you never wanted to depend on anyone. Well, here is your chance." I raised my palms in the air. "What are you going to do with it?"

"Is this why you brought me here? To teach me to fight?"

"To defend yourself," I corrected her.

"This is stupid."

Mia turned to walk away.

"Stupid?" I asked her back, and Mia turned around. "I bet you felt stupid when Ethan grabbed you and knocked you out. When you were tied up for days in that cabin, or should I remind you about the prankster, Mia? Nice nickname by the way, hardly a fucking prankster."

"Stop!"

"How did you feel? Because I feel like a tosser for not teaching you this before. That I didn't give you every tool necessary to protect yourself when I can't be there. Every day, it tears me up inside. Every scar on your body is a reminder that I've failed you. I'm not doing that this time, Mia. I'm fighting for you, but you have to fight for yourself too." Mia shoved me in the chest, but I wasn't backing down. "Are you getting mad, love?"

"Why are you doing this?"

"Because I fucking love you."

She went to hit me, and I snatched her wrist, spun her around, and slammed her back into my front, my chest heaving. "You always step with your left foot when you come at me. You're predictable and slow."

"I'm not doing this with you." She jerked her arm out of my grasp and walked away, but I grabbed her hips and yanked her back to my chest. I was asking for it, and if I wasn't careful, this could be grounds to never trust me again. But it was a risk worth taking.

After a brief struggle, I secured her wrists in one hand and pushed her against a tree. My entire weight pressed against her, and my other palm covered her mouth. Her silent tears fell over my hand, but I couldn't stop.

Not now. I was already too far in. "If someone comes at you from behind," I continued in her ear, "use that other hand and go for my face—for my eyes."

Mia threw her thumb backward and jabbed the soft tissue below my eye, and my first reaction was to take a step back, removing my hand from her mouth, which gave her the chance to turn and face me. Confusion swam inside those glazed brown eyes.

I nodded. "Let's keep going."

I showed her different scenarios and how to get out of them. With each one, Mia became braver, and the light gradually came back to life in her eyes. It was hard, being this close and keeping my head trained at the task at hand, but she needed this. Mia needed to know she could fight back, that she was strong enough all on her own.

Returning in front of her, I wrapped my hand around her throat to move on to the next move. Loose strands fell from her ponytail, framing her face. Mia's rapid pulse in her neck tapped religiously against my grip, her chest rising and falling in short breaths. Her glassy brown eyes locked on mine weakened me, and my hand relaxed from around her throat. I couldn't do it. Putting my hands on her in this way was hard enough, and I wished I'd just taken her to the gym.

"Keep going," she challenged me.

"I can't. I thought I could, but I can't."

Mia lifted my hand and placed it back on her throat. "What do I do next?"

Sucking in a breath, I pinched the bridge of my nose with my other hand.

"Ollie, I trust you," Mia whispered with tears in her eyes. "What do I do next?"

"All right." I ran a palm down my face and adjusted my hat. "You have a few options. First, you always want to drop your chin to your chest as soon as you feel a hand at your throat. Give them as little access as you can. You could grab my wrist with a free hand and yank it down. You could twist your body, throwing this arm up and over to use your elbow

160

to snap connection. Or you could lift your knee and jab it into my groin. It depends if your attacker is using one hand to your throat, both hands, or has you on the ground." Mia nodded, and I continued, "Go ahead, try one or a combination. But not the groin. I plan to give you children one day. Three of them, remember?"

Mia bit her lip and wrapped her tiny fingers around my wrist. When I thought she'd yank my wrist down, she surprised me with a twist of her body and throwing her elbow up, slamming it into my forearm, breaking the connection as I'd taught her.

Her knee came up, and I quickly blocked it. "I said, not the groin," I growled.

"Then you shouldn't have mentioned it." She fell back against the tree with a smirk. "Let's do it again. Don't be a baby. I know you can fight me harder."

Grinning like a fool, I shook my head before grabbing her neck. Her skin was soft under my fingers, pulse ticking at an all-time high. My eyes landed on her lips, distracted in the way they'd begged to be kissed. If Mia didn't hurry with a move, I'd lose all self-control.

"Make a move, Mia." My hand moved up the length of her throat, and she swallowed beneath as the pad of my thumb grazed her jawline. There was something in the chilled spring air, it smelled like roses dipped in desire, and the changing mood swirled inside our bubble. Mia grabbed my waist to pull me closer, and her breath shuddered in response to my growing knob pressing against her pelvis. With my free hand, I flipped my cap backward before my palm hit the trunk of the tree above her head. Though my fingers were dangerously around her throat, Mia had complete control over me.

Perhaps it was in the way she moved in a delicate defiance. Every breath pulled me closer until my nose skimmed her cheek, and my lips brushed her skin. My arm shook, and the only hope at this point was for her to breathe strength back into me by caving and kissing me already.

Instead, her knee came up and bucked into my lower abdomen, knocking all air from my lungs.

The blow sent me backward, and I automatically went down to the ground on all fours, my hands fisting leaves. "Mia," I croaked, then rolled over to my back. "What in the bloody hell was that for?"

"I don't know why I just did that." Panic buried in her voice, and she paced above me, the sun's rays appearing and disappearing, back and forth. "I'm so sorry. I'm so sorry. Ollie."

Groaning, I dropped my arm over my eyes to wait for the pain to subside.

I'd read the situation entirely wrong.

"Mia Rose, you're breaking my heart."

She fell to her knees at my side and pushed my arm out of the way. Horror marred her features as her eyes darted from my face to my stomach. She lifted my hoodie and shirt and pressed her lips against my tattooed stomach. "What on earth are you doing?" I chuckled, cupping her head and pulling her up so I could see her. I moved the loose strands from her face.

"I'm so sorry. I don't know what came over me or what just happened."

I raised my brows, laughing. "So you kiss my stomach?"

"I'm desperate." She shrugged.

A grin spread across my lips, and I jutted my chin. "How desperate?" Mia's top lip disappeared into a pressed smile in my hands, and I dropped my arms back, a fucking goner for her. "Come here." An impulsive plea, but I was utterly defenseless against her criminal smile.

Mia shook her head, lowering it until, finally, her lips clutched on to mine. A pivotal moment erupted, and suddenly, nothing else mattered. My heart skipped inside my ribcage, my lids fluttered close, and every worry detached, floating outside our space. My tongue pushed through her seams, until it stroked hers, back into a merciful slow dance of the two of us. The only strength I had was in my arms, and I pulled her fully on top of me, locked in sweet slow motion. Every small whimper coming from her throat had been fuel, and her tantalizing taste shot missiles packed with fireworks through my bloodstream, breathing me back to life.

She sank inside my arms, but I held her together. I always would. "Mia," I breathed into her mouth, not recognizing my voice. My hand gripped the back of her neck and the other on her hip, pressing firmly against the part that ached to fill her, and to keep me anchored from floating away…

A clearing of a throat sounded, and Mia broke away first to lift her head.

"Ollie," she whispered, but I was still under the spell from her lips. She smacked my arm. "We're in trouble."

I snaked my arm around her back, sat up, and looked behind me.

Two police officers stood there. Behind them, a family of five.

"Stand up," one of the men in blue said. "You two are coming with us."

FIFTEEN

"Magic doesn't dance in confinement."

OLIVER MASTERS

Mia

"Stay calm, love," Ollie whispered from beside me. "They have nothing to hold us. We weren't doing anything wrong."

My arms crossed and uncrossed from around my chest, pacing the length of the cop car. "I can't keep calm. I have court in a week. What if they arrest us for something stupid like open lewdness or destruction of nature."

"Destruction of nature? I don't know what you're talking about. That kiss was beautiful."

I snapped my head in his direction. "This is serious, Ollie."

Ollie's head was tilted back, facing the sky, and his eyes fell to the side until they met mine.

An unstoppable grin crept along his lips.

My arms crossed again, and my foot tapped on the pavement. "What's so funny?"

Ollie lifted his shoulder, his smug grin glowing. "You remember when we couldn't get you back through the vent, and I was terrified you'd get caught in my room? It was the first night after you returned from the looney bin. I was going mad, but you were shockingly calm. It seems like lifetimes ago."

I smiled, the memory invading my brain and simultaneously turning my worry to ash. "It does."

Ollie turned his body to face me and drummed his fingers over the top of the police car, his black cap secured back over his head. "It's going to be fine, all right? Just let me do the talking."

One of the two officers broke away from conversation off to the side and approached us. He looked to be almost fifty, but fit with salt and pepper hair. "Do you two know why you're standing here right now?" he asked, pulling his aviators from his eyes and folding them into the pocket of his uniform shirt.

"No," I said, as Ollie said, "Yes."

Ollie nudged me in the arm.

The cop crossed his arms. "So, what were you two doing out there?"

"Nothing," we said in unison, then exchanged glances. If I chanced a look again, Ollie would make me laugh, and this wasn't funny. We could get arrested.

The cop's eyes darted between the two of us. "Did you know that open lewdness was grounds for an arrest in the state of Pennsylvania?"

"Yes," I said when Ollie said, "No."

The officer laughed, amused by us, and I couldn't understand why. "Are you two married or something?"

"Engaged," we said in unison, and I rolled my eyes.

The cop lifted his brow. "Oh, this is great. You two have a long road ahead of you." The cop lowered the volume of the radio secured to his belt. "Since you're not from around here," he pointed at Ollie, "I'm going to let you off with a warning. But next time, try to keep actions that belong in the bedroom, in the bedroom."

"Thank you, sir." Ollie exhaled and grabbed my hand. "So, we're free to go?"

"Yeah, get out of here," he said through a chuckle.

With our freedom intact, we drove around every curve, dip, incline, and drop on the road, Ollie more confident and braver than before driving on the opposite side of the car. I had no idea where he was taking me and said, don't count on going back to my dad's tonight. With the windows down, and cold wind tangling in my hair, Ollie grabbed my hand from the driver side as an Ed Sheeran song played in our ears, a haunting beat tapping my chest. The only thing on our minds was the kiss and what was to come. His lips brushed over my knuckles before he pulled my hand over his thigh.

I was exactly where I should be.

This past week had been a whirlwind. Hell, the past two years had been a whirlwind. When Ethan dropped me off at my dad's, it stung at first. I'd thought I'd go back to the girl before Dolor and the last two years wouldn't have counted. I thought, for some God-awful reason, Ethan was the answer after everyone had taken off and abandoned me. With Ethan, I could have kept the person I grew to be and Ollie's memory alive because Ethan was attached to Dolor. But what I never expected, after all the misfortunes, heartache, and deceit, was Ollie showing up at my dad's doorstep.

The morning after Ethan had dropped me off, I'd heard Ollie in the kitchen talking to Dad and freaked out, jumped out of my window, and ran. Confusion and heartache was a terrible concoction, and it motivated all actions over the past week.

But Ollie stayed. And each day, he showed. For an entire week, he chipped away the black paint suffocating my heart all over again. There was something to be said about a love like that. I just didn't know the right

166

words. Maybe I'd ask Ollie. He'd weave words together like an epic string of notes on an electric guitar.

Not to mention that kiss.

We'd kissed before, many places, under many different circumstances, but that kiss brought me to new places and new beginnings. It was the kind of kiss that shook you awake and walked you out onto a candlelit floor under a galaxy raining warmth, euphoria, and the promises that everything would be okay.

Ollie pulled into a parking lot, the sign out front reading "Old Mill Inn." I'd remembered seeing the old churning mill up the hill off the main road, tucked away in a mountain. I'd passed by it numerous times before. My entire focus shifted to Ollie and the way he was trying so hard to hold back. The engine cut, and he forced his eyes in front of him. "You have three seconds to tell me no before I take you up to the room, Mia."

I started counting in my head, wondering if my seconds were shorter than his.

One.

Two.

Nope, his were shorter.

Ollie got out of the car, and I followed suit. My heart beat so hard, the vibrations hummed in my ears to the tips of my fingers. I knew what was coming. Ollie wore his emotions and needs as if it was written all over his skin. *Mia. Mia. Mia. Mia.* Down the lengths of his arms, chest, stomach …

"Bud, Mia. Mia, Bud," Ollie quickly introduced as he pulled me through the already opened door, Bud, I assumed, was holding with a sparkling smile painted on his face, dressed in a blue vest, blue slacks, and gray hairs branching in all directions. Ollie climbed each step of the narrow staircase in a hurry, desire emitting from his pores like a toxic poison, and I was already infected by it.

The red door before us had chipped paint with a number three inside a small frame above the peephole. Ollie released my hand only to shove his in his pocket to withdraw a key and fumbled with the lock. His hands shook from anticipation, and the silence screamed from desperately waiting for too long. Seconds ticked by, but it seemed like forever. This was happening.

As soon as we were both inside, my back hit the door, and mouths crashed. But this kiss wasn't hurried.

His hands slipped under my layers and over my skin.

But his hands were slow.

His heart exploded against my chest, his lips grazing neck.

But his lips weren't rushed.

And this was what it felt like to be in love.

Warm hands grabbed my face, and Ollie slid his mouth back to mine. Tongues stroked in sync, lips sucked, and his throbbing cock rubbed against my pounding heat when a chill ran down my spine. A whimper stuck in my throat. Ollie turned desperate, hips grinding between my legs, and his palms slammed the door on both sides of me without losing our cadence.

Don't hold back now.

And in an answered prayer, my pants were yanked down and discarded in an urgent need. Ollie's finger swiped through my slit to find me soaked. "Please," I begged, and he picked me up, pinned me against the wall, and wrapped my legs around his waist. Dizziness swept through me as my sex slid against his lower abs, and if he didn't hurry, I'd come from the friction alone.

Ollie freed his hard dick, fisted it in one hand, and thrust inside me, cracking me open. His eyes slammed closed upon an exhale, and our foreheads connected before everything turned into a whimsical love song.

There was no time for skin to skin, the connection alone drove Ollie's scattered emotions into full speed, proving with every grind that he felt safe in my arms, and I in his. Our hands linked and threaded above our heads, holding on as the length of him filled me and touched places we've been before, but still feeling like the first time, every time.

His hips, fastened to mine, skillfully moving like he was made for this, sliding his pelvic bone against my clit. The friction turned into a pleading life-line: *stay with me, Mia. Open your eyes and see me, Mia. Feel me, hear me, taste me, wake me, Mia.*

Yeah, Oliver Masters was made to make love, and I was made for him. So, I guess no one else stood a chance.

"Mia …" Ollie breathlessly hinted, and my name upon his lips pulled the climax out of me. I clenched and shook as he hit deeper. His mouth returned and his fingers curled around my hips to hold me down and attach himself to me. My fingers pushed through his sweaty hair as hot spurts pumped inside. And not long after, Ollie melted in my arms as our hearts begged to dance with one another, pounding inside our heaving chests.

Ollie buried his face in the crook of my neck, and we stayed there for a moment, clothes that felt like stone walls between us, but still connected and finally home.

"What just happened?"

"Magic," he whispered.

Our bodies spent, Ollie and I laid over the bed, staring up at the ceiling. We'd left our bags and burdens in the hatchback, not needing anything aside from one another, leaving us both in a comfortable daze.

"Okay, so I swear I was not expecting that. Hopeful, yes, but bloody hell … I was only supposed to take you to lunch." He laughed. "And don't make me drop you off, love. Stay with me for the rest of the week." His head tilted toward me, and ecstasy lingered in his eyes, still stuck in a high. Ollie was content—happy—which made me happy. "No Bruce or Diane. No Scott, no Dolor. Just you and me, here until the court date. What do you say?"

"We deserve this." It was supposed to be a thought, one that should've stayed in my head, but it still slipped my tongue. Things with Diane had gotten better. We could finally be in the same room without ripping each other's throats out, and though I was on the path of redemption, I don't think Diane or Dad could ever forget the wrath I'd brought into their home. The sneaking in strange boys, wrecking her car, and my destructive behavior over the last ten years.

Ollie obliterated my thoughts. "We absolutely deserve this."

But did I? "It's not—"

He sat up completely. "Don't say it, Mia. Don't even have those thoughts."

"You don't even know what I was going to say."

"I know you. I know you as if I wrote you myself. *It's not going to last,*" Ollie mocked. "Well, bring on the madness, the hurdles, every thrown rock, because I'm ready for it now. You are too. I know it. And what we did right there ... Mia, we got this. We so got this."

He felt it too. Of course, he felt it. Ollie felt everything. He was capable of feeling a worry before I ever voiced it. He'd always known when I was bothered before a frown crossed my lips. Ollie knew as if he'd written my pages. "What about after?"

"No more plans. I tried that already. For two years, I made plans and you see how that turned out. I published my work and planned to adopt Zeke. I bought a house and planned to marry you. I planned to meet you at three," he shook his head, "I'm not thinking about the future anymore. I'm thinking about here and now."

"You bought a house?"

"Yeah, love, I bought you a house. A home. We have a home, always."

Ollie's phone vibrated inside his pocket. It had been doing that all day, and not once had he retrieved it to see who it was. I tossed a few assumptions. Probably Laurie, his agent, or something that had to do with his work. "Are you going to answer that? It's probably important."

"You're important. Whoever it is can wait."

"They've been calling all day. Just see who it is."

Groaning, Ollie dipped his thumb and forefinger inside his front pocket. At this angle, I didn't have a chance to look at the screen, but a quick debate battled in his eyes before he decided to answer.

"This better be important," he snapped, but his long fingers stroked my hair calmly. Until they stopped. Ollie sat up completely, pushed his

170

legs over the bed, and dropped his head into his hands. "I don't have any answers right now."

I sat up and hugged my knees to my chest. Ollie's jaw flexed, and the vein in his neck popped. I was on one end of the conversation, and I didn't like it. Curiosity at whoever turned Ollie's entire demeanor around so quickly pinched my nerves. Whoever was on the other end was male and loud and shouting, but I couldn't make it out. The call ended, and he squeezed the device in his fist.

"What is it? What's wrong?" I didn't know if I wanted to know. Ollie pushed his fingers through his hair and ran his palm down his face. Then up. Then down again. Then his head cocked, and he searched my expression. I saw the question in his eyes—the wonder whether he should tell me or not. "Tell me," I gritted.

Ollie

Mia's eyes fell into slits, and they burned a hole into mine. I couldn't escape them. If I told her I'd been playing hopscotch with the Links to find her, she'd immediately recoil and ask me to take her back to her dad's. But I couldn't lie to her either. We had a week left before I had the option of taking her home. And after the phone call I just got, I didn't want to take her anywhere near the UK.

But I couldn't fucking lie to her.

So, I told her everything.

"What were you thinking?" she shouted, pacing the burgundy carpet of the room. Her arms flew around in the air, tears stained her cheeks, and this wasn't how I wanted this day to go.

"I couldn't sit back and do nothing."

"A fucking gang, Ollie? Go big or go home?" she laughed humorlessly, "You were finally doing something for yourself. You got out of that fucking life, away from your brother! And you'd risk it all?"

171

Something incredibly justifiable should have left my mouth, but she was right to a degree. Yeah, I'd risk it all. I could've told her none of it mattered if she wasn't with me, which was one hundred percent accurate. Mia had been missing, and I'd risked everything to find her. If we could go back in time, I'd do it all over again too. But the only reason my mouth slammed closed was that if the roles had reversed, I'd never want her to give up her dreams, risk her life, or take a wrecking ball to everything she'd accomplished for me. I'd want her to continue pushing forward. Mia was fucking right, but so was I.

Her palms raised in the air, and her eyes were a rare shade of gold. The tears and disappointment in them made them look even more lovely, and I didn't know how it was possible. "You have nothing to say?"

"I don't know what to say," I admitted.

"I want you to take me back to my dad's. I can't even look at you right now." She'd said it, but her eyes were still on me, not only staring at me but expressing love and devotion no matter how hard she tried to fight it. Sure, she was terribly angry, but her eyes anchored to mine, already regretting saying to take her back. But Mia was too stubborn for her own good. She wasn't going to change her words although she'd already changed her mind.

"All right, if that's what you want." *I know you like a book, love.* "But, I do have one thing to say." I stood and took a step forward. Her hands clenched into fists, and I wanted to reach out and take them in mine. "I wouldn't have changed a bloody thing."

The drive back to Bruce's was silent. She hadn't said a word, not even when I pulled into the driveway and noticed Bruce returned from work early, exiting his truck. After turning off the engine, I got out to shake his hand out of respect.

Bruce greeted me in slacks, a button-down shirt, and a laptop bag crossed over his chest. Mia blew past us like a child and I shook my head and held out my hand.

"What did you do?" Bruce asked with a laugh.

"Only love her. Too much, apparently."

172

He nodded, confused by my vague response. I wasn't about to tell him that his future son-in-law had done odd jobs for a gang to find his daughter. Perhaps after the wedding.

"Why don't you come by for dinner? It would be nice to have another guy around for once."

"A home-cooked meal? I haven't had that in … I can't remember how long. What time should I come by?"

"Oh, man. Six. It's Italian night, and Diane makes a mean Lasagna."

Lasagna had been invented and claimed by the British, not the Italians, but now wasn't the time to educate him. "I'm looking forward to it."

SIXTEEN

"You can't be both normal
and stand out against them."

OLIVER MASTERS

Ollie

"You have horrible taste in fashion," Bud stated from the chair, flipping through my book. "I remember the days we'd show up for dinner with the parents wearing a suit and tie."

"You're not helping."

"I suppose it's better than those rags you usually wear," he *tsked*, "millennials."

"Go to work, Bud." I shoved my foot inside my boot, wondering why he was still here.

Bud stood and adjusted his blue vest. "I'm five hours early. But you know what they say. If you're on time, you're late, and if you're early, you're on time. Well, I came up with that one all on my own. It's what got me the job thirty-two years ago. That and my charming smile."

"Surprised they didn't let you go for talking the guests out of the building."

"Someone's cranky."

Exhaling, I sat back over the bed with my other boot in my hand. "I got myself into a mess to get Mia back, and now I'm terrified it will be the very thing that will take her away from me."

"Quite a pickle you're in."

"Come on, Bud. It's not a bloody joke. Can you be real with me for five seconds? Be useful for a change?" Usually, I didn't talk to elders like this, but Bud was a cross between a fairytale character and Mr. Rogers.

"Advice is what you're looking for? All you had to do was say so. Take it from me. I was married for over fifty years, wanna know why?" I lifted my hands in a *get-on-with-it* gesture. "Most women want a man to take care of them, but the wild cards want to be treated as equal. Whatever it is, don't fight the battle apart. Fight together. Don't make decisions for her; make decisions together. Be the OG's, Bonnie and Clyde. Fast driving, guns blazing. You two against the world." He nodded and held up a finger. "Yup, I am one percent sure, that's what she wants."

My brows snapped together. "One percent? And what about the other ninety-nine percent?"

"Mia sounds like a wild card, and you wouldn't have fallen in love with the other ninety-nine percent."

You could tell the dining room hadn't been used in a while. Bruce was back in his relaxed attire, wearing loose jeans and a t-shirt, and he offered me a beer. I accepted to get me through dinner. Stepping into their home was like being locked inside a coffin six feet below ground. It was suffocating, hostile, and nerve-wracking, and no one had yet to say anything. No one had to. Diane's eyes were invading Mia's and my space, judging every bite, sip, and where our hands were.

Bruce cleared his throat. "Where were you born in the UK?"

"About an hour outside of London, but I don't live there anymore."

"No? Where do you live now?"

"Right now? Old Mill Inn." I laughed, trying to lighten the mood. No one else laughed.

"You should stay with us. There's no point in wasting money when we have an extra bedroom."

"He's not staying here," Diane snapped. "You can't just invite people to stay here without talking with me about it."

"It's okay. I didn't come here to intrude. I only came for Mia."

"Well, I'm ready for another beer." Bruce stood from the table. "Oliver?"

"Yes, please."

Diane glanced over at Bruce. "Haven't you had enough?"

It was amazing, really. Twenty minutes into dinner, and I'd learned more about communication and marriage than I would have from a counseling session. I slid my hand over Mia's thigh under the table, and she threaded her tiny fingers in mine. Regardless if she was mad at me, I'd never had to doubt we were in this together. Bud was right.

"You two have been together for what? Two years now?" Bruce asked, handing over an already opened *Bud Light*.

"Yes, sir." We cheered before he sat back down. Bruce wasn't so bad. He just had no more fight in him any longer.

"You should run now," Diane said through a small chuckle. "Do yourself a favor."

My knee bounced. I looked over at Mia. Her eyes locked on the untouched lasagna before her, and I offered her a few seconds to stand up for herself. She didn't. I looked over to Bruce, and he remained quiet. Mia's faced this kind of bullying for over ten years, and I leaned back in the chair. "You know, taking Mia and running far away from here doesn't sound like a bad idea."

A laugh cracked from Bruce, and Diane rolled her eyes. "You know what I mean."

"I know what you're implying. I'm just not entertaining the ludicrous suggestion."

176

Diane's eyes narrowed at me. Mia hadn't been kidding, she was more vindictive then Dex Sullivan, and there was something dark and buried behind those eyes. "You're the only fool at this table, Oliver. She'll do nothing but lie, cheat, and steal from you," her eyes darted to Mia, and Diane grimaced, "but only after she sleeps with half of your friends."

"Diane!" Bruce pounded over the table, and the beer knocked over.

I stood, taking Mia with me, but she jerked from my hold. "What did I do to make you hate me so much?" Mia cried out. "I'm sorry for what I did. I told you I was sorry. Every day I've been trying so hard, but I can't go back and change anything!"

"You want to know what you did?" Diane shouted.

Bruce stood and grabbed her arm. "No, Diane. That's enough."

"I lost my baby because of you. You killed my baby! The hell you brought into this home, the worrying, the anxiety, the panic attacks. You killed the only thing I ever wanted, and that is something you will never be able to change."

Mia froze at my side. Bruce hung his head. Diane fisted her hands, tears pouring. I turned my back to everyone else to face Mia, and I didn't know what to say. I tried to take her hand and pull her away, but she stood there, ready to face it.

"I'm sorry," Mia whispered, shaking her head. She looked to her dad and dug her teeth into her bottom lip. "I'm sorry, I … I didn't mean … I didn't know."

"It was a girl. I was supposed to have a daughter, and I ask God every day why you're here, and my daughter's not," Diane cried out. "I've tried to look past it, I've tried everything. It's not fair. You don't deserve to be here. You deserve to rot in hell."

"Mia," I turned back to face her, but she jerked from my grasp, bolted from the dining room, and ran up the stairs.

I was stuck, unsure if I should chase after her or put these two in their place. My mind raced and my fingers pushed through my hair. "I'm sorry you lost your baby, but that wasn't Mia's fault, and you know it! She didn't ask for this!" I raised my arms as my eyes darted back and forth between the two of them. Neither one of them said anything.

Diane cried. Bruce kneaded his temple with one hand, rubbed his wife's back with the other, and my mind raced, heat flaring over my skin and burning my eyes.

I paced the dining room, trying to calm but their silence only fueled my frustration. I slapped my hands over the table and looked up at them. "And you didn't just lose one daughter. You lost two. Mia's your daughter too, and she's been living in this house for over ten years, and you did nothing but push her away. She needed you! She needed both of you! Mia's been there this entire time, right in front of you, screaming for someone to bloody hear her."

I gathered a breath and wiped my face into my sleeve. My hands shook, and I allowed a few seconds pass to calm myself before addressing them again. Otherwise, I'd taken a chair to the glass cabinet behind me. "Thank you, Bruce, for inviting me to dinner. I know the kind of husband I want to be for her—one with fucking balls. And Diane," my eyes slid to her, "with all due respect, your baby is gone, but Mia's still here. Don't take that for granted."

They both looked at me, stunned, and I took off after Mia, climbing the stairs and barging into her room. My heart plummeted when my gaze landed on her opened window, but then I saw her brown hair blowing in the wind.

I climbed through the small window and took a seat behind her, stretching my legs out across the shingles. She sank between my legs and my arms wrapped around her chest.

There had been many times I'd sat under this same sky, dreaming of this very moment. In love, high off solid ground, and my girl in my arms. Any other time, I'd shout to the moon, and say we'd made it.

"I'm sorry," she whispered, her head falling back against my chest.

I looked down to see her face soaked, but eyes dry. "No, I'm sorry."

She tilted her head when her eyes met mine. "What are you sorry for?"

That things weren't easier. That I didn't find you sooner. That I couldn't take you away yet because of the bloody court date. But I settled on, "I think I just called your dad a pussy."

Mia laughed lightly through a sniffle. "Well, someone had to say it."

"Turn around, love." And she twisted in my arms, pushing her legs over mine. Mia shivered inside an oversized black sweater, leather looking leggings, and Christmas socks. I dipped my hands under her sweater to grip her sides as she rolled her hips closer. She blinked up at me, golden brown and bewitching. "Now, close your eyes." A smile fought its way over her lips. I lifted my brows, and Mia shook the hair from her face, lifted her chin, and closed her eyes.

"Where are you taking me?"

"We're not going anywhere, I just wanted to do this." I lightly kissed her, and afterward, she dropped her head into my neck and laughed.

We stayed like that for a while, under the starry sky. I stroked Mia's back until she fell asleep in my arms, thinking of all the baggage I'd left in the UK. My first and only priority was Mia, but if I didn't handle my end of the deal, it would follow us for the rest of our lives.

An hour passed, and I woke her up and helped her back through the window. She was half asleep, mumbling about '*a guy she dreamed about,*' and how he saved her, and I only told her that if he was real, give him my thanks. She passed out in bed, and I kissed her forehead before leaving. Mia was out cold in two seconds.

I walked down the stairs and noticed Bruce sitting outside on the back patio, looking out into the forest. At the last second, I figured I'd talk to him and pushed open the back door. Bruce was sitting in a rocking chair in front of a controlled fire pit, a cooler of beer resting at his feet. He turned to look at me before dropping his head back. "Take a seat."

Diane must have turned in early. Hesitantly, I sat in the other rocking chair and pushed my legs out in front of me. The lights from the fire lit up his crestfallen features, and he bent over to grab another Bud Light from the ice and handed it over to me.

I'd never been a beer drinker, but cracked it open with my forearm, not leaving the chap out here to drink by himself. "I want to apologize for what happened tonight, but the truth is, I can't," I admitted.

"You were right."

"Wish I wasn't."

"You know what's so fascinating to me?" He leaned in and planted his elbows over his knees and cocked his head. "My twenty-year-old daughter has a more mature relationship than I do. What does that say about me?"

"That your daughter has brilliant taste in men."

Bruce chuckled, leaned over, and clanked his bottle against mine. "You're a good man, Oliver."

"I'm sorry about your wife," I stated, looking out into the fire.

"Diane means well."

"I'm not talking about Diane. I'm talking about Mia's mum, Jackie. I'm sorry about what happened to her. I can't imagine ever losing Mia, let alone trying to get by each day." The toll it must have taken on him over the years. It made me sick just thinking about it.

"Jackie was a good woman, the love of my life. I think Diane sees that too. If it weren't losing the baby, it would be the fact I'd never fallen out of love with my late wife." He chugged from his bottle, then let out a sigh. "Nothing will ever fill that emptiness. Not Diane. Not fucking Bud Light. Trust me when I say, don't wait 'til someone dies to remind you what's in front of you. Know now. When I look back at it all, want to know when I was the happiest?" His eyes moved from the label peeling from the bottle to me. "We were so broke," he laughed, "Mia was only two years old at the time, sleeping in her crib, and our electric got cut off. Jackie and me, we moved Mia into the living room with us and lit a fire in the fireplace. Jackie hijacked the neighbor's Wi-Fi, and we curled up on the couch and watched *Rush Hour* from her laptop." Another laugh escaped him, and he pushed his fingers across the bottom of his nose. "The damn movie froze every five seconds. I think it was the longest movie we'd ever watched together, but I never wanted it to end. But Jackie fell asleep in my arms and the laptop died eventually, and it was so quiet. Right then and there, I knew I would never be happier. Shit, was I right."

It was quiet again, and the fire crackled before us as I digested his words.

"I'm marrying Mia."

"Are you asking for my permission?"

I shook my head. "Advanced notice." I should've asked for permission, and I'd thought about it out of respect, but Bruce nor Lynch had hardly been a father. Nodding, Bruce handed over another beer. "If you keep feeding me alcohol, I'm going to have to sleep on your couch."

"Please, I'd sleep better knowing you were in the house. I'm afraid a knife-wielding PMS-ing maniac will gut me in my sleep here." He laughed. "And I'm not referring to Mia."

"Ah, you're on your own with that one."

"You handled yourself pretty well in there. I've never heard anyone speak to Diane like that. She went straight to bed, and it's only—" Bruce glanced at his watch—"Shit, it's only eight-thirty. I'm getting old."

For hours, Bruce and I kicked back around the fire, talking and drinking. It was almost midnight before we turned in, and he threw me a blanket and pillow from a chest in the corner of the living room. I told him he was asking for it, defying his wife. He said she wouldn't leave her room, and I'd be safe. I clicked on the telly, turned down the volume, and a *Friends* marathon was on.

My eyes flitted open to see Mia standing above me, shaking me. "What are you still doing here?"

I pinched the bridge of my nose, still out of it. "Your dad got me drunk."

Mia giggled, and my gaze roamed over her bare legs, the lights from the telly bouncing off her ivory skin in the dark. She had little sleep shorts on and my MAKE LOVE NOT WAR tee. "What are you doing awake?"

"I can't sleep. Ever. I came down for a glass of water."

181

I lifted the covers as an invitation, Mia sank beside me, and I inhaled her jasmine scent. "Are you watching *Friends*? This is the one where Ross and Rachel take a break."

"Zeke never liked this one."

Mia laughed. "Zeke watched *Friends*?"

"Are you kidding? Zeke was obsessed with American sitcoms. *The Office* and *Friends* were his favorite. Played it all the fucking time."

"So, the real question is ... were they on a break?"

"That was their first mistake. You can't put a technicality on love. They were both right. They were both wrong. End of story."

Mia's shoulders shook, laughing, her arse rubbing against me, and my cock tightened inside my jeans. I had to control myself, being under her dad's roof and all, but my tipsy hands had a mind of their own as they dragged up her thigh, under her shorts, and grabbed a palm full of her arse. Mia turned in my arms to face me, and her laughter faded, eyes growing heavy under her long thick lashes. "Ollie," she warned.

"What?" I grinned, lifting her thigh over my leg. "I'm not going to bang you at your dad's house, Mia. That would be completely inappropriate." A nervous smile tugged on her lips, and I tilted my head. "Why are you smiling, love?"

"I'm just glad you're real," she whispered.

There was this feeling you get when someone was watching you. With my eyes closed, my soul twisted and turned inside me, tapping my unconscious brain and doing jumping jacks inside my skin, anything to wake me and confront the eyes peering down at me.

I pried my lids apart to see Diane standing over Mia and me with a coffee cup in hand, cringing as if she were in pain at the sight of us. It took seconds for me to put the pieces together before I jumped from the couch. Her gaze trailed over my tattooed chest to my jeans, and I looked down to see my knob bursting to get out.

My eyes widened.

Her eyes widened.

I grabbed a throw pillow from the couch to cover myself.

I'd never been embarrassed before, until that very moment.

My throat went dry, words utterly lost on me. This lady looked like she wanted to kill me. And suddenly I understood Bruce's fear. "I'm so sorry. I was up late with Bruce. He offered the couch. I didn't want to drive home under the influence," that *sonofabitch* left me to fend for myself, "I'll leave." Mia rolled over into the couch, her tiny body wholly hidden under the blanket. The only evidence of her was her brown locks sticking up from under the blanket. I looked back at Diane, who hadn't moved. "We didn't," I shook my head, "It's not what it looks like."

"Right, because that would have been disrespectful, you know … Fornicating on my white couch." She brought the white mug to her lips and turned to walk into the kitchen.

SEVENTEEN

"There's something about a woman
in a little black dress.
A cliffhanger, with nirvana in her eyes,
and the devil in her smile.
She left the dark side, yet it never left her.
One hell of an angel,
shamelessly tiptoeing as night turns to day.
She may look like every other girl,
but you'll never forget her name."

OLIVER MASTERS

Mia

Diane sat in the kitchen, staring blindly out the arched window beside the breakfast table. "Your boyfriend left," she whispered, her voice small and barren. "I made coffee."

I shuffled into the kitchen where her grief felt like gravity, compressing me into nothing. I didn't know what time it was, but it was still early, and the smell of coffee swirled through the cracks of her gravity, pulling me in. The mugs hung from a black tree stand beside the coffee pot, and I took a mug, poured the coffee, and added heaps of cream and sugar.

"I love your father, Mia," she began to say, not looking at me but out the window. "I do. I've always loved him."

"I don't know where you're going with this." It was too early, and I didn't have the headspace to decipher her.

Diane sighed, and she did that every time she was about to say something. I leaned against the counter and sipped from the mug, staring at the back of her blonde bob. She was in a fluffy pink robe, hair raveled, and not perfectly in place.

"It's not easy to fall in love with a man who lost his wife and daughter all at once. I'm a woman, so I'm expected to understand and mend the broken pieces. To turn a house into a home again. To connect with a girl who can't connect with anyone. To pretend marrying me should've fixed everything, and the disappointment after when it didn't."

"No one expected you to fix everything."

She shook her head, and her hair swung behind her. "When I couldn't, I thought for sure the baby would. Maybe if I got pregnant, having a little one around would be the answer. And now I realize, all the pressure placed on me, I was placing on my baby. Maybe I am the one to blame for losing her. And I don't know why I'm telling you this, anyway. You don't care about anything."

My fingers gripped the coffee mug that was still hot in my hand. "I'm trying to. To be honest, if I did know you were pregnant at the time, I probably wouldn't have cared. But, I'm trying now."

"So just like that?"

"Just like that." I kicked off the counter and pulled out a chair beside her. "Did you ever think we're just two women, both not filling expectations? All my life I was expected to remember, to feel, to relate, to understand. Now, I'm expected to have all the answers and know who I am. I'm starting to think we're never supposed to have it all figured out, and maybe that's the beauty of it all."

Diane swung her head to face me, eyes narrowing. "Who are you, and what have you done with Mia Rose?"

"I have no idea," I said through an exhale, and we both shared a laugh.

Diane and I spent the entire day together, shopping for new clothes, having lunch, and getting to know each other. It was a fresh new beginning for the both of us, but it would take time for us to mend all the broken parts we both shattered over ten years. The night before needed to happen, opening a gateway to hoarded grief and blame. And after the day came to an end, I'd accepted things between us would most likely never be perfect. I still hated her stiff hair, the way she dressed in Ralph Lauren, and the way she treated the waitress as if they had a disease because of her nose ring, but we were just two completely different people brought together by devastation and love.

Diane did love my father, and she was learning to love me too.

Days passed in a whirlwind. I'd spent the majority of my time with Dad and Diane, and Ollie kept his distance. I hated it, but he encouraged the time with them.

By the morning of the court date, I stood in front of the mirror, wearing a simple, sleeveless black dress Diane picked out. The hem hit mid-thigh, and the neckline was almost to my neck. The last time I wore a dress was the court date before Dolor, and I hoped this time around, things would go in my favor. My hair fell a little past my shoulders, and the only make-up I'd attempted was blush and mascara.

"Mia, you ready?" my dad called from the bottom of the stairs.

I didn't answer.

"Mia Rose Jett!"

I smiled. "Two minutes!" I glanced up from my black heels and smoothed down the dress across my thighs, worrying the judge would take my disappearance as a sign that I wasn't a changed woman. *What if he decides he's had enough and throws me in the mental institution? Or jail?* My smile faded, and nerves set in, creeping from my numbed toes up to my neck. Suddenly, the neckline was too tight, constricting, and I wanted out of the dress. Balling my fists, I tried to breathe, and the room swayed.

Then I felt his hands around mine.

I lifted my head, and Ollie stood behind me, wearing black slacks, an ironed white button-down shirt, and a knockout grin. His green eyes took me in, and he ran his palms up the sides of my arms. "Breathe, my love. It's going to be all right," he whispered.

"How do you know?"

"Because, look," he nudged his head in the mirror, "you've not only stayed with me, you've stayed with yourself. Not once have you given up. And if I'm not mistaken, you don't need me anymore." He cocked a brow and flashed a lopsided grin. "I think my job here is done." I slapped him on the arm, and Ollie dropped his forehead over the back of my head, laughing.

"In all seriousness," he continued and wrapped his arms around me. "You're absolutely breathtaking." His lips hit the rim of my ear, and the vibrations went through me as he rocked me back and forth in place. "I need six minutes with you alone."

"Six?"

"One minute to admire you. Two to taste you. And three to lose myself inside you."

"Only three?"

"If I'm being honest, I doubt I'll last that long."

The judge called my name, and Ollie gripped my hand before I stood and stepped up to the podium with my lawyer by my side. The lawyer was young, no older than thirty-five, and slender with side-swept chocolate-brown hair. He'd advised me before we entered the court room to be quiet and let him speak for me unless the judge questioned me directly. Roger was his name.

It all happened fast. The judge and Roger spoke back and forth in legal jargon as I froze beside him, trying to focus on the judge's hand movements and facial expressions. By the time I thought I had it figured it out, the judge had dropped the gavel and dismissed us.

I turned to leave, still unsure of what just occurred. Ollie, Diane, and my dad stood from the bench, and all their faces were blank. "What just happened? What did he say? Am I done?" I nervously drilled Roger out the door. I whipped my head around to see Ollie walking behind me, whispering to my dad. "It's bad, isn't it?"

Roger continued to ignore me until all five of us entered the hallway, and the courtroom door closed behind us. "Well," he nodded, "that went well."

"How well? Like *free* well?" I asked, looking between all four of them.

Ollie took a step toward me and cupped my face in his hands. "You're free, love. It's over."

"Don't do that to me!" I stomped my heel into the tile. "I saw your face, you looked like the judge sent me away again."

"I told you it would be fine. I wasn't surprised one bit with the outcome." Ollie kissed my forehead and turned to Roger to shake his hand. "Mia's dual citizenship still intact?"

"Yes, she can travel back and forth. No problem."

"Thank you, Roger, but I never want to see you again," Ollie said through a chuckle, and the rest followed suit, shaking Roger's hand before he left. I felt lighter, and Ollie turned to face me again, releasing a drawn-out exhale and his eyes glossy. He felt lighter too. "Let's get out of here, yeah?"

"Yeah," I agreed, nodding.

Diane and my dad joined us for lunch, and unasked questions lingered in the space between the four of us. *What now? When am I leaving? Will I be leaving at all?*

Ollie's hand slid to my bare thigh under the table as he reached for his tea, listening to my dad talk about the remodel he wanted to do in the kitchen. All I could focus on was the way his fingers dragged along the inside of my thigh, rising higher and higher …

"What do you think, Mia?" Dad asked.

My head snapped up, and I tried to lift my heavy lids. "mhm?"

"I prefer white cabinets," Diane interjected.

I moved my sweater over my lap. "Yeah, white sounds good."

Ollie tilted his head to face me just as his fingertips reached my panties. I let out a whimper when his thumb scraped across my sex over the thin material. "Mia, are you okay?" he asked with a smirk.

"Mhmm."

His finger pressed against my clit. "What about *your* kitchen?"

"My what?"

"Your kitchen back in Surrey. It's small, but we could do white if that's what you like." His finger dipped beneath the hem and trudged through my slit, and my thighs clenched as I grabbed my Dr. Pepper off the table and sucked from the straw. "Or would you prefer *open* shelving?"

The soda sprayed from my lips as my hips jerked forward.

"Mia!" Diane exclaimed, but I was too focused on Ollie's skilled and slender fingers, making love to me under the table as we all sat around for lunch.

"Excuse me. I think I left my phone in Ollie's car." I slid my eyes to Ollie who wore a smug grin. "Give me six minutes."

I got up from the table and hurried in heels through the restaurant and toward the parking lot, hoping Ollie would follow. It was mid-day, and I shivered against the wind in the vacant parking lot, pacing beside Ollie's hatchback. The sun shone high above as Ollie walked toward me with his hands in the pockets and a mischievous grin rising on his lips.

He walked past me toward the woods.

I spun around. "Where are you going?"

He turned to face me but continued to walk backward. "We have five minutes left. I don't have time to admire you. Now, hurry up, I haven't got all day."

I leaned forward as a laugh escaped before jogging up behind him.

Ollie had unbuttoned the top two buttons of his shirt by the time we reached a field behind a layer of woods. In a swift motion, he picked me up and laid me over the grassy bed of flowers, and pushed up my dress and my thighs apart. Hooking my panties, Ollie yanked them to the side, and his flattened hot tongue dragged through my soaked sex as a moan escaped the both of us. "I'm going to come from this alone," he whispered, then pushed two fingers inside me and curled. Over and over, his tongue stroked my clit. My hips bucked against his mouth, and I fisted flowers around me, pulling at their roots from the sensations threatening to erupt.

Ollie pulled his hand away to release his stretched cock, fisting it between us while lapping his tongue over my entrance. My head jerked back, and I raised my hips, aching for our connection. He growled and lifted onto his palms over me. "Tonight, you're mine. Tonight, we're taking our fucking time, and I'm doing what I want, Mia," he said, all in one breath. Nodding, I yanked his shirt down until our mouths crashed, and after one hard thrust, Ollie fell onto his elbow. "Jesus Christ, Mia," he slowly pulled out before slamming back in, his trembling lips hovering mine, "You feel so fucking good."

"Stop talking, Ollie," I cried through another mind-altering thrust.

"Not into the dirty talk, either?" He smiled against my lips, his hips rolling torturously, grinding to the wild tune we created. A moan came up from my throat as he ground into me again, and I tried to shake my head.

Ollie's fingers dragged down my thigh and gripped my ass as he took me deeper while his other hand caressed my forehead with his thumb. I tasted myself on his lips as our tongues collided, and his mouth moved from mine, down my jawline, to my ear. His breath hit, and my core clenched around him.

"I feel you, Mia," he whispered as I met his every grind.

Ollie sat up, eyes heavy and gaze licking over my body down to where we were connected. His fingers dug into my thighs, spreading me wider, and his other hand kneaded my clit. The buzzing white-hot flame lighted and drained the orgasm from me, and my sex contracted against his desperate beat. Legs shaking, I watched his green eyes adore me as I drifted inside a rapture, my lids flickering from the heavy intensity. Soon, Ollie let go, chasing the wondrous feeling.

With my body sedated and knees relaxed and parted, Ollie took his sweet time, kissing the insides of my thighs, my core, my sensitive clit, and licking my wounds as the field of wildflowers surrounding us danced with the brisk wind. I jerked against his warm tongue as he built me up into another climax. He was relentless and utterly shameless in his addiction, and his lips moved delicately against me, painting an illusion we had all the time in the world. Because with Ollie, time didn't exist, and nothing else mattered.

Ollie

Mia and I walked back into the restaurant, hand in hand with her delectable flavor skipping on the tip of my tongue. I picked a white flower from her hair as we sat at the table and averted the eyes of Bruce and Diane with a smile lingering over my face. One I couldn't shake.

"Get your phone?" Diane asked, all-knowingly.

"I must've left it at the house." Mia waved her hand in front of her and eyed the food that had arrived while we were gone. "Oh, man. This looks so good."

Diane rolled her eyes and sifted her fork through her coleslaw as Bruce remained quiet.

My phone buzzed, and I pulled it from my pocket to see it was Travis. He had been silent since I'd sent him a message to only contact me in case of emergencies, and this was his third time calling this morning.

"Excuse me. I have to take this." Answering, I stood back up. "Yeah?"

191

"I've been trying to reach you, where have you been?" Travis tried to get out through short breaths.

"Mia had court this morning," I explained, taking a step outside to the side of the building. "What's going on? Is everything okay?"

"No, Ollie. Things are not okay. I'm bugging out over here. Dex isn't fucking around. They fucking killed him, Ollie. They killed him to get to you. If you don't come back and give him what he wants …"

"Slow down, who's gone?" My gaze darted around until it found Mia eating on the other side of the window. "Who did Dex kill?"

"Oscar. He was shanked last night at High Down. Your brother is dead. Now, I don't know if he believes you two were close, but it was a fucking message. They can take anyone anytime they want. I don't know what to do, Oliver. They don't have your address, but I'm still packing up Summer and going to stay with her mom for…" his words fell into the back of my mind. The mobile shook in my hand, and the steady gaze I once had on Mia grew blurry.

My brother was dead.

Oscar was dead.

"Ollie, are you there? Are you hearing what I'm saying?" Travis shouted into the phone.

I dropped my head back and moved my fingers over my temples. "Yeah." I couldn't say more. My emotions betrayed me over a brother I'd once loved but learned to hate, but still always assumed he'd become this changed man one day, that I could help him change.

"Leave Mia there and come back and handle this. Give Dex what he wants."

"When's the funeral?"

"Funeral? You can't be serious. Your brother was a fucking wanker. He doesn't deserve a funeral."

"His prison sentence—*his fight*—is over," I reminded him through clenched teeth. "Stop punishing a dead man, it only thrives the hate that should be buried along with him. We are all worthy of closure."

I ended the call with Travis to ring High Down Prison.

They planned on burying Oscar tomorrow. I had to leave today.

"Mum! What have you done?!" Oscar shouts, rushing through the door, unexpected, dropping grocery bags in his wake as Mum clings on to me, crying.

Her entire body is shaking, and she's whipping her head violently, mumbling things I don't understand. Maybe it's because I'm crying, too, gasping for air.

Oscar rips me from her arms into his. He searches my face and tilts my head back into his hands. "Breathe, Oliver," he chants, pushing his fingers through my sweaty hair. "I'm here. I'm right here," a tear slips from his cheek and lands on my lips. I've never seen Oscar cry, but it's fascinating, and I don't know how it's possible, but his brown eyes go black when he snaps his head back to mum. "He's eight years old, Mum! Eight!"

"Oscar," Mum cries, "I'm sorry. I didn't … Come home. Please, I don't know what happened. I can't take this anymore …"

Oscar lays me over the mattress, and at the corner of my eye, he jumps from his knees and tackles Mum, his fists and threats flying, "If anything happens to him, you'll lose me too. You'll lose me forever, you worthless whore. I should fucking kill you." He slams her against the wall, and she curls into the corner.

Oscar returns to my side and cradles me in his arms. "It's going to be okay. I won't ever let anything happen to you," Oscar whispers, wiping the tears from my eyes in the warm bed for the first time as Mum cries from the corner of the room. He's eighteen now, big, strong, and safe. My brother. "Close your eyes, Oliver. Close your eyes and think about something else. You can go anywhere you want, just close your eyes and dream, brother."

It took me time to catch my emotions and shove them back down. Pocketing the phone, I walked back into the restaurant and toward the table, pulled out the chair, and took a seat. Bruce and Diane continued their conversation, arguing over countertops for the kitchen. I stared at the burger before me, lost my appetite somewhere back in the parking lot.

Mia's fingers drifted over my bouncing knee in search for my hand. "What is it?" she whispered, lacing her tiny fingers in mine. The touch of her hand steadied my heart rate, injecting strength. But I couldn't look her in the eyes. Oscar had tormented her, tried to rape her.

"Ollie?"

I swung my head and pressed my lips against her temple, slamming my eyes closed and inhaling a deep breath.

"Okay." She nodded and gripped my thigh. "Dad, we have to go."

"Sure, yeah." Bruce glanced at me and set down his fork. "Everything okay?"

Shoving my hand into my pocket, I found my wallet and threw cash over the table. I didn't know if it was too much or not enough, but my head was spinning, and Mia and I stood from our chairs. "It will be. Thank you both for everything."

Bruce stood and recognized the look in my eyes. "Yeah, it's been great having you, Oliver. I know you'll take care of my girl, better than I ever could."

Quickly but smoothly, we said our goodbyes before we took off into the parking lot. My only goal was to make it to the car without losing my grip, without punching something or someone. This was my fault. Oscar, though the piece of shit he was, was dead because of me. His death was on my hands.

"Ollie," Mia clutched my arm and yanked me back, "Ollie, slow down. Talk to me."

I took her hand in mine and kept moving forward. I had to bring Mia back home. I had to say goodbye again, and I didn't want to.

"Ollie!" She jerked her hand from mine once we reached the car. "I'm not going anywhere until you tell me where we're going."

"I'm taking you to your dad's," the words flooded out with tears stuck inside my throat, choking me. It was no coincidence there were cages surrounding hearts, stronger ones for the wild hearts that beat to a different rhythm. Mine was a different rhythm. My heart pumped to a different song entirely. "I have to go back, Mia, and you have to stay here."

"Bullshit!"

194

I gripped her shoulders and leaned over to face her. She was a different height in the heels. A height I wasn't used to. "Oscar died last night. They killed him to get to me. I have to go back, and as much as I can't be without you, I can't have anything happen to you either. You are my everything, Mia. Do this for me, please."

"No," she shook her head, "don't you dare leave me." Mia's hands clutched my face and kissed me hard, unlocking the shambles holding me down. I sank into that kiss, wishing our bodies could merge and become one. Wishing her soul could stay safe inside mine for eternity.

"I don't know what to do," I confessed with my forehead to hers, gripping the back of her head.

"I'm coming with you."

The OG's, Bonnie and Clyde. Fast driving, guns blazing. You two against the world. My wild card; my one percent. My lips landed on her forehead, hoping Bud was right in the fact we needed to start fighting these battles together. "Get in the car, love. We're going home."

EIGHTEEN

"The dark creeps nearer, consuming recklessly.
But we are together, and tonight she will sleep.
Soundlessly breathing, our hearts in rhythmic beats.
Because she is loved, unselfishly.
Diverging souls synchronize; a crossroad tale.
Stars align and fate intervenes.
I slay her terrors; sacred words as swords.
Because she is loved, wordlessly.
She rests her head; bodies melt under sheets.
I'll be here 'til sunrise,
With the weapon of a poet's lullaby.
Because she is loved, endlessly."

OLIVER MASTERS

Mia

Ollie sat on the opposite end of the taxi, drumming his fingers over his bouncing knee. It was three in the afternoon, UK time, and we hadn't even made it back to the other airport yet to retrieve his car before we'd entered into our first disagreement.

"I don't know why you're still upset with me. You had my back, then as soon as we boarded the plane, I get this." My hand waved back and forth, indicating the distance between us. He couldn't be farther away, gaze fixated out the back window.

"Of course, I had your back, Mia. I'll always have your back. But you were wrong."

"I don't understand." The douche back in customs had been an ass, asking ridiculous questions. Okay, perhaps I'd given sarcastic remarks and didn't answer each one of his perverted questions accordingly, but it still didn't give him the right. "If I was so wrong, then why stick up for me?"

Ollie dragged in a slow breath, stretched out his fingers, and let it go quickly. "I'll defend you, right or wrong, all day long in front of others, but as soon as we're behind closed doors, I get to tell you how ridiculous you were being. We could've missed our flight. They didn't have to hold the plane for us, and all he asked was what you did with that," he snapped his finger, "bullet thing."

"It's a vibrator, Ollie."

"You said, '*bomb.*'"

"I said it was the bomb." *Purposely.*

Ollie's eyes squinted as if I had insulted him. "And why do you have a vibrator in your backpack anyway?"

"You were rushing me. I just grabbed stuff from my box and shoved it in my backpack." Including my camera, film, pictures …

Ollie held out his palm and waved his fingers. "Give it to me."

"Why?"

"Because you don't need it anymore."

"What if you're out doing something, and I need a release?"

Ollie eyed the rearview mirror, where the taxi driver quickly pulled his amusing gaze away. "Since when have I ever not taken care of you?" Ollie raised a brow. He had a point, and his fingers flicked again. Groaning, I pulled the backpack over my lap and unzipped before shoving my hand into the front pocket and dropped the silver bullet into Ollie's palm. He manually rolled down the window and tossed it out into the busy afternoon traffic. "A fucking vibrator." He shook his head, laughing incredulously. "I'll lick circles around that thing."

"You just made a hitchhiker very happy," I pointed out. "I bet someone will pick it up and name it Wilson, keep it forever."

"One man's trash is another man's treasure," Ollie muttered under his breath. He was cute when he was mad, knee bouncing, fingers drumming, shaking his head. I slid across the backseat beside him, moving my hand across his stretched thighs. Heat radiated from the thin material of his slacks, and I clenched my thighs together to ease the effect he had on me. Ollie rolled his neck and faced me, and forgiving eyes hit mine. "Come here," he said through an exhale, then lifted his arm and dropped it around my shoulder, pulling me closer.

We arrived at the other airport two hours later. Ollie paid the driver, and the fee was hefty, but we couldn't get a sooner flight into the same airport he'd left his car at.

"What do you think?" he asked, tapping the hood of the black station wagon blanketed in dust.

I paused with my backpack slung over my shoulder and tilted my head. "It's...old."

Ollie rubbed the hood lovingly and whispered to the car's side mirror, "Don't listen to her, darling. She doesn't mean it." Rolling my eyes with a smile, I took a step forward as Ollie opened the back door and tossed our bags inside. "You don't have to come to the prison, Mia. I'll be fine. I can get you a room, and you can relax for a little bit." Ollie's hands moved over my hips, and he pulled me between his spread legs as he fell back against the car. I was exhausted. He was exhausted. But neither one of us let it show. "Oscar was horrible to you. I'm not expecting anything of you."

Oscar had been horrible to me. He'd drugged me, beat me, almost raped me, but he was Ollie's brother, and if he needed me at his side, I'd be there because that was what we did. We were always there for each other no matter what. I lifted my eyes to meet Ollie's, and his brow peaked, searching my face for an answer. "Tell me what you want me to do, and I'll do it."

Ollie's dimple appeared, and his fingers tugged on the bottom hem of the hoodie I was wearing over my dress until I was flush against him. Not the best fashion sense, but I'd never been into fashion. "Get out of these clothes," he whispered. "Take a proper bubble bath, order room service, get well rested. That's what I want you to do."

"Then that's what I'll do."

Ollie

It killed me to drop off Mia at the *Holiday Inn*, but it wasn't safe for her to be there, especially if the Links were watching. Dex Sullivan didn't get to lay his eyes on Mia unless I permitted him to, and I knew he was somewhere, watching. Dex knew I'd come.

I didn't have time to change, still wearing the white button-down shirt and slacks and a tiredness weighing heavy in my eyes. The heated car idled in the car park of High Down Prison, windows fogging as I waited to muster enough courage to leave the cabin of the station wagon. Rain beat over the hood, and a slew of black umbrellas marched across the lawn off in the distance, following a casket.

My fingers curled around the steering wheel until my knuckles turned white. I had the means to claim Oscar's body and give him a proper burial at a cemetery, but he'd made his bed, it was time he'd slept in it. Once upon a time, Oscar had saved me from my mum. He looked out for me, protected me. And if it weren't for him, I'd probably be dead. For that, I owed him my presence and closure.

I cut the engine, withdrew from the warm space of the car, and walked toward the huddled circle in the isolated burial ground of the prison. I stood off to the side. Rain dripped from the ends of my hair, down the bridge of my nose, and off my lashes. The white dress shirt clung to my cold skin, and I kept my head down as the priest spoke a few words, his voice drowned out by the rain.

The majority of the people who stood around the gravesite paid by the country were that of High Down employees and guards, but when the priest dismissed everyone, I caught a glimpse of raggedy blonde hair spilling from under a tilted umbrella. The woman was being consoled by, none other than, Dex Sullivan.

I tore my eyes away and commanded my feet to move, but they were cemented to the soggy ground as the two approached.

"Oliver," she stated, surprised.

I looked up and squinted through the rain. "Mum."

Black irises stared back at me, laying in the center of puffiness, bleakness, and redness. The years haven't been good to her, and her twitching fingers clung to Dex's trench coat as a source of stability.

"How dare you show up here," she spat, the frayed ends of her damaged hair flying against the wind. She seemed so small against Dex, who remained quiet at her side with a deceiving frown marring his face. "You have a lot of nerve."

"Nice to see you too, Mum."

"Don't you do that. Don't pretend like I didn't just bury my son," she gritted through clenched teeth and tears. Dex slid his arm around her waist and pulled her closer to his side. I flexed my jaw at how easily she rested against the man who'd helped conspire Oscar's death. Dex was probably still fucking her too, anything to get under my skin. "You know, that should've been you. I wished it was you, Oliver," she cried out, mourning the loss of her firstborn. The one she'd understood. The one she could relate to—the son who was just as sick as her and didn't make her feel bad about it.

"We both know I'm already dead to you. Let's not rip open old wounds." Telling my mum that Dex was the one who had Oscar killed wouldn't have done me any favors. She wouldn't have believed me. And Dex wouldn't have told mum about White Fox either. He wouldn't have told anyone. Dex wanted all the money for himself. And as soon as I could find a way to get him the money, I'd be done with all of this.

"Come on, Becky," Dex curled his fingers into her waist and steered her away, "you don't deserve to listen to this nonsense."

The two walked away, leaving me soaked and shivering in the cold rain. A tear slipped from my eye as the little boy in me watched his mum go. I'd spent years loving her blindly, even after the multiple attempts on my life. I'd be a liar if I said I never starved for my mum's love, or that it didn't kill me to watch her slip down the rabbit hole of addiction and her illness. I'd read many books, kept track of her symptoms growing up. It had all lead to a form of dissociative identity disorder, though she'd never listened to me or cared to seek help. Her only refuge had been a proper hit of heroin.

Back in the station wagon, I beat my fist into the steering wheel, over and over before turning the engine and backing out. A few miles passed when my eyes moved from the windshield to the rearview mirror, and I spotted a car following too close behind. I pulled off the street to let them pass, but they didn't. They pulled up behind me as another car passed by and parked in front of the station wagon, blocking me in. I got out, rain beating over my back, coming down hard, and threw my hands up in the air as I walked toward the car parked behind me. Two men got out, and I shouted curses against the thunderstorm brewing above.

One of them was Dex, and his lips moved, "Get him."

A force struck my head from behind, and I dropped to the ground, the gravel embedding into the side of my face. I tried to get to my feet when a boot kicked me in the stomach, stealing all the air from my lungs. My eyes squinted against the ice-cold rain, and I grabbed an ankle, tearing the bloke from a standing position, putting him on his arse before climbing over him. Before I could throw my first punch, I was struck again against my spine, temporarily disabling me.

"I warned you, Oliver," Dex shouted against the roaring thunder. I pulled myself up on all fours, trying to get back to my feet. When I lifted my head, lightning lit up the sky, illuminating Dex's vicious grin. A kick to my stomach flipped me over, and my back hit the curb. Then more blows and punches hammered over me. Two or three men, and no matter which way I turned, I couldn't get out from the bottom.

Eventually, they left. I'd heard the cars peel from the side of the road, gravel flying and hitting my face, but I couldn't move. I laid there in the frostbite under the raging storm, bleeding, shivering, and frozen. And my gaze fixed as blood trickled from my mouth and ran along the currents between pebbles, the rain washing it away.

I didn't remember how I'd gotten back to the hotel, but it was nothing short of a miracle—a saving grace.

"*Oh-my-god*," Mia cried, scurrying from under a throw blanket over the couch of the hotel room as I stood in a daze in the doorway, dripping water and blood. Tears gathered in her eyes as she touched my mouth. I turned my head away from her, hating her to see me like this. I couldn't protect myself. How was I supposed to protect her? Her voice and hands were panicked as she unbuttoned my shirt with a pained look in her expression, tears helplessly falling from her brown eyes. "I have to get you out of these clothes. You're shaking. You'll get sick." She made fast work at the buttons before peeling the shirt from around my shoulders. Her hands were hot against my quivering flesh. "Let me take you to the hospital. You need to go to the hospital."

I snatched her wrist. "No, Mia. You can't." They'd ask questions, file a police report.

"They could've killed you!" she cried out.

"Dex won't kill me. Not until he gets his money." I winced and clutched my ribcage, my entire body sore, trembling from the cold, and bruised from the inside out.

Silently, Mia unlatched my belt and unbuttoned my slacks before taking my hand and walking me to the bathroom.

Pausing in the doorway, I leaned into the frame to steady myself as she bent over to turn on the water. "I'm running you a bath," Mia muttered.

202

She was angry, and I couldn't blame her. I'd allowed my mum's presence to throw me off.

Voices from the telly competed against the water running from the bath, a crime show she had been watching still playing in the background. She turned and approached me, and her hair was piled high on top of her head, wisps framing her face as she slid off my belt. "Will you let me take care of you?"

I managed to nod and let her undress me. Both the slacks and boxers rolled down my thighs until the wet clothes hit the ground at my feet.

After sinking inside the bathwater, the hot temperature burned my wounds, but my shakes slowly declined before going away completely. Mia sat over the floor, leaning over the edge of the tub. "I'm so mad at you right now," she scolded, dabbing a hand towel over my busted lip. Another tear slipped down her cheek, and I closed my eyes, unable to see her like this.

"I'll be fine," I whispered, cringing. It hurt to breathe let alone speak. Mia dropped her hand and tucked her head over her arms on the tub. I'd seen her break down, punch walls, mirrors, letting out her absolute worst, but never had I'd seen her so defeated at my expense. My hand came up, and I wrapped my fingers around her neck and in her hair. "I promise. I'm going to be fine. It's going to be okay."

She lifted her head, her chin resting over her arm. "I can't lose you."

"You're not losing me."

"Promise me."

"You're never losing me," I repeated. "I promise."

Mia nursed my wounds and helped me into the bed. I'd been through worse before, but it seemed to make her feel better to help.

I spotted my book lying over the nightstand and asked her about it.

"They have a bookstore close by." She shrugged from the other room, picking up my wet clothes from the floor and disappearing into the bathroom, her voice trailing after her. "I went and grabbed a copy of Oliver Master's poetry book, volume one."

"Oh, yeah?" This made me smile. I'd left her a few ponies, and I knew how much the book cost. "I could've given you a copy, love."

Mia re-appeared into the room, cleaning and unable to sit still. "I wanted to buy it to support you. But it didn't occur to me until I was walking back to the hotel that you pretty much just paid for your own book because it wasn't even my money to begin with."

"Your money," I corrected her, wincing as I turned on my side so I could watch her.

Her brows bunched together. "Huh?"

"Everything I've built was for our future. It's as much yours as it is mine."

"Don't say that." She shook her head. "It's all your hard work. I haven't done anything to deserve it."

Mia walked around the room and slipped under the covers beside me in the king-sized bed, careful not to touch me, but I wanted her to. I tried to sit up, but an ache shot through my back. Groaning, I fell back into the bed. "Have you read the poetry, Mia?" White teeth dug into her bottom lip as her eyes locked on mine. Slowly, she shook her head, and my other hand came up to graze her jawline and down the base of her neck, despite the amount of pain coursing through me. "My love for you bleeds onto those pages. I write because I can't contain my feelings for you, but I publish because I want the entire world to know a love like ours exists." Her breath shuddered, and my thumb moved over her bottom lip. "It gives people hope, something to believe in. Something to never stop searching for."

"Will you read to me tonight? You know, if you're up for it."

I smiled. "I couldn't think of anything else I'd rather do."

Mia twisted in the bed, and I caught a glimpse of her arse peeking out from under my large tee she wore as she grabbed the book from the nightstand. Soft legs instantly tangled with mine, as she laid close to my side, jasmine filling my senses. Momentarily, I closed my eyes to cement this moment and stir the many memories of us these past two years. The

Links could do whatever they wanted to me, but as long as I got to come back to my home beside her, I knew everything would be okay.

I opened the book to the dedication page.

"A poet's lullaby," I read, then went on with the rest of the poem as her hand lightly moved over my chest, and my heart thumped against her palm.

"That's beautiful," Mia hummed against my neck.

"No talking, love. We'll never get through this book if you keep making comments," I pointed out, and she looked up from thick lashes, and I offered a grin before turning to the next page.

NINETEEN

"I'll cover her body
with A Starry Night
and paint her in the sky
because her canvas
deserves a Van Gogh
and the world should
be wishing upon her."

OLIVER MASTERS

Mia

t was a Tuesday morning, and we'd camped in the hotel until Ollie fully healed.

He was still asleep when the sun rose and yellow and orange rays swept through the hotel room through the partially opened navy blue curtain. His arm rested over his head as his face tilted away from me, and I took the time to trace my fingers over his sculpted features. My fingertip outlined his tattoos, hard chest, down his abdomen where bruises had changed colors, and over the curves of his abs. His body, branded in black ink, was the eighth wonder, and I'd wished I could hang him in the sky, his iridescent vibe raining over this somber earth. Maybe, then, people could finally stop and see the world the way he saw it and have a reason to smile again.

Ollie hummed in his sleep at my touch, and I lifted my gaze to catch his lashes fluttering and lips part as a breathy moan escaped. I waited until he stilled before moving my hand south, feeling the light trail of hair beneath my fingertips.

Last night, we'd laid naked, twined parts, anchored hearts, and twisted souls, and this was what love with him was like.

His gifted size stretched in my hand, swollen and warm, and I sank beneath the covers between his legs with a spontaneous smile. I dragged my tongue up the length of his shaft, and the muscles in his thighs tightened under my palms. "Jesus Christ," he said in a husky voice before I circled the end of my tongue over the bead of pre-cum, then taking him all in to my mouth.

Ollie's hips jerked forward and his fingers tangled in my hair as I sucked him slowly, stroking the sensitive spot with my tongue. The white and navy duvet was kicked off from over me before he pulled his knees up, and I looked up to see Ollie staring down at me through heavy green eyes.

I took him deep, and Ollie's head fell back into the pillow. "You keep doing that, I'm going to come."

"That's the point," I whispered, my lips brushing his tight skin.

Ollie's pleading eyes returned to me, and he pushed the hair from my face and ran his thumb over my bottom lip. I crawled up his torso until his nose brushed mine, and I straddled him, sinking over his arousal until inch by stretched inch, he filled me. Our fingers laced together as my sex clenched around him, grinding and rolling to an intense beat. His hands left mine to run the tips of his fingers along my curves, to my hips, and ultimately grabbing two handfuls of my bottom, meeting my every grind.

I bit down on my lip to fight the climax threatening to spill, but my legs were giving me away, shaking uncontrollably.

Ollie grabbed my hipbones, pinning my center to his until every muscle in his body tensed under his inked skin as he came undone. "Nobody controls my body like you can," he whispered into my hair. "You take me and make me crazy, love."

I laughed into the crook of his neck. "Good morning, by the way."

His hands roamed from my ass and over the scars of my back. "I knew I liked mornings for a reason." And his nose brushed mine once more before I rolled off of him and to his side.

"Ollie?"

"Yeah?"

"Why do I feel like this is the calm before the storm."

Ollie rolled onto his side and licked his lips. His mouth opened, about to say something, then closed, stuck in turbulent thoughts. "You're not going to like what I'm about to tell you."

Three minutes later …

"A cemetery," I questioned, my tone pitched and recovering from the story he'd gone over. Twice, because I'd asked him to retell it to be sure I'd heard correctly. "You buried the money in a fucking cemetery?"

"Yes." He nodded, resolved.

"Let me get this straight. You stole all the assets from your brother's prostitution ring and buried it next to George something's gravesite because …"

"*When death comes, it is never our tenderness we repent from, but our severity*, *George Eliot*," he quoted, which didn't help clear this up at all.

"I don't think Mr. Eliot wanted the earth around him disturbed by fuck money."

"First of all, George Eliot was a woman and a legend. Second, I think she'd find the irony amusing."

208

I rolled my eyes. "Very poetic, Ollie."

"Thank you," he said through a smile. "Tonight, we have to break into Highgate Cemetery to retrieve the money."

"Then you're just going to, what? Hand the money over to Dex?"

"That's the plan."

"How much are we talking?"

"Forty-three grand, give or take. But Dex doesn't know how much exactly. I'll give him half, and drop the other half off to Brad Burn's family. Leave the rest for his kids and wife. They don't deserve to struggle without a father."

"That's a lot of money you buried."

"I was pissed off whiskey and a grudge. Lost a grand somewhere between the car and the tombstone, I'm sure," he shrugged. "Not my greatest moment."

I shook my head, grinning.

Ollie stroked my side. "What?"

"Nothing."

"Tell me."

"They say you can't bury the money with you. You sure showed them."

Ollie's head fell back, a small cackle escaping.

"It's just … I'm glad you told me, you know. Including me in this. You can't take all your secrets to your grave."

"Oh, here we go."

"What?" I arched a brow. "Am I digging myself a deeper hole?"

Ollie's smile was contagious, and he tried shaking his head through his laughter.

"We're six feet deep into this mess," I laughed, "and I could go all day."

"You do that." He smacked my ass. "I'm going to shower. You coming?"

"You going to *bury* yourself inside me again?" Ollie turned his head and walked away, but I felt his smile linger as I watched his smooth tanned ass all the way to the bathroom.

The sound of water bouncing off the tile spilled from the bathroom, and Ollie poked his head through the doorway. "You'll be in *grave* danger if you're not in here in five seconds."

The car stopped in front of a cobblestone cottage, and my gaze snapped to Ollie, who wore a proud smile. "Welcome home, love."

"Ollie ..." I whispered, my eyes glued to the charming little house.

He grabbed my hand from my lap and brushed his lips over my knuckles. "Come on. I've been waiting for this moment for a long time."

Ollie cut the engine, and we both exited the car. My eyes landed everywhere, the gate with an empty bronze plaque waiting to be engraved, the tiny bridge arching over a creek, the mailbox, which was an exact miniature replica of the cottage. Vines crawled vertically up the front of the house, clinging on to the gray and white stone surface, and the front door was curved and chipped around the antique knocker. We'd left our bags inside the car, and Ollie opened the gate and let me walk ahead of him. "This is ... I'm ..."

"Gobsmacked?" he finished.

"Yeah, Ollie," I laughed, "I'm fucking gobsmacked. Houses like this belong in books. Fairytales. They don't belong in the real world."

"This is real, and this is yours." The door creaked open and we walked inside as he continued, "I haven't been here yet, so please excuse any mess Travis left. Him and Summer stayed while I was away. But they're gone now. It's just us ..." but I could hardly listen as I took in the nostalgic vibe the home transcended. We walked right into a small living room, and two thick wooden beams stood on both sides of us as a large leather couch sat against a wall, facing a fireplace. An old piano tucked in the corner. "Watch your step." He grabbed my elbow, leading me off a single step.

210

We walked through the living area, over the hardwood floors and toward the kitchen in the back, which overlooked a lake with a dock. The kitchen was small with open shelving, and I ran my fingers over the shelves, remembering what Ollie said back in Pennsylvania on my thoughts about them. Little did I know, he had been serious.

"There's only two bedrooms and two bathrooms. Figured less square footage and walls between us would be ideal. I never needed much, Mia. I'm a simple man."

"I love it."

"You haven't seen the best parts yet."

"There's more?"

Ollie grabbed my hand and led me to the master bedroom. The fireplace from the living room was a shared one with the master, and surrounding the brick were built-in bookshelves. Every detail was timeless, hand-crafted, and quaint. I followed him into the white bathroom where a free-standing tub sat against the back window, potted plants lining the sill.

"Okay, you're going to love this," he said excitedly, leading me out of the room and toward a narrow staircase lined in piles upon piles of books. "Ignore those. I've had books shipped, but I'm OCD about how they're organized. I told Travis to set them anywhere."

When our feet landed on the top step, it was a finished attic, complete with a dark room for my photography. Tears sprung in my eyes. "This is surreal," I said through a shaky breath. "Ollie, this isn't real."

"It's real," he smiled, eyes glassy, "I can't take all the credit. I put Travis to work. To be honest with you, I haven't been able to come here at all. Not until I had you safely back."

"This is your first time here?"

"It is. Travis did all right, yeah?"

"I can't believe this," I kept repeating. It was in front of me, but for some reason, I couldn't comprehend it. For so long, I'd never thought I was worthy of not only a place to finally feel accepted and at home, but with a man who was so opposite of me—who was everything I wasn't. A man who'd never stopped encouraging me or pushing me to be the best version of myself.

I held back my emotions until we walked through the back door of the kitchen and out onto the garden. A fire pit rested in the middle of our yard, and the cobblestone house blended over the ground, creating an illusion of a stone deck and a pathway out to the dock. "In the summer, this garden will be covered in flowers. Not sure which ones yet, but I suppose we'll find out soon."

Two chairs rested right outside the backdoor, and Ollie sat over a chair and pulled me into his lap, releasing a long breath. We sat in silence for a while, with his chin dropped over my shoulder.

"Well, what do you think? Want to make a home here?" Ollie asked as we gently rocked in the chair, the view of the water stealing our gaze.

Birds flew from tree to tree, singing, and I curled deeper against him. "It's perfect."

"Mia?"

"Yeah?"

"It's you and I, evermore," he whispered, and he shoved his hand into the pocket of his pants and held up a small burlap box between us. "I bought this ring in the village right after I saw the cabin fire on the telly. I knew, *God*, I fucking knew that was you crying out for me. And perhaps no matter where we are, our souls still speak to each other. It's the sweetest sound, and I've never doubted our music." Ollie opened the burlap box, and plucked the ring from inside. "I'd been holding on to this ring ever since, waiting for this chance to put it on your finger."

Ollie took my hand in his and slipped it on. Speechless, a tear fell down my cheek as I stared at it. The ring was round and simple, rose gold, with tiny diamonds surrounding a larger one in the center. It was perfect. "It's beautiful." I turned my head to face him, and his vulnerable green eyes shone back at me.

I dropped my forehead to his, and his nose brushed against mine before his lips did. "I love you, Mia," he whispered against my mouth before our lips locked in an unhurried and ardent kiss. Emotions

212

dominated both of us before we broke away, and I stuffed my face into his neck.

Ollie

"This is the ultimate serial criminal kit. Black attire, a shovel, gloves, and a flashlight." Mia laughed with her arms crossed over her chest against the car, her diamond ring glimmering in the night. "I feel worthless like I'm only along for immoral support."

"You're holding the flashlight," I pointed out, closing the trunk.

It was close to midnight, and the drive was about an hour to London. I made a turn onto Dartmouth Park Hill and drove until I found the same spot I'd parked before where the corporate offices bundled together. Just on the other side laid George Eliot and forty-three grand, give or take a thousand. The moon lit up the grey murky sky through puffed stringy clouds as if someone dragged claws through them. "We're here."

We had to be fast and invisible. And I jumped out of the car and rounded to the back as Mia followed in her newly purchased black jeans, black long-sleeved shirt, black puffer vest, and a black beanie fitted over her head. I looked the same, omit the puffer jacket, and adrenaline pumped through the both of us as I grabbed the duffle from the trunk, which carried the items we needed. The hike to the wall through the overgrown forest was short, and I was glad Mia decided to wear her combat boots. I shouldered the duffle and kissed my girl. "Ready?"

"As I'll ever be."

Once we hit the wall, I directed her to shine the flashlight down the length of the stone. "There's a door here somewhere. It blends into the rubble." Our feet sunk into the mud as we walked along the wall, my hand grazing the stone, feeling for the wooden door.

"I think this is it," Mia called out in a low voice a few feet ahead of me. "Do I just open it? How did you know this was here?"

I grinned. "I can't give away all my secrets."

"Taking it to the grave?"

"Yup." My thumb dropped down the lever of the handle, and I gave it a shoulder shove until the door gave in. We passed a layer of thick brush until we spotted a trail. The cemetery had an intense aroma of dying days and an irreversible past. A gothic Victorian eeriness lingered within the dense vegetation of canopied trees and scattered tombstones, embodying and transporting us back into an uncanny time. The moon bored down on us, bouncing off Mia's pale face as chills ran down my spine like it had the last time I was here. I nodded my head forward, and our boots and breaths bounced between us through the mud until we stepped foot on more solid ground. Harsh midnight winds ripped through her hair, but we were almost there.

I stood in front of George Eliot's faded tombstone. "*Of those immortal dead who live again in minds made better by their presence,*" I read, admiring the engraving for the second time.

"Mary Ann Cross," Mia added, staring at the tall gray stone.

"She took the pen name of a man so her work would be taken seriously."

"That's ... sad."

I shrugged and dropped the duffle, and it met the ground with a thud. "Times were different then."

Piercing the soiled earth beside the tomb with the tip of the shovel, I dug about two feet until Mia's flashlight glared off of the black plastic bag. Mia stood from a nearby tombstone, and I lifted my eyes until it hit hers. "Jackpot."

She crouched down beside me with the flashlight between her teeth, holding the duffle open as I ripped open the plastic and dumped handfuls of banded notes inside. The night was colder for May, below seven degrees Celsius, where our breath came out in thick clouds. Paranoid, Mia's eyes darted around her.

"You scared, love?" I asked, leaving no empty space inside the bag.

"No."

I worked the zipper. "You sure?" The place was creepy, especially in the middle of the night. It had taken me a few shots of liquid courage to come here alone last time, but I'd never admit that to her.

She cocked her head. "I don't get scared, especially of ghosts."

"I wouldn't say that too loud. You'll hurt their feelings."

I laughed as Mia's eyes bulged, and she shoved my shoulder.

Fuck, was she beautiful, even surrounded by death, like a wilted rose in the winter.

I patted the side of the bag before standing and filled the hole back in.

Our feet made quick work of high-tailing it out of there and disappearing into the woods. The moon wasn't our friend on our way back, and I depended on the little light put out by the flashlight and a sense of direction. It took us over an hour to find the door, which we'd left open, but now it was closed and airtight. "Shit."

"Don't say shit," Mia whispered from behind me.

"Fuck," I uttered in a breath, working the handle again.

"What?"

"The wind must've closed it shut."

"So, open it."

"I can't." I dropped the bag and planted my palm over the stone wall for leverage as I tried again.

"Ollie …"

"I'm serious, Mia. The bloody thing is stuck."

"You've got to be kidding me. I knew it. You've gone and pissed her spirit off." She huffed beside me. "What do we do now?"

"Plan B."

"Which is?"

"Camping out."

"You meaning to tell me, you show me our beautiful home today, and I'm spending my night in a cemetery." Mia groaned, but I couldn't see her anymore against the pitch-black night. "And I have to pee."

"You'll have to hold it, love. It's illegal to urinate on sacred ground." And I regretted the words as soon as they left my mouth.

"But it's perfectly okay to hide forty-three thousand dollars beside a famous dead novelist?" She gritted out in a whisper-yell, and I was sure her hands were flying, and I could only imagine her expression. "Is anything we're doing right now legal, Ollie?"

Her tone only meant I was in trouble. "All right, you're right," I pushed my hands through my hair and turned in place, "pop-a-squat, princess."

"Here?"

"I would rather you do it here than back at a grave."

She shone the flashlight on my face. "Okay, don't look."

"Mia, I can hardly see my own hand."

"And plug your ears."

Chuckling, I turned and hung my head, thinking maybe I should ring Travis to rescue us, but remembered I'd left my mobile back in the car. Mia shuffled inside her jeans, and a tree limb fell. I jerked my head around. An owl hooted overhead. The taunting night wasn't on our side. "Mia, are you finished?" I was ready to get out of the choking vegetation and back under the moon.

Another twig snapped. I whipped my head around.

"Mia?"

The silence screamed, playing tricks on me. I scanned the forest for her flashlight.

"Dammit, Mia. Answer me!" A hand grabbed my shoulder, and I twisted in place to see Mia jump from behind with the flashlight in her face, giggling. "Christ," I let out a breath and clutched my hammering heart. "That's not funny. You are not funny."

"What's wrong, Ollie? Are you afraid?" She laughed.

I shook my head and scooped the bag from the ground.

We walked back through the thick, overgrown brush to higher ground, Mia trailing close behind. We couldn't have been out here for more than three hours, which meant sunrise would come in no more than two. Tossing the bag at the nearest headstone, I took a seat and leaned back against the rock looking up at her.

216

The wind hadn't slowed and only blew more fiercely against her, sending twisted chocolate-brown strands to stick to her chapped, rosy-tinted lips. But the wind didn't throw her off-kilter. It was as if she summoned it, and nature followed her. The force in the air snatched dead leaves from the ground, floating and swirling around us, dancing right in her hair.

A night's spell.

I pulled my knees up and dropped my head back, mesmerized as she spoke, entirely captivated with the way her lips moved, the way the moon complimented her. Her black jeans hugged her hips so tight it could rip the skin. And I had to tear my eyes away to prevent myself from stripping her bare under the moon. We were probably already going to hell, and fucking her in a cemetery would grant us a one-way ticket.

Plus, Mia was the kind of girl to take your time with. An art. A canvas that deserved a Da Vinci. But I was weak against her, already gone. I reached for the flask I'd hidden with the money from the duffle, needing a shot of some booze—brilliant idea at the time, finally serving a purpose to calm the raging hormones Mia tended to call upon whenever she was near. I unscrewed the cap and felt the burn.

Mia tilted her head and narrowed her eyes. "Are you even listening to me?"

"Honestly, no. I can't hear anything over all that sex appeal."

Mia's shoulders relaxed, and her lips turned into a simple smile.

"Come sit down," I offered, pointing to the space between my legs, and she eyed me skeptically, taking the flask from my hand. She twirled in place, drinking from the antique bottle, then stopped in front of me and pushed her thumb to the corner of her mouth to catch a drip. As if she were snow, Mia drifted between my legs and anchored her hands to my thighs, her head falling back against my chest.

It didn't take long for her to fall asleep. It also didn't take long for the sun to rise and fight through the clouded skies and canopies. I wanted to stall a little while longer. And I held on to five more minutes of her in my arms before waking her and gathering our things. Sleepy, Mia sluggishly walked behind me through the brush and back to the secret door.

When we reached the stone wall, my gaze followed the length until they fell upon my secret door—wide-open.

I turned to face Mia, who had confusion painted over her face. "I thought you said it was stuck."

"It was."

TWENTY

"At the stroke of midnight
when darkness calls,
We're free to run
with the wild things,
to toss our masks,
French kiss like voodoo,
and wonder how
something so wrong
could taste so divine."

OLIVER MASTERS

Ollie

didn't want to leave Mia. I hated to leave her. But Dex Sullivan was
where I drew the line. I had to keep Mia far away from him. Dex knew
her name, which was enough to want to shove her into a box, lock it,
and push it under my bed to keep her safe. Of course, I had not done that,
but Mia had a way about her, putting herself in the aim of fire. And Dex
was a different breed than Dolor.

Dex didn't have any reservations when it came to murder.

Instead, I took her to the hardware store in the village and let her pick out paint and supplies. She hated the white walls. Said it reminded her of a mental institution. Why hadn't I thought of that?

Mia had picked a moss green named Nature's Cure, and I'd left her in the living room with the furniture pushed in the center and covered in plastic to keep safe from her. When it came to talents, anything paint-related didn't make it to her resume. Her fingers were created to only touch piano keys, a camera, and my skin.

I'd already had the number for a painter from London to touch up. Just in case.

I drove to the Links property in Grays South and parked on the curb. Adrian was hunched over on the front step, smoking a fag when I walked up. His eyes lit up when he lifted his head and immediately got to his feet to greet me. Our hands linked, and he pounded his fist against my back. "Oliver, you look like a whole new man. Where have you been, mate?"

Adrian's lip was busted and swollen, and a cut below his right eye.

"Around. What happened to your face?"

He snatched the cigarette from the edge of the step and pulled it to his mouth. "It's nothing."

"It doesn't look like nothing," I probed, and Adrian shoved his hand into his pocket and offered me a cigarette. "I quit."

He raised a brow. "Just like that?"

"Just like that." I gripped his shoulder. "How are the other two nitwits? Staying out of trouble?"

"You could say that."

James was the one to worry about. Adrian had an honest heart and good head on his shoulders, Reggi had already burnt his brain cells to a crisp, but the way Dex looked at James was the same way Oscar used to look at me. A project. A slab of wet concrete, begging to be molded and shaped into the perfect criminal. But I couldn't be everyone's hero.

"Dex is mad you left," Adrian warned, and then it dawned on me. Did Dex tear up his face because of me?

220

"I'm paying myself off and done for good."

"You can't just leave."

"I was never staying, Adrian. Dex and I had a deal. I'm following up on my end."

I entered the run-down house, and Dex Sullivan was aware of my visit. I'd texted him earlier that I'd meet him here with the profits from White Fox, enough cash to fund the makings of a new empire. It was everything he'd ever wanted.

Dex Sullivan wanted to be a king.

Except, the wannabe king was nowhere to be found.

"He's in the hot tub," James stated, coming from a back room. He barely looked at me, grabbed a beer from the refrigerator, and left through the back door. I followed after him.

Dex's arms were sprawled out on each side of him, head resting back against the tub, and eyes closed. I cleared my throat, and he lifted his head. Mischievous eyes met mine. "Nice of you to finally show up here, Oliver."

"You didn't leave much of a choice," I scoffed.

He held up a finger and fisted something below the water line before pulling up a hand-full of blonde hair. The woman it was attached to spun around to face me and curled inside his arm—my mum.

I turned my head. "Mum, get out."

"Anything we discuss can be discussed in front of her."

"Like how you killed her son?"

My mum twisted her head, and Dex laughed. "I did no such thing. We both know I'd never hurt my best friend."

"I'll leave your package inside. We're done here. I don't owe you anything anymore." I turned to leave.

"Mia Jett," Dex called out, and I froze.

Turning around, I flexed my shoulders back. "What did you just say?"

"You promised me White Fox."

"I'm giving you what's left of White Fox."

Dex squinted his eyes. "No, what you're giving me is fucking chump change. I want power. I want the same fucking prostitution ring that used to control this territory, the same ring you owe me. You know who reigns over east of London now? The fucking Links. Imagine my bloody luck when the bloke I currently work for is now my competition." My brow raised, and he continued, "The deal was White Fox, and the only way I can have it is if you kill the boss of the Links. You have to kill Ghost."

Dex had lost his fucking mind. Ghost was untouchable. No one knew who Ghost was, hence the nickname. His identity had been hidden for years. "What you're asking is impossible."

"I'm not asking you. I'm ordering a hit with no questions."

"Have you gone mad? What makes you think I'd do this? That I'd kill for you?"

Dex held up three fingers. "Mia. Rose. Jett." He smiled. "You'd kill for her, wouldn't you? If I'm not mistaken, you already have."

"You don't know what you're talking about."

"When your mum mentioned you went off to Dolor, I did a little digging and found a police report that you stabbed a young woman in the neck with a pencil after she attacked your girlfriend. Bravo, baby Oscar. But I found your weakness."

I slid my gaze to Mum, who dropped her chin, eyes fixed on the water. "I could just kill you, call it a day."

"But, you won't."

"Yeah? And what is stopping me?"

"Killing me doesn't protect your girl," he snickered as if he knew me. "You see, if anything happens to me, I have a man waiting to put a bullet through the back of her head. It shouldn't take much effort to find her. Surely, just follow your love-sick heart around." The single threat turned my blood to lava, and my heart plunged into my stomach at the thought. "Don't look so glum, Oliver. It should all work out."

The fury rising caused my hands to shake, and I crossed my arms over my chest to conceal my weakness for Mia, and the lengths I'd go for her. I didn't have it in me to kill another human. Murder was a job for Ethan.

Not me. "I'll do it. I'll kill Ghost," I lied, buying myself time to figure this out.

"I know you will, and I have a little friend here to help. Consider it my gift to you and your way in with Ghost. She was quite forthcoming when she found out she'd be working with you. I think you have yourself a fan." Dex blew out a whistle, the door behind me opened, and seconds later, fingertips gripped the side of my arm.

In my peripheral, blonde hair soaked my vision. Leigh. "What are you doing?" I whispered to her. She was innocent in all this.

"Leigh claims she's a virgin," he laughed, and my head jerked back toward him, "No, seriously. I can't believe it myself either. And rumor states Ghost fancies pretty young virgins."

"She's a child," I gritted out.

"I'm seventeen," Leigh argued.

I turned to her and clutched her shoulders. "This is ludicrous. You don't know what you're getting yourself into."

Dex interjected, "Calm down, Oliver. You'll kill Ghost before the exchange happens. Leigh will be safe, but you have to check her."

"Check her for what?"

Dex lifted his palm from the hot tub. "Well, her virginity, of course."

"Oh, fuck off."

"Either you will, or I'll make James do it, and I'm afraid James may take more than what's needed. Trust me, baby O, you don't want your virgin corrupted. She's your easiest way in, and with or without her, Ghost still has to go."

I grabbed Leigh's hand and yanked her back inside through the door, slamming it behind me. "What the fuck have you done?"

Leigh's hand rested over my bicep, and she looked up at me through sincere eyes. "I want to help you."

"You could get yourself raped or killed. You don't know what these people are capable of. And how did you end up in this mess?"

223

Leigh seemed insulted, and she dropped her arm. "I was looking for you! The last time I saw you was here and Dex promised you'd come back if I helped him. And you're back. You came back."

"Check that pussy, Oliver," James called out, coming through the door with a gun in his waistband.

I snapped my gaze at him. "Are you his bitch now?"

Ignoring me, he slapped a pill over the counter and shoved an open beer into my chest. "This is to help you through the night, mate." And I contemplated my options, which was close to none. I slammed the pill into my mouth and chased it with the beer. James slapped my shoulder before leaving, and I wiped my mouth with the back of my hand.

"You really want to do this?" I asked, turning to Leigh and raising a brow. "You'll let me touch you? You'll let me drag you into this mess? Risk your life? All for what?"

"I trust you. You won't let anything happen to me."

We walked into the bathroom, and I locked the door behind me and took out my phone, scrolling through Google search. "Take off your bottoms," I ordered Leigh, typing a question I'd never thought I'd ask into my phone and wondering how the fuck I was going to explain this to Mia. *"How was your day?" "Great, babe. Had to check a girl's hymen, how was yours?"*

After reading over the two-finger test with vision already blurring, I turned back around and glanced up from my phone to see Leigh standing shyly, completely naked. A perky set of breasts stared back at me, hard pink nipples, and teenage curves. "You didn't have to," I clutched her hipbones and dropped my head. "Never mind, just come here." I tucked my phone back inside my pocket.

Leigh stepped forward, her head coming to my chest. I wanted to get this over with, and picked her up at the waist and set her over the sink. Looking over her young skin, I shook my head. "Fuck, I can't do this." I backed away and pinched the bridge of my nose. It was wrong on so many levels. Mia, first and foremost. Legal, but still only seventeen. And a virgin,

224

nonetheless. "I need to make a call," I mumbled, shoving my hand into my pocket.

Dialing Mia's number, she answered on the second ring, "Picasso, here."

"I'm in trouble," I admitted.

"What's wrong?"

For starters, a naked girl was staring at me. "It's not over, Mia." I wanted to scream as soon as the words tumbled out. "Fuck, I have this girl here. They want to use her because she's a virgin—"

"Leigh," the virgin piped up, and I narrowed my eyes.

"What does he want you to do?" Mia asked on the other end.

"Stuff you wouldn't be proud of."

Mia sighed. "Whatever it is, I'll forgive you. Just do what you have to and get home to me in one piece."

I fisted the phone and wiped my face into my shirt, turning around. "I'm on some kind of drug right now." I wasn't going to lie to Mia. "I don't trust myself with this position I'm in."

"Ollie, I don't want to know. Just remember, it doesn't mean anything."

I drew in a deep breath. "I love you," came out upon an exhale.

"I know, but I'd rather you tell me in person."

"I'll see you soon." I clicked the phone and tucked it back into my jeans and narrowed my eyes at the body sitting before me. Leigh was just another battle I had to conquer to get closer to freedom. A conquest.

Leigh tilted her head, worry consuming her eyes. "Will this hurt?"

"I'm not going to hurt you," I promised.

"Will it feel good?"

"Leigh, I won't be able to concentrate if you keep talking."

"I'm scared it's going to hurt. At least try and make it feel good, Oliver." Leigh looked up at me through dark lashes. "Be gentle and make me feel good. Please."

"Okay," I said, waving her down to the edge of the sink. "But most likely, Ghost will do the same. He'll want to check you." I slammed my

225

hands on both sides of her, and lifted my head until our eyes met. "Have you ever been touched?"

Leigh shook her head, her blonde hair falling over her pert breasts. She had no idea what she'd gotten herself into with the Links, but I couldn't deny her innocence wasn't fucking with my head. I was confident it was the pill I'd taken. "Breathe," I coached her, spreading her legs open and running my fingertips down the insides of her thighs to put her at ease, so it didn't feel like I was about to assault the girl.

"Does it look okay?" Leigh asked. "You keep staring at my fanny like it's different."

It was different. "Your fanny is fine." Not the one I wanted to be looking at, but this was the position we were in, and I pushed her knees apart to get a better view of what I was dealing with as my hands continued to roam over her thighs to get her comfortable with my touch.

She bit her lip. "That feels good."

"Please, let's do this without talking."

Leigh shrugged. "I know you're not into this. Into me. I just wished the first time someone touched me cared, at the very least. It's fine. You can just shove your fingers inside me and get it over with."

She didn't value herself, which made me pity her. She didn't deserve this. "I'm not going to do that." I used two fingers to spread her pussy lips apart and soaked my thumb in my mouth before running it over her large bud. All this was completely unnecessary, but perhaps making her feel good would lessen the sting I'd heard about. I rolled my thumb over her clit, pressing against it and making circles.

Someone pounded over the door, and Leigh recoiled, slamming her legs shut. "What's the verdict, Masters?" Dex yelled, and I hung my head.

"Bugger off," I yelled back, dizzy and high from the drugs. The room grew hot, and I yanked off my hoodie. Leaning over Leigh, I pushed her stiff thighs apart again. "You have to relax." I cocked my head, knowing I'd have to work her up all over again. "Pretend it's just you and me right now," she was so tiny over the counter, and I gripped her thighs and pulled them apart, revealing herself to me again, "and we're somewhere else other than here," I pressed my fingertip against her opening, "that I'm someone you fancy, yeah?"

Leigh bucked her hips forward.

"That's right," I placed a palm over her pelvis to keep her still and pull her skin up, working her opening with one finger. "but don't get too excited or you'll hurt yourself." I offered a smile, and she sank backward with dark eyes on mine, rolling her hips forward. Her scent was the opposite of Mia's, and I missed my girl. I missed Mia's heat, her taste, the way I felt inside her. My stomach turned, pushing my finger a centimeter through her tight entrance, Leigh cried out, and I lowered my palm over her clit, rubbing up and down to take her mind off it. Surely, it couldn't hurt that bad, but I wouldn't know. "I'll have to get one more finger in there, and you're still not wet enough."

"It hurts."

"I'm sorry, I'm trying to be gentle." But fuck me.

"Lick me," she suggested.

"No," I scoffed, lowering my head and spitting on her sex. "I kiss my girl with this mouth." I moved my palm up and down over her flesh, soaking her folds with my saliva, and Leigh whimpered, grinding against my hand. She was loving what I was doing. The girl was playing me.

"I've never gotten off before, Oliver. Please, I bet it feels so good to feel your mouth on me."

"It does, you can ask Mia." I pressed my thumb against her clit as I gently stroked her entrance, in and out, and going further each time. Leigh's legs uncontrollably shook as she squirmed, but I stayed in control despite my high. Leigh's pussy was tight, and I had to be careful not just to find the hymen, but not break it, all while keeping her in the mood to keep her relaxed. She bucked her hips back, her knees closing in as her orgasm climbed. I withdrew, grabbed her thighs, slammed her bottom against my pelvis, and pushed down on her legs. "Stay still," I growled, then pressed two fingers back inside, gently pressing deeper until … There it was—her hymen. I quickly withdrew my fingers and rested my hands over the sink between her opened legs. "Good news. You're a virgin."

227

"You're not going to finish me off?"

I hung my head. "Nope."

"She's lucky," Leigh stated, referring to Mia as I washed my hands in the sink beside her.

"I'm the lucky one." I dried my hands off on my pants and pushed her knees together. "Keep your legs closed and don't let those boys fuck you." I had some sort of attachment to this young girl now, had to keep her innocence intact.

"You're leaving me?"

"Get dressed, Leigh." I snatched my hoodie off the ground and left her in the bathroom to find Dex.

He was in the kitchen with his bodyguards.

"Well?" he asked with a smirk.

"She's a virgin."

He took my hand and brought my fingers to his nose. "Fuck, you actually did it." I jerked my hand away. "Faint but delish."

"Don't fucking touch her."

"Did you get her off, Oliver? Don't tell me you left her high and dry here with a house full of horny blokes."

"I'm leaving. Your cash is already in your car."

"I'm calling Ghost's right-hand man and telling him I have a Virgin for sale. His turn around time is a few months or so. Your job is to make sure she stays a virgin until then and not to disappear again. Keep your phone on you."

What should've only taken an hour to get back home had taken me three. I had to make sure no one was following me. This was the only home Mia has known. I wasn't going to let anyone take that away from her.

I walked into our home, greeted by a fire burning in the fireplace and the living room walls a lovely calming moss green. All the furniture was back in its original state, and my brows lifted as I looked around. We'd been in the house for a little over two weeks now, and Mia set a few framed polaroid pictures from Dolor over the mantle. I walked by, admiring our first picture we'd ever taken in the center, surrounded by a photo of Mia, Zeke, and me, Jake and Mia, and one of just me writing in my journal. The piano was open, and my heart soothed inside my chest, knowing she was finally able to play again since we lost Zeke.

"Mia," I called out, dropping my keys in the wooden tray over the coffee table. I pulled off my hoodie and peeked in the kitchen before making my way to our bedroom.

The shower was going, and I removed the rest of my clothes, wanting to join her.

"Ollie?" she asked, hearing me from the bedroom through the cracked bathroom door.

Completely naked, I opened the bathroom door all the way and steam slammed into me. "Yeah, love. It's me."

"What took you so long?" she asked, and I pulled the curtain back and stepped in. "And what do you think?"

I looked her up and down. Water ran off her lashes and the tip of her nose as soap buds splattered over her ivory skin. Green paint was stuck in her wet hair and smeared against her cheek. "Perfection." I brushed my nose against hers, not wanting to touch her entirely until I washed this horrid night off me.

She pressed her lips together in a glowing smile. "I'm talking about the paint color."

"Oh, that?" I asked, squeezing soap over the loofah and quickly washed my body. I shrugged. "Eh." Mia shoved my shoulder, and I wrapped her into a bear hug. "I'm kidding, love. I love it."

Mia lifted onto her tiptoes and kissed me under the stream. "Thank you for coming home."

"Mia," I laughed, "why do you say thank you like I did you a favor?"

She lifted her shoulder. "Because you did."

TWENTY-ONE

"Chase her **wild."**

OLIVER MASTERS

Mia

t had been over a month since I'd arrived back into the UK, and Ollie
and I kept to ourselves, for the most part, making up for the lost time
and making the house a home. He had another book signing coming
up, and I was beyond excited to sit beside him and watch him with people
who read his work.

It was a short walk into Surrey where I would finally meet Travis and
Summer. The sun didn't set until after nine at night during the summers,
and the clouds lifted, allowing the sun to shine over us and promising little
to no rain. Most of the buildings were either made of brick or cobblestone,
outlined with wooden green or white details, and shingled roofs with
chimneys poking from the top. White flowers bloomed from the cracks of
the storefronts, and I peeked through the windows of the quaint shops to
see charming knickknacks, hand-carved details, and hometown feels. I

closed my eyes, breathing in the fresh air with a hint of flowers in the rain and gripped Ollie's hand. "I love it here."

"This is your home, Mia. You were born here." His comment immediately made me think of Lynch, and I wondered if he knew I was back or wanted to see me. Ollie paused at the crosswalk, and I glanced up, admiring him and his style. He dressed like he didn't care, in his hunter green pants, loose white tee, and a fedora.

I picked up the bottom of my gray cotton dress that met my sandaled feet as we walked across a cobblestone street to the other side. It was close to sixty-five degrees today, but I pulled my leather jacket tighter around me when a gust of wind swirled in the air.

"Do you want to stop for coffee?" Ollie asked, noticing the chill. "We're almost there but there's a coffee shop around the corner."

"I'm okay." I smiled, and he kissed the side of my head.

We made it to the restaurant, which classified as a pub, and found a seat outside under the trellis.

If we had the choice, we sat outside. Ollie didn't do well in confined spaces with his emotional intensity, and being too close to other people set off his anxiety. This past month, I'd learned more and more about him and how people's vibes could affect him physically, mentally, and emotionally. After two weeks of being here, we'd both agreed to continue seeing a psychologist, together and separately. It took a few tries to find one we both liked, but we'd finally found one in London from a referral Dr. Conway gave us. She'd searched high and low for someone familiar with Ollie's hyper-sensitivity and even pre-interviewed the lady over the phone just in case.

I'd confessed openly about my wicked thoughts, the ones of murder, but only to the counselor. I hadn't told Ollie about my demented dreams of death, and how it had been following me since I'd remembered my past. Ethan had understood, but would Ollie ever know the sick delusions inside my head? Would he ever understand that a single threat made me want to rip someone apart and watch them bleed out at my feet with a smile on my face? Or how the morbid thoughts kept me up at night while he was gone, and he was the only one who could soothe me with his poetic lullaby?

Ollie stood from his chair as soon as he spotted Travis and Summer, and I followed suit.

"This," Ollie looked down at me with a smile, "is Mia."

"It's about time," Travis said, pulling me in for a hug. "You know, Mia. I've been waiting a long time to meet you."

"I heard you tried to tell him I was dead. You wanted him to give up on me."

Travis frowned, shooting a glance over at Ollie. Summer laughed, noticing my sarcasm.

"I like her already," Summer announced, coming in for a hug of her own.

"You look like you're about to pop!" I tried hugging her back, but it was awkward with her big belly. "How far along are you?

"Four more bloody weeks. I'm due July 21st, and I'm so ready," she whined, rubbing over her belly in the flowy paisley-printed blouse hugging her stomach. Summer had golden hair and big, bright blue eyes. Her pale skin glowed against her navy shirt, and she set down her umbrella and took a seat. "Oh, fuck, Oliver. You didn't!" Summer grabbed my hand and looked at my ring, "You fucking did," she narrowed her eyes at Travis. "I'm having your baby, you bastard, and Mia already has a ring," Summer scolded Travis.

"In my defense, I told him to propose almost seven months ago," Ollie said, holding his palms out in front of him.

Travis shook his head. "Thanks, Oliver. Thanks for that."

"How did you do it?" Summer asked.

Ollie raised his brows. "Do what?"

"Propose. I love proposal stories."

Ollie snapped his eyes to me, and I clenched my thighs together at the reminder of me on the piano back at Dolor, and Ollie inside me.

"I'm not giving your chap here any pointers." He gripped Travis's shoulder. "He'll have to come up with his own."

The evening passed with laughs, drinks, and good food, and after a few hours, we said our goodbyes after promising to get together soon before the baby arrived.

On our way back to our cottage, Ollie pulled me into a shop beside a small bookstore that sold tea, coffee grounds, and bottles of wine with book quotes on the labels. He filled the basket with pastries and grounds and picked out a bottle of rosé wine. "*Love is longing for the half of ourselves we have lost*, Milan Kundera," Ollie read. "This is the one. It reminds me of a book I read."

"Perhaps *The Unbearable Lightness of Being?*" I laughed, tapping the label where the title of the book was listed.

"No, another book I read based on soulmates," he smiled at the memory. "I'll have to read it to you. After a few glasses of wine." He shook the bottle and placed it into the basket.

Halfway home, the sky parted and rain broke, and we ran the rest of the way until we reached our gate and crossed our bridge to our front door, drenched. Ollie dropped the bag in the kitchen as I started the bath, plugging the drain and sprinkling in bath salts. I heard his phone from the kitchen, which had been going off all night, but he didn't answer. It was probably Leigh again, who'd rang nonstop at least once a week and beg for him to come rescue her from situations she'd get herself into. At first, Ollie had left to help her, but after two times, he'd had enough and ignored her calls.

I slipped out of my dress just as Ollie walked into the bathroom, wearing only his boxer-briefs and fedora hat over his head, the bottle of wine in one hand. "Bad news. We'll have to drink straight from the bottle. I'll have to remember to get us wine glasses."

Laughing at his wardrobe, I turned off the water as Ollie set the wine over a wooden stool beside the clawed tub before shimmying out of my black panties and sinking into the water.

"Yes," he nodded enthusiastically, losing his boxers and following right behind me.

Together, we drank the entire bottle and sat in the hot water as our fingers pruned, Ollie still wearing his fedora, and me making fun of him for it. "But it's cool," he explained, grabbing my hips and pulling me over his lap until my sex rubbed over his arousal. I arched my back, dropping my hair into the water, and Ollie's hands trailed down the center of my chest.

His mouth reached for my breast, but the hat prevented him from going any further. Giggling, I leaned forward, and my forehead collided with his chin. A harder laugh clenched my stomach as I hunched over the side of the tub. Water splashed over the rim, and I tried to recover, but Ollie's frown only made my giggle fit worse, bringing tears to my eyes and losing my breath. "Lose the hat, Ollie," I said between spurts.

His eyes glazed over. He was drunk. I loved drunk Ollie. "I don't want to."

I tilted my head and flicked up the rim of the hat, and when my palm rested over his chest, my laughter faded. Ollie's cock jerked against me, and I leaned forward, pressing my lips to his neck. His pulse ticked against my tongue, and my hips rolled over him, desperate for friction.

"Oh, that feels amazing," he whispered, tilting his head to give me more access as he dug his fingers into my sides. "Don't stop. I don't want you to stop."

My lips moved up his neck and across his jaw and to his other side. Every inch of his tattooed skin begged to be touched, and I sucked, biting him slightly. His muscles tightened, all the way down to his groin.

I kissed his chin, then his lips, tasting the rosé lingering upon the soft edges. Intoxicated, my thumb ran over them before my tongue did. Ollie grabbed the back of my head and opened his mouth, catching mine, and his tongue slipped inside, falling into a wild kiss. Buzzing and utterly savage, he lifted me until our parts aligned, and I sank over his length. Ollie gripped the edge of the tub, his knuckles turning white, with his other hand in my hair. Chests crashed, and we both got lost in each other, grinding and letting this drunken haze keep us spinning and spinning…

234

Eventually, Ollie carried me out of the tub—in his fedora hat—and we laughed as he stumbled all the way to the bed, dripping wet.

We made love all hours of the night, pausing for pastries and to start a fire, then back at it until the sun came up … Because it was a Wednesday night, and Wednesday nights should be spent making out, making love, and eating glazed croissants. We would sleep when we were dead.

By five in the morning, we had the blankets pulled around us on the back porch to watch the sunrise, our buzz long gone but still drunk on each other.

"As long as I've known you, you've always woke before the sun. Now, me? I love mornings. But you? You like your sleep. Why on earth do you always wake up at sunrise, then go back to sleep for a few more hours?" Ollie asked, tapping the tip of my nose with his pointer finger. "One of the many wonders of Mia Rose."

I thought about it for a moment, compiling the right words to explain to help him understand.

"It doesn't last very long," I said through a breath, gazing up at the sky. "It's the tiniest moment, just when the sun peaks above the skyline, but the moons still visible—when darkness and light can co-exist. It reminds me of hope, and that I wasn't alone or lost in this world. A reminder that anything is possible, even between two beings such as the sun and moon who only meet for a fraction of a second. During that small moment, together, they can create something so beautiful across the sky. I hoped that could be me, you know? That I wasn't all bad, and possibly I could do something beautiful with my life too."

Cuddled under a live oil painting, pinks, blues, and purples made up the sky—a pastel dawn. I pointed up. "See, Ollie. Look at how beautiful."

Ollie stared at me for a moment. "I am looking, love."

I turned to face him, and his lips grasped on to mine, holding our kiss for a beat longer than usual. He said nothing more as we looked up into the sky, and watched as the sun rose beside the opalescent moon, a fiery orange, bleeding into the vast gray of the night, washing out the darkness like watercolor until the moon faded and stars turned to dust.

"It's moments like these that are impossible to capture in words, but I'll never stop trying," Ollie whispered.

Every morning I'd passed by the unused room off from the kitchen. Currently, it housed a desk, desktop computer, printer, and clutter, but Ollie preferred to write in his notebook in the garden or odd places throughout the house. Ideas sprung, and at any given time, he'd have his notebook folded into his waistband with pencils always tucked everywhere, behind his ear, in his pockets, between his lips.

This morning, Ollie had put on a pot of coffee and brought a mug to me in bed before heading out for an early meeting with Laurie, then mentioned he had to later check on Leigh to make sure she hadn't gotten herself fucked.

I spent the first few hours, sipping on the hazelnut blend in my darkroom upstairs. It was my solitude, with windows blacked out and a set up with expensive equipment.

At first, I only took pictures outside in the garden. Rose bushes, and various flowers had blossomed late in June. Until the day I'd met Cora down the pathway, a little raven-haired girl, no more than eight or nine, who liked to jump puddles in her yellow rain boots. Her mom, Mrs. Morrigan, always worked in the garden out front after it rained, and gave me a few pointers on how to take care of our flowers. On days Ollie worked, her and Cora would come by, and she'd teach me her green-thumb ways.

And the flowers were prospering, and so was my photography. People quickly became my favorite muse. Cora's mom was sick, and quite often, when Mrs. Morrigan was having a bad day, I'd take Cora into the village. Together, we'd people watch as I snapped stolen moments, frowns, kisses, smiles, seeing the true beauty of human kindness through a lens.

But today Cora had to visit her dad, and I made her a promise I would visit my biological dad too. It was easy to spill my secrets to a nine-year-old, but Cora's advice was always so simple. "Just go see him."

I was nervous about revisiting Dolor and spent the rest of the morning putting together a bundle of purple freesias, pink roses, and white lilies from our garden for Dr. Conway, and grabbing a to-go cup of coffee on my way out. The taxi waited outside our gate, and I climbed in with the flowers cradled in my arms. I had no idea what I would say or how this would go, but Cora's words replayed over and over, *"Think of the absolute worst that could happen, then the best. Most of the time, what will actually happen will lie right in the center."*

She'd said her dad told her that, and that life was too short to worry, and worrying gave you frown lines.

The taxi drove through the iron gates of Dolor, and the memories from my time here gave me whiplash. "We're here, love," the old man said from the driver seat of the taxi, which smelled like stale tobacco, wearing a wool driver cap over his head. He drove around the circular driveway and parked in front of the doors. I paid my fare, exited, and walked up the steps in loose faded boyfriend jeans, tan leather slip-on's, and a plain white tee, wishing I'd throw on the romper or the dress. I'd changed so many times, but there was no going back now.

I drew in a breath and opened the door.

"I'm here to see Dr. Conway, and Lynch," I almost stuttered, but remained cool as the new security guard studied me.

"Put the items over the conveyer belt and step through the detector." He motioned with his baton. "Arms at your side."

I did, and my heart was beating so loud as my mind betrayed me at the thought of them being able to hold me hostage again. Could they? I stepped through, and he traced my silhouette with his hand-held metal detector, paying close attention to my hips. "It's my phone. I'm a visitor," I reminded him. "Not a patient."

The security guard dropped his baton and looked over his clipboard. "I don't see you on the list for today."

"It's unexpected, I know. But Lynch will want to see me."

"Uh-huh," he grunted.

"Just … tell Lynch his daughter is here."

He looked up from his clipboard and grabbed a chorded phone from the wall. After a deep and muffled one-sided conversation, he hung up and returned to me. "We're waiting on an escort."

"I'll take her," said a low, burly voice. Just then, a large man with a scattered smile stepped forward. "I finally get to meet the amazing Mia." He laughed, his eyes twinkling.

I raised a brow. "Do I know you?"

"Jinx. I'm a friend of Oliver."

The big man was very talkative the entire way to Lynch's office, but I was thankful for the distraction because I was clutching the flowers so tight, the petals were wilting. And when we approached, Jinx knocked over the door before opening.

Lynch instantly stood and thanked him before motioning me to take a seat.

I was too nervous to sit.

"You brought me flowers?" he asked, walking around his desk and sitting over the edge. My gaze roamed over him, trying to find bits and pieces of myself. Did I get my sinister thoughts from him? Was there a darkness lurking inside him too? I'd looked at the man so many times before, yelled at him, challenged him, cried to him. He held the same tired brown eyes.

"They're for Dr. Conway."

"Of course." He swung his head to glance out the large window facing the Looney Bin, a place he'd sent me once before. "Dr. Conway. She isn't here."

"Oh." I shifted in place.

"Miss Jett," he cleared his throat, "Mia, what happened. Where were you?"

"I was fine." To this day, I kept my promise to Ethan and his secret. Perhaps I didn't owe Ethan anything, but despite what we'd been through, he was still my friend, and maybe I was the only person on earth who understood him. "I'm surprised you care, considering you didn't look for me."

Lynch dropped his head and shook it slowly. "That's not fair."

"Was it fair to keep this secret from me for two years while I was here?" Lynch had so many chances to tell me he was my father, but he didn't. "Why was I the last person to know."

"Because I had to treat you as a patient. Not a daughter. I planned to tell you, you know. On release day. But you'd already taken off before I had the chance."

I released a long and steady breath. "Well, I'm here now." I was done being angry. For so long, I'd been angry at everyone, holding so much pent up blame, rage, and grief. For once, I wanted to let it all go and not let those feelings tarnish this person I grew to be.

"Mia, I've been waiting for this moment, but I have no idea what to say. This is all new for me."

"This is new for me too."

He tapped his fingers over his desk and adjusted in place nervously. "So, where do we go from here?"

"I was thinking that maybe we could take it slow. Maybe you could tell me how you met my mom."

Lynch smiled. "I would love that."

Ollie

"Oliver," Dex sang, then laughed. "Your girl is here. You better come watch her."

"She's not my girl," I reminded him through the phone, already on my way because Leigh had texted me, begging me to rescue her. She'd said James ripped off her knickers and made her dance on a table.

It was two in the morning, and the bass from the music thumped from inside, but it wasn't the only house party going on at this hour. Constant parties went on up and down this street. Empty beer bottles littered the front steps, and I pushed my way through the door and into a house when a strong smell of stale cigarettes and even staler sex greeted me.

"Oliver!" Reggi exclaimed, and the rest of the crowd repeated, singing my name. I ignored him, my eyes scanning the bodies for Leigh. She was my ticket to Ghost, and without her, I'd never get the meeting or our freedom. Killing Ghost was my only option.

In a tight red strapless dress, Leigh swayed on top of the kitchen island as a bloke gripped her ankles, looking up her dress as she carelessly danced to hypnotic tunes with a bottle in her hand. Her blonde hair was a knotted mess over her head. Red lipstick smeared across her lips as she stumbled in red stilettos. I fisted the back of the bloke's shirt and yanked him backward. "Get the fuck off her."

The bloke flashed me a drunken smile and held up her red-lace knickers between his fingers.

"What did you do?" I threw a fist into his face, and the sea of people parted down the middle as he fell backward over the coffee table.

"Relax, Oliver," Dex said, gripping my shoulder. "Take a shot. This is a party."

"You should be watching her," I pointed out, grabbing Leigh's thighs to pull her down from the kitchen island. "I have a fucking job, a girl. I can't be here all the time." Leigh wrapped her legs around my waist, not letting off.

"You're right," he smiled, pointing at me, "You do have a fucking job. And I own you until Ghost is gone. Boys like us don't get to have relationships. You need to let her go. You need to forget her."

Forget her? Impossible. Mia Rose flowed through me, inked across every page of my soul. Did he not know you couldn't unread a book? If there was a chance, I'd find it. I'd want to read her over and over as if it were the first time all over again.

"I don't have to listen to this." I pat Leigh on the arse to motion her down. "Let's go. We're leaving."

Leigh clutched me tighter, her legs hugging my waist with her arms around my neck, clinging for dear life as she pleaded for me not to leave her here. Her bare arse was out, and every bloke who walked by ogled and moved around to get a better view, so I carried Leigh out of the house

240

and back to my car, unlatching her scrawny arms from around me to set her inside the passenger seat. She whined against my neck.

"I'm not leaving you, Leigh. I'm taking you home," I reassured her, and Leigh lifted her head and looked around, noticing we were outside. Her body slid down mine and she got into my car. I jogged around the front of the hatchback and climbed into the driver side before starting the engine. "Where do you live?"

Leigh didn't answer, and I turned my head to see her passed out beside me. I threw my head back into the headrest and let out a groan.

TWENTY-TWO

"Just like a book,
open her up and
crack her spine
for she doesn't want
to be admired.

She craves to be
devoured, provoked,
and to change
the fucking world."

OLIVER MASTERS

Ollie

// "hope she'll like it," Mia said from the passenger side as we drove to Hyde Park, admiring a photo of Summer in a vintage frame she picked out from the market.

Last week, Mia had done a maternity shoot for Summer, and we were meeting them at the British Summer Time music festival they held each year over the fields in London, wanting to get together once more before Summer had her baby.

I clutched Mia's hand, and her twelve freckles danced with her smile. "She'll love it." Mia's hair was cut short like the first time I'd met her, a little past her shoulders, and she tucked the framed picture back into the gift bag between her legs as I pulled the station wagon into a parking space. "You ready?"

The sound of an electric guitar was carried by the wind, pushing through Mia's locks as she twirled with Summer barefoot in the grass. Travis and I sat over a blanket in the grass while the girls danced in front of us as Pearl Jam played yards away on stage, and I kept my eyes on Mia as Travis talked my ear off, but all I heard was her laugh through the music. In a black romper and my fedora over her head, Mia lifted her arms high in the air as she spun.

"Earth to Ollie." Travis snapped in my face. "Still in that honeymoon stage, yeah?"

"What are you talking about?" I leaned back onto my elbows, and Mia turned to face me, a mesmerizing smile glittering her features. She waved, and I waved back.

"You know what they say about the first year."

"It'll be two years this fall."

"Bloody hell, I'm fucked." He sighed, leaning forward and dropping his arms over his knees. He twisted off the cap of his water bottle. "What's your secret?"

With Mia, it was easy. "First tip," I pat his shoulder, getting to my feet as *Last Kiss* started to play, "never let the girl dance alone, mate."

I approached Mia, grabbed her hand, and twirled her around. Her feet, pink painted nails, moved effortlessly over the grass until I had her in my arms. She clutched my shirt, and I tipped the hat back to see her face as I sang the haunting lyrics that touched a chord from what had happened last year. It was a testament to how far we'd come, and the hell we'd come back from—survivors.

Mia threw her head back. "Hold me, darling, just a little while," she sang. And we continued to sway until the only song I knew by the band came to an end. I kissed her once, twice, before sitting back over the blanket.

Mia and Summer continued to dance, and Travis shoved his shoulder into mine. "She's going to put my woman into labor if they keep dancing like that."

I chuckled, swiping my bottled water and stretching out my legs.

A dark cloud loomed over the two of us, blocking the sun, and I looked up to see Leigh staring down at me with tears in her eyes and her hands shaking. She was wearing a short jean skirt and a crop top, her long blonde hair in a braid. I straightened my back, sitting up. "What are you doing here?" My voice was in my throat. I cleared it and looked past her to where Mia slowed her dancing, watching our interaction. "You can't be here."

"Nice to see you, too," Leigh scoffed.

"Are you stalking me now?" I raised a brow, climbing to my feet. I tried to keep my voice low, but it was hard against my rising temper and the band playing in the background.

"I wouldn't have to if you'd answer my calls." A tear slipped from her eye. "You left me. I woke up in a motel room days ago alone without my knickers, having no idea where I was."

"Whoa, I didn't touch you," I argued, and leaned down to face her. I shoved my finger into my chest to prevent it from digging it into hers. "I didn't fucking touch you."

Travis's hand landed on my shoulder, and he pulled me back. "Calm down, mate. Let's take this somewhere else."

"No, Leigh, you can't just show up. How did you know I was here?"

"Summer posted about it. You wouldn't answer my calls, Oliver. You promised you'd take care of me, but you tossed me into a motel." Another tear ran down her cheek. "I was scared and alone, and you promised you'd look out for me."

I had done that. Leigh had been drunk, and I'd taken her to a safe place and left her plenty of money to get a taxi so I could get home to

Mia. I ran my hand anxiously through my hair. "We'll talk about it later. You have to leave."

"Sure, Oliver," Leigh crossed her arms over her chest, "I'll just find a ride with one of the hundred blokes here, I'm sure any one of them would gladly take me home."

"Don't be ridiculous."

"You forget I'm sacrificing a lot for you. I'm the one who has nothing to gain and everything to lose in all this. I'm helping *you* out, and this is how you treat me?"

I gripped her shoulders, my jaw grinding, and my chest heaving. "Have I not always dropped everything to save you from situations you got yourself into?" I shouted in her face as tears flooded her eyes. "What the fuck do you want from me?"

"Whoa," Travis yanked me back, staring at me with his brows bunched together. He looked into my eyes as if he didn't recognize me. He looked at me as if I was the bad guy. I shrugged his hand off me. "I'll take Mia home. You need to deal with this," he added.

I shouldered past Leigh to Mia, who stood fifteen feet away. Her hands were small in mine, and she looked up at me under the rim of the fedora through worried eyes. "Is that her?" Mia asked, knowing well of Leigh and the things I'd done.

"Yeah, love," I tilted her hat back and grabbed her chin. "I'm sorry."

"It's okay." She squeezed my hand. "I'll see you later?"

Nodding, I held her face in my hands and curled my fingers in her hair as I kissed her, making sure to leave an imprint of security and something to look forward to until I'd return home tonight.

During the hour car ride, I'd managed to calm Leigh down. "Up here on the left," Leigh directed as I drove through her posh neighborhood with large Victorian houses, knowing I'd been here once before. We pulled into a circular driveway, and it was the same house I'd met Jinx at months ago the night of release day searching for answers to find Mia.

"The party, it was yours?"

"Step brother's," she answered, twirling the end of her braid with her finger. "I live here with him and my evil step-mum. I suppose I'm your modern-day Cinderella, with daddy issues, and all."

I pushed the gear into park. "Listen, you can't just show up wherever I am and expect me to drop everything like I just did. Life doesn't work like that. You don't just get what you want."

"I'm fully aware."

"I don't think you are." I leaned back into the seat just as a man in his twenties came through the front door. He walked down the steps, twirling a set of keys around his finger, wearing a pair of athletic shorts and a tank top. "Who's that?"

"Samuel, my perverted stepbrother," she said through a sigh. "Thanks for the ride."

When I arrived back home, I walked through the front door to the sound of dishes clanking in the kitchen and the aroma of a home-cooked meal flooding my senses. The record player in the living room was going, soft tones of an acoustic guitar. I emptied my pockets on my way, dropping my keys, phone, and wallet over the coffee table before I'd reached the kitchen. Mia was still in her little black romper, barefoot, pulling a casserole dish from the oven. My shoulder rested against the archway into the kitchen, and my eyes rested on her.

Mia's hips swayed as she waved a rag over the steam coming from the dish to the beat of the song.

She cooked. Mia Rose cooked, and I was bloody impressed. Since we moved in, we'd managed to survive on takeout. She gathered her hair into one hand and pulled it off her shoulders, admiring her work. Her head tilted, and I watched from behind with a cheeky smile as her palm rested on her hip, leaning into it.

"Marry me," I whispered from behind.

Mia jumped and spun around. Her hand slammed against her chest as she let out a breath when our eyes locked. A smile emerged from the fear, and she shook her head. "I'm already marrying you, you idiot."

I grabbed her hips, lifted her in the air, and set her over the counter. "I'm asking for the life after this one," I leaned between her legs, and her arms hung off my shoulders, "because I'll always choose you. Above all else, I'll choose you in every lifetime."

Mia narrowed her eyes. "Do you feel guilty about something?"

"Yes, I shouldn't have left you."

"I'm a big girl, Ollie. I can handle another girl having a crush on you." My palms dragged up her smooth thighs until they dipped under the thin fabric of her romper. "I cooked," she added in a scattered breath.

"I see that." My fingers curled into her flesh beneath the thin bottoms, and I discovered she wasn't wearing any knickers. "What's the occasion?"

"We have company coming over in a little bit."

"It smells good, love." I fisted the center of the cotton shorts between her legs and pulled it up into a tight rope against her sex. Her eyelids grew heavy, and I looked down and moved the flimsy material to the side to see her bare, smooth center. The way her enticing sex moved when my eyes were on them made my knees go weak. I wanted nothing more than to spend the rest of my life with my mouth on her. "How much time do I have?" We'd christened every room in the house aside from the kitchen.

"I don't know," she struggled to say, her legs closing on me. "Twenty minutes."

I wrapped my fingers around Mia's ankles and lifted her feet to the edge of the counter, then pushed my hands down the insides of her thighs as I leaned between her spread legs. "Uh-uh, I got twenty minutes." And I wanted to spend every last one of them watching her orgasm.

The track on the record player changed, and I kissed along her neck, my slow hands skimming beneath the thin romper at her sides, finding her naked breasts. Mia's hands fell off my shoulder as she rolled her head to the side, and my thumbs grazed over her nipples. Her pulse beat like a drum against the tip of my tongue, provoking me and making me high.

"Baby," I whispered, a sucker for her, and my hands drifted south to the space between her legs. With both of my hands having a firm grip over her arse, I massaged her pussy with my thumbs, pressing against her tight hole and her clit. Mia shuddered, and my nose brushed her ear before my lips caught hers possessively before we both took off.

"Oh. My. God," she said slowly, breaking our kiss, and her head fell back. I couldn't keep up, my eyes darting back and forth to her lovely face and what my hands were doing to her. "I'll marry you again and again and again …"

A smile stretched across my lips, walking on air and a little off kilter with the fate of her undoing in the palm of my hands. She was beautiful, and I didn't know this high could dance with her.

With two fingers, I spread her apart and instantly fell under a spell over her pink center and little round clit. My eyes soaked her up, every hum, every flutter of her lashes, and every fucking movement of her hips.

I looked up, my gaze slamming into hers.

And I licked my lips before my mouth wrapped around her pussy.

Dragging my tongue up and down from her entrance to her clit, Mia's legs shook. I knew the password to her moans, and my mouth worked her like a French kiss until she fisted my hair, and her sounds escaped. Our first time in the kitchen with her clenched core pounding against my tongue, she quickly came.

My girl moved like rain against me, my tongue against her hole, tasting her particular taste I craved as my free hand pulled my cock out and stroked it. I was already rock hard for her.

When I came up, Mia grabbed my face and ran her tongue up my chin and over my lips. She liked the way she tasted as much as I did.

The tip of my cock pressed against her entrance, her pussy still contracting from her climax, and I slowly inched inside her, gripping her thighs to keep them down and steady. My gaze drowned in the way we connected. It was a beautiful thing.

"Ollie," she moaned, grabbing my face desperately. I kissed her palm, the blood rushing to one area as her walls squeezed my cock, stroking me as much as I was stroking her. "I can't handle it."

"Ride it out, love." She was still rolling in the ecstasy, and I moved my thumb back over her clit to keep her there. "This is all for you." I lifted my gaze to see the way she unraveled with every deep thrust, lovely lips parted, a blush crawling over her heated skin, eyes heavy on mine. Seeing the way she lost herself with me, I couldn't help my orgasm building, and my palms slammed on the shelving behind her to hold myself back as my intense grinds turned into a pounding.

My grip turned frantic, and suddenly, the shelf ripped from the fucking wall.

Pausing mid-thrust, the entire shelving unit collapsed, dishes falling and crashing to our tiled floor. I snapped my head to Mia with wide eyes, and she looked back at me the same way.

"Fuck it. Keep going," she whimpered, and grabbed the back of my neck and pulled my mouth to hers.

Our kiss turned needy, my fingers dug into her thighs, and it only took a few more hard and deep hits until Mia came again, her frantic climax draining my own.

Her head dropped into the crook of my neck, both our breathing shallow and harsh.

"What just happened?" Mia asked into my neck.

I chuckled. "I think we'd died and gone to heaven, love."

"I never want to leave," she admitted, pulling away. Her eyes bounced back and forth between mine.

"Then, we won't. We'll live here forever, yeah? To hell with this mess."

A lazy smile appeared over her flushed face. "Nice try, but you're cleaning it up."

Cora was a bright young girl, keeping us laughing through dinner. I was sure the pot roast Mia had made with cabbage and potatoes was terrific, but unfortunately ruined. In a matter of ten minutes, I'd driven to the closest restaurant to pick up food as Mia frantically cleaned. And when I'd returned, we transferred the food into another casserole dish that had survived our havoc. Mrs. Morrigan complimented on how delicious the food was, and I winked over at Mia. "It was my first time cooking. I'm surprised I didn't burn the house down," Mia said through a small laugh.

"Pretty close to it," I mumbled, chuckling behind the rim of my wine glass.

"Well, after you remodel the kitchen, you'll never want to leave it. It's going to be beautiful," Mrs. Morrigan pointed out before spooning another forkful of the roast.

We took the bottle of wine into the garden, and Mrs. Morrigan and I sat over our rocking chairs as Mia convinced Cora to help her pick a bundle for the kitchen. The weather had been kind to us over the last few days, only mid-day showers sprinkling under the sun. Mia carried a tin pail as Cora picked a cluster of pale pink roses, setting them inside.

"Mia's so good with her," Mrs. Morrigan mentioned with her gaze and smile pointed at the two girls amongst the flowers. Mrs. Morrigan's hair was black like her daughter's, but cut short and spiked up the back. A light wind picked up, and she pulled a thick knitted scarf over her bony shoulders as she shivered. "She's got a good heart, Oliver. Don't let that one go."

My heart rattled inside my chest. Finally, someone could see Mia the way I saw her, and I glanced back over at Mia, whose hair was pulled high on her head, her neck and defined collarbone exposed against the sleeveless dress she'd changed into. "I'd never dream of it."

My phone pinged, and I dipped my fingers into the pocket of my black jeans and opened up the message.

Dex: Be at my place tonight @ 11.

I typed a text back: **Busy.**

Dex: You can bring Mia. I'd love to meet her.

My jaw flexed. I quickly sent another text: **You have jokes.**

A picture came through. It was Mia wearing destroyed loose denim, a crop top, and her face hiding behind a pair of aviators with a market bag hanging from her arm as she crossed the street. It had to be taken just last week, which meant Dex had eyes on her, and my vision blurred from unfathomable rage.

Dex: **I'll see you tonight.**

I'd left the car running on the curb and jumped out, running toward Adrian and James, who were both covered in blood. James came up and threw another fist across his jaw by the time I'd reached them, and I pushed myself between the two and smashed my palms against James's chest to hold him back. "What's wrong with you, mate? Cool off!"

I turned back to see Adrian swiping his fingers under his nose, regaining his balance.

"He came at me!" James shouted, pointing the finger at Adrian.

Blood soaked both of their shirts, and there was too much for it to come from either one of them. I pulled my hands back and took a step off to the side, my heart pounding hard inside my chest. "What happened?"

"It was a deal gone wrong," Adrian frantically explained, gripping the back of his neck with both hands. "Reggi, man. He's gone. And it's all your fucking fault." He launched at James again.

I jumped to intercept and gripped Adrian's shoulders, I couldn't hear anything aside from my anger and the heavy thumps inside my chest. "No, no, no. Tell me it isn't what I'm thinking." I fisted his blood-stained shirt and smashed my forehead to his. "Tell me he's not dead."

"He's dead," James confirmed from behind me, and I pushed off Adrian and ran my hands through my hair over and over, shaking my head. "I didn't know. We were dealing with the fucking BOGs. They got one over us."

"You set it up!" Adrian shouted. "Admit it, James. You're jumping ship."

"It isn't like that, man. It wasn't supposed to go down like that."

My arms flew up at my sides. "You're scared, yeah? Dex is taking off, and you're scared he's not bringing you along." James had gotten nervous, made moves with the enemy for a place to go once Ghost was dead, and the Links would be nothing but a heap of rusty and brittle metal. "You're out."

"You can't push me out," James laughed. "It's not your call to make."

Without thinking, I grabbed Adrian's gun from around his back, knowing it was tucked into his waistband, and cocked it before pointing it at James. "It's my fucking call. You're done." James couldn't be trusted anymore. James had gripped loyalty in his fist and crumbled it as soon as he made that deal with the BOGs. I cared too much about Adrian to watch him fall to ash at the hands of fear. I'd known desperation, and how far some of us would be willing to go. I couldn't take the chance. "Run along, James. And if I ever fucking see you again, I won't hesitate."

James' eyes bounced back and forth between the two of us before he swiped his jacket off the lawn. "Watch your back, A." He lifted his chin, taking a step back. "At least I know I'll be protected when the Links fall."

Then James shook his head, turned, and walked away from us.

Adrian and I entered the home, and Dex was posted in the kitchen, counting money with a blunt between his lips. He held up a finger before licking it and sifting through the filthy heap of dosh, then pounded the stack over the counter and wrapped a band around it. "Take a look at the pictures and tell me what you think." He slid his phone across the counter.

One of his men died tonight, and Dex's calm behavior only fed the fury burning inside me. I snatched the phone from the counter, and my gaze scattered over numerous naked photos of Leigh. My finger scrolled through the shots, one right after the other of her lying over a pink comforter in a princess-style bed, breasts out, and a finger between her teeth. The last one was her on all fours, and her head turned back with a frown. "Who took these?"

"Hell if I know. They're good, right? I'm sending them over to my contact to confirm the appointment. She's perfect." He grabbed his phone from my clenched fist and admired her picture, smoke spilling from between his lips and over the screen. "Too bad we need her innocent for the exchange, the virgin's pussy is gonna make me a lot of money." His finger ran over the screen, and I looked up to see the sick bloke smile.

"We're not actually doing an exchange," I reminded him. "I'm killing Ghost before I hand her over."

"Yeah, right." Dex clicked off the phone when the screen turned black and pocketed it.

"Dex …" I hissed. "What exactly is the plan?" There was something he wasn't telling me, and I didn't like walking into this appointment blind.

"For right now, it's a need to know basis." He took another long drag of the blunt before holding it out in front of me between two fingers. "Don't fuck this up, Oliver. You have one shot at this."

TWENTY-THREE

"Let's get drunk on cheap rosé,
confess our darkest secrets and
create playlists of our best mistakes.
Kiss me like crazy
in this magical dark place
that doesn't have a name
but where we're both free."

OLIVER MASTERS

Mia

Baby Lehman arrived two weeks late on August 7th, and I'd fallen asleep in Ollie's lap as we waited in the waiting area for Summer to deliver him. There had been complications, and Summer was rushed into the operating room for an unplanned C-Section, but after a grueling sixteen hours, Ollie and I stood over the bed as Summer cradled her son.

"Do you want to hold him?" Summer asked, looking up at me through tired but joyous blue eyes.

"Oh, no. I couldn't." I'd never held a baby before, and I'd always destroyed everything my hands came across. "Trust me. You don't want me to hold your child."

"Here," Ollie spoke up, taking little Turner from Summer. The baby was tiny, tucking flawlessly inside his strong arms. Turner gripped his finger, big new eyes staring up at him, and the sight brought a ping in my chest. Ollie turned to face me. "It's okay, love." I caved to the pressure and held out my arms, and Ollie sank the baby inside. "See?" he moved my hair off my shoulder and over my back. "You were made for this."

Speechless, I brushed over Turner's soft arm with my pointer finger. "You guys made this," I whispered in amazement. "It's true. Love really does breathe life into this world."

"It's true. Couples who are always together end up talking like each other." Travis laughed, and I carefully rested Turner back into Summer's arms.

Hand in hand, Ollie and I walked back to the car after saying our goodbyes to the new family of three. He opened the car door for me, and I settled into the passenger seat, quickly wiping away tears that had fallen. It could have easily been from the lack of sleep over the last forty-eight hours since Summer first started having contractions, and maybe exhaustion was getting the better of me. But if I was honest with myself, it had been the way Ollie's eyes lit up at Turner and knowing I'd never be able to give him that.

"Mia, you're crying." Ollie turned in the car before starting the engine and took my hand. "Why are you crying? What's wrong?"

I rubbed my eyes, then shook hair away from my face before taking a deep breath. "I think I'm just really tired."

"Oh, no. Don't hide from me, tell me what's going on." His hand hit the nape of my neck, and he gave it a gentle squeeze before it trailed down my back. "Is it the baby?"

"Would you be happy if it was just us? For the rest of our lives, just you and me, no babies?" The conversation had always come so easily for us. We'd talked about our future, what we both wanted, and made jokes and deals about how many I'd owe him, but never thought I would be unable to give him one.

"Are you changing your mind, Mia? You don't want kids with me?"

I looked over at him, and his face was frozen, lips parted, eyes unblinking as he waited for the punch to the gut. "I do, I just can't," I wiped another slipped tear, "I can't have kids, Ollie. I haven't been on birth control since we left Dolor, and it's not like we purposely tried, but we never prevented it either. For months, you came inside me and nothing's happ—"

"Mia," Ollie interrupted. "You're rambling. I can't understand. What are you saying?"

"I'm saying this is my punishment for everything I've done." *For the morbid thoughts that go through my head.* "I know it. We haven't gotten pregnant yet, and I don't think we ever will. I don't think I can get pregnant, Ollie."

Ollie turned his head, his thoughts consuming him, and I wanted to hear what they had to say. I wanted inside his head, but then I didn't. I was terrified.

"You're sure?" he asked, and there were only a few times I'd heard his voice so clipped and distant.

More tears trembled at the corners of my eyes, and when I nodded, they fell without permission. "I'm sorry."

Ollie got out of the car, and my gaze blurred as my eyes glossed over from the disconnection, and I watched him round the car to the passenger side and opened my door. He crouched down beside the seat and grabbed my hands from my lap. "Listen to me. It's you and me, evermore. Remember?" I nodded. Ollie squeezed my hand, sucked in a breath, and let it out slowly. "Being with you is more than enough. You will always be more than enough. And if it's just you and me at the end of all this, we'll just have to keep our youth 'til we're seventy and put all the youngins to shame. We'll make out in public, dance in streets, and play footsie under the table at the book club meetings like two geezers in love. You and I, forever."

I smiled. "Evermore."

"Come here." He lifted me out of the car and pulled me into a tight hug.

"Tell me something you've never told anyone," Ollie asked, then sipped his wine as we sat outside with my feet in his lap. His thumb kneaded my sock-covered heel. "Something you've never told me."

"You know all my secrets," I said through a forced smile, guilt teasing me and my murderous thoughts. Perhaps Ollie really did know me, and I, him, but maybe there was something he wanted to get off his chest, and I leaned in, resting my elbow over the arm of the chair and dangling my wine glass in the air. He opened the door, and I couldn't hold it in anymore. "Okay, I'll bite. When I shot my uncle and watched the lights go out, I liked it. There was something about being there for his last breath, having control whether or not he lived or died. All the pain and shame he brought me for years just … slipped away, and I wanted to lay there in his blood and fall asleep in the peace of death from many nights of torment." Ollie stared at me from the other end, and I hadn't noticed the way his hand stopped moving over my feet. "His life was in my hands, and I took it, and I realize now that I liked it. And I'd thought about doing it again." I leaned back and took another sip of my wine, waiting to hear a reaction out of him. It was my darkest truth, something that had taken so long to admit to myself. "Your turn."

Ollie moved his hand again, pressing his thumb in the center of my foot. He took another sip before clearing his throat, averting his gaze to my feet in his lap. "When I fingered that girl, Leigh, I struggled to not imagine doing other things to her, you know. I wondered if she tastes like you. If my dick would respond to her the way it responds to you. If it would feel the same way." He quickly glanced at me before downing the rest of his wine. "But then the drugs wore off, and I feel sick about it. Because there is no me without you. It would never be the same."

I laughed. "So, you're a guy?"

"Hey, I didn't laugh about your thing. That took a lot for me to say out loud."

"I'm sorry, you're right. But, Ollie, that sounds completely normal to me."

"It's not. I have self-control. No woman can turn me on the way you can. But when I'm high on something, it's like this savage beast takes over my thoughts. I'm so scared something's going to happen with this whole Dex and Leigh situation, and you'll leave me for good. That I'll dig myself a deep fucking grave and have to lie in it without you."

"I'll bury you next to George Eliot," I stated simply. "Tombstone etched with, *Here lies Oliver Masters, surrendered to his savage cock and killed off by his blood-thirsty wife … Hyphen, poet.*"

Ollie lifted his finger in the air. "Can't forget the *poet* part."

"Never, and I'd never leave you, Ollie," I added, settling his worries. "This life is full of making mistakes and growing from them. And I want to make mistakes and grow with you."

Ollie lifted his wine glass in the air. "Here's to spilling secrets, making mistakes, and kissing with wine-stained lips."

And we cheered, kissed, and sat back like the conversation we'd just had was completely normal.

But after many seconds passed, Ollie lifted his head and returned his compassionate gaze to me. "Mia?" he whispered, calling my attention as his hands massaged my foot again. "I know, love. I've always known, and you never have to be afraid to talk to me about the things that go through your mind. No matter how dark, I'm here for it."

The hours carried through the night. Ollie flipped the pancakes over, singing to *The Beatles* and wearing his black torn jeans with the button undone and his faded tattoos on full display. We'd switched out wine for coffee as the night played on, and he, finally, made this moment real for me. I held out a plate as he dropped two stacks over it. "You know what time it is, love?"

"It's three a.m."

He winked and pointed the spatula at me. "I told you we'd be here, didn't I?"

Ollie

I had very little obsessions, and the history of bookstores was one of them. When I'd received the phone call from Foyles, which was once the largest bookstore in the world, and they had invited me to do a signing, I'd jumped from the bed, waking Mia in the process. It had been at ten in the morning when I'd received their call, and we celebrated, jumping over the bed for an hour before rushing to get dressed so I could show off Foyles and bombard her with facts of their history the entire way to the store. The signing wouldn't have been for a few weeks, but she had to see the place.

That was two weeks ago, and the memory of Mia and I walking across the brick storefront faded, and the long line of eagerly waiting readers took its place, clutching my book in their arms under canopies of umbrellas, hiding from the rain. "Foyles," Travis stated, pulling up to the curb and shifting the gear into park. "This place is legit."

"Thirty miles of shelf space. Used to be the largest bookstore in the world," I went on, going over the same information I'd told Mia. I couldn't help it. "Two brothers back in 1903, and now look. Over an entire century later, look at what it has become. You know, William Foyles supposedly covered the roof with copies of *Mein Kampf* to ward off bombs during the world war. It means *my fight*, and a bomb dropped right across the street, left a big crater. While they were fixing it, William fed the sappers sandwiches and ginger beer while they worked, and when the bridge was completed, they named it Foyle Bridge after him. Cool, right? Human kindness can go a long way, making and marking a dent in

259

history." I pried my eyes away from the brick storefront and crowd to see Travis's mouth pressed together and brows twisted. "What? It's interesting."

"It's annoying. Tell me, when you swallowed the encyclopedia, was it before or after your collection of history books?"

I'd forgotten my audience and opened the car door, wiggling my brows. "Whatever, man. Mia eats that shite up like it's candy."

The atmosphere inside Foyles was the opposite of Daunt Books. With four floors, clean and modern lines, crisp white walls, and glass railings, books became the main focus and only color inside the large building, which expanded over 37,000 square feet. My table rested on the bottom floor under words that read, *"Welcome book lovers, you are among friends,"* and after Laurie, Travis, and I set up, a Foyles' employer allowed the line of people in from the rain outside.

My second book signing and Mia couldn't be here to experience it with me. It pained her not to be here, but Cora's mum had a bad day yesterday and was in the hospital. Mia had been there all night and had messaged me this morning, saying she was bringing Cora back to the house so the two could get some shut-eye. I'd told her there would be plenty of other opportunities with events.

For hours, I'd signed, smiled, and took photos as Travis kept the line moving along, and about halfway through, I'd felt myself slipping.

I pushed my fingers through my hair when Laurie placed a tea in front of me, one from the café located inside the bookstore, knowing I was slowly losing it. She fixed the black-rimmed glasses covering her eyes and leaned down to my ear. "You only have an hour left, then you're done."

Nodding, I forced a smile as another girl approached the table.

Though I was utterly grateful for their support and presence, the excitement overload tested my nerves and stole my energy. It had been enough to cause my hairline to sweat and my vision to defy me. I sipped the tea before signing the next book, pushing my forehead over the sleeve of my shirt.

The next person tossed my book over the table, and two large hands gripped the edge as he leaned over. "We need to talk," he said.

I glanced up from my tea until my gaze settled on Ethan Scott.

My jaw clenched as he and his red hair violated my space.

It was the anger I'd felt first. A searing white heat rolled over my skin in waves, and I had no control over my next actions. Ethan was the reason I was in this bloody mess with the Links to begin with. The Leigh Situation. Dex Sullivan. The death of my brother. All to get Mia back from him. He was the reason Mia had once questioned me, our relationship, and even herself. She'd been through Hell's fire and came back with even more internal injuries than before, and his sinister eyes caused my fingers to twitch and my mind to blackout.

The table flipped up, tea spilling, and hands grabbed my shirt, attempting to yank me back as I launched at him. "I'm going to fucking kill you," I seethed, balling the neckline of his shirt into my fists and walking him backward against the line of people.

Gasping, the crowd parted, and shrieks came from somewhere, but my only focus was on Ethan as he tried pushing against me. We both toppled to the ground, and the painful memories washed over me. The waiting for her, the searching, the drinking, the crying, the agonizing ache inside my chest burned, reminding me of what life would have been like without her, and my fist pounded into his cheekbone, but I couldn't stop myself. Blood splashed up into my face, and Travis grabbed both my arms and pulled me against his chest.

A cold gust of wind hit me, and Scott and I stared at one another in an alleyway. I nursed my knuckles, holding them out against the rain and pulling the wound between my lips. Scott dropped his head back, rain falling over his bruised and bloody face, neither one of us saying anything.

"I'm sorry," Scott finally declared, lowering his head to look at me.

It was blatant I wouldn't be welcomed back at Foyles, a place I'd fantasized about since I was a kid. I dropped my head until it hit the brick, more upset with myself for letting my emotions win this time.

"I didn't mean for it to all go down the way it did," he continued. "I reacted. And yeah, I bloody took the girl, all right? I never hurt her. I got fucking scared, and I took her. That's it. When I realized what I'd done, I returned her."

A humorless laugh rolled off my tongue. "You returned her," I shook my head, "Thanks, mate, but she's not a fucking object, and the only reason you're breathing right now is because I'd promised Mia I would let you live."

My hands shook, ready to break the promise, and Ethan averted his eyes when he asked, "She's back with you?"

I raised my arms at my sides. "Where else would Mia be?" It wasn't supposed to come off arrogant, but Mia and I belonged together. I didn't understand why the entire world couldn't see and accept it already. I wanted my scream to shake this earth, shouting that love had and would always win. That nothing could tear us apart. If Scott had returned to rip her away, it would be the last mistake he'd ever make.

"Forget it, you're right."

"What are you doing here, Scott?"

"I went back to Bruce's, and she wasn't there. I had to make sure she was okay. When I didn't see Mia sitting next to you, I thought … Actually, I didn't know what I thought. Maybe she'd chosen me. That maybe I was wrong in letting her go. It was fucked up the way I left her. I don't know, I just wanted to see her one last time and to tell you—"

"I'll never trust you," I quickly said.

Travis's car pulled up at the end of the alley, and a few honks bounced off the narrow walls.

Glancing back, Scott climbed to his feet, his clothes heavy and soaked. "I thought you should know, I'm breaking Tommy out," he announced, and I turned my entire body back in his direction. "I know the promise you made to Zeke before he died, that you'd do whatever you could to free Tommy. Well, I'm breaking the bloke out. For Livy. For Zeke. For redemption …" he continued. I swiped my palm down my wet face and dropped my hands over my hip bones, unsure of what he was asking of me or where this was going. "And I don't want your help. Just take care of her, Masters. Mia deserves so much more than the horrors of this world, and you're the only person who can give her that. I'll take care of the promise you made to Zeke and free Tommy."

"It still doesn't change anything."

Scott laughed, pressing his hand against his bruised face. "I wasn't expecting it would."

Besides, it had.

As I walked back to the car, with Ethan Scott behind me, a burden I hadn't known was there, lifted. No longer did I want to kill him, knowing he'd take care of the last thing weighing me down since Zeke had died, and I dragged in a long breath as the rain slammed against my cheeks.

TWENTY-FOUR

"..."

OLIVER MASTERS

Ethan

The air was thick with a nightly rainfall on the horizon. The taunting threat of a storm simmered an eerie scent of destruction. An intuition, if you would? Or maybe the universe was revealing a fortune no one should endure, especially Mia.

Both of my helpless eyes peered through the window of their home. Mia played over the piano, a familiar tune floating through space between us. Brown hair twisted lazily over her head, wearing only a white tee and plaid pajama shorts. Ollie walked through the living space sipping from a mug in one hand, holding a book in the other. The fool's eyes glued to Mia before he dropped over their large couch and flipped open a book.

I should have left days ago, but had to make sure she was okay. It wasn't like I was obsessed with the girl, but Masters was too delicate to satisfy and entertain her fierce mind from spiraling to the pits of boredom.

I knew because Mia and I were the same. We weren't designed for contentment or a life consisting of marriage, babies, work, and routine. And even though I was the only one who could free her wild mind and feed the desires burning inside her, she chose Masters.

Ollie spoke, but I couldn't hear from here, and Mia turned to face him, a smile dazzling her features. She stood, walked over to Masters, and took his hand. The two disappeared from my view. I hadn't realized how much time had passed with me watching like a creep until the lights went out, and a chill ran down my spine.

I bet he couldn't fuck her like I could, and a laugh fell from my lips and onto the empty street, their mailbox my audience. Laughing, because all I could picture was Masters struggling to maneuver her parts during a lousy game of foreplay. Laughing, because he was inside with her this very moment, having the chance, and I was still standing out here in the cold.

My laughter died, and I made the half-mile journey back to my car. Mia was okay, and it was all I needed to make sure of. It took every bit of strength not to burst through their front door and tell her I was sorry for leaving her the way I did, but I'd already made my decision, and she made hers.

When I got into my car, my reflection in the rearview mirror greeted me.

Masters took me by surprise back at Foyles. I had been under the impression Foyles was a safe territory with his fans surrounding him. The last thing I'd expected was for him to launch at me in public and on display. Perhaps I underestimated the pussy all along, but that was the second and last time I'd let him paint my face with his impressive fists. If he had taken what was mine, I'd probably attempt to kill him too, not even bothering with a fucking needle or hanging. I'd chop him up into pieces and spread them over New Forest National Park, where the wild animals could eat away the rest of him.

But Mia chose him, and I had to respect that.

She was never mine.

So, Masters was safe.

Dean, my best mate with connections, called on my way to the motel. Over the last few weeks, the two of us had been making arrangements for Tommy's escape. There was no way I could move on without freeing him. I'd tried that already. As soon as I'd dropped Mia off at Bruce's and made it halfway across the states, a calling nagged from above. I'd never forgotten the way Zeke used to look at me back at Dolor, and I've been feeling that tormenting gaze deep within my dark soul ever since. He never had to ask or say the words, but he and Tommy both had known I was their only chance. And because Tommy was the man my sister fell in love with, freeing him was the last thing I needed to do before the monster inside dissolved to nothing.

I'd be free too.

"You should see this town, man. I'm positive this is where they snatched up the cast for the movie *The Hills Have Eyes*," Dean said into the phone.

"Haven't seen it," I clipped out. I never watched the telly. It bored me.

"In any case, of all places, this is where Luke brings us. My brother has lost his fucking mind."

Dean was still vague about who they were and what they did, but I had always rolled with the conversations and the little bits of information he fed me. He needed to vent, and I needed the distraction. "Sorry, man. How are we looking on time?" Dean needed to be here for Tommy's escape, and I was going stir crazy being in the same town as Mia and Masters, itching to change my mind and take her back against her will. Seeing her only made me miss the chaos and challenge. My puppet. The warm side of my bed.

A heavy sigh came through the other end of the phone. "Depends on Luke." Family came first. Dean's loyalty was his religion. If he weren't doing me favors to make this mission a whole lot smoother, I'd do it myself. I needed Dean, and the lifespan of my monster were in the hands of his brother. *Cheers.* "Give me six months. I know it seems long, but trust me, man. Six months, and I'll be on the red-eye coming your way. Keep yourself busy 'til then."

Suppressing a groan, I nodded as if he could see. "Six months. I'm counting on you, mate. If you're not here in six months, you'll be freeing two chaps from prison."

"Six months. I'll call you after the holidays to check in. Stay out of trouble."

The phone disconnected, and it dropped over my lap as I turned into the flat I was renting under the fictitious name and identification Dean mailed me.

Ben O. Verbich.

The bloke had a sense of humor, and I finally had a timeline to plan around.

But tonight, I wasn't going to let Masters be the only one to smash. For over a year, Mia fucked with my head to the point I haven't buried myself inside a fanny since laying eyes on her. The night, and every night after this, called for straight rum and a local slag, the only two things able to warm me through this long, cold winter and turn Mia into a stranger.

In six months, Mia Rose Jett would be nothing more than a memory.

In six months, Dean would be here, and we could finally free Tommy.

In six months, the monster would be gone.

TWENTY-FIVE

"Lovers dip their feet in galaxies
and run with the unknown because
dreamers belong among stars,
and soulmates make love
to adventure."

OLIVER MASTERS

Mia

October's cold front blew angrily while Cora's little hand clutched mine as she stood over her mom's grave in a bright yellow dress with sunflowers printed sporadically, cowgirl boots covering her feet. The weather was only getting colder as we entered the month, but the sunflower dress was important to Cora as she fought back shivers. Friends and family of Mrs. Morrigan had left a while ago, but Cora wasn't ready to say goodbye.

I glanced up to see Ollie holding both of Grammy's hands as they spoke, but the distance between us ate their words.

Soon, Cora would have to leave to live in Ireland with her grandmother, and though it was incredibly hard for me to say goodbye to the first friend I'd grown close with since I came back, I had to be strong and remind her of all the new adventures she'd experience. A new country, new friends, new flowers to dance with, and new puddles to jump in. "This is just where her body lays, Cora. But no matter where you are, her spirit is with you. It's never goodbye."

"You're just saying that because my mum is dead. You're saying that to make me feel better," she whispered. "I'm not stupid. I know what it's like. My dad's dead too."

Though she came up to my chest, I still crouched down and smoothed my black lace dress under my thighs to not physically talk down to her. "You have two guardian angels, Cora. They are watching you now, and it's your job to make sure you give them the best and most beautiful life for them to see until you're all together again."

"Do you have a guardian angel?"

Smiling, I nodded. "And I hear Ireland has castles, and rolling hills, and fields of rare pale purple flowers …"

"Does it rain in Ireland?"

"It does."

"Do they have boys who tell stories like Oliver?"

I laughed at her choice of words. "They have boys who tell stories everywhere. There is not a shortage. I can promise that."

Cora looked up to the sky and closed her eyes, her black hair twisted around her lightly freckled face as she wordlessly communicated to her mom and dad. Perhaps she was saying goodbye, or maybe she was praying. A gust of wind twirled, picking up loose petals from the bundle of flowers cradled in her arms, and they ended up in her hair. "Thank you," she whispered with a smile of innocence and strength.

We helped Grammy pack up the car with Cora's things and stood outside our cottage behind the gate. Cora blew hot air against the window from inside the car, and her little finger pressed against it, drawing a heart and a flower. Ollie's arm hung over my shoulder, and he pulled me close to his side as we waved the two off. The rattling exhaust pipe sputtered a cloud of smoke before the old town car took off down the road with Cora's nose pressed against the glass, waving back.

"Let's go to Gibraltar," I stated, both our eyes on the back of the town car. "Ten-ten-twenty-twenty." It was almost a year ago when we'd made the promise. But at that time, it wasn't just a promise. It was so much more. A future. Plans. You and I. Evermore.

Ollie's head snapped to face me, and his arm fell off my shoulder. Green eyes bounced between mine. His lips parted. "Holy hell, you're bloody serious."

"I'm totally serious. Let's go. Right now, Ollie. Who else has to die to remind us to start living? Blind, no plans, let's just pack our shit and go to Gibraltar and get married. Ten-ten-twenty-twenty, Ollie. I'm so ready." Ready to marry him. Ready to be Mia Masters. Ready to finally feel the ocean against my feet, itching for those icy cold waves of freedom since I'd told him back at Dolor in our first year.

Dimples deepened as a smile spread under his sparkling green eyes. It was the same smile I'd seen across the room during breakfast back at Dolor, at the end of hallways as classes changed, and in his dorm as he watched me dance in the middle of the night. Through all the death and darkness we'd been through, it was his smile shining light over our shattered life. It crumbled walls, clutched hope, and pulled us from the depths of despair—a single smile, and as if it was not enough, he kissed me.

We talked through our plans for the trip as we shoved clothes in a large suitcase, deciding on driving to the Port of Portsmouth and taking the ferry to Spain. We would figure out the rest upon arrival, both of us on a natural high and unable to think clearly.

"Don't forget the passports," I called out, changing out of the black lace dress and into something more comfortable for travel. Ollie came through our bedroom door with our documents in hand and laid them over the suitcase. He'd already changed into his grey joggers and a black hoodie, his brown hair styled into his backward wave. His eyes glued to my hips as I shimmied into a pair of ripped high-waisted jeans. "Stop, I can hear your thoughts from here, and we don't have time. The ferry leaves in two hours."

"There's always time for pleasure."

"Not the way you do it," I pointed out, my eyes traveling down to the bulge straining inside his joggers, and Ollie did nothing to hide his arousal.

He raised his brows. "See something you fancy, love?"

I took off my bra and tossed it over his head, and Ollie caught it mid-air before he flung it behind him, picked me up, and threw me over the bed. "Six minutes," he breathed into my neck, his length digging against my core. He pushed my arms above my head and moved his mouth over my already hard nipple. "All I need is six minutes." His hands cupped both breasts before they dragged down my sides. "One to admire you. Two to taste you. And three to lose myself inside you." And he hooked his fingers into my waistband, peeling them off me. "Six minutes."

Ollie took twenty-one.

The drive to the Port of Portsmouth was only an hour, and we arrived just in time for the last call to board the white ship with the navy-blue Brittany Ferry logo, heading to Bilbao, Spain. I'd never been on a boat before, and my eyes feasted on a whole new world living within the walls of the ship. Walkways around the outskirts of the ship lined in glass, overlooking the vast blue ocean. Everywhere my eyes landed, I noticed new shops, dining areas, bars, and stages for entertainment. Certainly, we couldn't fit everything inside a thirty-six-hour window on the ship before we reached Spain.

When we reached our small room, complete with two twin-sized beds, we'd noticed our suitcase had already arrived. "Don't worry, love. We won't be sleeping."

"Crap-bag!" someone yelled, and the single name had my jaw drop, my heart in my throat, and my eyes bulging from their sockets. Ollie lifted his shoulder as a smug grin formed, and he nudged his head to behind me. "I was wondering when there would be a fucking wedding. Maid of honor, remember? I called it …"

"Jake," I cried, twirling to see him standing in the doorway, still rambling with one hand planted over the doorframe. Liam hunched over behind him, arms filled with bags and out of breath. "How in the world…when…what?"

Then I was in his arms, and Jake lifted me off the ground in a bear hug. "Ollie sent a text, said it's time. You think I'd miss my maid of honor duties?"

"I told Ollie three hours ago!" I turned to face Ollie, who had his arms crossed over his chest as he relaxed against a table in the small room. Tears fell freely down my face. "I told you like three hours ago! How?"

Ollie only lifted his shoulders again in response.

Jake pumped his fist in the air. "I'm maid of honor bitches!"

The mid-fifties temperature brought strong winds against the ship from the Bay of Biscay, and the four of us bundled up at the stern of the boat. With the sunset came a fiery sky, burning the day into the same colors you'd see on a battlefield. It seemed like forever had passed since Mrs. Morrigan's funeral and saying goodbye to Cora, but it was only hours ago, and we'd conquered the somber day, and the night was near. The dying sun's reflection bounced off the deep blue bay, creating stars over the water. Ollie held me closer.

Dinner had passed, and we sipped on spiced apple hot toddy's. The warm bourbon mixed with cinnamon slithered down my throat, warming my chest through the cold winds of October.

"I still can't believe it," Jake shook his head, "Lynch is your dad."

"Bloody hell, I fucked the Devil's daughter," Liam muttered, hair cut short, matching Jake's. "Forgive me, Lord, for I have sinned."

"Don't remind me, mate," Ollie growled.

"Lynch isn't so bad," I said, leaning back against Ollie's tall frame. "We have lunch once a week now in Shere Village. He has this dry sense of humor I've never noticed before. But enough about Lynch, I want to hear what you two have been up to."

Jake and Liam exchanged a smile, and Jake turned to face me as Liam ran his palm down Jake's covered arm. "We're moving in before the holiday."

"Oh, Jake, that's amazing." I grabbed his free hand and gave it a squeeze. "Where are you guys moving to?"

"Liam's actually from Manchester, and I'm from Windsor, so the long-distance has been killing us over the last six months. As long as we can both find work in or outside of London, that's where we're going." Jake glanced over at Liam, his blue eyes lighting up. "Liam has a job with a tech company but believes he can transfer. I'm back in school, working part-time."

"What are you in school for?" I asked, my eyes sliding between the two of them and noticing the way they smiled at each other.

"I want to get my teaching degree."

We spent the rest of our night catching up while our drinks overflowed. Eventually, the chatter settled, and the four of us curled up over the poolside chairs, wrapped up in pillows and blankets under galaxies and the matte black sky above. Ollie and I tangled with one another, looking up at the stars. "Thank you," I whispered, my head resting into his warm neck. "For Jake. Not so much Liam, but I suppose they're a package deal now."

Ollie's chest rumbled against me as he quietly laughed. "It wouldn't have been the same without Jake here." His palm held my cheek as he pressed his lips against my head, then returned his eyes toward the sky. "You say there's something about sunrises, but for me, there is something about the mid-night sky. When the lights go out, the world opens up. Quiet. Peaceful." A shiver ran through Ollie, and he released a long exhale. "The unknown isn't so scary when it's this spectacular."

"What are you proposing?"

"I say after the wedding, after I'm done with Dex, we take off and travel the world. I can collect my poetry and get my second book together, and it would be a great opportunity for your photography. We can tag-team the Earth. You and I. What do you say, love? Are you ready for an adventure?" The excitement in his tone moved through me—an electric current of curiosity.

I didn't ask about our home, about Lynch, or the life we'd made in the last five months. Traveling had always been Ollie's dream, to meet people from all walks of life and experience the greatest wonders this world had to offer. And I wanted nothing more than to capture every single smile and spark in his eyes. "I've been ready."

With one eye barely opened, I was staring at a little boy who was staring down at me, wearing a puffer jacket with his head covered in a knitted cap pulled tightly over his head. "Mum!" he called out, pointing down at Ollie and me with a twisted expression. "Are they dead?"

"Zeke, dear, leave those two lovebirds alone, will ya?" The mom called back across the back of the ship, and the wild organ inside my chest flipped at the sound of his name.

The boy ignored her, taking a step closer as the sun beat down over us, fighting against the harsh sea winds of the early morning. "Are you in love?" he eagerly asked, and a lump formed inside my throat. Attempting to shake the shock consuming me, I nodded. "Is it forever? Because mum says when two people sleep together, the love is forever."

My head snapped up to Ollie, whose still and asleep with a blanket pulled halfway up his face, his eyes closed.

"Well?"

It was bright, and I squinted my eyes as emotions threatened to spill out over the stern and into the blue waters. "Love is forever," I confirmed, easing his troubled mind. "We are forever."

The boy smiled, turned his back to me, and took off running across the ship to his mom, shouting, "They're not dead, mum. They're in love, forever!"

"Oh, that's good, dear," his mom celebrated, sending me a wave.

I waved back and curled back under the covers, eyes wide open with every hair raised over my chilled skin, gazing out into the sea with an unbidden smile.

With Ollie, I'd learned to believe in the impossible, in the unexplainable. With Ollie, magic existed. I could have simply marked it down as a coincidence, but Zeke's presence washed over me, and I knew there was nothing else it could've been. Zeke had visited me, and perhaps it was his way of letting me know he would watch us get married from the Heaven's above.

Ollie stirred against me, breaths coming out as light moans as he woke. "Did you miss your sunrise?"

"Yeah, but I got something better."

Ollie

After thirty-six hours of sea, I was ready to be back on solid ground. The ship had docked in Bilbao, Spain at approximately six in the morning, and it was still dark as we stepped off the ship. Jake had kept his word, and he and Mia had stayed awake all hours of the night, planning the small wedding while pounding drink after drink. Both of them dragged behind Liam and me, Jake whining and Mia hiding how terrible she felt under my fedora as she quietly kept up.

Rolling the suitcase behind me, I paused to adjust the backpack over my shoulder. "Come on, love. Only a few more feet, and you'll have your steaming hot coffee."

Mia grunted, notifying me that she was still alive. I glanced back and saw her tangled brown hair, loose ripped jeans, and combat boots, tiny inside one of my hoodies that was three times her size.

We reached the snack bar at the port, and Liam and I grabbed four coffee's as Mia and Jake took a seat at the closest available table. It was still dark, everyone half asleep. "We're in fucking Spain," I dropped a coffee in front of Jake as he groaned, "time to wake up, mate."

"I hate you, Jake," Mia stated, and I chuckled, handing her the coffee.

"It's October seventh. We have three days to make it to Gibraltar to get married on ten-ten-twenty-twenty. We could either take a train across Spain, which takes thirteen hours or rent a car, which would take ten if we drive straight through," I explained. "I say we take a car. It'll be cramped, but we'll have more freedom."

Liam raised his cup to his mouth. "Car sounds good to me."

"Mia?" I asked, moving my hand under her hair to massage the back of her neck.

"Yeah, I'm down for the car."

"Sun rises in,"—I clicked on my phone and looked at the time— "two hours. We can grab breakfast and do a little sightseeing before we head out."

Enterprise didn't open until after eight, so we took a taxi to Casco Viejo, and I'd asked the driver to drop us off at his favorite place to have breakfast. My Spanish was a little rusty, his English newly developed, but together, we made it work. My three traveling companions fell asleep in the backseat as I struck a conversation with the driver. Talking to strangers had always been easy for me, as long as it wasn't in crowded areas. I thrived in intimate environments such as this—just me and Antonio, with an adventure before us and sleepy heads behind us.

In the twenty-five minutes to Casco Viejo, I'd learned Antonio just celebrated his sixty-fourth birthday with his seven children, and fifteen grandchildren, with one more on the way. He'd lived in Spain his entire life, born in Madrid, and moved to Bilbao on a whim. He had dark eyes with unruly grey strands curling from his lively brows under his Panama style hat. At around seven in the morning, his smile brightened the narrow streets of the city before the sun did.

"El Tilo de Mami Lou," Antonio announced, pulling the taxi in front of the Belgian bakery. "Perfecto, para la dama con un paladar dulce, eh?" he wiggled his bushy brows.

I'd told him my fiancé had a sweet tooth, and the old chap delivered. "Perfecto, gracias, Antonio." And I tipped him extra from the currency I'd exchanged back on the ferry.

Mia's eyes lit up as soon as we walked into the bakery with black and white checkered flooring under our feet. A glass display case before us held cupcakes, cakes, pastries, and loaves of specialty homemade bread. The quaint bakery had a baroque-style interior with bistro tables and chairs. I ordered both of us cappuccinos, complete with a dollop of whipped cream and cinnamon, and two glazed croissants. Mia added a slice of chocolate pumpkin bread before we found seating outside the building, situated across from the beautiful Arriaga Theatre, lit up by spotlights in the early dark of the morning.

"Oh-my-God," Mia moaned after her first bite into her croissant, "I needed this so bad."

"Ah, she's awake." I laughed, sipping the cappuccino. Mia nodded, then took another bite.

About forty seconds later, her croissant was gone, and she was already licking the melted chocolate chips from her fingers as Liam pardoned himself to use the loo.

We spent an hour walking up and down the Riverwalk beside the Estuary of Bilbao, stopping when the sun peeked above the historic buildings. Pale pinks, blues, and yellows bounced off the water from the changing sky, and the vintage lamp posts lining the channel went out, one by one, as the daylight arrived. A new day, a new adventure. I caged Mia inside my arms against the railing, her hair whipping under the fedora, as we admired the moment, taking it all in. I dropped my eyes to see hers closed with a lazy smile complimenting her face and dipped down, my mouth grazing the rim of her ear. Her beauty mixed with the morning breeze stole my breath, and suddenly, I forgot what I was going to say.

With marvel lit in Mia's brown eyes, the four of us walked up and down the seven streets of medieval Casco Viejo. Her camera dangled from around her neck, snapping picture after picture. We stopped and ate lunch at the Mercado de la Ribera, which was a traditional market composed of local farmers inside the walls of the Art Deco-styled building. The entire space was open, and natural light poured in through the ceiling, reflecting off the luminous flooring as merchants and travelers busily exchanged small talk and money by the delicate floral interior. We didn't stay long and crammed a lot in half a day before we rented a black suburban at a nearby Enterprise before taking off to our next destination.

Though there was another route almost an hour faster, we took the one leading us through the city of Madrid. In the rearview mirror, I glanced back where Mia and Jake fell fast asleep shortly after pulling out of the Enterprise. "They'll sleep the entire way to Madrid," I said to Liam beside me, who had his window down and eyes on the busy road out in front of us.

Never in my wildest dreams did I expect to be sitting beside Liam on my way to get married. During our time at Dolor, the two of us never particularly cared for one another. It wasn't until I'd slapped him, waking him up from denial when we finally turned a page and developed a friendship. Liam cared for Jake, and Jake was one of Mia's best friends, so in return, I couldn't have left the two out on an important day. Though the bloke had fucked my fiancé once upon a time, that was water under the bridge. Her old habits … which died hard once I came along and showed her the truth. I'd always felt the light in her, it illuminated mine.

"Who would've thought," Liam muttered, almost hearing my thoughts. "It seems like forever ago when Oliver Masters was this untouchable god at Dolor who I despised."

A laugh sputtered from my lips. "Untouchable god?"

"People listened to you, looked up to you. We were locked inside a world of criminals and users, but you …" he shook his head, "You have no idea, do you?"

"No, mate. I have no idea what you are talking about."

Liam looked back at Jake before sinking into the passenger seat. "You inspired a lot of people, Jake included. He talks about you, you know. All the fucking time," he exaggerated. "How you were the first person to talk to him and accept him. When we first got together, I was jealous, which I can admit now. But if it weren't for you, Jake wouldn't be going back to school to teach or stand up to his father. Hell, he looked up to you, mate. He saw the way you were with Mia—with Zeke, Bria, Maddie—and grew balls and a new outlook on life. You made a positive change inside Dolor, and it still blows my mind."

"Being kind can go a long way," I quickly pointed out.

"Sure, there's kindness, but then there's genuine compassion. You have a spark for people and life. You're a good man, Ollie. You sure as hell make me want to be a better one for Jake."

"It's a never-ending journey." I didn't like talking about me, so I switched gears. "Moments will come, and life will happen, but no one is perfect. We're all going through this life expecting everyone else to think, walk, and talk like us, but that's where we get it wrong as a society, because different just works. Individuality needs to be embraced. So if Jake fucks up, don't be so quick to turn your back against him, and vice-versa. Choose each other. There's my Ollie-Lesson of the day."

Liam laughed. "Thanks, mate."

The conversation rolled smoothly after that, and five hours later, we reached Madrid.

In Spain, dinner wasn't until around nine at night, and we stopped at a skivvy petrol station so I could fill up the tank, and so the two bums who slept the entire ride could freshen up and change. Mia returned to the SUV wearing ripped dark denim, so tight it could break the skin, with a casual grey tee partially tucked into her waistband, leather jacket, and combat boots. My heart stopped when my hand on the gas trigger didn't,

279

gasoline overflowing out of the tank and over my shoes. Jake barked out a cackle as he slid inside the backseat with a bag, popping candy into his mouth. "Every time," I mumbled to Liam, placing the nose of the nozzle in its resting place. "That girl gets me every bloody time."

TWENTY-SIX

"I'm yesterday's child toasting with old friends
while the night is young; buzz still fresh.
And if I'm supposed to die tonight,
slice me open with a smile
and kill me with a kiss."

OLIVER MASTERS

Mia

"HELLO, MADRID!" Jake shouted out the window from the back seat, fist pumped high in the air toward the tops of the city buildings. "It smells like this city never sleeps!"

I glanced at Ollie beside me. "And what does that smell like?"

Jake pulled back inside the Suburban as Ollie made a left down a busy, narrow street. "Like sewage, onions, and garlic," he dragged in a breath through his nose, "Yeah, it smells like someone dropped New York City right in the middle of Italy."

"You've never been to New York or Italy," Liam reminded him through a laugh.

"Hey, I heard about it."

The four of us walked through the doors of Cacao Restobar, where Edison light bulbs wrapped and dangled around tree trunks from the ceilings, and the walls curved in natural brick. The other side gave the illusion of a cave, and we found a table against an iron-bar-covered window overlooking the city. I tapped the window with my finger. "This reminds me of Dolor."

Liam rolled his eyes. "Fuck Dolor."

Ollie surprised me, being the only one who knew a lick of Spanish, and he ordered all of our drinks and food after insisting we trust him.

"That was impressive. How the hell do you know Spanish?" I asked, arching a brow.

Ollie pressed his lips together, fighting a humble smile. "How was I supposed to travel the world and talk to people without learning how they speak?"

Liam leaned into the table across from him, intrigued. "How many languages do you know?"

"Started teaching myself a long time ago, I know a tad here and there. For the most part, it's all similar once you master one, the rest comes easy. Spanish, Italian, Greek, French … I can understand it, but I'm rusty speaking since I don't speak them often."

Liam's eyes bugged out, and he dropped his fingers over his head and made a bomb sound, mimicking his mind being blown.

Our drinks arrived, decorated with fruit and flower garnishes. Ollie clutched his glass of water, and we all toasted to Madrid, friends, and Ollie's Spanish speaking skills.

After eating traditional tapas and pinchos, we walked down the colorful Cava Baja street with multi-colored banners and cloth draped above us. The locals strummed their guitar strings, beat their drums,

282

playing hypnotic rhythms up and down the crowded alleyways as people swarmed around us, dancing and enjoying the night.

"Just drink, mate," Liam said over the music to Ollie. "We'll get a hotel here tonight. It's your vacation. Enjoy yourself."

Ollie turned to me and shook his head.

"Oh, for God's sakes, Ollie." Clutching his hand, I yanked him to the nearest outdoor bar and ordered him a mojito to loosen him up.

And an hour later, Ollie had a permanent smile coasting between his dimples. In black jeans, a long-sleeve gray shirt, and bright white trainers—what he'd call them—Ollie danced behind me, his hands moving down my sides and clutching my hips, pulling my backside against his front. The beat of the music surged through our movements and echoed down the festive street. As if he were an extension of me, Ollie matched my every rock and sway. Breathing grew heavy, sweat licked our skin, and I turned in his arms when his forehead dropped to mine. With our buzz heavy and alive, Ollie licked his lips as I rolled into him. "Ah, bloody hell, love."

Giggling and stumbling through a hotel, we took an elevator up to a rooftop bar where a glass bridge laid above the city of Madrid. Fresh cold drinks frosted our hands, and the four of us admired the skyline, having complete three-sixty views. Strong October winds hit us from all directions, and my hair blew wildly. "Don't look down," Liam announced, and the rest of us looked down against his instruction through the glass bridge. People, cars, and lights scrolled under our feet as if the world had flipped upside down, and stars twinkled from below.

"This is incredible," I whispered. "You can see the world from up here."

Liam wrapped his arms around Jake, and I'd never seen Jake's blue eyes so captivated, but he wasn't looking at the view. Jake was staring into Liam's eyes. It was my favorite view tonight thus far.

And in our only night in Madrid, we claimed it as ours.

The following morning, we all woke up in the same hotel room, moaning and groaning. Liam fell asleep beside the toilet over the bathroom floor while Jake slept comfortably in the second queen-sized bed. During the entire hour, we all took turns in and out of the shower while Liam and Jake comically ignored one another.

Liam stuck to Ollie's side at the front desk while Jake and I fetched the SUV. "You should just talk to him. He's mad you left him in the bathroom," I explained as Jake pulled the car up to the entrance of the hotel to wait for Ollie and Liam.

"It'll be fine. We go through this all the time, and I think he gets off on it. Liam's dick-whipped. He'll get over it by the time we make it to Gibraltar," Jake said, and I pinched my brows and narrowed my eyes. "What? Don't believe me? This is our thing. We fight over stupid shit just to make sure the other still cares, and to have a reason for angry sex."

"Angry sex is actually a thing?"

"It's totally a thing."

Jake transferred to the back seat with Liam as Ollie slid in the driver's seat with two coffees, and for the next five hours, we rode in a comfortable silence to Gibraltar.

I kicked my feet onto the dashboard and left the window halfway down. Ollie's hand rested over my thigh as I drifted with the peaceful breeze, racing across the country of Spain, on the move to celebrate a fantasy we'd dreamt up in our heads for so long. The view captured me with every passing mile, and the warm sun hit my face as my hand surfed through the wind outside the window.

Ollie turned up the radio, the broken promises turned down, and he looked over at me, his eyes dancing with his knock-out smile. A child lived within us, seeing the world through brand new eyes and expecting nothing, only chasing freedom with the open road as our muse.

I could picture it, traveling all over the world with him. Excitement pumped inside me at the mere thought, and I kept my eyes open to not miss a damn thing.

And at around noon, we arrived. The giant crescent Rock of Gibraltar rested at the edge of the peninsula, and Ollie parked the car in front of the crystal blue waters and white sandy beach. I jumped out of the SUV, rushing to the shoreline without waiting for anyone else.

"Mia, take off your shoes!" Ollie shouted through laughter behind me.

On the way down, my fingers worked overtime to undo my laces before kicking off my boots and socks, leaving a trail in my wake. Emotions burned in my throat. Tears stung behind my eyes. The memory of us from two years ago invaded me.

"What's the first thing you're going to do when you get out of here?" Ollie asks, his fingers threading through my long locks as I lay over his chest.

I didn't have to think about it. "Put my toes in the water. What about you?"

"Find you ... then take you to the ocean," Ollie simply says, and he can't see, but I'm smiling. "I want a life with you, Mia. I've never wanted anything more. Do you think we can survive the next two years? Think we'll be able to make it?"

A sigh leaves my lips. "God, I hope so."

There is a sudden skip in his breathing. "I can't lose you," he whispers.

"You won't."

Sand flew up as I ran, and I didn't stop until my bare toes hit the ice-cold shoreline, and a wave crashed against my ankles. My eyes slammed closed, hoarding tears that shouldn't fall.

Then Ollie's chest rested against my back as our fingers intertwined. "Now, love," he whispered into my ear from behind. "Now, open your eyes."

I blinked my eyes opened, and tears fell freely. Each one for everything we'd been through to get us here. The darkness. The torment. The death. One by one, they slipped over my cheeks as Ollie wrapped his arms around me. The water swimming between my feet was a reminder that this world was so much bigger than Dolor and the miseries of our past. Undiscovered moments, untraveled territories, an entire journey laid out ahead of us for the taking. We'd made it this far but would never forget where we came from or who we met along the way.

It was October 10th, 2020.

Ten-ten-twenty-twenty.

Jake had everything under control, and no matter how many times I silently repeated this to myself, it didn't ease the nerves working against my bloodstream. Ollie and Liam had kept themselves busy yesterday as Jake and I went dress shopping. "You have to wear a dress, Mia. You're not an animal for crying out loud," had been his exact words when I'd told him I was good with a shirt and jeans. And I'd bought one against my better judgment, hoping not to be overdressed for the occasion and having no idea what I'd see Ollie in once we would arrive.

My reflection stared back at me in the mirror as Jake played with my hair, taking maid of honor roll into a whole other level. "Do you have any idea what you're doing?" I asked, music playing from my phone somewhere over the dresser, hiding among the makeup and tools he was using.

"Shhh …" he said, patting the top of my head. "You're distracting the artist."

"Artist is pushing it."

Jake twirled the desk chair around, turning me away from the mirror. "No more looking. You'll see when I'm done."

As soon as a groan left me, a knock sounded over the hotel room door.

Jake dropped the wand over the dresser and told me to sit tight with a finger out in front of him. "And don't look," he added before disappearing. The door opened, and Jake let out a squeal, coming back into the room. "Okay, I'm officially with the wrong bloke," he gushed, and in his arms was a bouquet of origami roses with burlap and a light pink ribbon tied around the wooden stems. My heart jumped inside my chest, and I fought back the happy tears threatening to ruin my mascara.

Jake examined the roses. "What book are these from?"

286

Struggling to breathe, I plucked a rose from the bouquet, and my eyes landed over Ollie's poetry. "Ours. It's our love story."

Jake handed me a note, and a tear escaped from the corner of my eye as I opened it.

Mia,

   I know what you're thinking, but no … it's not our love story …

With blurry vision, I let out a small chuckle.

   This is everything I've written since the day I met you. You give me so much love and life, my heart could never be big enough to contain it. So, I bleed onto paper, call it crimson love. Call it poetic. But it's not our love story, because my love for you never ends. You and I, we've been rooted since the beginning of time and continue to soar past the moon and sun, the two very beings you watch every morning during those small sacred moments in hopes of becoming as alluring. What you may not understand, is that you have so much light and beauty already living inside you, you bring galaxies to their knees and stars dim with envy.

   You are my sunrise, love.

   I'm telling you this now because I'm afraid I'll have no words the next time I see you. I've spent these last few months filling every promise I'd made to you so that way, as I write the following words, you have the belief they're not empty. I promise always to be the man worthy of every second spent in your presence. To be worthy of your smiles, triumphs, kisses, and yes, even tears. Thank you for making the dreamer in me never want to sleep again …

Evermore,

Ollie

I released a long breath through trembling lips, unable to hold on any longer. I had to see him. It had been a little over twelve hours, and Jake placed rules my heart couldn't take.

"No, no, no ... Stop!" Jake insisted, holding out his arms to the sides. "Mia Rose, you will *not* ruin this for me!" Pulling my hands over my face, I wiped the tears as Jake growled, pulling tissue after tissue from a box. "I knew it. As soon as I saw that letter, I bloody knew it ..." he continued to mutter as he blotted the tissue under my eyes. "There, and no more happy tears. You'll see the man in an hour. Then you can cry all the fuck you want."

A little over an hour later, Jake and I stood in front of the floor-length mirror attached behind the closet door in the hotel room as his fingers kept touching my hair.

"Jake, he's waiting," I whined, bouncing over the carpet barefoot. "It's fine. I'm fine."

The dress was a mix between bohemian and beachy, with lace detail down to the floor. What took Jake over an hour on my hair could've taken me ten minutes, my locks framing my face in semi-natural waves. The makeup, however, was impressive. I'd never known how to use the tools, and Jake applied heavy eyes with bronze cheekbones and rose-pink lips. My freckles still shining through the light blush.

"One last thing," Jake disappeared as I admired his work, "ah, here it is." He appeared behind me and fitted a flower crown over my head. "Absolute perfection."

"I don't even know what to say." Shocked could never cover it, I was gobsmacked. "I never thought I'd ever look like this, or even be standing here in a white dress. I'm getting married. This psychopath is getting married," I spun around, "I don't deserve this, Zeke. I don't deserve him. This is too much," I rambled, freak-out mode setting in.

Jake crossed his arms, smiling.

"Why are you smiling? What's so funny?"

Both of his palms landed on my shoulders. "You just called me Zeke."

I shook my head. "No, I didn't."

"Yeah, you did."

My fingers grabbed my temples, massaging circles as I paced the room. "I'm officially losing it."

"Mia, listen to me. You calling me Zeke means you feel him. He's here, ready to watch you marry Oliver fucking Masters. Do you really want to disappoint Zeke?"

"You think so? He's here?"

"Of course, he's here. He's the one walking you down the aisle."

Ollie

Mia was late, but it could be because of Jake. Liam kept reminding me of that every five minutes in hopes of lifting the nerves off my shoulders, but it didn't help. Memories from six months ago, waiting outside the gates of Dolor for her to meet me, wouldn't leave. The memories only tormented me.

The three of us stood beside the Rock of Gibraltar over the white sand, the ocean as our witness. There were no chairs, no music, no family—only Liam, Christy, and me, waiting for Mia and Jake to arrive. Christy was the lady marrying us, with short blonde hair, wearing a conservative pink dress. She wasn't a local, and I only knew this because I couldn't stop asking her questions about herself to take my mind off the time. Christy got married in this exact spot four years ago and never left Gibraltar. "This is the same spot John Lennon got married," she informed me, standing under an arch beneath the evening sun.

"Oh, yeah?" I knew this, *God*, I already knew, but my head was in another place…Wherever Mia was at the moment.

Where are you, love?

I adjusted my collar and smoothed down my khaki slacks, thinking maybe the letter I'd wrote freaked her out. But as soon as that thought came to mind, a slight wind blew through us, easing all my doubt. The last two years played out inside my head, and how I fell in love before her lips ever collided with mine. My head dropped back to face the sun, speaking against the cool October breeze. "Thank you, brother." I closed my eyes when Liam tapped my shoulder.

My head snapped forward and ... *Mia* ...

There.

She.

Is.

There is my girl, my evermore.

And there went my hands, shaking.

I pinched the bridge of my nose to fight what my emotions were doing as Mia stood across from me, twenty feet away. I wanted to run to her, but I couldn't bloody move. I wanted to tell her how beautiful she looked, but couldn't move my lips from the shape of my smile. The only thing I could do was swipe my shaking palm down my face to remove the tears to see her better. She was fucking real, and she was here.

Mia walked toward me with her heart-stopping smile, and the entire world silenced. Christy had already started talking, but I couldn't hear anything aside from my heart pounding in my ears. Jake stood behind her, and I hadn't noticed him walking over at all. The only thing in front of me was Mia, consuming all my senses.

I clutched both of her hands into mine. "Hi, love," I whispered, lost in her coffee-brown eyes.

"Hi," she whispered back, gaze darting between Christy and me.

Christy asked if we had anything to say, but 'Hi' was the only word I could manage, and I knew this would happen. Mia had always stolen words right out from this bleeding poet's mouth, shaping them into stars and lighting up the sky.

"I have something to say," Mia said, surprising me. Christy nodded, giving her the floor, and then I felt stupid for being so weak in that moment. "You wrote me a letter today," Mia smiled with glossy eyes, "and I wasn't planning on saying anything, because you've always been better with words and explaining how you feel. So, this may not come out right ..." I squeezed her hand, letting her know it was just her and me, and she fought back the tears before continuing, "but your letter, it reminded me of those sunrises I watch every morning, and that sacred moment when light and dark can co-exist, making something beautiful across the sky. I've always been the dark, but you've always been the light, Ollie, and together, our love burns in color. You are my every beautiful sacred moment, and I promise to stay for the rest of my life."

Mia's hand came up to wipe my eyes, and I kissed her palm.

Christy continued, and we exchanged vows.

Mia said, yes. And an explosion went off inside my heart as I took her tear-stained face in my hands, desperately catching her lips with mine. She tasted like the ocean and freedom, and I sank into that kiss. Lips moved like water with that kiss. Tongues slowly grazed, hearts wildly pounded, and planets collided with that kiss. I wanted her to take me away and live inside our feelings forever. The cheering went off around us, and our foreheads connected when I opened my eyes. "I love you, baby."

Mia smiled with a natural glow in her golden-brown eyes. "I love you."

TWENTY-SEVEN

"You are my most unexpected plot twist,
reminding me to never get caught up in
the deadly routine of life.
And for the first time,
I am not afraid."

OLIVER MASTERS

Ollie

insisted on carrying Mia over my shoulder through the door. We'd
spent the last few hours celebrating, dancing, and drinking with Liam
and Jake.

Mia was officially drunk. Or perhaps I was the one wasted. I couldn't
tell anymore.

Everything after the ceremony was a blur.

"Oh-my-God," Mia whispered from behind me.

I paused halfway through the hotel room with my arm holding the
back of her thighs. Mia had danced in the ocean at midnight, soaking the
bottom of her dress where sand clung to the lace. "What is it?"

"We don't have any fucking pictures," she called out, smacking my arse.

"Oh, there are pictures, love," I laughed, then continued my trek to the bathroom, "of you dancing, doing shot after shot, and not to mention, the tabletop incident." I'd noticed the balcony doors wide open, wine glasses set out, and a bottle of champagne prepared in a bucket of ice outside on the terrace. Music played inside the room with rose petals scattered across the bed. The Rock Hotel was posh, and Jake must have planned this out for us.

Mia cringed in my hold. "I didn't."

"You did."

Surprisingly, I made it to the bathroom without dropping her and halted in front of the mirror. My stance swayed, but my eyes fixed on the way her bum looked in the reflection over my shoulder. Mia wiggled in my arms, her laugh bouncing off my back.

I pulled up her dress to get a better look, and the white lace knickers clung to her sex like a second skin. "For the love of God, Mia," I breathed our, moving my free hand up her bare thigh and over her perfect round arse. My knob stretched inside my pants as the buzz rushed to the one place craving to be inside her. The way she looked from behind arrested my gaze, flaring animalistic desires within me.

"Ollie," she whimpered, but my fingers continued to wander, grazing up and down her sex over her white lace.

"Stay still, love. I just want to look at you." I stretched her knickers to the side with one hand to reveal her. My lips broke apart, my balls tightened, and I couldn't remove my eyes from the view as oxygen held inside my lungs.

Of course, she didn't listen, pressing her bottom against fingers as I stroked her, wanting more. The liquor flowing through me forced my two fingers in my mouth, then over her tight entrance, making circles as she glistened. I watched, kneading her tight hole and inching them inside, my thumb scraping over her little clit. Mia's legs shook, and my fingers curled. A fire blazed across my skin down to my groin. "You have no idea what this is doing to me right now. You are so … fucking Christ, Mia." I quickly walked to the bed before tossing her over, changing my mind on the shower. I needed her now, and she laid over the cloud-white sheets in her wedding dress as I stood over her, taking her in.

The dress hugged her tiny frame, a deep dip down the middle of her chest, and my eyes touched over every inch of my wife. Mia lifted her arms over her head, where the flower crown fell, and she turned her head outside the balcony before her brows pinched together. "Ollie …"

A lump lodged inside my throat at the way she looked, and I tried to swallow it back down before saying, "Yeah?"

Her eyes slid back to me. "A fucking monkey is watching us."

"What?" I laughed, unsure if I heard her correctly or if the number of shots I'd taken distorted her words.

She pointed toward the balcony. "A monkey is staring at me right now."

I looked back, and sure enough, a brown monkey was sitting over the railing of the terrace, staring right back. "Your bloody right." I snapped my head back toward her. "What do we do?"

"I don't know." Her eyes darted back and forth from the monkey to me. "I can't get naked with it staring at me, Ollie. It's weird."

And I was certain the little ape wasn't going to ruin the night or my chances of Mia not undressing for me. I marched toward the terrace and waved my hands out in front of me, with Mia giggling from behind. "Bugger off!" I whisper-shouted, and the monkey's eyes moved behind me to Mia once more before taking off to the next balcony over.

I turned back, and my gaze collided with Mia's, who was standing at the foot of the bed with a delicate smile. The strap of her dress fell off one shoulder, and her eyes captured me, begging for me to take her out of it. A few steps forward, and I towered over Mia and fell under her spell, utterly lost in her. A dizzy spell of a moment, making me weak and empowered, unsure whether or not to fall to my knees or tear off the dress and cross lines, limits, and horizons.

My fingers danced over the straps to behind her, and I unzipped the dress down to the base of her back. Mia allowed the dress to slide from her body to the floor, pooling at her feet, and my heart slammed inside my chest. She stood bare, and the tips of my fingers skimmed over her lines, from her collarbone down the length of her arms. My fingers itched to touch all over her, drowning in wanderlust for this woman.

Mia looked up at me with tender eyes, goosebumps glittering over her ivory skin. A blush graced her cheeks. Golden suns glowed in her eyes. Ecstasy tugged on her lips. I dipped down and kissed her, already a goner.

Mia gripped my biceps as I walked her backward toward the bed. The backs of her knees hit the edge before she sat, and my lips moved like a scream, my slow hands like a whisper. My chest burned from my thrashing heart, ready to break free from its cage and soar with hers. Emotions caused my hands to shake, and Mia pulled away. "Stop thinking," she whispered against my lips, her fingers hooking onto my belt, "let go and make love to me, Ollie."

My belt came undone. My button and zipper came undone. My bloody mind came undone as she pulled my pulsing cock out and trailed her tongue along the bottom of my shaft, and the soft beat of the music followed my fingers through her hair. A breath stuck in my chest as she took me deep, and I leaned forward from the pressure climbing. Her neck twisted, conquering a different angle and threatening my control. And when her eyes lifted to mine, I struggled to pull away.

But I did … because I needed our connection more.

Laying her back across the bed, I crawled between her legs and up her torso. Mia's nails dragged down my back as my breath hit her neck before my lips did. Chests grazing, my palm slid down to her thigh, and I wrapped it around my waist.

Then I entered her slowly until all of me was in all of her. I wet my lips as she held my face, moving my mouth to hers. Together we chased highs, star-gazed, and transcended time, a wild eclipse between the sheets, flying within our supernova. The moonlight came from outside the terrace, tracing shadows across her skin, but the shadows couldn't erase the colorful feeling burning between us, just like she'd said.

Bodies slick. My name upon her lips. Her taste on mine. We reached our heaven. Earth quaking, body shaking. Sinning and worshipping, there was an innocence battling a fury, and all night was spent up in flames, over and over, as if it were our own religion.

By the time her head laid upon my chest, my heart pounding against her cheek, I wanted to wrap us up in the stars and live there forever. It was moments like these I would tattoo over my flesh so I could always be beautiful, and she could always admire the way she made me feel.

It was true, there should be a lifetime of these moments, but there was also a small fleeting pinch inside my chest, reminding me the worst has yet to come. Mia fell asleep in my arms, but I stayed awake, fighting off the demons after my sunrise closed her eyes. There was still a man to kill, and a problem to take care of. Ghost and Dex. I'd promised her forever, but I was still outrunning the desperate decisions of my past.

Mia

We'd broken away from Liam and Jake to explore Gibraltar. The weather was perfect, low seventies, and I slipped into cut-off jean shorts and a cream-colored blouse with a floppy woven hat Ollie had bought for me in Madrid. I grabbed my camera before we were out the door in search of coffee. We'd never been heavy breakfast people, a few pastries, and we were always good to go. But there had been many nights we'd eaten breakfast for dinner, and Ollie's chocolate chip pancakes had quickly become my favorite.

It was a hard hike up the steep Mediterranean staircase to the Highest Point of Gibraltar, sitting 435-meters above the white sandy beach where we married just the day before. Another tourist took a photo of the two of us standing over the moor, the wind threatening to blow us away. From up here, you could see Africa's coastline across the Strait of Gibraltar.

"You see those mountains off in the distance?" Ollie asked me against the wind, his eyes glistening with the view. I nodded, and he continued, "That's Morocco."

After we'd walked back down, we explored St. Michaels Cave and the Great Siege Tunnels before heading into town for lunch. Over two plates of fideos al horno, which was nothing more than a fancy macaroni, I showed him all the pictures we'd taken. "Look at this one," I gushed.

"These are brilliant," Ollie shook his head with a mouth full of food, "I want them in my next poetry book."

I set my camera down as heat rushed to my cheeks with the same smile I always wore whenever he was around. "Ollie, you don't have to say that just because I married you."

"I'm saying it because they're seriously good. My next book, my poetry, and your photography. I don't know why I haven't thought of it before." As Ollie took his next bite, a shriek belted from my throat when a monkey snatched my camera from the table beside me and took off through the town. Ollie dropped his fork and bolted from the chair, taking off after the uncanny thief.

I snatched our backpack off the ground to run after Ollie. "Ollie, don't, he will bite you!" I shouted, more than fifteen feet from behind.

By the time I caught up, Ollie had the monkey cornered with a crowd surrounding him, and he crouched down as the small ape examined the camera in his little hands. "Give me the camera, mate," he firmly stated, and I crossed my arms over my chest, holding in laughter.

"He'll bite," a bystander said, shaking a finger at the monkey, and I wanted to say, "I told you so" until the man standing beside her intervened, "No, he's British. He's good."

The two went back and forth, bickering about Gibraltar being under British control when Ollie turned to hush the crowd. The people silenced, and Ollie held out his hand to the little guy. "Hand the bloody thing over."

"He's not going to just hand it over because you asked," the lady mumbled to herself.

Ollie and the monkey entered a staring match, his outstretched hand between the two of them, and the crowd stood frozen with a curbed breath, waiting. And after a few beats of suspense, the monkey dropped the camera beside Ollie's hand over the rock pathway. Ollie scooped the camera into his hand and stood, and the monkey took off into another direction. Probably the same one from the night before. I remembered that look in the monkey's eyes. He had it out for us.

The crowd cheered, and Ollie slipped the strap over my head and planted a kiss on my lips.

"Told you." The man rolled his eyes and held up his palm. "It's because he's British," he explained to his wife standing beside him.

Later, we met up with Liam and Jake at the hotel after a much-needed nap. It was our last night in Gibraltar, and we spent it sitting over the beach with our toes curled in the sand. The enormous cliff laid to our right as the sunset painted pinks and purples over the sparkling water. Jake danced over the sand by himself with the beat of a band playing from a nearby hotel as I retold the story of Ollie and the monkey.

"Oh, yeah. Our tourist guide talked about it today," Liam said with utter fascination brewing in his eyes. "Legend says, the monkeys alerted the British during a surprise attack, which prevented the French and Spanish from ever gaining control of Gibraltar. So, as long as the monkeys remain, so do the British. An unspoken bond between them," he lifted his brows, "Pretty cool, yeah?"

"Ah," I looked back at Ollie, who was sitting beside me, "Now it makes sense."

"So, the monkey just handed over your camera?" Jake asked through heavy breathing.

I lifted a shoulder. "More like dropping it beside his hand."

"Dodgy little bastard," Ollie muttered.

We'd returned to the UK the same way we came, but this time, Liam had driven straight through from Gibraltar to Bilbao as the married

298

couple cozied up in the backseat. The four of us had to spend one last night in Spain before taking the next available ferry across the Bay of Biscay to the United Kingdom. We could have simply flown back, but had left Ollie's car at the port anyway and didn't mind the ride. Ollie and I were made for adventure, our only home within each other.

Exhausted, Ollie pulled the car in front of our cottage but laid his hand over my thigh as I went to get out. "Mia, wait," he stated, and I turned back to face him. "I know what you're probably thinking right now, that once we get out of this car, it's back to the real world. One with the Links and Dex and Leigh—"

"Ollie …"

"No, listen to me for a second." He threaded his fingers with mine. "No matter what happens, we're going to get through it. Look at how far we've come. We're a force, love. A force no one will be able to withstand. As long as you're by my side, I'm not scared, are you?" Biting my lip, Ollie smoothed his hand down my hair before clutching the ends as I slowly shook my head. He kissed my forehead before saying, "I'll get us out, Mia. I promise to do whatever it takes to keep you safe, and me out of this fucking mess."

The temperatures were below fifty in the night as we exited the old car. I had to give it to him, though. The beater managed to survive many miles so far without any problems. Ollie grabbed the luggage from the trunk, and we walked through the gate of our unnamed cottage.

When we made it through our front door, he flipped on the light and released a long exhale. "Home sweet home," he said through a sigh, but all my attention narrowed to the gift left in our living room.

Over our coffee table sat a dozen pink roses in a vintage glass vase, and I walked over to the flowers and picked them up at the base. "Oh, Ollie, they're beautiful. Did you have Travis leave these?"

Looking over, I caught Ollie scratching the back of his head. "I don't think so."

I arched a brow. "You don't think so?"

"Mia, I'm so tired, I honestly don't remember, but it does look like something I'd do."

Laughing, I examined the flowers for some sort of note or card. "There's no note," I said, and Ollie yawned from the entryway before I set the vase back over the table. "Alright, Romeo, let's get you off to bed."

"I'll call Travis in the morning."

TWENTY-EIGHT

"Is the chaos
following me,
or have I simply
become addicted to
chasing the chaos?"

OLIVER MASTERS

Halloween had passed, yet the spooky vibe lingered among the streets of Surrey as I drove to Thurrock to meet Dex for a job. Between traveling and working on preparing for a new volume of poetry, I'd blown off most of Dex's calls.

I couldn't keep this up, and Dex only grew more annoyed with where he stood on my list of priorities.

The group of men huddled around the bar at Jack's Pub, and I spotted Adrian with an easy smile and glazed eyes. Dex and his two other men pushed drunken Adrian around in amusement, and I stood over them, most of the blokes shorter than me, to assess the situation.

Smith, one of his men, noticed me first and squeezed my shoulder. "Nice of you to show up, mate."

"I was busy," I said, my voice vacant. There were a million other things I'd rather be doing.

Dex stood from his barstool, and the men subconsciously took a step back. "How was the wedding?" he asked with an all-knowing grin. *Bloody hell, he knew.* And if it were up to me, and under entirely different circumstances, the whole world would know Mia Rose was my wife. I'd climb the tallest mountain with a smile and six-pack of Red Bull to chisel our two faces into the rock with those exact words etched above our heads. But this very news was enough for Dex to know how deep my love for Mia ran. It meant another card in his back pocket, and another lure to keep me coming back. His sinister gaze confirmed it. "Ah, I understand. Our friend here gets married," he turns back to face me with a hand over my shoulder, "and what happens in Gibraltar, stays in Gibraltar."

Smith slid a shot in front of me, and I picked it up and slammed the liquor down the back of my throat. "Something like that."

Adrian shot up from his chair and held his drink above his head. "To endings and new beginnings," he shouted in amusement, but his eyes recked of grief, still mourning the loss of our mate, Reggi. I'd been gone for weeks, and Adrian was left alone to deal with the pain after I'd kicked James to the curb for switching teams.

The next breath I sucked in filled me with guilt, and it slid down to my lungs and fed my heart. I pulled Adrian off to the side, and his dead stare never faltered. "How are you doing, my friend?" I asked, low, hoping he was sober enough to make conversation.

"Fuck you," he spat, shrugging my arm away. "All this talk about brotherhood and trust, you're just like the rest of them, so you know what? Fuck you, and fuck your new wife too."

As soon as the words left him, my hand snapped over his jaw, squeezing it in a firm grip, and I twisted his head to the side and lowered my mouth to his ear. "You're hurting right now, I know. I feel it, mate. But if you so much as disrespect her again, that pain you're feeling? Nothing less than a glorious high compared to what I could do."

Shoving Adrian's head backward, I let go and returned my attention to the group. Dex's gaze was fixed on me, an amused smirk playing behind his shot glass. I adjusted my hoodie before throwing my finger up for another drink. With Adrian drunk, James gone, I was on my own, and the night was still young—and a job still ahead.

After about an hour, I'd walked Adrian to my car and let him pass out in the backseat. Dex and I were going over plans. "The thing is, Ghost doesn't make appointments. As soon as I get the time and address, I'll call you, but you need to pick up your bloody phone." Dex lifted his finger in my direction. "Are we going to have any problems?"

"No." I wanted this to end as much as he did, and I'd realized the only way for that to happen was to kill Ghost.

Dex rested his glass over the bar. "I'm going to need more than that."

I leaned in and squinted my eyes. "You think I get off on your presence? I can't fucking stand you. Trust me when I say, there won't be problems. I'll answer, kill that bastard, and be done for good. And if it were up to me, it would have been done months ago."

"Situations such as these need planning. Ghost won't be alone, you know. As soon as you walk in and take the shot, his men will kill you before you're able to take a step in either direction. You're an amateur, Oliver. The reason why you're in a mess, to begin with."

The thought of Mia ever losing me punched a hole in my chest. The pain and suffering I knew she'd face were enough to call back the fear. A month ago, I'd told her I wasn't scared anymore. But I was a liar. I was terrified. "Then why choose me to do your bidding?" I nudged my head toward his entourage. "Why not them?"

"It's simple. If the plan goes up in flames, you're disposable," Dex scoffed. "Plus, don't forget what I've done for you. You made your bed, now shut the fuck up and lie in it."

"You still haven't told me this plan of yours," I pointed out.

"I'm working on it."

Since Adrian was in no shape to take on the job tonight, I left him at the Links house and drove with Dex into BOG's territory with Smith behind me in the backseat. Deliberately, Dex was moving his chess pieces across the board, taking out competition one by one. Once Ghost was killed, the BOGs would still be an issue on the east side of London. As far as I understood, no one within the Links knew of Dex's devious betrayal aside from his inner circle, which, unfortunately, consisted of me.

This all started with me.

Me and my desperate deal to find Mia had been the first move in his inconspicuous game, giving Dex all the tools he needed to take over and light a match under the Links from the bottom.

Under Dex's instruction, I turned off the headlights and pulled up to an abandoned warehouse on the opposite side of town. Magazines loaded, first round chambered, the ominous sounds of criminals handling illegal weapons played in the car, having a much better beat than any MGK song. Dex's eyes slid over to me. "Going in clean, baby O?"

"I have one bullet, and I'm saving it for Ghost."

Dex chuckled under his breath and turned to face Smith in the backseat. "Alright, simple grab and go," he tossed black cloths over our laps, "we'll take him back to the house and question him. They'll be in the middle of a deal inside that building, and I prefer taking him after, not before. The other player can't know."

"Sounds easy enough," Smith confirmed.

Then Dex added, "My sources say James may be with him for training, which could be a snag. And if that's the case, we have to separate the two. Oliver, that's where you come in. James is useless to us. He's new and won't know anything. After the buyers leave, we'll snatch the BOG while you get rid of James."

"What do you expect me to do with him?" I asked, having no intention of murdering anyone tonight, especially James. He may have been responsible for Reggi's death, but I already had enough blood staining my conscience, and plans for the bullet burning a hole in my pocket.

Dex's black brows pinched together. "I don't care what you do with him. Kill him, turn his lights out, fuck him in the arse. Just be quick and get back to the car."

The three of us abandoned the car and surrounded the building. I went in through the back while Dex and Smith went in from the side. Hidden behind a wall, I peeked around the corner to see four men in the middle of a drug deal, James present. I shoved the black cloth over my head and lifted the hood of my hoodie, spotting Dex through a window at the side door, waiting.

It felt like forever had passed as the four chit-chatted inside the empty warehouse, their voices hushed. I wiped my anxious palms down the front of my hoodie as sweat built inside the black cloth over my face. At this point, we didn't have a clue which way they would leave, and I bounced on my toes in anticipation.

Finally, the blokes broke apart. The two buyers left out the front, a large duffle under one of their arms, most likely containing the drugs. James's eyes bounced around the warehouse as the other BOG's lips moved beside him, recounting cash before walking in my direction. It made sense why Dex wanted to grab afterward, may as well take the filthy lucre too.

I pulled back my head and glued my body against the wall until a shuffle echoed off the cement walls, which was my cue. I walked out from the direction James hadn't expected and appeared behind his back while Dex, head covered, tried to get control of the BOG we needed. Smith had his weapon pointed at James, and James had a chance to retrieve his pistol, but it only hung from his hand, pointing at the floor. Smith had full control of him, and I came up from behind, grabbed the gun from his hand, and slid it across the floor toward Smith.

James turned to face me, and I grabbed him from behind in a chokehold and dragged him back into the hallway as the other two moved out with the captured BOG. James was stronger than me, always had

305

been, and he fought against my hold until I pulled his arm behind his back into a lock, where one simple move would snap it in half.

Once the sound of the door closing reached my ears, I knew the other three were out of the warehouse and on the way to the car. I didn't have much time. My back slammed against the wall, and I slid down with James's back to my chest, both of us on the ground. He struggled, but I had control and wanted to get this over with. With James's entire weight on top of me, my lungs crushed, making it harder to breathe. I fought for air and the moment to pass, and as my arm around his neck tightened, I counted down the seconds before he was out.

"Oliver," he rasped, his free hand clawing at my arm around his neck.

With my cover blown, my eyes briefly closed in an attempt to detach myself from the situation emotionally. James had been one of mine. I trained him. I was there during his drunken episodes when he confessed his fears and weaknesses. I used to be someone he looked up to. And, here I was, the one who had two proper grips on him at the moment, one on his neck, the other on his arm behind his back, and I twisted him to the side to ease him off my heaving chest so I could gather enough oxygen. "Stop fighting me. It will be easier for you."

"He's going to kill Adrian."

I'd barely made out his gravelly statement and eased up my hold around his neck. "What are you talking about?"

"Dex," he said in a collected breath. "Adrian and I know too much … Dex never planned on taking us with him. Once you finish off Ghost … Adrian's as good as dead. I heard everything, mate. I didn't have a choice…but," he croaked. "There's still time for Adrian."

"Know your target, you always have to be ten steps ahead," I'd repeated to Dex, to my boys, to Oscar. Except I hadn't been the one ten steps ahead, I was far behind and just now catching up as it hit me all at once, and I let go of James.

Dex had planned on killing off my three boys all along.

Adrian, James, and Reggi never stood a chance.

306

An enraged tornado touched down inside me, and I stood, throwing my fist into the cement wall. Over and over, my fist pounded, hand deforming, but I couldn't feel a bloody thing. James pushed me forward, and my body slammed against the wall before I flipped around and turned my anger on him, and with one clean hit against his skull, James fell back. His massive body thumped against the concrete floor with a loud echo mocking me.

I waited a few minutes to cool off before heading out of the warehouse and back to the car.

Sliding into the passenger seat, Dex was leaned back behind the wheel, flipping through stacks of cash. "What took you so long?" he muttered, and I turned back to see the black sack over the BOG's head with Smith beside him, a gun clenched in his hand over his lap.

"James is strong, gave me a run for my money," I said, casually, holding my fist out in front of me to examine the damage. It wasn't the time to confront him, not with his mate behind me and a dodgy drug dealer at his side. Smith could very well be on his hit list too, or the only man he wanted to bring along on the ride to rule.

And the entire way back to the Link's house, I kept my mouth closed and eyes out the window, devising a plan of my own. It had been too late to save Reggi, and James had made the impulsive decision to switch teams. Good for him, but where did that leave Adrian? My only option was to get him out before I'd pull the trigger on Ghost.

The house had always been a large heap of trash, but the neglect only worsened since I'd been here last. Empty bottles and take-out rubbish scattered across tables and counters, and more holes decorated the walls meant for hanging pictures of loved ones.

Dex sat the BOG over a chair and tied him up. Once the BOG was secure, Dex turned his attention to me. "You can go now, baby O. I got this."

I pulled bottled water from the fridge, unscrewed the cap, and took a gulp with a raised brow. "No," I chuckled, "I'm staying if that's all right with you." Dex planned on exhuming details from the BOG, and it was time for me to be in the know. With a flick of the wrist, I pointed the base of the bottle at him. "Carry on."

For half an hour, I grimaced as Dex tortured the man for information, demanding names, locations, and dealings of their boss—the BOG's leader. Dex wanted to know who was in charge, and his sick, menacing smiles only confirmed he was enjoying it as my stomach rolled from the heart-wrenching screams. By the time the man passed out from the pain, Leigh had strolled through the door with my mum on her tail.

Rolling my head back, I reached for my bottled water sitting over the counter beside the whiskey. I would need something heavier to deal with the two of them, but the only thing I wanted was to be back home with Mia, sober. Dex greeted my mum with a smack on her backside as Leigh approached me with a smile, and I stood from the barstool to leave.

"Holy shit, what happened to your hand?" she asked, taking my injured hand into hers. The blood had since dried, and I couldn't move my fingers without searing pain shooting up my arm. It wasn't broken. It was shattered.

I pulled my hand from her grasp. "I'm fine."

Dex washed his hands in the sink, looking between us. "The BOG isn't talking."

"I'm told I have a way with people. Perhaps I could give it a go," I offered.

My mum approached the kitchen, glancing over at me as she wrapped her arm around Dex's waist, and he flashed her a short-lived smile before his eyes returned to mine. In an instant, the mask he'd wore dropped, and his expression turned cold with a void. "He'll be out for a while. You should go. Better not keep the wife waiting."

My mum's head jerked to mine when Leigh gasped.

"You married her?" Leigh asked, a frown marring her features.

I dropped my elbow over the table, and pain skyrocketed from my fingertips to my shoulder. I winced, saying, "Of course, I married her."

"Yeah," Dex chuckled, "and that's the problem because the only person you should be committed to is me."

308

"Oliver?" my mum asked, her voice small and careful, and it sent my heart into my throat. "You got married?"

"It wasn't what she said, Mia, it was the way she said it," I explained as Mia wrapped my hand. She was sitting over our bathroom counter as I stood between her legs with my arm out between us. "Four years, Mia. For four fucking years, and she didn't visit me once. Hell, she testified against me when everything went down with Oscar and Brad. Even when I saw her at the funeral, she could barely look at me. But as soon as she found out I got married …" I shook my head, "it was almost as if she cared."

Gently, Mia pulled my double-wrapped fist to her lips, kissing my knuckles lightly. "All better."

A grin fought through my perplexity. "Thank you."

"What happened after she said that?"

Breath rushed out of me, and I lifted a shoulder. "Left without saying anything." I leaned my good hand over the edge of the counter beside Mia. "You know, she lost touch with reality a long time ago. Paranoia, hallucinations … it almost killed us both, and all I ever wanted was for her to quit using and get help. But, Mia, that look in her eyes tonight—"

"You think she stopped?"

Pushing off the counter, I scratched the back of my head. "I don't know. Maybe Oscar dying woke her up. Or maybe I'm that six-year-old kid again, getting his hopes up. I can't be sure, but I can't trust her either." Every time I saw her, torment broke out inside me. Multiple times, Mum had tried to kill me, and those were memories that could never be erased. Time and time again, Mum had proved she was a hopeless, incurable disease, one I'd never want in our future.

But the way she looked at me …

Mia reached for my uninjured hand and pulled me back toward her. "She still doesn't know Dex killed Oscar, does she? It's weird, her hanging out with him."

"I told you Dex and Oscar were mates growing up, and Dex and my mum fucked off and on since he was young. If I'm not mistaken, she took his virginity."

"What?"

I nodded. "Yeah, so the bloke has a soft spot for her, and vice versa. If I told her Dex was responsible for killing her son, she wouldn't believe me anyway."

My past had quickly caught up to me, bleeding out into everything I treasured. And the only smart thing to do was push Mia further and farther away from it all. But like I said before, love turned us all into fools. Mia's steadfast soul anchored mine, and she was the only reason I'd stayed sane through it all. With a sword in one hand, she was clutching my other, and I was hardly hanging on.

TWENTY-NINE

"If a love hasn't grown wings
from the depths of your soul,
ripped open your chest,
and perched on the rim
to lick your bleeding heart.
It wasn't a love after all."

OLIVER MASTERS

Mia

'd never had the most brilliant ideas. From experience, most of them ended in either handcuffs, a hangover, or looking into loveless eyes after a harsh fuck. I'd just hoped this idea of hosting Thanksgiving dinner wouldn't end up in flames.

Ollie wouldn't be back home until after midnight, and I had only tonight to prepare a dinner for seven people and a baby. Jake, Liam, Travis, Summer, and their baby Turner were joining us, along with

Lynch. Ollie had found a nine-foot wooden table at an antique shop for half off, and spent the last few days refinishing the wood back to its original charm. Tomorrow, we were having Thanksgiving dinner at our house, and I was responsible for the food, or lack thereof.

Since arriving in the UK, I only got around by cab or taking my bicycle into the village if I needed something. I refused to learn to drive here, and it drove Ollie insane. But to be honest, the opposite sides scared the living hell out of me. I'd tried once, and drove his dear car into a ditch. It took three men and a pick-up to drag the beater from the muddy valley off the road. After that, Ollie found a purple bicycle, complete with a basket and a bell. What started as a joke turned into my most reliable transportation.

But there was no way the bicycle would be able to carry the groceries back from the store. Knowing this, Ollie had left his car. And I stood outside my front door, staring at the old, rusty station wagon with determination in my posture, twirling the keys around my finger.

After a few close calls—*okay, a lot of close calls*—loud honks, and British insults from other cars passing by, I'd made it to the village in one piece. Dark clouds broke apart, and I grabbed the umbrella from the backseat before getting out and running through the misted rain. We were nearing the end of November, and the temperature was cruel. People rushed over the cobblestone path and ducked into their cars as I idled under the roof's eave, closing the umbrella and stomping out the water dripping from my Sperry boots.

I entered the store, the bell chimed, and the cashier waved over at me from behind the counter as I grabbed a buggy. The Yankees back in the states made the locals here seem like fairy godmothers from Pleasantville, and I was tired of keeping up with the smiles and small talk.

Strolling through the aisles, I snacked on a bag of Mini Cheddars as I tossed the items from my grocery list into the cart when my buggy crashed into two girls, one with who I recognized.

"Hi, Mia," Leigh said. And though I'd only seen her once, I'd never forgotten the face of the girl who took the majority of Ollie's time. But seeing her this close, she couldn't be more than twenty-years-old. She wore black leggings and a cream satin tank under her black puffer jacket with an older lady at her side. My eyes darted back and forth between the two.

The other lady's eyes relaxed. "So, you're Oliver's Mia?"

"Nope, wrong person," I lied, trying to maneuver my cart around them, but Leigh grabbed hold of the end and pulled it back in front of her. Closing my eyes, I sucked in a long breath.

"Can I help you with something?" I asked upon exhale.

"I'm Oliver's mum," the older lady said, and her gaze roamed down my body before they flicked back to my eyes where they settled. Her expression transformed from conflicted to concerned, and her eyes watered. "I … I just wanted to introduce myself. Take care of yourself, Mia," she quickly turned to Leigh, who had her palms in the air, and Oliver's mom shook her head, "Come on, we're leaving the girl alone."

Before I could get a word out, Oliver's mom gripped Leigh's arm and pulled her in the opposite direction as Leigh whisper-shouted, noticeably upset. Then the two disappeared around the aisle, leaving me with nothing but confusion from what just happened.

Once my body thawed from my frozen state, I checked out, made it safely home, and spent the rest of the evening recapping the events from earlier in my head. Ted Bundy's documentary played on the TV over the fire burning in the fireplace, but I hadn't paid attention to the last twenty minutes, too busy mulling over the run-in, and why Ollie's mom was so quick to leave. No matter how hard I tried to shake it away, her reaction to me had buried into my brain.

The uncanny feeling of someone watching me raised every small hair across my arm, followed by goosebumps. My coffee turned cold, and I leaned over and set it down on the table before pulling the blanket across my lap, looking out the window. Our white curtains were partially drawn, and all I could see was the black night. I grabbed my phone off the arm of the couch and texted Ollie to find out if he was on his way.

It was very seldom when Ollie left me home alone, but this past month he had been gone about once a week to deal with Dex and the Links. He rarely went into detail and hated talking about it, and over the past few months, I learned it was better not knowing. But it wouldn't be long before Ollie would walk through the door, dripping with regret. The week before, he'd taken me over this couch and released his shame and guilt inside me before spending the rest of the night writing in his notebook. Every other night, he'd make love to me slow and fuck his poetry hard. But night's such as this, when he'd come back from that house, it was the other way around.

Of course, I never minded, having once said Ollie carried the burden of a thousand lost souls and had the heart of a thousand angels, and the only way to release his pent-up emotions was through me.

And on cue, he walked into our home wearing black joggers and a jean jacket over his hoodie with his hair in chaos. Bruises had colored his cheekbones. The bandages had unraveled from around his hand. The winter chill had kissed his lips. Then Ollie lifted his head. The same green eyes where a museum of knowledge, dreams, and books about love stories lived, found mine as if the sun came out in the dead of night. Screaming thoughts turned to whispers, and Ollie dropped his guard, knowing he was back with me in his safe place.

The smell of cinnamon and apples swirled inside our cottage, and I was busy pulling the last pie from the oven while Ollie stood over a bonfire in the backyard with Lynch, Travis, and Liam. Fanning the pie, I fixed my eyes out the window, admiring the four men as Summer nursed Turner over the couch in front of the nine-foot table behind me. Ollie had pushed the furniture against the wall to make room for it temporarily, and after Thanksgiving, it would be going back outside.

A fire crackled in the fireplace, and Jake and I worked together, tag-teaming setting the table over low music playing from the speakers above my piano. After spreading out a placement, Jake looked up with a dramatic sigh. "I have to admit, Mia. Over two years, Lynch scared the pee out of me. Literally. Like, he literally made me piss my pants. I'm so on edge right now, and I don't know how to act around him."

Laughing, I crossed my arms over my chest. "Just be yourself."

"That's exactly what I'm afraid of. What if he gets mad the pie is gone, decides to blame the gay one, and throws me upstairs in your darkroom."

I rolled my eyes. "And what do you call a really annoying gay man?"

Jake's shoulders slumped, and his eyes narrowed. "What?"

"A pain in the ass."

Summer giggled from the couch.

"And, Mia?" Jake pointed at me. "When the comedian pumped his sense of humor inside you, did you laugh?"

"Okay, touché. But we got a baby in the room …"

"What's Thanksgiving without a little banter, yeah?" Summer asked, standing and laying Turner down in the pop-up playpen beside the couch. "Should I grab the boys?"

My gaze scanned over the table where a complete Thanksgiving meal laid out. Turkey, gravy, stuffing, mashed potatoes, green bean casserole, and cranberries sitting over a festive tablecloth, candles lit, and drinks poured. "Yup, we're ready for them."

Jake walked around the table and threw his arm around my shoulder. "You did well."

"Wait until you try it before you say that," I said through a laugh, hoping it tasted as delicious as it appeared.

After everyone was inside, oohs and aahs echoed from the other three men with their gaze sailing over my masterpiece. We all took our seats around the table and lifted our wine glasses for a toast before the feasting.

"I'd like to say a few words," Lynch disrupted from the opposite end of the table, and I lowered my glass as Ollie's palm rested over my thigh. "First and foremost, I want to thank Mia and Oliver for inviting me. It's been over twenty years since I had a home-cooked Thanksgiving dinner. And Mia," he cleared his throat, "we've come a long way with still a long way to go, but I couldn't be prouder of the lady you've become in such a short time. Thank you for giving me a chance to be a part of your life. To Mia and Oliver, everyone."

"To Mia and Oliver," my family echoed, clinking their glasses with dazzling smiles.

Ollie squeezed my thigh, leaning in, and I met him halfway. Our lips touched briefly before his nose brushed mine, and he faced the eager eyes around the table with his hand in the air. "All right, dig in," he called out, looking handsome with his hair styled in his usual messy wave, black pants, and a grey sweater. The swollen and red bruise under his eye changed colors but didn't bruise his spirit.

After dishes passed around and plates filled high with food, everyone did just that and dug in.

Thankfully, the food wasn't too bad, and I didn't kill anyone. Over the next hour, we laughed over memories from our trip to Spain, heard Lynch's crazy stories from his earlier days at Dolor, and listened to Travis and Summer explain about life with a newborn in the house.

"So, what's next for the two of you?" Liam asked, eyes darting between Ollie and me.

The only people in this room who knew about Ollie's dealings with the Links were Travis, Summer, Ollie, and me. Everyone else was clueless as to the double life Ollie had been living since Dolor, the criminal activity he was involved with, and our future of traveling the world put on hold until he could get out.

Ollie's eyes met mine when a boyish smile crept along his lips. "I have no bloody clue, mate. But whatever is next, we're ready for it."

Bubbles floated over the hot bathwater, the scent of rose and bergamot bursting in our bathroom and seeping into every inhale. "Thanksgiving was a success," Ollie said, sitting over the small wooden barstool and rinsing the soap out of my hair with the shower spray. "The food wasn't half bad, so why the frown?"

316

I waved my hand over the water, collecting bubbles and blowing them from my palm. A few popped, and the rest drifted until it latched on to the subway tiled wall as I thought through my next words. "I have this sick feeling in my stomach that this is the calm before the storm, and it's only a matter of time before we are swept away. This whole thing with the Links …" I shook my head and dropped my hands under the water, "Don't forget, you promised me, Ollie."

Ollie turned off the sprayer and pushed up his grey sleeves to his elbows before leaning in. "You are not losing me, love. It's going to be okay."

"How do you know?" It seemed as if I'd been asking him that same question since our eyes locked the first time.

A smile graced his lips. "I just do," he whispered, giving me the same answer every time.

"Ollie—"

Ollie's elbow dropped over his knee as he held his pointer finger over his lips. I snapped my mouth shut, caught by the daydream look in his eyes. The tip of his finger met my chest and my heart slammed against it before it made the journey to his. "Remember?"

I nodded. "I remember."

A gesture so small but meant the world.

I stood from the bathtub, and Ollie wrapped a plush white towel around me to dry off before he picked a novel from the bookcase in the bedroom and joined me in bed.

As soon as the book opened, his angelic voice silenced the corrupt thoughts circling in my head, calming me, chasing evil, and bringing me to new heights and distant worlds where terrors, demons, and beasts weren't welcomed.

It was two A.M. when I woke from the sound of our gate slamming right outside our window, and I turned over in Ollie's arms to find him asleep on his side with his lips slightly parted. The wind howled, the gate

317

slammed again, and footfalls pattered, the eerie notes spilling through the cracks of our front door.

"Ollie," I whispered, shaking his shoulder. "Wake up."

His eyes slowly blinked before they found mine under the moon's light. "What's wrong?"

"I think someone is outside the house."

"Check it out, Mrs. *I'm-not-afraid-of-anything.*"

"It's Mrs. Masters, now, thank you very much. And, no way. You go check it out."

Another slam, another scuffle, and Ollie sat up from the bed and reached under the mattress to pull out a gun. My eyes widened, jumping back and forth from the weapon to his tense posture as he stood and slipped on sweats and a hoodie. Ollie tucked the small gun behind his back and grabbed a flashlight from the nightstand. He tried flipping on the lamp but the power was out. "Stay here and don't move."

"What are you doing with a gun?"

"I'll be right back," he replied, ignoring me. "Make sure your phone is close by."

Ollie disappeared from our bedroom, and the sound of our front door closing rebounded off the walls inside as I sat in the dark. The only light was the moon, and my eyes fixed on the clock sitting on the bookcase. Every second waiting was long and agonizing, and my heartrate refused to obey the steadfast beat of time. Since the age of eight, I'd stopped being afraid up until the moment I'd met Ollie. I had never been a scared girl, but the one to be scared of. And, with everything to lose, I was fucking terrified.

The small tormenting voice in my head talked back, showing me every worst-case scenario, and I hadn't heard the front door close when Ollie appeared in the doorway. "There's nothing out there," he said, setting the flashlight on the nightstand.

I released a relieved breath. "I'm sorry. I could've sworn I heard footsteps."

Ollie shrugged off the damp hoodie and slid the gun back under the mattress. He planted two hands over the bed to face me. "It's bad out there. It could've been the rain, love. *The Office* re-runs?" he asked. "The electric is out, but I can hook-up the laptop and use the internet from the mobile."

I nodded, and Ollie grinned before the two of us pulled the large fluffy duvet and a few pillows off the bed and dragged everything into the living room. With the laptop set up over the coffee table, Ollie pushed play, and we sank inside the blanket when Ollie dropped his head against the back of the couch and let out a laugh.

The show had barely started, and I glanced over at him. "What's so funny?"

"Déjà vu." Ollie lifted his head and his eyes landed on mine, his smile infectious. "Back in the states, your dad, Bruce, told me a time when it was just him, your mum, and you. It's the weirdest coincidence …" he shook his head and pulled me closer until my head rested against his chest. "This moment with you, Mia. I'm the happiest man alive, and I don't want you to fall asleep without knowing that."

He never did tell me the story, and I'd made a mental note to ask him about it another day. We spent the rest of the stormy night tangled up in one another, slow hands roaming, and the pitter-patter of rain competing against the laptop and our light breaths and heavy moans.

THIRTY

"Here we are again

my chilling shadow,

staring back at me

with the deathly trace

of a wilted rose

and the touch of

a tomb stone.

Here we are,

sweet insanity.

Climb inside and

give me the peace

I so desperately crave."

OLIVER MASTERS

Ollie

The situation between Mia, Leigh, and my mum was not lost on me. For two weeks, I'd waited until the right time presented itself to confront Leigh. She hadn't been at the Links house the week before, but as soon as I walked into a party Dex held at the Links location, through the crowd of bodies and thick smoke, my eyes immediately found her. The vibrating beat of the song pumped through the speakers and blasted into my ears, and I walked closer to see Leigh's skirt bunched at the hips, eyes glazed, and laying back across a bloke's chest on the couch. Her breast was in one hand, the other between her legs. I cocked my head, and the junkie across from them had a blunt between his lips with eyes fixed on the show.

My mouth watered, tasting fury, and I grabbed Leigh by the hair and yanked her off his lap, dragging her between people and into the hallway. I shoved her forward, her cheek pressed against the wall. Leigh whined, pissed drunk, and hardly hanging on.

"What the hell is wrong with you?" I screamed into her ear over the music, but she couldn't form a complete sentence, mumbling incoherently. She slid down the wall, and I managed to scoop her into my arms and carry her into the bathroom. She was blacking out, and panic replaced the anger, charging every nerve. In a frenzy, I laid her in the tub and flipped on the shower, spraying cold water over her lifeless form.

She was out, and I dropped to my knees, patting her cheek. "Come on, Leigh," I shouted, every movement desperate. I flipped Leigh on her side and shoved my finger down her throat until her body heaved. Leigh lurched forward as contents came up and shot from her lips while my fingers pushed her hair back, trying to hold myself together.

After nothing more came up, her eyes squeezed shut as she cried under the cold water. I fell back until my bum hit the floor and dropped my head over my free arm, the other refusing to let go of her. "Why do you always do this to yourself?" Exhaling, I lifted my head and swiped my palm down my face. "You can't keep doing this. You need help."

Leigh shivered under my hand, and I helped her to her feet and out of her soiled clothes. She stood naked in the tub, and I averted my eyes, turning the water from cold to warm. "You'll need to wash the chunks from your hair. I'll get you clean clothes from my car."

Leigh's teeth chattered. "Thank you, Oliver."

"Yeah," I muttered, locking the bathroom door behind me before closing it. Initially, I'd come here to confront Leigh and talk to Adrian, but never planned on a party and saving her again. I sent a quick text to Mia, letting her know it was going to be one of those nights before returning to the bathroom. I lightly knocked over the bathroom door when Leigh opened from the other side and peeked her head around to make sure it was me.

I held up some clothes between us. "Here, get dressed. I'm taking you home."

Mia

After receiving a disappointing text from Ollie, I made myself a cup of coffee before climbing the stairs to my darkroom, bypassing Ollie's stacks and stacks of books piling over the wooden steps on the way. On top of my client list building due to word of mouth, a huge job opportunity had come in to capture images of a local model to advertise a jewelry brand. Officially, it was a step into the big leagues with my photos inside magazines. Thousands of people would see my art, and I couldn't be more nervous.

I had a lot of favorite spots in the house, but the darkroom was, by far, my favorite. After begging Ollie to move the piano into my darkroom, and him refusing, he'd purchased me a tabletop keyboard and set it up under the window beside my laptop. Inspiration could come from anywhere, and whenever I needed a break from editing, designing, and developing, I'd roll my chair over to the keyboard, flip it on, and drown myself in the notes flowing through my fingers.

No one was allowed up here—no one aside from Ollie. Stepping into the room, negatives of my favorite photos scalloped from wall to wall, mostly of him. Ollie was my favorite muse. Here, I could admire parts of him when he was gone. His smile. The squint in his eyes. The angles and edges of his body. And all the candid moments I'd caught him without

322

him noticing. In here, I could crop, distort, change, filter…but never of Ollie.

The walls had been painted black, including a black-out curtain over the stained-glass window. Against one entire wall sat a work counter, processing sink, holding sink, and print washers. On the opposite side was the heavy-duty equipment I'd saved up for over these last few months.

After hours passing with hushed music playing in the dark from the laptop, and toying around with film, I'd fallen asleep over my desk and woke up to sounds coming from downstairs. Lifting my head, drool stuck to the side of my face, and I swiped my forearm across my cheek and mouth just when another sound clashed from below.

I slowly stood from the chair and tiptoed to the window, and Ollie's car wasn't outside in its usual spot. Heart pounding, I whipped and scanned the room for my phone. I'd left it downstairs.

It could very well be Ollie, but usually, he'd find me as soon as he walked through the door. He'd already be up here. He'd be the one to wake me.

It was someone else.

And the single thought drove all fear into existence.

Slowly, I walked across the hardwood floors until my shaky palm wrapped around the door handle. Afraid to make a sound, I held my breath as the door pulled open with a small painful creak.

I peeked my head out and gazed down the steps to where the kitchen was. A girl was leaned over the counter with my phone in her hand, the bright screen beaming over her face. But her back was to me, and though I couldn't see her, I knew it was Leigh.

She'd broken into my home.

I'd left Dolor a long time ago, but apparently, Dolor never left me.

With my gaze pinned on her back, I went through every scenario of how this would go. It was just her and me here, but this was my house. Leaving the door cracked, I pulled back behind the wall and released a breath while planning out my next moves. Knowing she had relations with the Links could mean she had a gun, but so did I. Under my mattress.

While her back was still turned, I made swift and quiet moves down the stairs to make it across the living room and into my bedroom. Each step closer was a threat, but my feet still moved forward with eyes trained at her back, knowing every turn of the house better than anyone. All the lights downstairs were off, and as soon as I made it through my bedroom door, I slid to my knees, pulled up the blankets, and shoved my hand under the mattress on Ollie's side.

My heartbeat pulsed in my ears, and my eyes burned when my fingers never touched metal. I lifted the mattress. The gun was gone. Ollie took it with him.

Suddenly, a rope wrapped around my neck and tightened, cutting off airflow to the point I could no longer breathe. My eyes bulged, and I clawed at the rope, trying to pull it free. Leigh shoved my face into the mattress and pressed her knee into my back, yanking back tighter. My chest burned and my limbs fought, terror consuming my every sense as the twine cut into my flesh. "I'm sorry, Mia," she said, "but you have to go."

Ethan transported me to this place before. The place where I could drift into a world where only Ollie and I lived.

I felt myself slipping to that place.

My heart thumped.

It was warm and quiet.

My heart thumped.

Only peace and freedom.

My heart thumped.

But green eyes flashed before me. Promises, dreams, and a fight to never let go. My eyes squeezed shut as a single tear slid over the soaked sheets, and I threw my head back until a jolt of pain erupted inside my skull. The rope loosened, and my chest begged for oxygen, gasping and coughing as I flipped around to face her. Leigh launched back at me, and I bent my leg back and kicked her between the legs before standing to my feet.

Before she was able to steady herself, I took off to the kitchen. My cell phone was gone, and I grabbed the home phone off the wall. After dialing 9-1-1, my entire body shook as I snatched open drawers in search of a knife. I'd set the kitchen up, placed everything in their spots, but couldn't get my mind together to find a single knife. The call disconnected, and I tried calling again in a desperate panic. By the time my fingers clasped around the handle of a knife, Leigh had gripped my hair and yanked me backward as the knife crashed to the floor.

The two of us fought in a power struggle, hair pulling, fists flying, gasping for air as we both begged for a solid breath. Once I managed to maneuver and pin her to the ground with my legs straddling her waist, she punched my left temple, and my entire body flew to the tile. A deep moan from the pit of my stomach escaped. I lifted my head to see the knife had slid across the floor and against the counter.

Inch by inch, I crawled across the floor as blood dripped from my face onto the tile. But the adrenaline and fight to survive temporarily numbed the pain.

"Bloody hell, I underestimated you," Leigh muttered under her breath. "You're one crazy bitch." She stood over me as I laid over my stomach, crawling and eating away the distance between me and the knife as the taunts continued.

Once the tips of my fingers touched the knife, I grabbed it and kicked her legs out from under her. Leigh fell on her back, and I shuffled back over her, pressing the cold metal to her throat. "You walked into the house of a certified psycho," I reminded her. "You haven't seen crazy." Her dark eyes went wide, and she froze beneath me. Digging the edge of the sharp knife into her flesh, tears held in the corners of my enraged eyes as thoughts of slicing her open invaded me. It would be so easy. I had her right where I wanted her. The pulse in her neck slammed against the silver blade, and I couldn't pry my eyes away.

Struggling to hold myself back, I reached my arm up and over the counter for the phone to call Ollie to stop me from killing her.

He picked up on the first ring.

"I'm sorry," he immediately said, and the sound of his voice granted the tears to fall from my eyes. "I dropped Leigh off hours ago, but had to go back for anoth—" he paused, hearing my harsh breathing from the other end. "Mia, what's wrong?"

I bit my lip as Leigh stared at me from the ground with tears in her eyes and a knife to her throat. "Ollie …" I croaked through a whisper. Sucking in a quick breath, I let it slowly release between my lips, my knife-holding hand shaking against her throat, threatening to stab her in the neck and watch her bleed out. The war inside wasn't over. It would never be over. It was always there, lurking, waiting. Evil thoughts blurred. Visions of her life slipping away, her eyes closing, the void taking over the both of us. It seemed so peaceful. Final. And I was exhausted. "… I'm going to kill her."

"Who, Mia? Talk to me. What are you doing?"

"Leigh. She broke in. I'm sitting on top of her. A knife to her neck. She can't leave this house with her life. This is my home. Our home," I rambled as Ollie muffled the phone and talked low to someone else to call the police. "Ollie?"

"I'm right here. I'm on my way. Listen to me, Mia, I'm begging you. Don't do this and stay with me on the phone," his voice was frantic, and Leigh swallowed with tears staining her cheeks. "Are you listening to me?"

A beat passed, and Leigh wiggled under me to try to break free. I pressed the edge of the blade against her flesh, and the teeth bit into her skin. Blood trickled down her throat onto the tile. Leigh stopped. "Yeah," I whispered.

"Close your eyes, baby," he calmly said. "Are they closed?" I slammed my eyes closed and tried to inhale through my nose as I fought the urge to cut deeper. I nodded, but he couldn't see and continued anyway, "Over two years ago, back in my dorm, you came through the vent with this crazy belief that kissing was more intimate than sex. Do you remember?"

I nodded, sniffling.

"Mia?"

"I remember."

326

Ollie let out a breath. "Then you slid over my lap, and my heart stopped inside my chest. I couldn't think. I could hardly breathe, love. But when your eyes hit mine, a change happened. Inside you. Inside me. Your eyes, they lit up, and I was no longer afraid. You went on, talking about science and this forbidden kiss, and all I could think about was the fact you eventually would be gone, and the panic returned. I never wanted to lose that contact. I never wanted to be without you," he choked and paused to take a breath. "I dragged you closer, laid my head to yours, living in that moment for as long as possible. Because you managed to give me something I'd been searching for my entire life, Mia. You gave me you, all of you, without even realizing it,"—chaos erupted as police broke through the door, guns raised, and the knife slipped from my trembling hand onto the tile as I fell back against the counter with the phone clutched to my ear, tears spilling from my eyes— "The funny thing about it all, you were wrong all along, love. Sex, a kiss … it took way less than that. I only said those things at the time … Because, so badly, I just wanted to keep you talking. I just wanted you to stay with me for a while longer."

Men in suits and gear dragged Leigh away while another one gripped my arm and pulled me off the floor. The phone dropped, breaking once it hit the tile.

Blue lights flashed up and down our street from outside and through the windows of my home. I sat over my couch with two officers standing before me, questioning me about what happened with a blanket wrapped around my shoulders.

It wasn't but minutes later when Ollie ran through the front door. He pushed through the two officers and crouched down before me, examining my face, my eyes, with worry and terror etched in his. "Mia?"

I shook my head. "I didn't do it."

Ollie grabbed the back of my head and kissed my forehead before our heads connected.

And we stayed like that for a moment, my body still trembling from the close call until the officer cleared his throat and dropped his card over the coffee table. "If you have any questions, here's my number."

"What will happen to her?" I asked, and Ollie stood and sat over the arm of the couch beside me, his hand never leaving mine.

The cop closed his spiral notepad and adjusted the hat over his head. "It's too soon to say, but from what I can see, there may be a chance for Leigh. She'll most likely end up at the reformatory school in Guildford—A place called Dolor."

THIRTY-ONE

"All-consuming love does not
Lurk in shallow waters.
It's in the deep
Where you can't see the bottom."

OLIVER MASTERS

Ollie

A week had passed. Refusing to go to the emergency room, Mia healed on her own. My little explosion of hope. I could never fathom or understand the internal struggle she'd faced at that moment, the need to kill when your entire being had been threatened in your own home, but she had been strong enough to fight it.

We were halfway to Christmas, and Dex hadn't made the call yet or gone over the plan. The police had arrested Leigh, which put a kink in his plan, and if he'd known, he would've called. Either way, we couldn't use her anymore. But with or without Leigh, I was prepared to use the bullet

I'd saved. I was still ready to kill Ghost more than ever. It was the only way.

"What about this one?" Mia asked, standing beside a Christmas tree.

Rosy cheeks, hidden eyes behind large black glasses, and hair piled high, I admired how tiny she stood against the monster of a tree. Mia's fingers tugged the frosted branches, and ice chips fell. "Think it'll fit inside the door?"

"No, definitely not," I said through a chuckle. Mia frowned, wearing black jeans, combat boots, and a large grey trench coat over a plain black hoodie. The sun would set soon, and we didn't have much time. "Think small, love. We'll put it in front of the window in the living room, yeah?"

"The one by the piano?"

I shook my head. "On the other side of the front door. Closer to our room."

"Oh, yeah. Okay," Mia jumped in front of another tree, "this one!"

The tree had half the height and half the life, but it would fit. I walked toward her. "You're sure? This is the one you want?"

Mia bounced on her toes, the daylight dying. "Yes, now let's go." She blew hot air into her hands and tightened the coat around her. "It's bloody cold out here."

I chuckled. "Stick with your accent, love. The only British in you is me."

The chap at the tree farm had helped tie the tree on top of the old station wagon, and it held steady the entire way back to our cottage. I'd set up the tree in the corner by the window, and Mia sat on the floor with decorations she'd collected over this past week from the village scattered around her. She'd changed out of her jeans into pajama pants, Christmas socks warming her feet.

Flames danced in the fireplace, heating the small house as old Christmas tunes played from the record player, and I was in the kitchen, making homemade hot chocolate using the milk chocolate bars I'd picked up from a shop in London. Once done, I topped both mugs off with candy canes and walked back into the living room where Mia had the corner of the ornament box between her teeth.

"Is it giving you a hard time?" I asked, chuckling, and walking toward her, but I knew better than to help her. For the most part, Mia was determined and never asked for help, wanting to do everything on her own.

She growled into the box, and I sipped from my mug while handing her the other.

After a back and forth battle between Mia and the packaging, I strung the lights around the tree and pulled out a box of our things from Dolor. Between the two of us, we'd saved every origami rose I'd given her. But the one that we hung first, was the one she'd ripped apart and I'd pieced back together again. The rose rested in the middle of the tree, and I looked over at her to see tears in her eyes.

"I'm so sorry," she waved her hand in front of her face. "I don't know why I'm so emotional right now."

I pulled her into my arms, and she pressed her face into my chest. My hands smoothed over the back of her head. "As long as they're happy tears, love."

My mobile phone rang, and Mia pulled away, sucking in a long breath. "I'll be okay," she laughed, "you should get that. It could be Dex."

Mia was right, and I walked over to the fireplace and grabbed my phone from the ledge to look at the screen. My heart flipped inside my chest. *Dex.* I answered.

"I need you to come by the house tonight," he stated. "We have to go over a few things."

Mia's watery eyes watched mine for a reaction.

"Yeah, I'll be there."

The call disconnected, and I pocketed the mobile and walked up to her, clutching her face in my hands. "I have to go."

"I know."

"What's the emergency number here, love?"

She rolled her eyes. "*9-9-9*, not *9-1-1*."

Nodding, I forced a grin. Leaving Mia had always been my biggest, repeated mistake. One I'd been making over and over again for months now, but I'd always come back to her. "Wait up for me."

"I always do."

It hadn't been the call I'd been anticipating, but I also didn't want to drive across town to see him tonight—especially with the chance of him knowing Mia was involved with Leigh's arrest. My knee bounced under the steering wheel, tensions rising as I pulled in front of the chain-linked gate against the curb. No music played from the house, which only meant one thing. Tonight meant business.

I blew hot air into my hands and rubbed my palms together, my feet moving forward up the path toward the door. Upon entering, Dex, Smith, Adrian, and another guy I'd seen with Dex stood in the kitchen, huddled in a circle while Mum sat over the torn couch in the living room. "Baby, O," Dex called, waving me over to the group of blokes. I passed Mum, and her apprehensive gaze never left mine, causing my palms to sweat. Dex stepped to the side, making room for me. "I have to ask you something, mate. Do you know where Leigh is?"

He'd always been straight to the point.

My eyes darted around the circle, looking for an indication on which answer I should give. The three other men stared back at me, eyes utterly blank of all emotion, aside from Adrian. He seemed clueless and out of the loop. "No, haven't heard from her."

Dex's hand slapped the back of my neck before he squeezed. "That's lie number one," he pointed out and faced the other men. "Leave us."

After looking back and forth between each other, the men dispersed out the back door. Mum rose from the couch, but Dex lifted his palm toward her, gesturing for her to sit.

Then he turned to face me. "Our virgin's gone," Dex continued. "Hadn't answered or shown up for a fucking week. Do you know how hard it is to find a willing participant who's a fucking virgin? Leigh was perfect. And imagine my surprise when I found who had her arrested."

Dex knew, and my heart jumped into the pit of my stomach. "Mia had nothing to do with this," I growled.

"Mia just became your biggest problem," he said slowly. "Your wife took every chance of you walking out of Ghost's office alive."

My lip twitched, and I crossed my arms over my chest. "What are you talking about?"

"I had a meeting with the BOG leader, and we made a deal. It turns out Leigh was worth more than I'd anticipated. So, a pretty virgin with a tight fanny up for grabs in exchange for a raid by BOGs men. Once we got word of the time and place, they'd be your distraction to get you out of there. Now, we don't have anything to exchange. Leigh was your one-way ticket, and now you're on your own. There's no time to find another Leigh."

If Leigh was worth as much as he'd said, he wouldn't have exchanged her for my life. The BOG raid was so nothing fell back on Dex. Another step ahead. The only person Dex looked out for was himself. He was nothing more than a little fish in a vast ocean with the appetite of a shark.

A shark who had planned to kill me all along, but only after he'd used me to do his bidding. He'd said it. I was disposable. And I'd made a promise to Mia.

I'd promised she would never lose me.

"Fuck you," I whispered, my eyes darting over the counter as the puzzle became clearer. Slowly, I lifted my chin until our eyes met. First the news from James about Dex's plans with Adrian, now this? My voice increased, the rage spilling into every word, "It was never over, was it?" My clenched fist pounded over the counter. "You think I'd give up my life to build your empire?"

There was humor in Dex's narrowed eyes. "You fed me an opportunity, and I took it. You're killing Ghost, and *if* you make it out alive, you can leave. You have my word."

A dry chuckle stumbled from my lips. "Yeah? And what am I going to do with that? Throw it at you?"

Dex gripped my collar and yanked me forward until our foreheads collided. Spit flew from his lips as he screamed, "You will kill Ghost."

"Go to Hell," I stated, pushing him off me, and he stumbled backward. "I'm done with this bullshit. Find another bitch."

I turned to leave when Dex's voice touched the back of my neck. "You know what your Mum said once she found out Oscar's death was your fault?" Dex's tone was calm, practiced, and I paused in the middle of the living room and slid my gaze to her, "The only way to break you, was to break your heart. And I thought to myself…She's exactly right. Oliver's fucking heart. But what exactly makes Oliver Masters heart beat? I mean, he willingly gave up over forty grand in exchange to find a fucking security guard. He drives an old station wagon for crying out loud, so it was never money he wanted. And sex?" He chuckled. "The young chap fingered a tight hole but didn't smash. And for a while there, I almost believed the wanker sucked cock. But that only left one thing: family. And I'm not talking about his brother or Mum…because we all know mummy dearest tried to get rid of him a long time ago. He never forgave her for the poisoning, the suffocation…"

With my gaze locked on Mum, my eyes burned. Tears slipped down her cheeks, and she tilted her face to the side, breaking the connection like a popsicle stick. I slammed my eyes shut and turned around to face him.

Dex flashed a smile. "Well, you know how that story went."

"Get to the fucking point."

"Point is, it was never *what* made his heart beat, but who," Dex shoved his hand into the pocket of his pants and retrieved his phone. His eyes fixed to the bright screen as his finger scrolled. "Jake, Travis, and little Turner, who's grown so much," he grinned, and my muscles tensed, "but then there's Mia. As soon as I laid eyes on her, mate, I about wacked myself off right then and let her watch. The girl is beautiful. I mean, look at her." Dex held up the phone, the screen faced me, and it was a picture of Dex and Mia talking in the streets of Surrey, Mia's hand pointing ahead as if she was giving him directions.

I blinked once, fear having a tight grip on my heart, and Dex pushed the phone back into his pocket. "You will kill Ghost, Oliver," he continued. "And as long as the job gets done, I'll make sure nothing ever happens to any of them. Chances are, yeah…you'll die in that room, but you can at least die knowing Mia is safe. And if you so much as try to take me out before then, my boys standing right outside know the deal. Mia's dead, all the bloodshed would be on your hands, and you'll go back to prison for life." Dex lifted his palms in the air and tilted from side to side, imitating a scale. "I'd say, things aren't looking too good for you, mate."

A scream ripped through me in the cabin of the car as I raced home to Mia in the middle of the black night and under the same moon I'd dreamed under countless times. I passed every car in my way, going well over a hundred miles per hour on M25 after the Queen Elizabeth II bridge.

My hand pounded over the glove compartment for it to open, and I shuffled inside for the stale pack of cigarettes, needing something to settle the anxiety. I lit the cigarette, an orange glow between my eyes, and inhaled the menthol, but the nicotine never eased the anxiety tearing me apart. Mia wasn't safe, and there was only one way to make sure no one would touch her.

I had to break my promise.

I had to let go of her hand.

When I reached our cottage, my gaze fixed on our Christmas tree, pouring white lights from inside the house through the window as my feet flew up the steps and through the front door. Mia jumped from the spot in the corner of the couch, the blanket falling to the floor. "Ollie, what's wrong?" she asked, walking toward me in my MAKE LOVE NOT WAR tee, her hair still damp from the shower.

Her hand reached for my chest, but my heart couldn't take it. "You have to go," I said, clutching her wrist and pulling it away. I walked into our bedroom and stood in front of the closet, and Mia followed close behind. "You can't stay with Summer or Jake." My hands shook as I pulled down a duffle from the top of the closet and turned toward her dresser. "You have to go back." Every drawer I yanked open fell to the floor, and my hands automatically grabbed clothes, shoving them into the duffle while a fire blazed behind my eyes. I couldn't see clearly. I couldn't think clearly. The only goal consuming my brain was getting Mia back on a plane to the states—to get her as far away from here as possible.

"Ollie, stop!" Mia cried at my side, yanking clothes from my hands and pushing me away from the dresser. "I'm not leaving you!"

Turning, I gripped her shoulders and bent down to face her. "I fucking lied, Mia. Does this look like the face of someone who isn't afraid?" I asked her, and my own reflection bounced off her golden-brown eyes. Raw. Vulnerable. Stripped to the core of my soul. "Because I'm terrified! I can't allow anything to happen to you. This is the only way!"

Mia squinted her eyes and shoved my arms off her. "You're a real son of a bitch, you know that? What happened to *you and I?* What happened to staying through this together?"

"There's no *you and I* if we're both fucking dead," I shouted, and Mia turned, so I stepped out in front of her with my finger pointing at the wall. "You're getting on that plane, Mia! You're going be quiet, listen to me for once in your life, and get on that fucking plane."

My gaze locked with hers, both of our chests heavily heaving. By this point, Mia's eyes were bloodshot, soft lips trembling, and my heavy heart slammed inside its brittle cage, no match against her and the power she had over me. My breath held, tears sprang in my eyes, and a finality crossed her expression.

She'd made up her mind.

Mia walked around the bed, grabbed a pillow, and headed for the living room. "Make sure to clean up the mess when your done with your tantrum," she barely whispered through her tears. A desperate growl

336

erupted from deep in my throat, and I grabbed a drawer and threw it across the room, drilling a hole through drywall above the bed.

Then I crumbled to the floor against the dresser.

Hours passed, and the only sound in our home was a show playing over the telly and Mia's soft sniffles from the living room. I'd been in this same position the entire time, bent at the knees and my legs numb. Utterly drained from the toll of emotions happening within me, my limbs were weak as I got to my feet and made my way to her.

Mia's back was to me as she laid over our leather couch, her brown hair spilling off the pillow and over the edge. "I'm sorry," I whispered, and she turned over at the sound of my voice to face me. Her eyes were swollen and cheeks so red, her freckles were lost, but still so goddamn beautiful. "I'm scared, Mia."

"I know, I am too," she admitted, then moved back to give me room. I peeled off my hoodie and tee then slipped out of my jeans before sinking onto the couch beside her. She immediately warmed me, and my fingers pushed through her hair as she shook her head. "I'm not leaving you, Ollie. There's nothing you can say or do to make me leave. I'm staying with you. No matter what happens, I'm going to be right here with you every step of the way."

The right thing to do was tell her I was a dead man—to prepare her for the inevitable, but I couldn't find it in me. It was better off anyway, Mia not knowing. She'd only do something incredibly stupid like beg me not to take the call and run away from it all. But we couldn't force Travis, Summer, Jake, and the rest of them to take off with us. If we ran, Dex would be out for blood. He'd take away everything that made my heart beat inside my chest, most importantly, Mia. And if dying meant she'd be safe, I'd die a thousand deaths.

"Promise me something, Mia," I said as her shallow breaths hit my lips. Mia lifted her eyes to mine, and she nodded once. "If one night I don't come home, don't wait for me. Instead, close your eyes and go to sleep, that way, no matter where I am, I can still be with you." Her eyes bounced between mine, and I swallowed. "Dream of me, all right? Promise me you'll do that."

Mia's lips parted and eyes glazed over. "I promise."

I abandoned the couch and picked her up, carrying her in my arms back to our bed. She didn't say anything about the hole in the wall, the broken drawer lying beside our bed, or the clothes draping over our wooden headboard. Mia only kept her eyes on mine as I laid her over the mattress and slowly undressed her.

The only way I could get through this moment was to keep myself together when all my body and emotions wanted to do was break apart at the thought of this being our last time. Her ivory skin glowed against the white sheets of our bed, and I took my time, running the tips of my fingers over her lips, down her neck, and over her breast. Every inch of her had branded into my mind, but tonight, she'd sear into my soul so I'd remember us far after death.

My fingers grazed down her stomach, and it slightly rose and fell beneath my touch. I flicked my eyes up, and her bottom lip caught between her teeth, her eyes closed. "Open your eyes, love," I whispered, and her thick lashes blinked open.

I continued my journey, her entire body shuddering when my fingers brushed her sex, and her thighs broke apart under my silent command. Mia's eyes fluttered, and a breath caught in her throat as my eyes drifted down her torso. My heart hammered, and her tender core starved to be kissed.

I crawled between her legs and up her torso until my nose grazed hers. My mouth moved down to her neck to kiss the spot below her ear just once. "The first time we made love," I whispered over her throat. "I asked something of you before it happened. What did I ask you to do?"

Mia's back arched, and her nipples grazed my chest before she said, "You wanted me to remember the moment and the way you made me feel."

"Yes." I grinned, moving my mouth back to hers. "Hold on to this too."

338

And we made love that night like every other night, and though I was unable to hide the way my heart danced to our last song, she would never notice or see the difference. I'd never held back when it came down to the two of us, and Mia always had the power over me.

The girl was a design, a form of art. Painters, musicians, nor novelists could capture or mimic the way she lit galaxies beneath my flesh or make my heart beat to the tune of *River Flows in You*. Even the most talented would be jealous of the way she moved like paint across my skin into my bloodstream. For over two years, I'd poured her through every line, word, and syllable of poetry, but could never get it just right.

An absolute wonder.

I'd spent the last few years falling in love with her, and I could die easy knowing Mia Rose was strong enough on her own. She never needed anyone. It was true, I'd pushed her to bring her back, but she'd always been the one to save herself. Perhaps that was my purpose in this lifetime with Mia, to remind her the struggle and fight along the way could be just as beautiful as the freedom she'd find once I was gone because … we were once together, and it was beautiful.

THIRTY-TWO

"Once a poet falls
in love with you,
you will never die."

OLIVER MASTERS

Ollie

t was Christmas day, and we had a full house earlier for a gift exchange with Lynch, Travis's family, Jake, and Liam. Smiles and laughter had filled the room as everyone enjoyed my famous hot chocolate, and the Christmas music Mia played on the piano. Nearing the end, Jake and Lynch had teamed up for a game of charades, both pissed off a shared bottle of spiced eggnog. How the two of them had won was beyond me.

After everyone left, a Mazzy Star song blessed the speakers, interrupting the Christmas vibes. Mia shrieked from the kitchen and ran toward me in a snowflake printed red sweater and leather pants, forcing me off the couch. "Dance with me," she asked, and she never had to ask twice. I pushed the coffee table out of the way, and we danced in our living room in front of the fire, the colored lights from our Christmas tree glimmering in her eyes. "When can I give you my present?"

We'd talked about this. I'd told Mia not to spend heaps of dosh on me, then she had mentioned the first year was paper. I'd told her it was for anniversaries, not Christmas, but Mia never liked to follow the rules, and my heart had clenched at the thought of not making it to our first anniversary, so I'd agreed. Paper it was.

With her arms wrapped around my shoulder and an eager smile tugging on her lips, I went to open my mouth when my phone chimed.

The air grew thick. My stomach turned at the slight sound, and I tucked my hand into the front pocket of my pants to retrieve my phone and held it out to the side.

My mobile lit up. *It's go time.* The three simple words across the screen paralyzed me.

My eyes wouldn't move from the screen, and a beating struck in my ears. My fist clenched, and my pulse ticked from the pads of my fingers against the phone.

"Ollie, what is it?" Mia asked, but her voice sounded distant, lost as my insides screamed.

The room spun, Mazzy played, and it felt as if the entire cottage was submerged in water.

"Ollie?" Mia asked again, touching my face.

Her tiny hand clutched my chin to move my eyes back to hers, and I wet my dry lips before swallowing the agony back down. "I," I paused to clear my throat of emotions, "I have to go." It came out as a question. *Did I have to go?*

Of course, I had to go. It was the only way to keep her safe.

"Now?" Mia tilted her head with a frown. "It's Christmas."

"Believe me when I say, I don't want to. It's the absolute last thing I want to do, love. But I don't have a choice." I forced a smile, and it took every bit of effort. Mia studied my expression, seeing straight through it. I averted my gaze and lifted her arm from around my shoulder to bring her palm to my lips, pressing a kiss inside. "I have to go change."

I left her standing there in the living room to make my way to the bedroom. The only thing keeping me sane and steady was the fact she'd be safe and free. It was the only thought chanting inside my head over and over while I quickly changed into a pair of black jeans, a white tee, and a black hoodie. Hopping on one leg, I pulled my black boots on in the doorway to look out into the living room. Mia was busy dragging the coffee table back in place and picking up mugs from the side tables, cleaning, which she rarely ever did. This time, I'd left the gun under the mattress for Mia in case she needed protection, hoping she'd never have to use it. I hurried to the antique wardrobe to retrieve a letter I'd written for her, the second gun Travis had gotten this week, and a box of bullets.

My eyes darted back and forth around the wardrobe toward the door, catching Mia folding a blanket and laying it over the couch, and my shaky hands slid bullets into the magazine. I'd do whatever it took to come home to her, and this time, I was going in fully loaded. After making sure the safety was on, I tucked the gun behind me and closed the drawers.

Mia was in the kitchen, her back to me, and I paused mid-step on my way to her, only to spin back around to breathe. Oxygen turned scarce, scattering in and out from between my lips as my stomach twisted into knots. With one swipe of my palm down my face, I collected the tears and dropped my head back in search of any strength left within me before turning back around.

My hands clutched Mia's hips, whirling her around to face me. I held her face in my hands, and she said nothing with glassy golden eyes. Naturally, my body leaned into hers, pinning her to the counter, and I closed my eyes to inhale through my nose. The distinct aroma of jasmine after it rained, and I ingrained it into my soul.

I tucked a strand behind her ear before kissing her, my lips latching on to hers, and my mouth moved softer, my tongue grazed slower, and my lips sucked harder, holding on for longer than I should have before reluctantly pulling away. Our noses brushed before our foreheads connected. "I'll always be in love with you, Mia," I said, grazing my thumbs over her cheeks and down her pouty lip. "Remember your promise?"

"Don't wait up for you," she whispered, and I nodded against her. Mia released a breath and wrapped her arms around my waist above the weapon, not noticing. "Do you remember your promise to me?" she asked, blinking up to me.

"You're not losing me," I lied, because it was the only way, and pressed my lips against her forehead before leaving her arms to head toward the door, my heart warning me.

"Hey, Ollie," she called out once my hand landed on the doorknob, and I froze by the sound of my name upon her lips. I didn't turn back around, I mentally couldn't do it, and her voice traveled between us. "I love you too."

I'd called Dex on my way to Thurrock, and he went over the details before sending the address to my phone. The meeting would take place in two hours at a storehouse ten minutes away from the scaffolds I'd climbed as a kid. With time in my favor, I sent a quick text to Adrian to meet me at the same location we'd burned the drugs after the BOGs raid, which seemed like lifetimes ago.

Adrian's two-toned Civic idled beside the large building, and I parked beside him before opening the glove box for a cigarette. My eyes landed on Mia's Christmas gift sitting inside, and all the muscles in my body flexed, my knee bouncing. After a few pounds of my heart, I swiped the pack, slammed the glove box shut, and joined Adrian by the barrel.

With a quick shake and pat on the back, we lit up.

It was silent between us at first, and I dragged in the smoke until the burn hit my lungs as we both stared off into the abyss of nothingness. The moon loomed overhead, the night too peaceful, too calm for what was about to go down. My thoughts had tangled into a holy mess of Mia, and if I didn't say something now, I'd probably lose it. "Remember when we came here after the raid?"

"Yeah, mate," Adrian threw his head back and chuckled lightly, "I thought you'd reached nutter status after burning the BOGs drugs and filthy lucre."

I flicked the cigarette butt, and ash floated to my boot. "Besides, I didn't."

In my peripheral, Adrian cocked his head. "What do you mean? I watched you do it."

Shaking my head, a thin layer of smoke seeped from my mouth and mixed with the cold air. "You only saw what I wanted you to see," I pointed out, pulling the cigarette back to my mouth and walking the few long strides behind the station wagon.

Adrian followed, and I shoved the key inside the lock of the trunk until it clicked and popped open. Lifting the floorboard, colorful heaps of banded money rested in the cracks, and Adrian's young features lit up with a cackle. "Are you fucking kidding me?" He turned to face me, and I lifted my hand over the top of the trunk hood and leaned in. "That has to be at least ten grand sitting there."

"It's thirty," I corrected.

Which was pocket money to the hoarder in me. Mia would be all right. I'd made certain of it. I'd spent this past week going over the finances, and there was enough to where Mia would be taken care of for the rest of her life. And it was true, I never expected to be the one-hit-wonder poet, but I'd finished my second manuscript in the nightstand along with the letter. Mia would have the choice of either handing it over to Laurie to share with the world or cherish it for herself. It may even be worth more once I was a goner. Either way, it had always been the two of us woven in every word on every page, poetically making love to her for eternity.

"I need you to do something for me, mate." The sincerity in my voice seized his attention. "It's important to me."

Adrian tilted his head and crossed his arms. "Yeah, Oliver. Anything. You know I'm good for my word, and you're my boy. I'm loyal to you, always have been."

"I'm going to text you an address once I leave, and I need you to take the money in the black bags and deposit them on the doorstep of the house. It's already split up." The drop off for Brad Burn's family. I wished I could do more for the family.

"What about the rest of it?"

"The rest is yours." My arm dropped from the trunk, and I flicked the cigarette over the cracked concrete. "I had every intention of getting you out from under the Links, and it may not be enough to take care of you forever, but it's a bloody start. You're a good man, Adrian. And I promise, there's so much more out there. This world is too fucking beautiful to be spending your days drowning in drugs, cheap liquor, and meaningless sex. Don't waste it, A."

Adrian rubbed his palm over the top of his buzzed head before gripping the back of his neck. "I don't understand." He shook his head, big brown eyes trying to read me. "What about you? What about Ghost?"

"It'll be all right," I reassured him. "I'm trusting you'll do this for me then?"

"Yeah, of course."

For the following five minutes, we got to work loading his car, and after finishing, I cut our goodbye short and slid into the station wagon with a few minutes left to spare. Adrian drove past me, and I shoved another cigarette in my mouth and opened the glove box to swipe Mia's gift. My fingers shook as they creased the lines of the tattered paper, making it perfect.

Instead of pulling up to the front of the storehouse, I drove around the back. Though this was a business deal, men such as Ghost wouldn't let anyone pass through the front doors without being patted and checked for weapons or wires. I had to find a way to get my gun inside unnoticed, and most of the exits wouldn't open from the outside.

A harsh wind stung my eyes as I tried the last door without any luck. Only a single street lamp buzzed about a quarter of a mile away, giving

345

me little to no light. I took a step back and glanced down the side of the building. Three doors aligned, and I could only leave my weapon out in front of one of them. If I chose wrong, this entire plan would burn.

I laid the gun flat against the brick wall at door number three, left the car behind the building, and walked back toward the front with my hands shoved deep into my pockets and anxiety at an all-time high. Earlier, I'd given Dex my own instructions on how this was going to go without Leigh. Ghost was under the impression he'd pay half now before we'd meet once more to deliver a locked-up virgin. Ghost was under the impression this was just another business deal.

But it wasn't.

We were both dying tonight.

A few men greeted me at the entrance, and one patted me down and checked under my hoodie for wires. "I'm clean, mate," I reassured, scanning the inside of the storehouse. Numerous storage units with bright blue doors lined the halls of the compound, a few opened, but couldn't see what was hidden inside at this angle.

"You're late," he growled. "Where's your mot?"

The beefy man's neck was thick, blue veins popping beneath his flesh—fifty pounds of face, and probably a heavier liver. If one couldn't tell by the blondish-red hair or icy blue eyes, the accent would've given him away, an Irish fellow who was a long way from home.

"You don't bring the present to the party unless you want someone to open it," I said with a grin. The chap narrowed his eyes, and I shook my head. "The exchange isn't happening until I get my first payment, let's not pretend we don't know how this works."

The Irish man looked over at another bloke. "The boyo's a real chancer, ya? Let's get on with it." He nudged his head, and I followed him down the line of storage units to the back, his mate close behind me.

My eyes flicked into storage rooms as we passed, stacks of containers in some while men lifted, carried, and organized whatever was inside. In other units, women young and old shuffled through clothes hanging from free standing closets, wearing an emptiness in their eyes.

And my feet kept moving until we reached the end of the line, where the hallway broke off into two opposite directions. Three offices laid out before me, and to my horror, Irish man made a left when I'd been counting on him to make a right. Rooted in place, he turned back to face me. "Something the matter?"

I forced a step forward. "No, all good."

We stopped in front of the door, and the Irish man was quick to open and usher me inside with a gesture of his hand. "It'll be a while. In the meantime, sit, and enjoy the entertainment on Ghost," he emphasized with humor in his tone.

I took a step inside the room, the door shut behind me, and I halted in place when a familiar face stared back at me from against the desk. Utter chaos swam inside her dark brazen eyes. "Mum?" my voice hiked.

"Oliver," she rushed out, yanking me away from the door and in front of her. My eyes darted around the bare room for answers as she gripped my hand, "We don't have time. You have to listen to me—"

"What the fuck is going on?" Words left me, but I couldn't hear them, and I jerked my arm away and took a step back as her expression softened. My heart hammered inside my ears, and I clenched my jaw as I tried to make sense of it all. "Did Dex fucking send you? Of all people, he sent Mum to make sure I killed him? Or did you want to see me die? Has the last twenty fucking years of torture not pleased you enough?" I shouted through a whisper and turned and pushed my nervous hand through my hair before grasping it. "No, you have to fucking go." My hand hit the doorknob for her to leave.

"Oliver, stop!" her stringy blonde hair smacked her cheek as she jumped out in front of me. Her hand squeezed my bicep, and I flinched.

I looked down at her hand and back into the terror in her eyes. "Don't fucking touch me," I seethed, walking her backward into the wall and dug my finger into my chest. "You don't have the right to touch me, to talk to me, to fucking watch me die. You lost your bloody rights."

"I know, Oliver," she cried. "I was a terrible mum. The truth is, I never deserved you."

"I don't have time for this," I shook my head, then looked around the room for something to keep the door open to retrieve the gun lying on the opposite side of the building. Ghost would walk through that door any second.

"No, listen to me," she cried, following my erratic pacing. "I got clean, baby. And once I got clean, I could finally think clearly! You can't do this, Oliver! If by some miracle, you made it out of here alive, it's not over. He planned to kill you all along," she frantically rambled.

I whipped around. Time was ticking, the rage was building, and my hand shook as I vigorously tapped the side of my head. "You don't think I fucking know that?"

"No, you don't know everything!" she cried out.

"I have two seconds before they get here, and you had twenty fucking years to make it up to me!" I whisper-shouted inches from her face, my teeth clenching.

Mum's shoulders sank, and she wiped her tears with the back of her hand. "Let me do this for you. After everything I've put you through, let me be a mum for once. Let me do this."

"No," I shook my head, vision blurring as I took off my boot to wedge in the backdoor. "they'll kill you. I've already accepted my fate." I whipped around and reached for the back door.

"It was Dex who ordered Leigh to kill Mia to make sure you'd go through with this."

I paused and turned around.

That couldn't be right. I'd known girls like Leigh before. "No, Leigh was jealous of Mia."

"No, Oliver. Leigh would've done anything for Dex. She would've done anything to feel a part of something, to feel a part of a family. Who knows if Dex would ever leave Mia alone. And you can't do this, Oliver. Mia needs you. The baby will need you."

I froze.

My lungs froze.

My chest froze.

348

I couldn't think.

"What?" I whispered, my head slowly shaking and my eyes squinting, unsure if I heard her right. I couldn't have heard her correctly, but my heart must have. Hard and heavy hits slammed inside my chest, an extra skip than before.

It was loud and eternal.

"Mia's pregnant," she blurted, and tears froze in my eyes. "I saw her four weeks ago. She had that glow about her, one only a mum could see. I'll never forget that look in her eyes, Oliver. If you do this, you're not only risking Mia's life. You'll risk your baby's too. Who knows what Dex would do once you're dead."

As soon as she said that, the door opened, and everything that followed seemed to happen so fast in slow motion.

A tall man in a suit took one step into the room when Mum pulled a gun from under her skirt, pointed it at his head, and pulled the trigger. A thunderous *Bang!* pierced my eardrums as the man collapsed to the ground. A ringing ruptured in my ears, my hearing temporarily impaired, and my eyes darted around when Mum's lips moved, "*RUN!*"

Two men launched forward over Ghost's body, and I turned and ran for the exit as another shot rang out, whistling past me.

I'd made it through the door, the cold wind slammed against my face, turning my tears to ice when Adrian's Civic pulled up with the window rolled down. "Get in," he shouted, and I quickly rounded the car and slid in just when open gunfire blasted from inside the building, one right after the other, each one ripping my heart to shreds knowing Mum was inside.

I'd left her there.

Mum was dead, and I'd left her there.

My palms pressed against my ears as I screamed out, and Adrian peeled out, tires sliding and asphalt spraying.

What have I done?

I pounded over the dashboard, my anger ripping through me.

"*Mia needs you. The baby needs you,*" Mum's paralyzing words replayed, and I ran my palms up and down my heated face as Adrian sped through the alleyway, but the fury only fueled the malicious thoughts pulsing inside my head.

I shoved my hand into my pocket and pulled out Mia's Christmas gift, creasing the paper over and over with trembling hands in a rage-filled daze.

It would never be fucking over.

My family would never be safe.

Not as long as Dex was alive.

"Adrian," I fumed, and cocked my head to face him. "Take me to Dex."

THIRTY-THREE

"And we all know
how the story ends.
For once, let's go
out with a little
m y s t e r y
and a whole lot of
m a g i c ."

OLIVER MASTERS

Ollie

Adrian sped through the run-down streets of Thurrock to Dex's house, and I couldn't stop the rage flaring up inside me. My hands shook, eager to wrap around his throat and steal every bit of life he threatened to take from me. My jaw clenched, holding back from tearing Adrian's arse apart for not going fast enough. And my chest and lungs burned from holding back the Saint trying to talk sense into me. *Bitch, It's not your fucking turn.*

My knee bounced at an impossible speed. My ears still rang from the same shots that took Mum's life. I gave up trying to calm myself down a long time ago. Dex had sent Leigh to kill my wife—*my baby.* Sweat and infuriated tears poured down my face in the dead of winter. I couldn't feel the cold. I couldn't feel anything aside from the madness. My clenched fist pounded over the middle console. "Hurry the fuck up," I screamed out.

Adrian jumped at my side and gripped the steering wheel. "You need to think about this. Stop for a second, and think about what you're about to do."

I cocked my head to the side. "Don't fucking question me."

"What the bloody hell are you going to do?"

I'm going to crack the world open and swallow them whole.

I'm killing them all.

The Honda hopped the curb, and before Adrian had a chance to come to a complete stop, I jerked open the car door and jumped out.

Flames. Red, yellow, and searing orange flames blazed through my hazy sights as I sprinted up to the house and through the door with no weapon, no gun, only me. Vengeful, enraged, and on the warpath, anger ripped me open and controlled me. My emotions turned into ammunition, and at this point, I wondered if I cut my own flesh, if I'd still bleed because the power roaring inside me made me believe I was invincible.

And if I'd die tonight, perhaps my immortal anger would bring me back to life.

Three men lounged in the living room when I'd busted through the door, none of them expecting me.

Dex jumped from the couch, and his smile quickly faded when his confused eyes locked with mine. Smith stood beside him, eyes bouncing between Dex and me, and I picked up the small telly over the three-legged table and pitched it across the room and into the side of Smith's thick skull, and he instantly went limp and fell over the couch.

Dex's eyes widened as he reached behind him for his gun, and I flipped up the coffee table into his face just as the gun went off, the bullet punching a hole through the ceiling. The sound of the gunshot couldn't affect me. Nothing could throw me off. Not until all three of them were dead.

The single thought of her kept my mind racing, my feet moving forward, and my reactions moving quicker. The third bloke took off to the kitchen where his gun sat over the fridge, and Dex pushed the table against my chest, shouting vulgar threats. I gripped the edge of the table and threw it against the wall, and a window shattered.

Dex threw a punch, but I dodged his fist and landed mine into his jaw. He fell back against the couch, and I snatched the dropped gun from the floor and snapped up, pointing it at the runaway bloke's back.

It all happened so fast.

A bloodcurdling scream shot up from my pained heart, and I pulled the trigger, again and again, firing at his back. The color of red stained my vision as blood sprayed over the white fridge, and the bloke dropped to the ground, head bouncing off the tile.

By the time I looked back over to Dex, his fist connected with my jaw, and I tumbled backward but quickly steadied myself. I lifted the gun at Dex, and he backed away as the sound of another gun cocking echoed to my side.

Smith.

My eyes slid to him, and he stood off to the side with his pistol pointed at me.

"You don't want to fuck with me!" I screamed, my hand shaking and tears streaming down my face. "I'll fucking kill you!"

A single gunshot cried out, ripping through my side. My eyes bulged. Tears stopped. The impact jolted me back and knocked the air from my lungs. I fell back against the wall, the gun heavier in my hand and gravity dragging me down.

Mia, my baby ... I grasped at every ounce of strength to pull myself up against the wall and waved the gun in Smith's direction, refusing to stop until they were all dead.

Desperate, I pulled the stiff trigger, and a thunder sliced the air as a bullet tore through the center of Smith's forehead, blood painting the wall behind him.

A second wind jolted a rush inside me like a shot of adrenaline. Despite the burning pain and the warm blood seeping from the bullet hole at my side, I stormed over to Dex.

He slowly shook his head, panic invading his senses, and before he could get a word out, I slammed the base of the gun into the side of his head.

Dex fell back into the couch, and I gripped his black hair, yanked his head back, and dug the tip of the barrel under his chin.

"Alright, I get it," Dex's voice shook with his palms in the air. "I get it, Oliver."

Flashes of Mia and I went off like fireworks in my head. The first time our eyes met in the mess hall, her small smile in the bathroom when we first talked, the late-night rendezvous', chasing her in the library, reading to her, the lovemaking, the fighting for each other, the tears, her golden eyes, the paper roses, the dancing, the stars, the sunrises, proposing, our drunken nights, the wedding ... Falling into this maddening love that stayed forever and ever ...

"No," I wiped my face into my sleeve and cocked my head, "you don't fucking get it."

And I pulled the trigger.

"Oliver!" Adrian shouted, my eyes weighing heavier and heavier. He'd taken off my black hoodie, and I had it pressed against my side, but it wasn't helping. My white tee soaked in blood. It was everywhere. The color of rage. The color of love. *How is it possible?* "Hang in there, mate. We're almost to the hospital."

354

"No," I croaked, shaking my head. With the gun still in my grip, I clenched both my eyes from the white blistering pain, my body begging to pass out. But, I knew Mia. She was waiting up for me. "Take me home."

"You'll never make it," Adrian nervously explained, whipping the car to the right, and my head dropped over the passenger side window.

I lifted the gun and balanced it over my thigh, pointing it at him. "Take me the fuck home," I seethed through gritted teeth. We couldn't be more than ten minutes out. I could make it to her.

"Fuck, Oliver!" Adrian slammed his palm against the steering wheel once before he shook out his hands and released a drawn-out breath. "I'll take you home, but I know you, and you won't shoot me." His voice shook, and his hand came down over the gun as he took it from my clenched fist. "You have to trust me, mate. *Blindly*. You have to trust me blindly, Oliver. You hear me?"

Nodding, my hand relaxed over my thigh as Adrian drove with his knees, wiping down the gun with his shirt. Going well over a hundred miles per hour, he dropped the gun inside the door pocket and snatched his mobile phone from the cup holder, punching in numbers before bringing it to his ear. Adrian's wide eyes flicked over to me. "Yeah. This is Officer Adrian Taylor," he turned his frightened gaze back to the road, "I'm undercover with SC and O ten. I have a twenty-three-year-old male in critical condition. Gunshot wound to the abdomen. I need an air ambulance…"

My brows pinched together. "A?" It hardly came out against the pain.

Adrian cocked his head back to me as he continued into the phone, "My location?" his breathing was heavy and voice shaken as he looked over my condition, and I squeezed my eyes closed as we hit a turn. "The Masters cottage in Surrey …"

The rest drifted as I shifted to my side, cringing from the pain, and with two fingers, I pulled out Mia's Christmas gift and clutched it into the palm of my hand. My head rocked against the window, and I turned my gaze to the sky, pinning it on the iridescent moon for the rest of the way.

In record time, Adrian pulled outside my cottage. My insides were on fire. The pain was unbearable, and every slow and short step toward our front door felt like a mile as our Christmas tree glowed through the window. Adrian shouted from behind me before the car door slammed, but I kept going with her gift clutched inside my fist, probably ruined. But she had to know.

Once I reached the front steps, I shoved my bloody hand into my pocket and pulled out my keys. After a few attempts, the door opened, and I collapsed against the door frame.

Then there she was, coming from our bedroom and appearing before me in her red pajamas and her hair a wild mess.

Her presence, it was overwhelming.

I dropped my arm to my side.

Mia.

I only saw her, and she saw me.

Horror flashed in her eyes, but I couldn't wipe the smile from mine. I made it home.

"We're having a baby, love?" I whispered, and Mia's hand flew over her mouth, tears slipping down her cheeks as she nodded.

A relieved breath escaped me as I sank down the door frame. Mia ran toward me, catching my fall as a scream sliced through her lovely lips and pierced the cold winter night. Together we slid to the floor, and she clutched my head against her chest as my numbed body laid out in a pool of warm blood. Desperate cries echoed through the black night as her trembling hands ran through my hair over and over.

Mia was right. There was something peaceful about death, especially in her arms. I could stay right here forever, listening to her heart beating. I'd memorized that sound. I could pick her heartbeat out in a lineup. But just as much as I'd known the sound, I felt it hard and steady inside my chest.

Because her heartbeat mirrored mine.

Adrian tried to calm her and laid his hand over her shoulder, but Mia jerked and screamed out against him, shaking her head. The ends of her

356

soft hair grazed my neck like the times she'd rolled her hips over me when we made love. I glanced up to see her cheeks soaked, eyes bloodshot, and snow flurries dancing wildly in her hair when my eyes became heavier.

"Ollie, please," she cried, sobs sputtering through her trembling lips. "Open your eyes. Keep them on me."

The pain was dissolving. I wasn't scared anymore.

With the little strength I had left, my eyes blinked open, seeing the snow fall toward me under the same moon I'd talked to as a kid. My clenched fist opened at my side, and Mia's gift laid in my palm. The only gift I could give her on our last Christmas—*freedom*.

The paper airplane fell from my fingers, and I looked up to see her screaming out, but her cries didn't make it to my ears this time. Mia beat against my chest, but I didn't feel it. Bright blue and red lights flashed all around, and I blinked once more to embed her golden-brown eyes into my soul.

And, finally, we were free …

Note from
Oliver Masters

I'm a dreamer, but I'm not afraid. Not anymore.

For my entire life, I'd lived in a fantasy. I'd created my own world and got lost in it because I couldn't believe in the reality around me. I was certain there was light and good out there. People who were kinder. Places that were warmer. Genuine smiles, honest laughs, and selfless love. It couldn't all be a lie, because they were in stories. And inside every story, there was truth. Anything real was once imagined, and I found comfort in that, and until I could either find this world I'd believed in whole-heartedly or face my reality, I'd bring myself to the one I'd imaged because it was easier—safer.

I let Mia into my world, taking her away from the dark.

Together we danced, kissed, and made love behind the gates of our heaven.

And it was beautiful, poetic even.

I'm a man, but I'm not afraid anymore.

I'm not afraid to cry.

I'm not afraid to dream.

And I'm not afraid to pour my entire heart into her.

I wear my heart on my sleeve because I'm not afraid to get it broken. It was never mine anyway, it was everyone else's. It was my mum's when she made foolish mistakes, but she did the best she could under her circumstances. Perhaps she hasn't always done the right thing, but she loved me the only way she understood how.

It was my brother's because, despite the sickness inside his head, I couldn't blame him. He was raised by a prostitute, with a brother who constantly escaped the harsh reality, and numerous punters with loads of advice on how to make it through in life. Perhaps he hasn't always done the right thing, but he loved me the only way he knew how.

My heart was with Ethan because he loved Mia enough when I couldn't. He protected her when I couldn't. When the cruel world failed him, failed his sister, he did the only thing a person in his position would only think of. I see that now more than ever. And I admire his strength, his loyalty, and his devotion. Perhaps he hasn't always done the right thing, but he loved Mia the only way he knew how, and I hope one day he'd be able to find love again …

My heart was with the father I never knew because he brought me into this world. Perhaps he decided not to be in my life, or maybe he never knew I existed, either way, it still lead me to her.

No, my heart was never mine. It was everyone else's to mend, shape, slice, and stitch, all making me the man I am today. And for that, I love myself. Because whatever condition my heart is now in, Mia still treasures it all the same.

I'm still a dreamer, but I'm not afraid anymore.

Because I found her.

All I had to do was open my eyes.

EPILOGUE

"Sometimes I'm terrified of my heart;
of its constant hunger for whatever it is it wants.

The way it stops

and

starts."

—Edgar Allan Poe

Mia

would never forget the day he'd slipped away.

Surrounded by blood and snow, sobs had broken through my desperate pleas as I held his head against my chest. His gaze had locked on mine, a wistful freedom collided with wonder in those green eyes, grasping on to the belief of forever. I'd never seen his shade so vibrant. It had caused my entire being to fall into a somber eclipse, spiraling faster and faster with no end, no walls, only darkness.

And then he blinked his eyes once more before they closed.

The flesh from my bones, the blood in my veins, the oxygen in my lungs, all of it had crumbled, breaking into small pieces yet still holding on by a thread—the thread was my heart. It had pumped on auto-pilot as if it couldn't associate with the rest of my body. It's thumping sounded in my ears, and I'd wished it would stop, but my heart was not ready to let go. It had continued with the same steady beat, refusing to give up what was right in front of me. *Open your eyes*, I'd thought—well, desperately begged.

And I'd waited.

Two seconds had passed—waiting as my body weakened from his disconnection, and my heart continued to pump.

Three.

Then the paramedics had ripped him from my arms …

That was three years ago.

A soft pink glow spilled down the hall, and I followed the light, stopping just before I reached the door with a coffee mug in hand. The soft giggles coming from her room was music to my ears, and I turned the corner and leaned into the door frame of her bedroom. Origami roses and paper airplanes hung from her sky painted ceiling. Jake had her room set up while we were traveling, and had it ready just before returning home for Christmas.

Under the constellations and origami shapes dancing above, my eyes found hers.

They were beautiful. Rare, yet duplicated. A color so familiar. It was the color of the reflection of palm trees across a shoreline when the sun was at its highest point in the day. The color was the perfect timing when three of God's creations collided: the sun, trees, and water.

The color was Ollie's.

She smiled that innocent smile from her bed when her dimple kissed her cheek, then curled inside his arms.

Ollie's gaze flicked up at me from the book, and he froze with that daydream spark in his green eyes. A matching smile spread from her face to his. "Uh-oh," Ollie snapped his head to our little girl. "I'm in trouble."

"*Big* trouble. You," my eyes narrowed at the brown-headed green-eyed wild child, "are supposed to be asleep by now. And you," I slid my gaze to Ollie, "are supposed to be … Well … Do I really have to finish that sentence?" I nudged my head to young ears.

Grinning, Ollie closed the book. "Yup, she's angry. Daddy's in trouble." He sat up in her bed and pointed out the door with panicked eyes and a smile. "Run, Ever. It's too late for me, but you still have time!" In a frantic, Evermore turned, slid off the edge of the bed until her little toes touched the wooden planks, then ran toward me, giggling. I scooped her up with one arm and nuzzled my face in her neck as I carried her back to the bed. Ollie pressed his lips together to hold in his chuckles. After Ever was born, we haven't been able to get pregnant again. Yet, I couldn't be happier. All we ever needed was our Evermore, anyway. "One more, then it's Mummy and Daddy time."

Ollie wiggled his brows. "Oh, yeah?"

Blushing, I laid next to Ollie with Ever settled between the two of us. Ollie opened his book, and I rested my head over his shoulder as he turned the pages to her lullaby. His enchanting and elegant voice arrested my heart. And I blinked up to catch his lips move and eyes blink slowly as he read to our daughter, never taking granted of a single beat.

"Lay your head, Evermore, for there is nothing to fear.
Love will slay the monsters; velvet skies are warm and clear.
Drift to sleep, Evermore, you're free to touch the moon.
Soar and dance with stars; Mum and dad will see you through.
Get lost in adventure, Evermore, but never stray too far.
Stay with me in my arms, even while you're gone.
Sleep with angels, Evermore. Soon the sun will rise,
But only when morning whispers,
Now open your eyes."

And we were together,
and it was beautiful ...

Thank You!

It's January 24th, 2020, and I finally wrote the epilogue after sitting on it for so long. Yes, two weeks until the release day. Which, if you are reading this, the date has come or passed. I'm telling you this because I want to admit to you how scared I was to finish this story. I was TERRIFIED. I could hardly get through edits and beta reads without turning into an emotional mess. I was so close to not adding the epilogue simply because I never thought I'd be able to end the story the way it deserved.

But I did it.

Wherever you are sitting right now, I want you to do me a favor.

I want you to close your eyes and find what your heart beats for.

Once you find it, or if you have known all along, give it your everything. Cut yourself open and pour your heart into it. Don't just chase it, become it. Breathe it. Live it. Never allow fear, uncertainty, or insecurities, or any soul or thing take it away from you. It's right there, and it's yours. The rejection you may face will never amount to the regret. You can learn to overcome rejection, but regret will haunt you for the rest of your life.

Six months. My entire life changed within six months, and I have so many people to be thankful for. I've been blessed with the best team at my side, book-lovers who adore these characters, life-long friends, new opportunities, and the list goes on …

To the READERS — Every morning, I wake up unsure what I ever did to deserve any of you. Every day, I see all your messages, and though it takes me a while to respond to contain my emotions (yes, I'm Ollie in a nutshell), they touch my fucking heart. It may sound so simple, but thank you. Thank you for reading. Thank you for understanding the story and the characters. Thank you for your tears, for your laughs, for your frustration, for your patience, for relating, for learning, for finding pieces of yourself inside these books and sharing it with me ... Thank you!

To the ladies on the STREET TEAM — Each one of you have a piece of my heart, and though we only started this team within the last two months, I couldn't have asked for a better group of ladies. Your constant enthusiasm, excitement, and passion fuels me every fucking day. From the bottom of my heart, thank you for believing in me, wanting to spread the word, and always on your A game. I love you all!

To the ARC ARMY —The talent, passion, and drive stirring within this community is unfathomable. By far, the favorite part of my day is when I get a message from you all. Thank you for your beautiful graphics, for sharing and spreading the word, for the hilarious meme's, and trusting me with this story. I hope you find that I've done it justice because it was you all in the back of my mind as I wrote the epilogue. Here's to a happy ever after, forevermore.

To the LOVELIES — During the most stressful days, you all keep a smile on my face. I know I haven't been as active lately, but I still see the way you ladies interact with each other, and it warms my heart. Thank you for staying so positive and accepting of each other. Thank you for always celebrating with me and becoming the one place I can escape to. You all are my safe haven. **Oh, and Christy L. ... I told you I'd take you to Gibraltar ;)**

To my KASSY — Dude, I fucking love you. Like, that's it. And I'll say it over and over. And thank you for beta reading SWM, EWIG, then NOYE. And thank you for being understanding and patient when I know deep down you wanted to strangle me these past couple of weeks while dissecting NOYE. Thank you for not just holding on, but carrying me through this, giving your complete honesty, and never holding back. In one year, we made it together. There is no other way I'd rather have it. Always and forever … (PS: There are 7 "ands" because I know that's your favorite word and lucky number.)

To ANNIE — I wish this entire world can see what I see in you. Thank you for always being there without question and being my emotional support through the passing of my Nana while writing NOYE. I know it's been a rough few months for the both of us, but despite what's happened, you've never put me on the back burner, and for that, I'm forever grateful. Thank you for your perfect beautiful eyes and proofing my books. You are my Adrian Taylor—my most unexpected plot twist. My ripcord. This is going to be a busy year, partner. Buckle up! I love you!

To SHALEY — You are beyond amazing and more. If it weren't for your hard-ass pushing me to make deadlines, we probably wouldn't have seen this book for another few months. Thank you for your constant reminders to keep me on track, for leading the street team in the best possible way, for your guidance, your knowledge, for always willing to help, but most importantly, thank you for your friendship. You have made this ride so much smoother.

To LUCIA — That quote in the prologue is for you, woman. It's only been a few months since we crossed paths, but it didn't take long for me to look up to you and admire the woman you are. The kind of woman I strive to be. You are every bit encouraging, strong, fiercely passionate, and dedicated. Thank you for pushing me to get on a schedule, turning me into a morning person, and, without you ever realizing, reminding me to never second guess myself. At the end of the day, these are our stories, and we're sticking to it …

To MICHAEL, CHRISTIAN, & GRACIE — You are the three I bleed onto these pages for so my love for you will last forever, even when I'm gone. XO

To my MOM — *"Yes, Mom. I know, Mom, Okay, Mom."* Thank you for your constant nagging, reminders, willingness to help, trips to the post office during big orders, and celebrating all the small victories with me. I love you, and I'm ready for that breakfast date now.

To AMANDA, DANIELLE, & KAYLEE (and Steve)
You three will always be my favorite story to tell.

To the rest of my friends and family all over the world,
Thank you!

ABOUT THE AUTHOR

Crafting stories and stringing words together since a young age, most times I live in imaginary worlds. Other times, I live on an *island* somewhere in Florida with my loving husband, two kids, and lazy Great Dane, Winston.

My writing style is unapologetic and emotional, striving to push buttons, hearts, and limits within romance. I would say my books fall under all sub-genres, from gothic romance, suspense, to fantasy. I want to write everything.

A lover of music, especially a good electric guitar solo, I can rap most Eminem songs, dance, dabble on the piano, but also enjoy using power tools and a paintbrush. When I'm not writing, I'm either enjoying family movie/game nights, sleeping (probably sleeping), traveling, or planning my next book adventure … with one hand on my laptop, and the other holding a can of Red Bull.

I LOVE HEARING FROM YOU!

Facebook & Instagram: @nicolefiorinabooks

JOIN THE BOOK CLUB ON FACEBOOK:

https://facebook.com/groups/littlemissobsessivebookclub

SIGN UP FOR THE NEWSLETTER

https://www.nicolefiorina.com

n i c o l e   f i o r i n a

Printed in Great Britain
by Amazon

18620628R00212